J.W. GARRETT

A REALMS OF CHAOS NOVEL

REMEON'S CRUSADE

bhc press™

Livonia, Michigan

Editor: Denise Baker

Published by BHC Press

Library of Congress Control Number: 2020933869

ISBN: 978-1-64397-117-9 (Hardcover)
ISBN: 978-1-64397-118-6 (Softcover)
ISBN: 978-1-64397-119-3 (Ebook)

For information, write:
BHC Press
885 Penniman #5505
Plymouth, MI 48170

Visit the publisher at:
www.bhcpress.com

Dedicated to my husband, who puts up with
my writerly brain at all hours of the day and night.
Thanks for sticking with me through it all.
Love you always.

BOOKS IN THE
REALMS OF CHAOS SERIES
SUGGESTED READING ORDER

REMEON'S QUEST: EARTH YEAR 1930

REMEON'S DESTINY

REMEON'S CRUSADE

REALMS OF CHAOS TIMELINE

1929

Jack and Sam meet. Jack begins work in coal mine

1930

February, Remeon's Quest: Earth Year 1930 opens

Jack and Harry held captive on Remeon

1931

Jack returns to Earth after short return visit
to Remeon to see Whisterly and Arista

Jack and Harry work on Hoover Dam project
Jack and Harry serve in WWII

1947

March, Remeon's Destiny opens

Thomas captured. Visits Remeon for the first time

July, Thomas returns to Earth

July, Remeon's Crusade opens

1948

Jack and Thomas return to Remeon

THE CHARACTERS AND DEFINITIONS OF REMEON'S CRUSADE

MAIN CHARACTERS

JACK: Worked in the coal mines of Utah before being transported to Remeon in 1930. Husband of Whisterly

HARRY: Jack's best friend, transported to Remeon with Jack in 1930

SAM: Jack's mentor on Earth; died in a mine collapse in 1930

WHISTERLY: Head of the council on Remeon. Jack's wife

THOMAS(CALLED STEPHEN ON REMEON): Lives on family farm in Virginia. Transported to Remeon in 1947; Belle's brother

BELLE: Thomas's sister. Lives on family farm in Virginia

ARISTA: Daughter of Jack and Whisterly, first in line for Head of Council of the Day Watchers

SIMON: Son of Jack and Whisterly. Second in line for leadership of the Night Dwellers

DANIEL: Son of Jack

VINIQUE: Sister of Whisterly, second in line for Head of Council of the Day Watchers

JANUS: Leader of Night Dwellers

MILA: Left the compound to become a Night Dweller, former maid of Whisterly's

GREAT GRANDMOTHER ARISTA: Witch and grandmother to Whisterly, great-grandmother to Arista and Simon

DAMOND: Former Council member; was betrothed to Whisterly; killed by Jack and Whisterly

REMEONITES: People of Remeon. Procreated using a laboratory due to the effects of the virus PR 251 on reproduction

DEFINITIONS

PR 251: The virus that has been infecting Remeonites for generations—the cure derived from human testing is now being disseminated

UNIVERSAL TRANSLATOR: Device which allows all races to communicate on Remeon

TELEPATHY: All Remeonites (and humans who've been on the planet) can communicate via telepathy and can prevent others from accessing their personal thoughts with barriers they construct in their minds. Invasive telepathy is considered a crime on Remeon

TRUE NAME: Holds controlling power on Remeon. With the knowledge of another's true name one can read all thoughts and compel another to act as the instigator wishes

COVEN: Gathering of witches, housed in magical basement in the Compound

GRIMOIRE: Magical tome filled with spells and passed down through the generations

MAGICAL BASEMENT IN THE COMPOUND: Where the coven and grimoire reside. Ceremonies as well as lessons in magic take place here

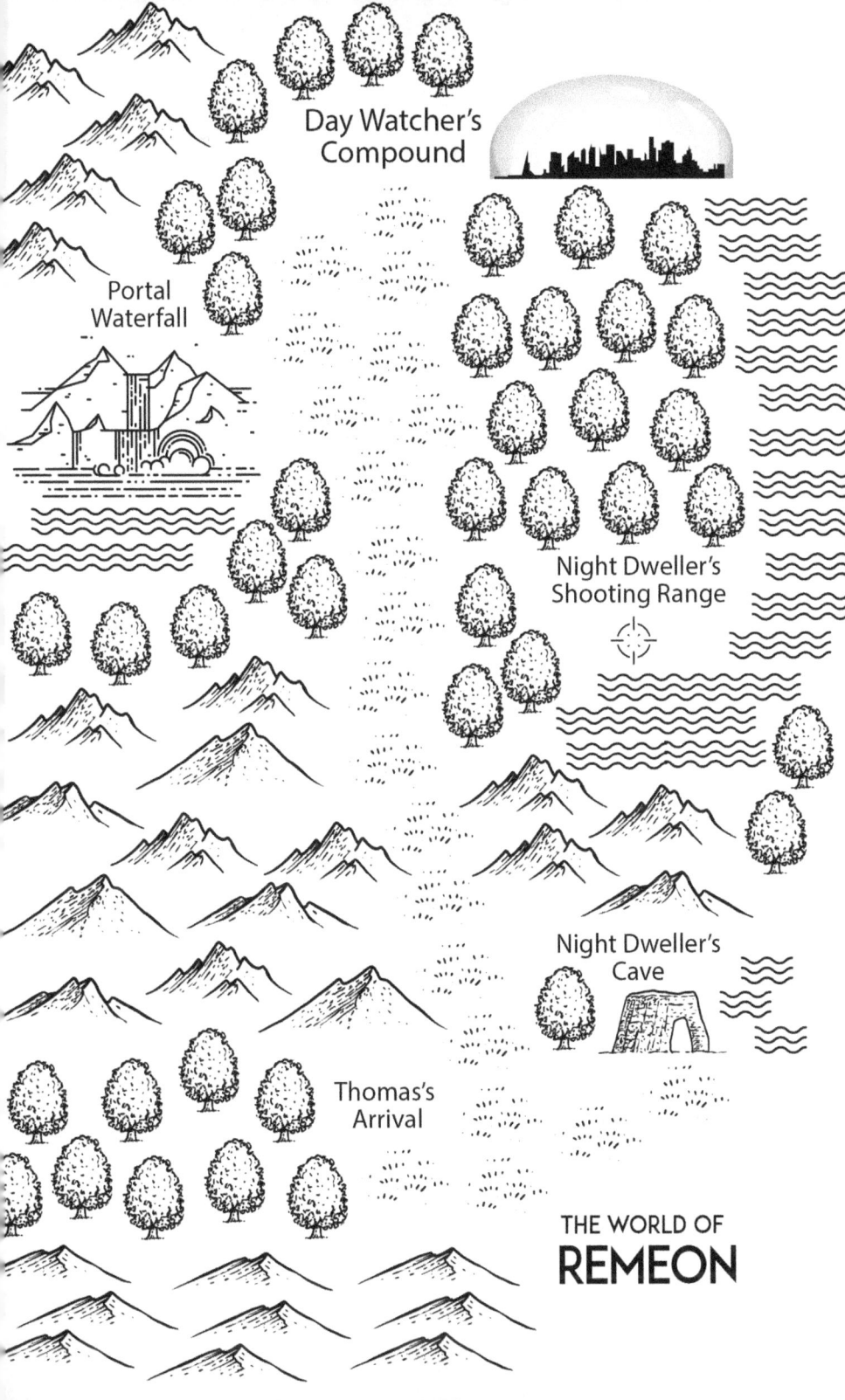

Day Watcher's Compound

Portal Waterfall

Night Dweller's Shooting Range

Night Dweller's Cave

Thomas's Arrival

THE WORLD OF
REMEON

"I loved her against reason, against promise, against peace, against hope, against happiness, against all discouragement that could be."

— Charles Dickens, *Great Expectations*

REMEON'S
CRUSADE

CHAPTER 1

1947, EARTH

TIME SOMEHOW HAD a way of making even Jack's life appear "normal." For a person kidnapped and taken to the planet Remeon in 1930—who, while there, then married Whisterly, a witch, gained powers of telepathy, and returned to Earth with said powers, after fathering two children—well, that *was* his normal.

Jack lingered on his second cup of coffee as he mused over his telepathic conversation with Whisterly from earlier in the morning. When their thoughts were already intertwined, it was easiest then for their reflection to flow freely, before the stress of the day had gotten to both of them. Jack sighed. He'd all but given up on returning to Remeon for now. So much had happened during those sixteen long years since he'd left. To both of them. And evidently a cure for the disease ailing the Remeon people was now imminent.

This had been Jack's and Whisterly's latest hurdle.

They'd argued repeatedly about it. Disagreeing via telepathy wasn't nearly as satisfying as in person, so he'd dropped it, temporarily, once again. *Hell, I don't give a damn about all that shit.* Whisterly and Vinique had cleared his name, had cleared him of murder. That was what had mattered so many years ago, the last time he'd seen Whisterly and Arista. Killing Damond, the bastard, had been self-defense, and ultimately the council had agreed.

More factors presented complications now, however, like Whisterly's body being in stasis. *That's the real reason for the distance.* But he'd not give up. Jack couldn't fight the grin taking over his face. With the cure in trial and being distributed, Whisterly would soon be healed. *No more excuses.* What then? Would she finally agree? *She damn well better.*

The grin disappeared as his brows knit together. Would she always throw more obstacles between them? Jack sucked in a breath and shook his head. *No, it's closer than ever. I can feel it. Our time is finally almost here.*

He took another sip of his now-lukewarm coffee and returned his attention to his book, *That Hideous Strength.* The final page awaited him. C. S. Lewis was a favorite author of his and Harry's. Soon they'd trade, and Harry would get to finish this series as well. *And what is Harry reading? I can't remember.* Whatever it was would be next on Jack's list, when they could find the time to meet. Jack turned the final page, contemplating the ending, then closed the cover.

Damn, that was a good book.

The ticking sound of the clock drew his attention in the silence. *Where is Daniel?* He should be ready by now. Gulping the last bit of his coffee, he stood, then paused, the coffee's heavy aroma urging him back toward the kitchen. A third cup before work sounded tempting, after getting Daniel out the door. "Daniel? Where are you? Sometimes you take as long to dress as a girl. Come on, son!" Jack heard feet hit the floor, then scuffling, followed by drawers banging. *Yeah. Not dressed yet.*

"Coming, Papa."

"You have exactly five minutes to be dressed and presentable to the outside world, or I'm coming in there to *help* you."

His thoughts still on the lack of punctuality of his son, Jack strolled into the kitchen with his cup. From the window he eyed the barn—his workshop. Things were going well. His small construction business here in Provo, Utah had taken off since returning from the war. And soon he hoped to finally convince Harry to join him, to be his partner. Honing their skills on such huge projects as the Hoover Dam had been a great experience for the eager duo.

And, in those early days after the life-altering events on Remeon and before the war, they'd gone to where the work was, garnering experience, learning the trade. Over the years, Jack's focus had turned toward design and planning for construction. He'd been grateful to the Freemasons during those years, who'd helped drive him toward his goal.

These days he gave back through their organization, and the unique sign for his business branded him as a member. Could others pick out the additional symbol hidden in his signage—one of the few other guiding forces that had shaped his life through the love he shared with Whisterly? The image of a pentagram seared inside him, harboring within it a link to his love. He needed it close each and every day.

Jack turned toward the clatter of the slamming bedroom door, pulled from his reverie. He suppressed the smile that fought for control of his face and cleared his throat instead. "Ah. There you are." Leaning against the entryway to the kitchen, Jack concentrated on the eight-year-old in front of him. Thick black curls, recently tamed with a brush and water, clung slightly to the boy's forehead; the outfit, although hastily put together, matched and was reasonably clean. Daniel's chest heaved from his recent activity. Squatting, Jack outstretched his arms to his son. "Come here."

The dark cloud on Daniel's face lifted as Jack tackled him in a hug, pinning him to the floor amid a cacophony of giggles. "Okay, I can smell the toothpaste from here. I think you're good."

His face turning solemn again, Daniel nodded. "I did everything. Honest… I'm ready to go."

Jack stood, then wrangled his son from the floor, and bent low to plant a kiss on his cheek. "I believe you. Now scoot. Head on over to the Millers' house. I'll see you later this afternoon."

Assuming a definitive air well beyond his years, Daniel threw his arms around Jack's neck for a final hug, then disappeared out the front door. Jack watched from the door until his son dropped out of sight.

Coffee. More coffee. It had been such a help that the Millers had agreed for Daniel to spend some time there with their son, Mark, who was about the same age as Daniel. Jack had been an only child. He wanted his children to have the companionship of other kids, during the long afternoons as well as weekends, if Jack had work piled up. So far, it had worked well for the boy to go there occasionally. Daniel completed chores here at home as well as at the Millers. Responsibility needed to be practiced daily to truly be ingrained in young men.

Jack refilled his cup. He blinked as a flash of memory assaulted him. The stench of gunpowder mixed with blood and sweat filled his nostrils, and instantly the years fell away. His friend Henry lay dying in his arms, his life force pumping steadily into the ground. Henry's mouth moved, but Jack couldn't hear in the din surrounding the battle, so he lifted up his helmet and leaned in to focus on Henry's barely audible words...

Shaking his head side to side, Jack cleared the intrusion from his mind. Daniel was his son in all the ways that mattered, just as surely as Jack had belonged to Sam, his mentor and father figure. DNA wasn't a necessary ingredient—only love, which Jack possessed for the young boy in abundance. Jack's best friend Harry and his wife, Maggie, helped constantly. Daniel knew them as aunt and uncle. Harry, Henry, and Jack had fought side by side in the same platoon, creating a bond that even death couldn't break. Henry was a brother and another in an endless sea of senseless losses.

Jack took a substantial gulp of his coffee as he focused on Harry and chuckled. Someday soon, Jack expected to hear that Maggie was pregnant, and they would have a little one of their very own. His friend walked around with a stupid smile on his face all day long. The whole world knew Harry was happy, and Jack didn't begrudge him one second of it—not one second. It was so well deserved and a long time coming.

Coffee in hand, Jack concentrated on the items needing completion today, making a mental tally in his head as he walked. A steady hum interrupted his thoughts, piercing the silence. Always on alert from his military training and his time on Remeon, Jack froze, attempting to isolate the source. His jaw dropped, immediately followed by his cup. The space before him turned murky, and, in a span of seconds, the swirling matter took shape.

Jack?

Whisterly! He reached for his wife's form, solidifying before his face, but grasped only air. Jack's heart wrenched. She was in pain. He felt her agony as it coursed through him. Tears stung the back of his eyes. *Baby, what is it?*

Her body fought for breath through the commotion going on around her. Raspy sounds left her throat. Jack reached for her extended hand that glowed only inches from him. *Dying... Be... trayed... Love... you, Jack... Always... true...*

A sob rose in his throat. *I love you, baby!* A flicker of recognition registered on the pained image that hung in air. The next second the mass lost its shape and dissipated like it was nothing more than a morning mist. Speechless, he stared where her form had been. Then Whisterly's telepathic presence, his constant companion since he was seventeen, left his body.

A boiling rage rose within him. Jack threw a punch, landing it solidly in the kitchen wall. And as his hand met a wood stud, a vague crunching sound erupted. Jack slid to floor and grabbed his head. A barbaric wail emanated from him. It felt as if a piece of his brain had been torn from him, more brutal than any wound he'd received in combat, even more savage than the telepathic attacks at the hands of Damond on Remeon.

The cryptic message repeated in his head over and over again, not unlike the scribbled final words he'd forced himself to read from

Sam so many years ago. The broken message cascaded through his mind, over and over. Jack's eyes flickered then closed.

What seemed like only seconds passed. He woke and found strong arms wrapping him in a hug.

Sam.

The cool shade of their tree shielded his eyes. "Sam," Jack croaked, "tell me it's time, for real now. She's…gone. I don't want to be in a world where I can't have some part of Whisterly with me. I always believed there would be a chance, someday. Don't send me back. I'm begging you."

A gentle wind swayed between them. Sam shook his head and held his son as he cried. "Not yet, Start-Up. You've work left to do."

"Yeah? Well, I don't give a damn," he screamed. "Let someone else work for a change."

Sam's green eyes held Jack's watery gaze. "Remember, Jack. There's hope. All's not lost. Believe it or not, these trials have a purpose. But for now, rest."

"Jack, Jack... You need to wake up."

Jack pushed back at the intruder. "Go away." The sound of a chair scraping across the floor grated on Jack's nerves.

"You're at the hospital Jack—gave us quite a scare."

"I said, go away Harry."

"Your son needs you."

Jack glared at his friend. After pulling himself up, he leaned heavily on an elbow, examining his bandaged hand. "I doubt that. I'm no good for anyone right now." Jack eased himself back down on the hospital bed, ignoring Harry's worried gaze.

"You have about ten broken bones in your fingers and hand." Harry sighed. "You know what? These doctors here don't understand what's wrong with you. They think you're deranged—losing it due to the war."

Jack shrugged and wiggled his fingers, a grimace attacking his face. "Sounds plausible. Let's go with that."

"Really? You want a permanent trip to the funny farm? If not, you need to convince them you're all right."

Jack met his friend's gaze. *I'm not all right, Harry.* The back of his eyes stung, tears threatening to expose the depth of his hurt, and he blinked them away.

Harry leaned forward and pulled Jack closer, surrounding him in a tight hug. *I know, Jack. I read your thoughts. When I found you sprawled on your kitchen floor, I thought you'd had a heart attack and died. And you did have a heart attack, of sorts. You scared the shit outta me.*

Jack avoided the wounded look on Harry's face as he scooted away and leaned back against his pillow. "Please tell me that Daniel didn't find me like that."

The lines in Harry's forehead scrunched together as he let out another heavy sigh. "No, he didn't. I came when I could tell that something was wrong. I got there first."

"I'm grateful for that at least. Where is Daniel?"

"He's with Maggie and me. She's spoiling him rotten, by the way. She's smitten with him, I'd say."

A ghost of a smile crept along Jack's lips. "Yeah, he does that to people."

"Listen, Jack. I know nothing I'll do—"

The smile that had inched onto Jack's face dissolved. "Whoa. Stop right there. Don't even start. I can't do this right now."

"If not now, then when? The pain isn't going away."

"You think I don't know that?" Jack bowed his head. Then, with a shuddering breath, he forcibly regained control and added, "She came to me, Harry, in an apparition. I saw her die, right before my eyes."

"Jack, let me help," Harry whispered.

Jack saw the pity reflected in Harry's face and turned away. "You can't. Nobody can," Jack hissed back at him. "She's gone. Forever. Now go get one of those damn doctors. If I need to put on a show so I can get the *hell* outta here, let's get it moving. Give me five minutes."

Harry released a shaky breath, then rose. "Okay, Jack. I'll do as you ask, for now."

VINIQUE ROSE EARLIER than her norm. A nagging unease seemed to be a constant companion for her as of late, trickling through to her core. Had it really been almost six months since Whisterly's death? Along with all the other fallout, Vinique's own witchcraft training had stalled. With her mentor gone and her new responsibilities as Council Chair ever looming, her time hadn't been her own. And, well, she'd had her own grief to deal with.

Now Vinique would need to be the mentor, and what a job before her. Outside her window, the shifting colors in the sky caught her attention as she prepared her tea. Grateful for the distraction, she sat at her desk and sipped her drink, while the flurry of muted tones in the sky transformed, heralding a new day.

Over the years, Whisterly had mentioned her expectations to Vinique in the event of Whisterly's premature death. Namely, Arista's training. Whisterly had been on the precipice of initiating her daughter into the coven. That too would fall to Vinique. With all Arista had been through, Vinique had consciously deferred this task. So much needed discussion now.

Ideally this dissemination of knowledge should have flowed from mother to daughter, lessening the shock. Vinique's chest tightened. That wasn't to be. Training would fall on her shoulders alone. But a few other points needed to be addressed first.

After Whisterly's death and the initial shock of her letters had been revealed to Arista, Vinique told Arista about her father, Jack Livingston. Vinique had disagreed with Whisterly on this point of secrecy, but with Arista about to take up the Council Chair, she needed to know. Vinique's love for Whisterly would never wane. But

Vinique would concentrate her efforts on decisions going forward for the living.

Another item was left undone—Jack's letters to Arista. They'd been kept separately from Whisterly's own missives. And timed by her mother to align with Arista's initiation and training, Whisterly had planned to give Jack's letters to their daughter, adjusting their release to life events whenever Whisterly could, as Jack had intended. The idea being that Arista would now be old enough to understand the content of these personal letters.

Since finding out about her father, Arista had been searching and uncovering information here and there and had even resorted to using Stephen on Earth to find Jack. No doubt she would locate him soon. *Then what? A visit? I need to get to the bottom of her plan. Quickly.*

Grabbing paper, Vinique wrote down her mental notes; at least it might help her organize the mess of duties that had piled up. Vinique paused. One item deserved to be at the top of her list, foremost in her mind if not in her actions. She wrote the words along the top of the page: *Visit my sanctuary.* It would center her, give her needed direction, and, gods, she had missed it—the coven, her own training, the discipline. Her life had taken a back seat. From her perspective, it felt like an eternity.

The void that Whisterly had left in Vinique's life—in her heart—had stifled her just like with everyone else whose lives Whisterly had touched. Going back to her own training in the seclusion of the basement represented a gigantic step forward for Vinique. Would Whisterly be among the coven now? Vinique didn't know how that worked, and honestly she was somewhat anxious about the matter. At least, though, it would be something, a connection again.

Nobody possessed the depth of Whisterly's knowledge of witchcraft now—well, except Grandmother. As the disease had whittled away at Whisterly day by day, her body's ability to endure magic had eroded. The last few years she'd devoted most of her energy into honing her ability to jump from one body to the next, using both live and dead hosts. Her most recent efforts, right before her death, had been fully successful, for all the good that did her now.

Even with her depleted strength, Whisterly should have lasted to receive the cure, which now brought healing to so many Day Watchers. Vinique's heart still ached, knowing that Whisterly didn't witness the final fruition of her life's work.

Many times in the days since Whisterly's death, Vinique had traveled the corridors which led to the basement, then continued on by it. A thin mist veiled the entrance now. Passersby didn't know of its existence, so they weren't aware of the oddity. Truthfully it was easy to miss. But someone or something had put the new barrier there. Or had Whisterly somehow left this token in her passing?

Suddenly she couldn't wait. Couldn't wait to know what existed beyond the mist. Was it Whisterly's new home? Vinique only now saw how she had been on the edge of dereliction in her duties by not returning sooner. She was in charge now. The baton had passed to her, and she'd done nothing with it as of yet. Abandoning her list, unfinished, Vinique rose, dressed, and found herself on the perimeter of the mysterious haze within the quarter hour.

Whisterly's key hung around Vinique's neck. At times during the past few months she had sensed the key as a weight pulling her down into a deepening abyss, but, in actuality, had it been an anchor, encouraging her back home?

Since Whisterly's death, Vinique had worn it daily. The original key to the basement remained in a lockbox still in Whisterly's office, and the last copy belonged to Jack, Whisterly's lifelong love. Vinique's heart went out to him. His suffering must be unbearable. She stopped to make a mental note. If Arista didn't reach Jack, then Vinique must. Soon.

As she pulled the key from its resting place, Vinique reached for the doorknob with her other hand. Mist or not, she knew it had to be there. Her hand claimed the doorknob, and after inserting and turning the key, the door gave way with a quick twist of the knob. Her senses came alive in the musty stale air as she descended, step by step into darkness. *Illumine.*

Vinique continued on, her path ahead now bathed in light from her quick spell. Beneath her feet, the wet cobblestone slowed her progress, but Vinique landed each step more confidently than the last on her way to the hidden passage.

Ducking into the room on her hands and knees, her gaze immediately turned skyward. She stood and waited and, closing her eyes fully, immersed herself in the surroundings. The cool dampness seeped inside her, and although already one with the magical tome so many years ago, its spell drew her closer, nearer to its pages. Within seconds she knew her grandmother would be by her side, chiding Vinique for her extended absence.

Vinique closed her eyes and raised her arms to her community, and as the book flung open, its pages twisting and flipping in response to Vinique's mental command, light flew up from her fingertips, perfectly highlighting the coven before falling down again, effectively choosing its page within the grimoire. The dazzling blaze hit the designated spot, creating the signature mist that hissed from the page's surface. Seconds later her grandmother appeared in full form and donned her waiting gown.

"Well, child, I'm glad you finally decided to return. My gentle urgings weren't working as well as I'd have liked." A snarl-like smile twisted the old witch's lips.

"I know. I've been remiss. But I needed time to begin my own healing process. She was my half-sister, my mentor, and, above all, my dearest friend."

The old woman plodded closer and patted her granddaughter's hand. The cool touch sauntered through her, clearing her thoughts. "Remember, dear. Matter is matter. Recall your training on elemental magic? Whisterly isn't gone. Transformed maybe, but still here. You'll always have her, in one form or another."

Vinique scanned the coven members who hovered nearby, not sure whether in her desperation she had hoped to find Whisterly among them or not. Vinique's gaze settled on her grandmother, the silent question made clear.

"No, child. She's not among us. And, even though I feel her presence, I can't isolate it... yet."

Vinique's gaze bore through her grandmother's form. "You can't? What does that mean exactly?"

"The possibilities are endless. Each witch's journey is unique. She may still find her way."

Vinique's brows rose in question. "And if not?"

"Before we discuss this further, let's talk about Arista's training. I sense we will need her talents within the coven sooner rather than later."

Vinique nodded. "Absolutely. But Arista has needed this time. She lost her mother to a violent death. She's in love for the first time, and she doesn't yet realize her lineage is made up of witches."

The ancient witch lumbered closer to Vinique and lingered by her ear, as if she were sharing a closely held secret. "She realizes more than you know, and she's strong, just like her mother. If we are to have a chance, we must have her committed among us and fully trained in her own specific area of elemental magic. Soon."

"Understood. I'd planned to talk with her later today, about many subjects, her ancestry as a witch being only one of the topics. Assuming she's willing, and I believe she will be, I'll have her back here for immersion in a few days."

"Sit, child, and let me give you a brief rundown as to why her involvement is crucial. Now our timing needs perfecting. And, if we can move quickly, I daresay the situation may not be as dire as you believe."

Vinique quieted, while her mind ran maniacally with questions. She wasn't sure where to begin. "I'm all ears and open to anything, if I'm understanding you correctly."

"Well said, child. Open, indeed, as is our entire coven."

During their conversation, the witches who'd been hidden by the darkness loomed just outside the brilliance that the book exuded. But Vinique could see them now when she focused her gaze beyond that perimeter.

"Combined, we are a powerful lot. Through the ages we've had a hand in many shocking feats, and this time will be no different. Every witch knows any task begins with a way forward, and, through that path, grows hope. Now, where hope reigns, anything is possible. Whisterly had it. I have it. You have it. We all do."

The silent agreement of her sisters in the craft filled Vinique's being.

"Are you ready to harness the gifts before you?"

Vinique's eyes glistened with unshed tears. A tiny glimmer shown through amid the shadows that she'd let creep into her mind, until they had almost taken over. How had she not seen it? She bowed her head as a tear fell down her cheek. "I'm yours."

The coven circled Vinique, and, through their combined link, her grandmother shared the illumination of her years and their collective plan.

VINIQUE SLOWED AS she neared Arista's chambers. The letters she clutched in her hand felt like an impending trap, their aging words waiting to be exposed. She'd felt completely confident when she'd set out only moments ago. Now that confidence waned. *So much information and so soon after her mother's death.* Vinique's thoughts returned to the basement and yesterday's enlightening visit. It would all be worth it. Too much time had already been wasted. Vinique nodded to the security detail, knocking, then proceeded through the door. Arista was expecting her.

Vinique eyed Arista from across the room, her head still bent over her work. *Her resemblance to Whisterly is striking and growing stronger. But I still see Jack peeking through there as well.* "I hope this is still a good time for you."

"Absolutely." Arista flashed Vinique a smile. "Just let me finish this thought, and I'm all yours for the remainder of the afternoon. Help yourself to a drink. I'll be right there."

Vinique poured herself some tea and chose a chair. *Hopefully the afternoon will be enough time to get all this out.* Relishing in the rich aroma, she buried her face in the cup and let her thoughts drift as to the best approach with Arista.

Arista plopped down beside Vinique with an audible huff. "Whew. I'm all yours. No. Wait. I think I'll join you and have some tea." Minutes later she returned, cup in hand. "Shoot."

Vinique placed her cup on the table beside her. Her eyes gravitated toward the letters in her lap.

Arista followed Vinique's gaze. "Are those for me?"

Vinique nodded, making a last-minute adjustment in her planned order of discussion topics. "We'll get to these. As I mentioned before I came, we've got a lot of ground to cover. Bear with me."

"Continue."

"Some of what I have to say, you won't find pleasant. So I'll just dive in."

A wry smile twisted Arista's lips. "No need to mince words with me."

So much her mother's daughter. "Let's start with Stephen."

Arista scrunched her face. "Stephen? What about him?"

"Is he aware you performed the mating ceremony, right before he left? Did you two talk about it beforehand? It was abbreviated. But all the components were there."

Her eyes downcast, Arista shifted uneasily in her seat. "Well, no… We didn't discuss it in detail. I'm not sure why this is important now. You said the items you wanted to bring up were imperative."

"This is crucial to our council—vital in fact. Now you can never mate with a Remeonite."

"And I didn't want to be forced to do so," Arista said, raising her head to meet Vinique's cool gaze.

"You will need to continue the bloodline. It is one of your responsibilities. You are close to the same age now when Whisterly conceived you and your brother. Do you plan to have children with Stephen?"

Arista's face colored. "I can't answer that. Possibly."

"You need to discuss all this with him, let him know what you've done without his knowledge or consent. And his expected responsibility."

Arista bowed her head. "Now?"

"Yes. Soon, very soon. Look. There are extenuating circumstances—your mother's death for one. A mating has never been negated to my knowledge, but maybe we could take it to the council…"

"No," Arista snapped. "I'll talk to Stephen soon. What else did you want to discuss?"

"Many, many items. Try to relax. I'm not attacking you. We must get our council and our bloodline in order." Vinique reached out and covered Arista's hand with her own. "Arista, I'm your aunt. Whisterly's half-sister. And I'm a witch, trained by your mother."

Arista's opposite hand still held her tea. Spilling a healthy portion, she led a shaky hand to set down her cup. She drew a deep breath. "A witch…? You and my mother?"

"That's right. Whisterly was preparing your training right before she died, but I'm ready to take your mother's place, to fulfill this role, in her absence."

"All these years—she never once mentioned this to me. Why not?" Arista whispered.

Vinique nodded. "I realize it is so much to take in, which is why I waited to have this conversation. I have Whisterly's words here within these letters. And later volumes of the letters, which you already possess, detail my place in the bloodline."

"Damn letters! So much has been hidden from me through the years. And I thought I knew my mother. What a joke." A tear slid down Arista's face.

Vinique squeezed her niece's hand. "Arista, we're part of a sisterhood unlike anything you could possibly imagine. Open yourself to it. You'll feel it tugging at you. You've most likely felt it before, but without the immersion, there isn't an avenue forward. You're the same age now when Whisterly began her own training. The timing is perfect."

Arista searched Vinique's face. "So I'm your niece? Did my grandmother know of our connection?"

Vinique exhaled a breath. "We weren't completely sure. Whisterly traced my lineage to her mother. It's what brought us together. With the proliferation of test-tube births from that time due to the virus, it was difficult to track down. However, ruling council members participated in this activity to a much lesser degree, so my birth from Trista's donated egg was documented clearly. We aren't sure if Trista knew though. She was already extremely sick when Whisterly confirmed our relationship. Since we were sisters, my training in the craft began immediately." Vinique paused, meeting Arista's eyes. "You see, Arista, witchcraft and its teachings are an integral part of our council leadership. And it has been as far back as we were able to track."

Arista loosened Vinique's grip on her hand suddenly, as if she were burned or in pain. "This is quite incredible… Yet I feel the truth of your words deep within my being." Arista walked to the window and focused on the activity happening outside, the silence hanging heavy between them.

"Shall I continue?"

Arista turned. "There's still more?"

Vinique rose and walked to her side. "Yes. A bit."

"Did my father know about this?"

"About Whisterly being a witch?"

Arista nodded.

A smile wrapped across Vinique's lips. "Absolutely. He helped her discover her true self."

"Vinique?"

Vinique raised a brow in question.

"I'd like for Jack to come here. I want to meet him."

Perfect. This is going better than I'd envisioned. "Let's work on making that happen. I'll help you."

"And Stephen too."

Vinique hesitated. "Even with the progress the Night Dwellers have made on the cure, he may still be in considerable danger from Simon. What's the last you've heard from our operatives? I've been out of touch on this particular piece."

Arista spread her arms forward, indicating the couch before the pair. "Simon no longer has a medical need for Stephen. So the Night Dwellers have progressed substantially with their cure. Just like we've seen complete healing in patients with PR 251, they've begun to see similar results. Death rates remain highest among those individuals who have lived with the disease the longest, since the disease progression is nearing its final stages."

"I see. Let's set another time to discuss Stephen. Agreed?"

Arista nodded. "Agreed."

Vinique reached for the letters at her side and splayed them in front of her niece. "These are from Jack. I was there when he gave them to Whisterly. He wanted you to have these when certain life events occurred. Whisterly had envisioned giving these to you in conjunction with those events, as they happened." Vinique placed the envelopes in Arista's hand. "I'm not the keeper of these though. You decide how you'd like to read them. I suggest sticking to Jack's original wish—he put a lot of thought into these."

"I'm speechless that he'd care enough to do this." Arista took the letters and held them against her chest. "Thank you. And I will."

"He loves you dearly." Vinique beamed at Arista. "Now, on to my last topic. Suffice it to say, Whisterly was a master witch. She fought off attackers, scryed, created apparitions, and jumped between hosts of the living and dead when she was your age. Your potential is limitless, Arista. We have a whole coven of witches waiting to meet you and to assist in your training, especially your great-grandmother Arista, your namesake. I've set your immersion for tomorrow. That is, if you agree to be trained and hold sacred and secret the practice of witchcraft, continuing the lineage of our family bloodline and birthright. The decision is yours." Vinique sipped her lukewarm tea again and studied Arista. "So I'm curious as to your thoughts regarding your path. I have an inkling from my quick read of you, but tell me. Do you feel compelled to continue?"

It was Arista's turn to grab her aunt's hand this time. "At the beginning of our conversation I'll admit that I was frightened." Arista's downcast eyes turned slowly toward Vinique. "But, as we talked, a calmness permeated through me that wasn't my own. It was you, Vinique. You brought that to me, through me. I'm still somewhat apprehensive, but knowing you and my mother have gone through this journey before me I'm ready, ready to accept my path—my destiny. I've been floundering lately. Deep inside this feels...right and, at the same time, strange to even speak these words, but I'm excited in ways I never dreamed possible."

Vinique pulled Arista forward, surrounding her in a hug. "So glad to hear that," she said. "We desperately need you. And we have a lot of work ahead of us. Your schedule will be rigorous, starting with your joining with the grimoire, the magical book of spells. This initiation will begin your journey into witchcraft that your mother and father began for you years ago."

"They did?"

"Indeed, they did. You are already bound by bloodline to the craft, solidified through blood magic. Your immersion will confirm your personal choice."

Arista gasped. "I can't wait to begin. Where is the craving coming from, Vinique?"

"Your acceptance. I can feel it within you already. And now I can tell you the final piece." A ball of emotion hung in Vinique's throat. "Your great-grandmother has searched for Whisterly's presence to bring her into the coven, just like those who have preceded her. She was unsuccessful," Vinique finished in a whisper.

"Wh... What does that mean?" Arista stammered.

"Hope, Arista. Hope that Whisterly found a way somehow. And it means we have to dig to uncover the clues available to us."

Arista screamed and fell into Vinique's arms. "I can't believe it! Now! Let's start now!"

CHAPTER 2

EVEN WAITING OUTSIDE the building, the hospital's antiseptic odor still hung in his nose and clogged Jack's throat. And worse, it provoked painful memories, beginning with Sam. Jack scanned the cars approaching—still no sign of Harry. Jack took a long draw from his cigarette. Then exhaled, covering the pervasive stench with smoke.

Sam had never made it to the hospital during that awful disaster in 1930, but some of his friends did. Jack still remembered that day and evening in excruciating detail as the search for Sam ended amid the blood and guts of his fellow mine workers. The night of the accident Jack had been heavily sedated after he'd gone on a fighting rampage, then spent several days lost in a sorrow-filled haze.

Next came the adventure of Remeon, coupled with the invasive tests that had incapacitated him and Harry for days on end, the pair of them stuck in the clinical offices of the Remeonite doctors. The staff there didn't care about them as patients, or about their pain, only the results to their battery of experiments.

Combing his memory, Jack tried to recall the number of times he'd been in a hospital or aid station as a result of battle-inflicted wounds. *Let's see. Somewhere in the vicinity of six or seven.* Enough to stay far away from the pain and sadness he associated with these institutions. A flash of memory hit him. Jack pushed down a sudden gag reflex, his senses filled with hot, heavy air and thick green foliage.

Munitions captured his range of vision, the battle unfolding once again before him. His ears rang with the constant stutter of machine gun fire, while deep in his solitary pit—mired in sludge and human waste—he stared through the wooden bars high above his sweat-and-filth-slicked body.

A car door opened, followed by an emphatic slam. "Papa!"

The small voice wrenched Jack free from the Guadalcanal memory. Taking one last draw, he stomped the cigarette under his boot.

Jack's face transformed into a broad grin as he crouched and reached out for Daniel. The eight-year-old hit Jack's body with a solid *thud*. Had he really been ill, the force would have toppled him to the ground. "Wow, easy now. Are you training to be a linebacker?"

"Sorry, Papa." Daniel eyed Jack's heavily bandaged hand. "Did I hurt it?"

The easy laugh that escaped Jack felt foreign and out of place to his grief-stricken heart. "No. See?" Jack knocked his hand against the metal chair beside him. "I have a cast to protect the bones while they heal."

"Oh. Good." Jack stood, and Daniel clasped his arms tight around Jack's waist. "I'm glad you're okay."

Jack leaned over and kissed his son on the top of his head. "Me too."

Harry threw open the car door. "Come on, you two. Finish the reunion in the car."

"Let's go, Daniel. Uncle Harry's waiting. Go on. I'm right behind you." Jack grabbed his small suitcase with the few necessities that Harry had brought him and followed his son to the car. Jack closed the door behind Daniel and folded himself into the front seat. "Thanks for coming, Harry."

Harry let out a bark-sounding laugh, then glanced at Daniel in the rearview mirror. "This guy wouldn't have it any other way.

Nonstop talk all morning. *When are we going? Let's leave. My dad's waiting...* You've trained him well, Jack."

Jack winked at Daniel. "Haven't I though?"

"If it's all right with you, I told Maggie I'd bring you back to the house. She's fixing this elaborate meal as we speak, so you can't really say no, huh? Whada you say?"

A few seconds passed. Jack gazed out the window, lost in thought.

"Hey, I can beg off if it's too much for you and take you straight home."

Jack turned toward Harry. "No, sounds good. I don't feel much like cooking tonight."

"Well, okay. She'll be pleased."

Harry sat back with a smug smile resting on his face, like he'd just wrestled a beast and won.

Jack chuckled. "Really, I'm looking forward to seeing her. It's been a little while, a few months right?"

Harry shifted his position in his seat. "About that. I thought I was gonna have to tie her down to keep her from the hospital."

"Thanks for that, Harry, and keeping Daniel. Being away from him those three days I spent in that place made it seem like so much longer. But I didn't want anybody else there. Still not real fond of being around people in general right now. I can't guarantee I'm gonna be great company."

"I know. But we're family, not just people."

Jack nodded and gave his attention to the countryside outside his window. Soon the repetitive motion, along with some lingering pain meds, lulled him to sleep.

Gravel spit from beneath the tires, waking Jack.

"Here we are," Harry announced. "Looks like Daniel is out too."

Jack stretched, then tossed a glance toward the back seat. "All you need to say is *food*, and he'll be wide awake."

Harry slammed his door and met Jack on the opposite side. "Truth is, he didn't sleep so well with you gone. He's finally relaxing a bit."

Jack crawled into the back seat. "Hey, buddy. Let's go inside. Aunt Maggie is fixing dinner." Daniel's eyes shot open, and his body stiffened. Then, as he focused in on Jack, a lazy smile crossed his lips, and he allowed Jack to lead him from the car.

"Hi, sweetheart." Harry held open the front door as Jack and Daniel trailed in.

"There you are. Finally." Maggie rushed from the kitchen, squeezed her husband's hand, then took Jack in her arms, and kissed his cheek. "I may not be able to speak telepathically to you like Harry, but I love you as a brother just the same, and I'm so sorry about Whisterly."

Jack's glassy-eyed gaze met Maggie's. "Thank you," Jack whispered as their two foreheads met briefly.

"Who's up for a drink?" Harry called from the kitchen. Jack lifted his chin toward Harry. "I know what you're having, Jack. Maggie?"

Maggie squeezed Jack's hand and whisked away a stray tear. "A glass of wine would be great, honey."

"Coming right up."

Daniel yanked on Maggie's skirt. "Aunt Maggie, what's for dinner?"

"Oh. I need to get back in the kitchen. Fried chicken and mashed potatoes and biscuits. How's that sound?"

"Yummy!"

"How about you go in your room and play? The food will be ready in about twenty minutes."

Daniel disappeared, his quick footsteps echoing down the hallway.

"He's perked up," Harry said, handing Jack his drink.

"He's fine. What did I tell you? It's all about the food."

Harry joined Jack on the couch. "Harry, do you think about Daniel's dad much? His biological dad—Henry?"

Harry shook his head and took another large gulp of his drink. "No. Not really. Why?" Then not waiting for an answer, he continued. "You well know, it was a godawful time. I don't dredge up those memories. Sometimes they come back on their own, but I don't go looking for 'em."

"I had a flashback earlier today, while I was waiting for you at the hospital."

The lines in Harry's forehead deepened. "Wonder what sparked that?"

Jack downed the last of his drink. "Hell, I don't know. Maybe the painkillers. While I was in there, I had some of the same old nightmares again too."

"Might just have been being back in a hospital brought it all back."

Jack shrugged. "Maybe."

"When Henry pulled us from those pits, we were barely human." Harry shook his head, as if he could rid it from his mind. "I try not to think about it. Or the weeks we spent recovering after that. I'd rather just leave it as a blur."

"Except for the fact that Henry died, pulling us from that cesspool."

Harry laid his hand on Jack's shoulder. "What are you getting at? I remember. I was there too."

Jack cleared his throat. "Well, we were both there when Henry died in my arms. He gave his dying breath to make sure his son would be taken care of."

"Right… We both swore to that."

"Harry, I need to try to find out what exactly happened to Whisterly." Jack ran his fingers through his hair. "But first I need to get my head on straight again. Without her in my thoughts, things are… different. Empty… Dead." Jack let his own thoughts drift and stared at Harry. "No. I don't want to talk about it. I need to know though that Daniel, my son, has a place, 'cause I'm not sure where this will lead me. Well, I take that back. Remeon is where the answers are. So most likely I'll end up there. Eventually."

Harry nodded.

"Well?"

"Jack, do you really have to ask? You know Daniel has a place here, a home here. I swore an oath to Henry as well, and besides, we both love the little guy. But are you sure you don't want me to come with you? All kinds of hell could break lose—then what?"

"Then I'd take comfort knowing that my best friend was keeping my son safe, and that he'd be raised right, by people who love him. Daniel deserves that." Jack paused and met Harry's stoic gaze. "I need you here."

Harry took Jack by both shoulders. "He's got it, Jack."

Thanks, man.

Harry clapped Jack solidly on his back.

"Who's ready for another round?" Maggie yelled from the kitchen. Seconds later she appeared, drinks in hand. "I figured the answer would be yes."

"Ah, bless you, wife of mine."

Jack cracked a grin. "And you said you couldn't read minds."

Maggie raised a brow. "Officially, no. But I've been around you both long enough to know you rarely stop at one."

The dinner's aroma reached Jack. "That smells much better than the hospital food I've been consuming."

"Come on. Let's eat, you two, before it gets cold. Daniel! Wash up and come eat."

ARISTA TRIED FOR the third time since Vinique had left to return to her work. Arista had briefings to review, an agenda to finish for the next council meeting, and two additional meetings scheduled later in the afternoon. *And my dead mother to locate, or is it my undead mother?* A shiver ran up her spine. *What did it all mean?* Ugh. It was pointless. She couldn't focus on work.

Arista pushed back from her desk and twirled her chair, giving her a perfect window view of all the day-to-day happenings surrounding her. Her breath caught in her throat. The focal point of her office never failed to draw her attention. She could lose herself for hours, just observing life through the Remeonites below. After hearing she had descended from a family of witches, the people-watching activity lent an air of normalcy to her thoughts.

The connection to all these people was real. It pulsed through her veins, alive within her. But her mind wouldn't stop spinning from all the new information. Noise rambled in her head. Contemplating her odd situation, she willed her heavy lids to fall. The room began to spin.

A flurry of activity whirled within her vision as the years turned back. Arista cracked opened her eyes just in time to see her mother scoop her into her arms. "Let's go, little one. Lots to do today."

Arista studied her mother. From her vantage point her mother appeared tired and thin. A layer of stress lined her words, and an uncharacteristic nervousness filled her being, yet she exuded youth, and an echo of hope glimmered in her eyes.

"You're coming with me today. I'm sorry. There's no other choice. I've loaded Vinique with other activities, so you must promise to be good."

A cooing sound left her lips. The realization hit her. Arista was little more than a baby. This had to have been shortly before Whisterly checked into the infirmary and activated her hologram. With the wisdom of her current years, Arista evaluated her mother's condition solely from her appearance. Whisterly's eyes peered out from deep within her sockets, and, reflected in those eyes, a plump baby squirmed—Arista.

A dress cinched tight about Whisterly's thin frame, and from where Arista clung to Whisterly's arm, bones protruded under a thin layer of skin. The advanced state of PR 251 showed in her mother's features, but within, a different story played out. Determination, desire, and drive coursed through her brain waves. There, where it mattered, Whisterly's strength didn't waver.

Snug in her mother's arms, they traveled down well-known hallways, then followed a steady downward darkened path. Arista didn't recognize the cool damp room that Whisterly tucked her within. Her mother spoke a series of words, and illumination filled the space. Then, from her secure niche, nestled between blankets, she watched mesmerized as her mother's disease-filled limbs twisted and flowed effortlessly to a soundless rhythm, swaying with a lithe grace that drew in Arista, giving her insight into her mother's soul.

Arista must have slept, but when she woke, her senses jolted to attention. A fireball ascended to the ceiling, exposing an intricate web of drawings, which startled Arista, as figures pulled from their resting places and joined her mother. The body of women convened a ceremony. Her mother opened a huge book; then, as its pages flickered and fell away, Whisterly held her hand high, while drops of blood leaked from within her fingers to the exposed papers. Deep murmurings echoed from the group of women, kindling a kindred spirit. Arista felt herself sway with the gathering; then the commotion stopped. A woman's voice addressed Arista.

To you, our visitor, we welcome your old soul and wise spirit. You were uniquely chosen by birth. We await your arrival.

Arista let the words flow through her and settle inside her core. Her great-grandmother Arista welcomed her. Arista closed her eyes again and basked in the primal stirrings surrounding her.

The passage she'd experienced shifted. She blinked, and her office rippled before her eyes once again. The small slice of life she'd witnessed inspired Arista. These were the footsteps she'd follow behind. The passion and drive simmered within her now, just below the surface. Instantly she knew what had led her to this moment. An awakening: foreknowledge of events to prepare herself for and familiarity with those who had come before.

An array of papers lay strewn across her desk, forgotten, poised to pull her back to a detailed analysis accompanied by lengthy summaries and charts. *Not today.* Her priorities had changed, and she knew they'd never be the same again.

Arista entered her personal chambers. Maybe, just maybe, she'd reach him. She settled in a chair and focused on Stephen.

Stephen? Are you there?

Arista? Hi. I'm here but not to Provo yet. Didn't I tell you when I'd be arriving?

Yes. You did. I'm early in making contact. I just wanted to talk to you.

Ah. I'm good with that.

Arista felt Stephen's smile flow through her, and her lips tugged up in return.

Do you have much longer to go?

Quite a ways. A few hours yet.

I can feel your movement. You're on the train, aren't you?

Yep. For a long time now.

It's almost like I'm there with you.

I wish you were. Instead it's just me, this old man snoring beside me, and my sore backside.

Thanks for agreeing to help with this.

Sure. You know I'd do anything for you.

Arista's heart fluttered. *I know, and it means so much to me.*

I can tell.

Stephen, I'm trying to work out a visit. I'm not sure when or how yet. But I need to know if you're open to the idea. I feel like it's been ages since we were together.

Arista waited for his response, knowing she'd feel any true emotions behind his thoughts.

Open? Of course I'd be open. I love you. Remember?

Arista sighed when a tingling sensational reverberated through her.

I remember. But I don't mind being reminded, often.

When she sensed Stephen's laughter, Arista joined in. *I miss you… And there's so much happening. I hope I can talk to you in person. If I can work out details on this end, will it be a problem for you at home?*

I'll deal with that one way or another. I miss you too. And if you can make it happen, you can be damn sure I'll be there. I can't wait to hear all about what's going on! I can sense you're holding something back though, even from so far away. Is it something bad?

I taught you well. No, it's not. But I'd rather talk to you about it in person.

All right. I can wait. I just don't like bad news hovering over me. Reminds me of doctors.

Understandable. I'm so excited to meet Jack. Even through you, I'm nervous about it.

I'm expecting a hard-ass soldier, so I'm a little nervous myself.

Reach out to me when you're closer.

You got it.

Thomas—his given name on Earth, was called Stephen, on Remeon—stood up to stretch, then climbed over the sleeping man beside him, catching his braces on the seat in front of him in the process. Thomas wrestled them free within a few minutes but still garnered plenty of attention from those passengers closest to him. He trailed through the car, trying not to clang his leg braces together.

As he met the gazes of those he passed, they averted their eyes. *Idiots. I wish I could connect with each of them personally and let them know what big jackasses they are.* He'd hoped the dining car would be clearing out with the dinner service almost done but no such luck. Thomas squeezed in to one of the few open seats and ordered meat loaf and mashed potatoes.

The terrain raced by him. And, even with night approaching and the darkening view outside, Thomas peered out the window, hoping he wouldn't get pulled into conversation. Tomorrow he'd take off his braces for the day. They weren't necessary *every day* now, but they were a pain to carry around as well. *Someday soon, no one will know by looking at me that I had polio. Then maybe I can have some real discussions with people about something other than these things.*

"Young man, your dinner."

"Yes. Thank you."

Thomas imagined his family sitting down to dinner at home. His parents had been real troopers since he and his sister had returned from Remeon. They'd given him space and more freedom to come and go how he pleased. Without questions or reminders he got his chores done. Life on the farm wasn't the big deal it used to be somehow, now that he'd experienced life and death on Remeon.

It would be another thing altogether to ask his parents to let Thomas return to Remeon. His parents had been worried and pushed almost beyond their breaking point with both him and his sister affected by Remeon events. Maybe he wouldn't ask them. His folks were in a good place now and seemed happier than ever. It might be best not to mess that up.

He shook his head as he argued silently with himself. *I promised to be honest.* When he and Pa had talked man to man upon his return, Pa had said he'd listen to Thomas about anything—as long as it was the truth. He'd told them everything about Remeon, even about Arista.

Thomas opted for coffee as he remained in the dining car, still deep in thought. Whatever secret Arista held was big. He could tell. And he missed her like hell. He'd be forthright with his parents and hoped they'd understand. But, when the time came, he'd be going back. One way or another.

The busyness of the dining car noticeably relaxed. Thomas maneuvered back into his seat. Energized by the coffee, he reviewed what he'd memorized to say to Jack. First impressions were important, and he'd be meeting Arista's dad. Eventually, if things went the way Thomas hoped, he would go to Jack to ask for Arista's hand in marriage, if she'd have him.

Yeah, he'd need to make a *very* good impression.

Amid the silence and the steady *clickety-clack* din of the train, Thomas's knee moved up and down to its own rhythm.

HIS NERVE LEFT him as Thomas approached the house. He perched behind a line of trees on the perimeter. Hitching a ride from the train station took no time.

Now what? What if this isn't the right house? Maybe I should go back to the courthouse—check again, just to be sure.

What's wrong, Stephen? You came all this way. Well, you said it was a long way from home. You can't turn back now.

Hell, yeah, Provo is a long way from home. I'm doing this for you.

I can tell you're on edge. It's all right.

He's your dad. I'm forgetting everything I memorized on the trip here.

Thomas checked the address, verifying it for the fourth time. *This has gotta be it. We've ruled out the other ones.*

Just go ahead and do it. Knock.

Arista, we need to be sure. I've come all this way.

We've gone through this. We are sure. Knock!

Thomas walked to the porch, hit the front door with his knuckles three times, and waited.

I guess he's not here.

Inside the house Thomas heard the solid *thud* of shoes hitting the floor, steadily getting louder as they advanced toward him.

Shit. He is here.

We did it!

Not yet we didn't.

Thomas watched as the doorknob twisted, just before the door creaked open.

"Hello."

Well, tell me what he looks like.

Tall. Real tall. Blond hair, blue eyes.

"Hello? Is there something I can help you with?"

"Uh, yeah. Actually there is. Sorry to bother you. I believe you fought with an uncle of mine in the war. Could you spare just a few minutes to talk with me?"

Thomas watched while the man's mind worked. If he said no, Thomas would move to plan B.

"It's a bit unexpected but sure. I guess so. What regiment was he with?"

The man turned, his focus distracted by someone's voice inside. Seconds later his attention settled again on Thomas.

Regiment? I guess I should know that. Damn.

The man's eyes narrowed.

To Thomas, it seemed as if they drilled right through him. He stuck out his hand, hoping to deflect the question. "I'm Thomas. Pleased to meet you."

The two shook hands.

"Thomas, I'm Jack. Come on in."

Wow! It worked. I'm in.

Good job. Remember. Listen to me. I'll try to help if you get into trouble.

Marveling at the wonder of telepathy, Thomas smiled inwardly. He wasn't a master at this form of communication by any means, but Arista had taught him the basics, then worked with him more in depth after his abduction at the hands of Simon. So far, Thomas had been able to keep Simon from his thoughts here on Earth, while at the same time, Arista and Thomas could communicate at will.

The knowledge of one's true name held special power on Remeon, and Simon knew Thomas's and Belle's true names. However, only if they were on Remeon could that power be utilized. Still, Arista believed something else aided Thomas and Belle, and it had to do with Belle and her abilities. Arista hadn't been more specific, except to say Belle was uniquely suited to telepathy, and that somehow she'd been shielding Thomas, likely without even Belle realizing her feat.

None of it made any sense to Thomas. How could his little sister do such a thing? Just one more question that needed an answer during his upcoming trip back to the planet… Soon. The lines of his face bent into a smile. He couldn't wait!

Thomas stepped into the entryway and scanned the room before him. The high ceiling and large wooden beam overhead drew his gaze upward. "Wow, I've never seen anything quite like this."

"Oh, that. It is unique."

Thomas noted a hint of pride in Jack's voice.

"I built this house. That's what I do. If you like this, wait until you see the kitchen."

"Could I?"

"Sure." Jack led the way and waved Thomas along. "Now, what do think of that view? You can see the sunrise peek in every morning, just about there," Jack indicated, pointing outside.

Thomas nodded. "I bet it's incredible."

"Indeed, it is. My second-favorite place in the house."

Thomas raised a brow, wondering, but not particularly expecting an answer. He didn't really know the man after all.

"The living room there, where you came in, it's grown to be my favorite. After serving in the war and being constantly wet, or sick, sitting by a fire—enjoying a good book and a stiff drink—not much that can match that, with an exception or two."

An infectious grin lit Jack's face, and Thomas felt himself respond to Jack's good humor and honesty.

I like him, Arista. I like him a lot. He seems…genuine.

"Can I get you something to drink?"

Thomas's gaze immediately darted to the amber-colored liquid on the side table next to a leather chair where an open book lay. It was only just past noon.

"That'd be whiskey. How old are you?"

"Six…Sixteen," Thomas stammered.

"A man then. What's your pleasure?"

"Uh…" Thomas shifted his weight and felt his knee start to give way. *Damn.* Regretting his decision to leave his braces behind, he grabbed for the nearest wall. A second later Thomas felt Jack's strong arms steadying him.

Thomas grasped Jack's forearms, willing his legs to move forward. The pair froze, eyes locked on each other. *Damn it to hell.* All that squatting outside had stressed his legs. What a great first impression.

Jack's gaze drifted down the length of Thomas's legs, then back up again. "Lean on me, and let's get you a seat."

"I'm all right, really." But, with his legs still not cooperating, all he could do was accept the seat offered—Jack's seat, the closest—the leather chair. "Look. I'm sorry." Thomas heaved a deep breath, preparing himself for a long explanation.

"Now, what will it be?" Jack interrupted. "Got plenty of this." He chuckled as he grabbed his drink and downed the remainder.

"No, thanks. I'd love some of that coffee though. It smells great."

"Coming right up." Jack disappeared into the kitchen.

I can't do this, Arista. You should see this room. He's had so many commendations, articles framed from newspaper stories, pictures of his buddies from the war I bet.

"Here you go. It's black."

"Thanks."

Jack took a seat next to Thomas and placed his own refill on the side table.

"Papa?"

Jack turned his attention to the voice. "Daniel, come meet our visitor." Daniel took slow deliberate steps toward his father. "This is Thomas." After a little nudge Daniel crossed the small space between his father and Thomas and stretched out his hand.

"Please to meet you, Mr. Thomas."

Thomas shook the small hand. "Very good to meet you as well." Thomas eyed the child, glancing back and forth from Jack to Daniel.

They don't look alike at all, Arista. Cute kid though.

Hmmm.

"Go on back to your room, or sit here with us. But if you stay here with us, you must mind your manners."

"I'll go back to my room, I think, Papa, until lunch."

Jack laughed and pushed Daniel's backside back the way he came. "Suit yourself." Jack took a deep breath and released it. "Now, where were we?"

Thomas cleared his throat. "Polio. I had Polio." Thomas shrugged. "I, uh, didn't want to wear my braces today." Thomas glanced quickly at Jack, then plowed forward again, afraid that he'd lose his nerve if he didn't. "Listen. I'm not here about my uncle." Thomas's gaze drifted to the walls again. "Not that I wouldn't love to hear about all this."

"You're not?"

"No."

A wry smile rested on Jack's face. "I was wondering when you'd get to the real reason for your visit."

"You knew?"

Jack nodded, his eyes scanning the wall. "Don't mind talking to you about the other as well, as soon as we clear this up between us."

Thomas reached for his coffee and gulped down several large swallows.

"Not that I haven't enjoyed watching you squirm, just a little bit."

Arista… I think I'm in that trouble part you mentioned.

I can see why my mother fell in love with him.

Okay. So you have the information you need?

"No, I don't think I do, Thomas," Jack interjected.

Loud laughter echoed in Thomas's head. *You're no help.*

Invite him back to Remeon, Stephen. Vinique and I can pull him through the portal.

Jack leaned back and sipped his drink. "So I'll just put my cards on the table… I've been reading your thoughts since you came in here. I sensed your connection to Remeon when you walked in."

Thomas rearranged himself in his seat. "Why didn't you just tell me? If you knew why I was actually here…"

"You came to me. Remember?"

"I didn't feel you inside my head."

"Good. I didn't want you to. I'm betting I've had many more years of telepathy experience than you. And… I learned from the master." Jack raised his glass, as if making a toast, then tipped back his glass, emptying the remainder of his drink. "I can feel Arista with you. I haven't tried to connect with her directly—I wasn't sure she wanted me to."

Stephen, I'm sorry to put you in the middle of this. But I had to know what he looked like, how he acted. I was afraid, afraid he'd tell me no.

"Thomas, tell her yes. I'd love to see her, and, if she wants to talk to me telepathically, I'd like that as well."

Thomas sighed. "That's a relief."

"How about some lunch? I'll answer your real questions, and maybe you can tell me about your trip to Remeon, especially how you've come to know my daughter. That would be way better than me pulling all that from you. Huh?"

"Much." Thomas ran his fingers through his hair. "Mainly due to my stupid disease, I was abducted, along with my sister, and had mostly a very unpleasant experience, with the exception of meeting Arista."

"You were the one."

"The one?"

"The final one who ultimately led to a cure."

Slowly a grin reached Thomas's face. "Yeah. I guess so. Arista said the people are being healed in record numbers."

"Sounds like we have quite a bit in common." Jack stood. "I'll fix us some lunch. Can you manage?"

"Sure can. Traveling just put some extra stress on my legs. After resting a while now, I should be fine."

"Let's go then. Now that we've gotten to a truth between us, can we keep it that way? I'm hoping to get to know you better, since you obviously have an interest in my daughter." Jack turned, almost slamming into Thomas as he tried to keep up. "And, Thomas?"

What did I do now? Thomas raised his eyebrows in question, waiting. Jack patted him firmly on the shoulder. "I can't thank you enough for bringing my daughter and me together again."

Relief flooded him. Thomas released the breath that he'd been holding, and the smile that took over his face reached his eyes.

Oh, Stephen, I can't believe I've been without him all this time.

Jack busied himself, preparing lunch. "Have a seat. And start at the beginning. I want to hear all about your time on Remeon."

Thomas drew in a breath. "Well, to start, I'm known as Stephen among the people there, 'cause of the *true name* thing. My first encounter was with Whisterly. She guided me to the compound."

Jack paused his preparations and focused on his visitor.

Thomas stared into the distance. "She was the most beautiful woman I'd ever seen." He met Jack's stoic facade. "That is, until I saw Arista." Heat rose in the younger man's face, and Thomas yanked at his shirt around his neck, suddenly feeling constricted.

Jack carried two plates, loaded with sandwiches, and set them on the table. "Please, continue."

DURING HIS DRIVE to Harry's, Jack contemplated how different his experience on Remeon had been from Thomas's. And, although both were brutal, it pained Jack to discover that the majority of Thomas's injuries, physical and psychological, had been inflicted by Simon, Jack's own son. Bile rose in his throat as he pushed aside the memory of the conversation for now.

He threw the gearshift into Park and grabbed the book, *That Hideous Strength*, in the seat beside him. He associated the book with Whisterly's death now, since he'd finished reading it right before she had appeared to him, and he didn't mind at all handing it over to Harry.

His feelings of powerlessness and helplessness had been growing ever since that horrible morning. In his heart Jack knew, if he'd been with her, like he'd wanted to be all these years, that he could have done something to prevent it. His obsession over Whisterly's murder consumed his waking hours and tormented his nights, and with no outlet, no formal grieving process, it ate away, day by day, at his insides. In the six months since her death Jack had found no way to reconcile himself with her passing. How could he?

At the same time, memories had been resurfacing from the war…snippets encapsulating the horrors and atrocities…provoking the same feeling of powerlessness. From years of trying, he knew he wouldn't completely overpower the darkness of that pain, but he sure as hell could beat it into submission. Now meeting Thomas added a new layer to the mess of confusion in his head.

As Jack had feared, Simon was out of control and cruel—even from Remeonite standards—inflicting pain for his own pleasure. And so now, finding his son, after all these years of begging Whisterly to bring Jack back, so he would have a chance to know Simon… well, it would finally happen, or Jack would die trying. Maybe he was already too late.

Going back to Remeon would unearth emotions that he'd attempted to bury long ago… Reconnecting with Arista, well, there weren't words to express how happy he'd been over the opportunity to see her again. Life was less without Whisterly. Very little mattered. Jack growled out a sigh, shifting his focus. Only Arista, Simon, and Daniel were important now.

Jack approached the door, but before he could knock, Harry stood before Jack and pulled his best friend in for a hug.

"Come on in. How's the hand?"

Jack shrugged and held it up. "Cast's off. Been off for a long time. Fine, I guess." He stretched his fingers on his right hand. "It's amazing what time can do for physical injuries, isn't it?"

Harry nodded. "So day after tomorrow is the big day?"

Jack held out the book to Harry. "This is a great book. I think you'll like it." Jack ran his fingers through his hair, then paced the length of the family room. "Yeah, that's right, day after tomorrow."

Harry set down the book, watching Jack prowl back and forth. "Are you okay with it? Going back?"

Jack paused and nodded. "I am. It just would have been a damn sight better to have been there earlier."

"Let me see if I can find my book for you. Then we can have a drink."

"Sure. Don't know when I'll have it back to you though."

Harry grinned. "What? No time for reading on Remeon?"

Jack gave Harry a side-long glare. "God only knows what's waiting for me there. Whether I read it there or not, something from you, from Earth, will help me."

Harry came behind Jack and put his hand on Jack's shoulder. "You got it. Here it is."

"Hmmm. *Cannery Row.* Is it any good?"

Harry nodded. "Very good. I think you'll find it worth your time. Some of the characters…well, they remind me of us, Jack."

Jack turned the book over in his hands. "Is that so? Steinbeck, huh?"

"Yep. Are you ready for that drink now? You're stalking around like a caged animal."

Jack met Harry's gaze. "Yeah. That's about right."

"Come on into the kitchen. Sit." Harry held out the whiskey. "Drink."

"Thanks. Keep 'em coming." The pair sat in a comfortable silence for a while, not feeling the need to fill it, the clinking sound of bottle meeting glass every so often, ensuring the next drink, the only sounds in the kitchen.

"Harry, do you want kids?"

Harry eyed his friend and took another swallow of his whiskey. "Where did that come from?"

"I don't want all my issues to scare you away from having kids. In the end, they're all that matters. Our legacy. You and Maggie would make great parents. And I'm looking forward to a little niece or nephew one day."

A crooked grin took over Harry's face. "Let's just say it's not from lack of trying. With any luck it'll happen soon."

Jack clinked Harry's glass and polished off his drink. "How about another?"

Harry refilled both glasses. "Can we toast to Whisterly?"

Lifting his drink, Jack paused, nodded.

Harry raised his glass. "To you and Whisterly. She'll never really be gone, Jack."

Meeting Harry's glass, Jack fought the tears that pushed at the back of his eyes, always so close to the surface, straining to be set free. "No, no she won't."

Harry glanced at Jack over his glass, then set it down on a long exhale. "Jack, I'll just say what I'm thinking, even though you probably already know it."

Jack chuckled and hung his head. "You're right. I do."

Harry leaned in closer to Jack. "I'm worried about you."

"Spending a lot of time in my head, are you?"

"As I said, I'm concerned about you. You've not given yourself time to grieve. So, yes, I have."

Jack looked down at his hands and spoke softly. "Even with all the time that's passed, with me on Earth and her on Remeon, there was always a chance before…"

"A chance?"

"For us to be together as a family. Now that's gone, along with Whisterly." Jack swallowed his drink. "I can't deal with it. Not being a part of her is like asking me not to breathe. I can't explain that to people. So I just don't."

"But I'm the one person on Earth who gets it, Jack, after all the hell we've been through."

Jack nodded, then reached for Harry telepathically. *I can't. If I do, it'll make it real. Sometimes I still feel her in my head. After all this telepathic shit, am I finally losing it, Harry?*

Harry's eyes misted. *If it helps, I'll stay out.*

Jack's brows knit together. *I don't care if you're in here. I'd kick you out if I did.*

"While you're on Remeon, you'll look for Simon?" Harry asked, returning to vocal communication.

A searing pain grabbed Jack's gut. "I've got to try, Harry. He's my flesh and blood, just like Arista, even if he has done some horrible things. I can't abandon him, like my father did to me."

Harry sucked in a breath, then met Jack's pained gaze. "Your situation was completely different."

"Maybe, but not to Simon. He's never known me, and to him, I can guarantee you that's all that matters."

"You know what, Jack? Talking to someone who doesn't know about any of this might help. Get an objective perspective."

Jack pushed back his chair and stood. "I just told you that I can't. Stop the psycho crap, and fill up my glass, would ya?"

"Okay, Jack. Sit down, and let me catch up first."

"Besides, there's nothing left to say. She's done. I'm done. What else is there? Damn her!" Jack sat down again and leaned heavily on the table as he scooted his glass toward Harry. "It's empty. See? And I *need* it full."

"Sure thing."

Harry refilled both glasses, and Jack grabbed the whiskey bottle. "Leave it." After quickly downing his next drink, Jack gripped the neck of the bottle and plodded around the room in awkward motions.

Harry crossed in front of Jack and spoke in a hoarse tone. "For Christ sake, Jack, let me help you."

Jack grabbed Harry's arm to steady himself and took a long swig from the bottle; then he met Harry's glassy-eyed stare. "Now don't you start. One of us needs…to keep shit together." Jack backed away and, meeting resistance, slid to the floor. He raised the bottle to his mouth again and drank deeply. "Harry, I'm…not, go…nna… make…it…this time," Jack said, slurring his words and shaking his head.

Harry joined Jack on the floor and pried the bottle from his fingers, then held Jack tight. "Yes, you are, Jack. Your kids need you. I need you. You'll hang around here with the rest of us, damn it, and put one foot in front of the other, just like you always do. I'll not have it any other way."

Jack raised his head and tried to home in on his friend. "Was that an…order, Harry? Can't give me…orders. … I outrank you." Jack's body went limp.

Yeah, I know you do. You stupid oaf. Harry ran a hand down his face, attempting to rein in his own emotions. Grabbing Jack under his armpits, Harry half-dragged, half-carried his friend to the couch, then heaved him on it. *Jesus, you're heavy. This used to be easier.* After yanking off Jack's boots, Harry covered him with a blanket. *Rest, Jack.*

Harry set to righting the items Jack had tumbled through, picked up the bottle, and laid the glasses in the sink. A sudden noise caught Harry's attention, and he turned toward the door.

He forced a smile. "Maggie, I didn't even hear you drive up."

Maggie's eyes settled on the disarray of the room in front of her. "So I see." Harry pulled Maggie toward him and held on tight. "How's our Jack?" she whispered.

Harry shook his head. "Hurting like hell. And I have no idea how to help him. I'll bet no one else knows about Whisterly but us. How can Jack get through this if he never mourns her?"

Maggie stared at the empty bottle. "You two drank all that?"

A raspy chuckle rose in Harry's throat. "Yeah, well, the drunk guy on the couch drank most of it, and a little bit spilled."

Maggie walked to where Jack slept and kissed him on the forehead, then rejoined her husband. "You don't look too stable on your feet either." Harry opened his mouth to protest, and she silenced him with a kiss. "You're a good friend and practically dead on your feet. Come on. Let's go to sleep."

Maggie started toward the hallway, and Harry took her hand, sliding her back in the folds of his arms. "In a minute. I need another one of those first."

Maggie leaned in, and they met in slow kiss. "Now are you ready to go to bed?" She arched her brows in question.

Taking his wife's hand, he led her toward their room. "Bed, yes. But sleep can wait," he whispered.

CHAPTER 3

SIMON EAGERLY WAITED for the hour later this evening
when he'd escape the cave of the Night Dwellers. Even after
all these years he still craved time away, needed to follow the same
routine that his mother had ingrained in him years ago. The short
respite from his underground existence gave him the unencumbered
opportunity to sift through his thoughts, and those of others, without constant interruption. Especially now.

While the Day Watchers were celebrating the delivery of the
cure to their masses, hordes of Night Dwellers continued to die.
Deep-seated anger boiled up from his gut. The cure lay on the horizon. At least with the vaccine in place, the discovery of new cases
had been dwindling.

Meanwhile, reported deaths continued, their numbers steadily
rising. *Still*. Making his rounds, Simon's lip curled under in a snarl
as his nostrils filled with the stench of diseased flesh and stale body
fluids. Making a daily appearance inside the infirmary helped to
bolster his image among Night Dwellers.

But the truth—that he could barely stand to set foot in
the place since his brother's death from the disease months ago,
compounded by Simon's own infirmary stay due to injuries inflicted
by Stephen—threatened to bubble up quite literally now as he
fought the urge to vomit.

From his short distance away, Simon scanned the hospital beds to find Janus, the commander of the Night Dwellers, and the only father figure Simon had ever known. Just as he'd watched his younger brother, Willie, die and his mother, Mila, years before, now came Janus's turn. How the mighty fall. Janus had sworn he'd never succumb to the disease.

Then, when he did, he had maintained he'd outlast everyone and would survive until the cure became available. Simon took several steps closer, examining Janus's face as he did. The leader's chances appeared slim to none.

Simon sat in the chair next to Janus and attempted a telepathic connection. Janus preferred this method of communication since their visits frequently included tactical and strategic updates. None of those would occur today, however.

The man struggled to simply breathe. Raspy puffs of air pushed through him, followed by coughing fits, which appeared to fight Janus for the little strength he had left.

"Janus, I'm here."

His thin eyelids opened. "Simon? Is it you?"

Simon stared into the murky stillness of the man's eyes. Janus fumbled about him. Simon knew what his mentor wanted. His awkward jerks were an attempt to reach for Simon's hand. Simon couldn't, wouldn't touch him. Janus's body exuded the essence of the illness which would soon kill him. A death cloud clung to the man. Simon had never felt it so strongly.

Why couldn't others feel this? He didn't hear anyone discuss matters such as this. *Am I the only one?* A shudder pulsed through him as he edged away from Janus. Killing a man was one thing, but watching death sink its claws into a person, bit by bit, was quite another.

Through the older man's eyes, Simon saw himself fall from an extended beating at Janus's hand. Then Simon's own screams had echoed inside his thoughts as Janus had probed Simon's mind, punishing him. Simon disconnected the telepathic connection.

Similar events had occurred repeatedly throughout his younger formative years. Janus taught Simon how to be mentally strong, how to find others' breaking points, and, at that time, how to gather the weak minds under his control, ultimately delivering peace through compliance.

Janus's mantra circulated in Simon's head: *Everyone seeks to be led. We will be that for them.*

Simon sighed as he studied his mentor of old. *Now here he lays. In the end, just another death.* Seeing so many Night Dwellers fall to this insidious disease, one after another, death had become commonplace, expected. Did Simon love these people? No. But he needed them to fight. Only one, Mila, his mother, held a place in his heart.

Since her passing, Simon used his pent-up rage from those lost to this disease to fuel his assault on the Day Watchers—Whisterly's tribe.

The man in front of Simon didn't love him either. In fact, most of the methods of torture Simon used on others, he'd experienced firsthand from Janus as he drove Simon to be a better leader, to use Janus's own words. Even with that knowledge, Simon endured these…encounters. How else would he finally exact his revenge upon Whisterly, except to make it to the top?

Sick as it was, Simon focused all his attention on just that, until about a year ago when he began to exact what he needed from others. His insides tingled as he remembered the first time. The power… The control… The submission… Strange how it worked though. The craving… it grew with each consumption. Some nights the need seemed insatiable.

"Yes, it's me, Janus."

"Come closer. I can't hear you."

Simon scuffled about in the chair, feigning the action of moving in toward the bed. Then he spoke louder. "Is this better?"

Janus nodded, then came another bout of coughing. "Status… of…the cure?"

Simon leaned in nearer to the old man's ear. "Very close now. Won't be long. I'm sure you can hold on," Simon lied. The doctors were convinced Janus would not make it through the night. This would likely be the last time Simon would see him alive.

At one time Janus had served a purpose. He had found them shelter, procured a means for steady supplies, driven the doctors mercilessly as they researched a cure, and of course, had planned the initial exodus from the compound, freeing all his people from the control of the Day Watchers' council. But now, with the Night Dwellers under Simon's command, for all intents and purposes, Janus was only a dying figurehead.

The man mumbled incoherently beside him. Simon scooted farther away, taking the opportunity to draw a fresh breath from a greater distance. A doctor glanced at Simon, then stopped, hovering over Janus.

Simon rose. "I'll leave you to your work."

"No need to leave. I'm only checking vitals."

"How's he doing?"

"Not good, I'm afraid. As we expected, his organs are shutting down. Feel free to stay as long as you'd like. He's not in any pain. His passing to the next realm should be a smooth one." The doctor tapped the buttons on the console next to the bed.

"I have some matters to attend to, but please inform me when he passes."

The doctor nodded. "I'll personally see to it."

"I'll stop by later, Janus. Rest well." At last. Escape. Simon fought the urge to run from the room. The sense of weakness and lethargy combined with the stench of decaying tissue ensconced within the room had permeated his being. He needed to be free.

As he walked intently through the halls, he drew deep breaths, cleansing his body from his visit with Janus. On his way out of the cave, Simon grabbed a collection bag, then disappeared into the cool night.

He kept to a steady, brisk pace, with the knowledge that soon his leg injury, compliments of Terron, would give him trouble. Even though it had "healed," his leg wasn't 100 percent, and the doctors weren't sure it ever would be, thanks to Thomas's and Terron's betrayal. Simon's hand gravitated to the scar at his side when his thoughts turned to Thomas. Even with the knowledge of Stephen's true name, Thomas, Simon had not been able to exert enough control over Thomas to prevent the pair's betrayal. And thanks to them, Simon would have lifetime reminders of his failure with these injuries that wouldn't quite mend.

Before the Day Watchers had so quickly transported him off-world, Thomas had given Simon a gift. Through the special link Simon had forged with Thomas, Simon gained disturbing knowledge regarding his father, information he'd kept deeply hidden since that revelation. Information he'd need to confirm. Even more data was lost as Thomas neared Earth, managing to sever their telepathic link.

Could it possibly be true?

Simon would need proof because it was just too incredible for belief. Thomas being an outsider, something must have gone wrong in the information exchange during those last few seconds before Thomas had left, Simon reasoned, damaging the thought transfer.

Simon aimlessly trekked through the forest as he often did when he wrestled with difficult issues. No easy answers would be forthcoming. If the information were correct, his true father had been human.

How will I live with the shame?

Since pulling this knowledge from Thomas, Simon had fought to come to grips with it, without success. There had been more, more thoughts he'd tried to gain that had slipped from his grasp, along with Thomas. His departure had been too quick. The link evaporated.

The cure that the Day Watchers enjoyed, and that would soon be in the Night Dwellers possession as well, was derived from a human—

could that be the source of Simon's own immunity? His mother's union with a human, if that were true, may have provided him with additional protection against PR 251. Simon bit back a laugh, relishing in the irony as his plan formed. A perfectly sweet revenge.

With Janus's death imminent, he needed a successor. One who wouldn't ever fall. One with Simon's blood. Eventually following these thoughts through to fruition, the next generation would be united under his true defining leadership, encompassing Night Dwellers and Day Watchers alike.

Janus had turned weak, his mind limited. Simon would take the people full circle in a much grander style than Janus had ever conceived. Simon would end the war between the two factions for good and emerge the victor.

He returned to the cave and handed his sack to a waiting guard. "My companion for the night, is she waiting?"

"In your quarters, per your instructions."

Simon took a step closer to his guard. "And what is her age?"

The guard's voice dropped to just above a whisper. "Her age matches your own, sir."

"Excellent." The smile on Simon's face transformed into a hideous grin.

"Sir?"

"Yes? What is it?" Simon, eager for his recreational activity, charged through the entrance hall.

"Our Commander and Chief has died. I received word minutes ago and was asked to relay that information to you upon your return."

"And so you have. Resume your duties."

Simon dashed through the corridor to his quarters. Nodding to the guard stationed there now, he entered the room and closed the door behind him. At the noise the young girl waiting for Simon turned her gaze toward him. As he seized her thoughts, Simon felt a defiance rise within her. "Well, now, this is a pleasing change to the women who serve me." Simon discarded his shirt while the girl inched away toward the wall. He chuckled. "Yes, please do make this fun."

Simon delved further into her brain, and her breath caught. He prowled closer as her eyes widened. Within inches of her face now, his hand trailed down her throat; then, leaning down, he possessed her mouth. Their connection pulsed through his limbs, her fear surging within, encouraging him. Simon pushed his own negative thought energy into her brain waves, and she slid to the floor. Beads of sweat dotted her forehead, and her breaths came in short pants of air. "That's it. You're mine now," he murmured next to her ear.

She whimpered.

Simon bent and slipped the dress from her shoulders. "Perfect. Let's begin."

THOMAS SCALED THE steps to his bedroom, wondering if he'd made a mistake telling his parents at all. He could have just disappeared. Heaving a deep breath, he twisted the doorknob and entered the room. The darkness and cool night air coursing through the window calmed him.

With January here now, the need for Thomas's help on the farm dwindled to almost nothing. His pa hadn't pushed him, but since returning from Remeon Thomas actually wanted to help in the fields. And, with the healing that had taken place in his legs, he'd made a significant contribution. The proud look on his pa's face was all the evidence Thomas needed to know what his pa thought of Thomas's accomplishment, small in comparison that it was.

After his adventure on Remeon, the two men had communicated more than they ever had in the past. And his father treated him differently. Thomas couldn't quite put his finger on it, but he liked it. It made him almost feel like an equal…almost. For now, at least, his pa wasn't shoving the farm in his face constantly. His father had been right about one thing. The process all clicked, coming together like a well-oiled machine, from planting to harvesting and selling.

During the weeks following their return from Remeon, Thomas and Belle had relayed their story to their parents in bits and pieces. These installments—Thomas's idea—gave their parents time to absorb the details to the fullest extent. Well, from the pieces they'd been given anyway.

Thomas and Belle had decided and agreed upon in advance the particular information that they would tell their parents. Things like, the extent of Thomas's injuries and how close he came to dying had been glossed over. And to Belle's credit, she understood, complied, and had been happy to tell about her part in finding her brother and participating in his rescue.

While Thomas and Belle could still communicate telepathically with each other on Earth, they still couldn't read their parents, a fact Ma and Pa were quite happy about. After each session, Thomas asked if they had any questions and typically was met with blank stares. When his parents spoke alone, he'd been sure that they must have voiced concerns over their son's sanity.

But then an odd thing happened. Thomas's parents came to him, and in some cases to Belle, independent of one another and asked questions. With the exception of those details he and Belle had agreed to keep between themselves, they both answered their parents' questions.

An acceptance with the events reached, it appeared they'd all cleared a hurdle. His parents had witnessed the outcome of the telepathy between their two youngest children. What could they do? They accepted it and their children, including their special clairvoyant gifts.

But tonight hadn't gone as well as the prior months' discussions had. At least his parents had spoken just with Thomas this time. From the fear evident on both their faces, their concern for Belle consumed them both. Thomas didn't want to tell them this now, but he believed Belle would return also. He didn't like admitting it, but her telepathic abilities surpassed his own. She just seemed to fit in on Remeon. Pieces of the latest conversation with his parents played over and over again in his head.

"So you're going back now because of this girl—"

"*Arista*, Pa. You know her name's Arista. And she's meeting her father for the first time, who's also from Earth."

"I see."

His father had reached for his mother's hand as she started to cry, while Thomas studied his own hands intently, waiting for the next question.

Pa continued. "Do you love her, Thomas? I'm not sure why you would do this if you didn't. From what you've told us before, you've got enemies there."

Thomas nodded and met his pa's gaze. "Yes, I do have some enemies on Remeon. But I do love Arista, and I'm going back to help her through this any way I can."

Pa stood and covered the short distance to his son in two broad steps.

Thomas heard his mother gasp, and when he felt his father's form towering above him, Thomas stood, meeting his father face-to-face. The two didn't speak as they studied each other.

Finally his pa broke the silence. "I don't want you to go, but I'll not keep you here against your will." A strong hand fell on Thomas's shoulder. "You sound clear-headed, and your plan is thought through. We won't stand in your way."

Thomas reached toward his pa. When his arms surrounded Thomas, he'd let out a heavy sigh as relief flowed from him. Feeling the lighter touch of his mother behind him, Thomas turned and embraced her also, her gentle sway differentiating her contact. Then they'd both silently withdrawn, and joining hands, left their son in the family room alone.

Scaling the stairs, Thomas drew in a deep breath, appreciating the chill dampness in the air that would most likely bring rain to their fields tonight. "I had a feeling you'd be in here." Sliding into the chair next to his bed, he clicked on the lamp, the sudden light revealing his younger sister.

She giggled. "Well, tell me already...how'd it go...or should I just pull it from you instead?"

Thomas couldn't resist. The stern look that had taken over his face dissipated, and he joined in with her laughter. How would she manage alone with their parents in his absence? Once Belle had "recovered," Ma had encouraged Mary to move to town, to be closer to her work. Her seamstress skills were in high demand, and, although uncertain at first, Mary eventually agreed that the change made sense.

Truthfully, upon hearing the experiences her siblings had gone through, Mary seemed fearful of remaining in their house, as if that had anything to do with it. Ma had said Mary had been through a lot, including stepping in where Ma and Pa could not when they were totally consumed with the strange circumstances of their two youngest children. "Let's give her space," Ma had encouraged. Now Mary had it.

"Better than expected," Thomas offered.

"That's it?"

Thomas leaped on the bed, bouncing his sister high as he landed, beginning another round of giggles. "They're concerned for me, but I can tell they're even more worried that you might follow after me."

"*Hmm.*"

"Yeah. They have pretty good instincts, huh?" Thomas stared down his sister, who avoided his gaze. "Belle?"

"What?"

"Come on... I know you've been thinking about it, returning to Remeon. And, even if I don't pull you through the portal, Vinique easily could."

"Maybe… Would you play a game of War with me?" Belle avoided the question, exposing the deck of cards in her hand.

"Sure." Thomas said through a grin. "If you don't mind getting beat again." The two played silently. At first, Thomas took the lead; then Belle came back from behind.

"I am getting better." Belle beamed at Thomas.

"Look, Belle. I'll be fine. You'll know what's happening. You don't have to worry about me."

Belle rolled her eyes, looking very much like her older sister, Thomas mused. "I can't do much from here, can I, Thomas?"

"Your job, and it's a big one, is to talk to Ma and Pa. Give them updates every now and then. Let them know that I'm all right."

Belle stared at her brother, her eyes clearly communicating her thoughts. "And what if you're not?"

Well, yes, that too, I guess, he said telepathically. Thomas leaned forward until their foreheads met, joining their consciousnesses. Then, as he read her thoughts directly, Belle's fears seeped through. Tears drifted down her cheeks.

I won't get sick again, Belle.

She shook her head. *You can't say that. It's happened before. You don't know, and the doctors don't either.*

Thomas rocked his sister. *I can't live like that, Belle. If there's one thing I've learned from being sick, it's that I want to live, not stay hidden in a room with my braces on, waiting for something horrible to happen. And you shouldn't either.*

Thomas sat back and forced his sister's chin up, even with his. "I'm going, Belle, and I need to know you're with me."

Belle nodded. "Will you take the rock I gave you?"

Thomas shoved his hand in his pants pocket. "Of course. It's always with me." He pulled the rock free and held it out to Belle. "See?"

Belle sniffed and wiped her eyes with the back of her hand.

"What do you think about Ma and Pa coming to the portal when I go? It might help them understand."

"Watching you disappear, you mean?"

"That's part of it, yeah. It's something they can both see, to help them believe and take part in somehow."

Belle's eyelids fluttered. "If that's what you want, Thomas," she said with an exasperated sigh. "Either way you'll be gone. That's what matters to them and me." She stretched as she lay across the bottom of Thomas's bed, then curled herself into a ball.

"Belle?"

When she didn't answer, Thomas covered his sister with a blanket, then undressed and flipped off the lamp. A shiver hurried him under the covers. He threw the layers over his shoulders, and grateful for the warmth, he tunneled deeper. Tomorrow would be a big day. *Night, Arista. I'll see you soon.*

Sleep well, Stephen.

SIMON WOKE WITH the new morning and peered at the young woman, Dawn, beside him. At first she'd been defiant, then quite literally petrified. Simon's lips curled into a teeth-baring grin. He'd reveled in every second of his control over Dawn, which she had seen the wisdom to embrace. It was rare now, since Simon excelled at this skill, but some of these girls died, by accident of course.

Each one had opted for this path in noble service to the cause. Still, they were screened and chosen carefully. The leadership desired strong Night Dwellers, and these unions often resulted in births, a duty he took seriously. So he'd partake once again before she left him this morning.

Her breaths came in even slow waves. Simon initiated their connection. A calmness flowed through her. Carefully he entered her thoughts. He didn't want to be detected just yet. Inching through her pathways, he felt her body awakening, resisting the intrusion. She mumbled something incoherent in her sleep. Any second she'd open her eyes… *Now!* Simon seized control as her eyes shot open, meeting his gaze.

The fire he witnessed there encouraged and inflamed him. His hand inched down her throat.

Dawn wriggled underneath Simon, gasping, panting for the air he'd deprived her body. Then, as she gave herself over to him, her eyelids closed, and her stiffened limbs relaxed.

You're learning. Much quicker than last night.

She winced and sucked in the air available now to her.

Ah, surrender.

WHILE SIMON SHOWERED, Dawn took her time dressing, checking that nothing felt out of place. Even though she had been conquered, she didn't want to appear so. Maybe she had conceived an heir, and with it would come an elevated status and eventually a better life. As she exited, Dawn drew in a deep breath, then exhaled, absentmindedly smoothing the wrinkles in her dress. *Had it been worth it for what she might gain in return? Time would tell.*

Thirty minutes later Dawn left the commander's quarters.

SIMON RETURNED TO his empty chambers. He chuckled; he'd need to have her again and soon, hers being one of the best choices in recent memory in fact. Checking the time, Simon dressed.

Soon the three applicants would arrive, with no idea why they'd been summoned. He considered each one in turn. Errol had been with Simon the longest, trained by him, by far the best weapon's trainer, and could be depended on in a fight. Despite Terron's betrayal when Thomas was taken, Errol had remained committed. Now Simon counted him as one of the strongest among his team.

Aldwin, a few years older and trained by Janus, stood out as a candidate. He had it all: brains, brawn, loyalty, and seemingly a commitment to the cause.

Lastly Travis, average upon initial evaluation, but his strength lay in his mind. Telepathy suited him, and he controlled his environment with ease. While he was a decent marksman and could throw a mean punch, people followed him because he compelled them to. Their weakness drew him, and in return he easily commanded their will.

Simon clicked the button to return the message. "Send them in." The men filed in and stood at attention.

"Sir!"

Simon crossed in front of his desk, then leaned against it, taking on a casual air as he examined the men before him. "At ease. Sit." Simon raised his arms, indicating the small gathering. "You three are here because I need a second in command. Janus passed last night. And now, under my leadership, the Night Dwellers will undergo a few changes."

Simon let his chin fall to focus his gaze on each person in turn, delicately probing for signs of anxiety or fear. "Each of you is well qualified, even though your individual strengths would bring a different balance to the table. Only one can be second in line, another will be third. If you are judged to be the last choice of your lot this morning, your existence will terminate. Now. Today. In this room." The trio turned to look at one another over the small table they occupied.

A face-encompassing grin glowed on Simon's face. "I can see I have your attention. All of you have proven worthy in battle and commitment to our cause, but I need to see your ability to strategize and lead, before you get placed in a new position." Simon shrugged.

"Let's face it. We're not immortal yet. So, at any point in the future, you may find yourself in the highest leadership role among us. What would you do?" Simon paced the length of the room, then stole a glance at the three men who sat in stoic silence before him.

"Here's how it's gonna go. Each of you will need to imagine you're leading the other two. Choose your strategy, garner support, and the odd man out, he loses. Telepathy will be your communication of choice. I'm already deep into your thought waves. I'll know your decisions as you make them." Simon pulled a pistol from his desk drawer and laid it beside him.

"How can we all assume a leadership position at once?" Aldwin blurted out. "It'll be chaos. It won't work."

Simon nodded. "Indeed, it will be chaotic, disjointed, uncertain, confusing—much like combat. Ascertain your situation and act, or you will die." Simon paused, looking at each one directly. "Any other questions or *observations*?" A full minute passed. Each man drew his weapon. "Then we'll begin on my mark… Now!"

The three threw their chairs back, and telepathic energy filled the space. Simon marveled at the rapidity of the communication back and forth. He'd not set a time limit, but the intensity rose as the intellectual banter passed freely among the three. Simon experienced their thoughts as the position vied for jockeyed between them. The combination of their styles mingled, then evolved. And quite the model of civility, each presented and supported their reasoning for their personal position to the other two.

Inwardly Simon felt a winner emerge, with a close second and a distant third. He concurred, nodding, signaling his silent approval. Three sets of eyes set upon each other, their gazes locked. Crouching, they prowled around the table, as they held their weapons, sights set on the other two. With a loud grunt Aldwin threw the table in the air, toppling the other two men. Grabbing the legs and using the table as a shield, Errol and Travis drove toward Aldwin, pinning him to the wall. He leveled his weapon at Errol and Travis.

"Don't try it. You'll be dead before you can get off the shot," Travis warned.

Aldwin let out a weak chuckle. "Seems I'm gonna be dead either way, so why not take you with me?"

"Your plan was to follow another's lead," Errol said, setting down his weapon. "How will you be a second if you choke under pressure?"

"Great question. Why don't you answer it, Aldwin?" Simon inclined his head. "You've had more *training* than the other two."

A hysterical high-pitched laugh tore from Aldwin. "You set us up to fail. It just happened to be me. Could as easily have been one of the other two."

"And you did it brilliantly," Simon sneered. "But I disagree on your logic. If you crack here, you'll cave when you have a team of soldiers following you also. We can't afford that."

"Go ahead. You've made your choice."

Simon shook his head. "No, *you* made it. In order for this experiment to work, the stakes had to be high and the pressure real. Because you really could lead people to their deaths. I had already decided to keep all three of you, if you were all truly up to the task. Clearly you're nowhere close."

Aldwin waved his pistol at Simon. "You're not half the leader that Janus was. And you never will be."

Travis fired, hitting Aldwin in the hand, forcing him to drop his weapon.

"Traitor!" Aldwin spat back.

"That's true. I'm not Janus. But I learned from him. Got what I needed." Simon's eyes narrowed. "You, however, cowered behind him. And I've been blind to it until now."

Aldwin clutched his bleeding hand. "This isn't the first day I wished I'd chosen the Day Watchers—"

"Shut the hell up, stupid," Errol yelled.

Aldwin scoffed the words away. "Go on. Get it over with."

Simon stared at him, considering.

"I'll make it easy for you." Aldwin reached for Simon through the link he'd already established. The link that had betrayed him, confirming his own failure to act. He seized Simon's thoughts digging, thrusting deeper.

Simon smirked. "This isn't a place you want to be. Trust me, Aldwin."

"Trust? No one here trusts you."

Simon plowed through the gray matter of Aldwin's brain, experiencing the crackling and sizzling with him as he tore through the doomed man's cerebral cortex. It lasted mere seconds. Aldwin slumped, dead where he landed. His body just didn't know it yet as it flopped over the table, swaying slowly side to side, blood still dripping from the bullet wound in his hand.

Disgust twisted Simon's face as he took in the full measure of the man, lifeless before him. "It's decided. Travis, you'll train as my second. Errol, you'll be third in line for command should the situation warrant. Now go, and send someone in to clean away this putrid mess."

CHAPTER 4

ARISTA TURNED THE key over in her hand. As she twirled the metal between her fingers, its coolness seeped into her skin. Sliding her hand over its bumps and groves, she memorized each one. Whisterly's key. It belonged to Arista now. After their conversation, Vinique had left it with her. Tonight Arista would use it before her initiation ritual tomorrow night, the joining with the grimoire.

Bowing her head, Arista slid the necklace around her neck. The key plunged swiftly underneath her dress, the chill it exuded dissipating as it met with the warmth of her skin. Determined to uncover a few answers tonight, Arista left her chambers.

Throughout the day, apprehension had gotten the better of her. Even after Vinique's assurance that this initial step, while somewhat of a shock, would go smoothly, Arista's mind roamed, searching and unsettled, compelling her to investigate the heritage she was about to embrace. She found it difficult to reconcile that the mother she knew so well—kind and loving but also strong and decisive—could have this hidden existence. The turmoil within Arista threatened to explode.

Coinciding with her initiation would be the arrival of Jack and Stephen. Her heart fluttered at thought of seeing Stephen again. And she'd have to tell him what she'd done in her desperation right before he'd gone back to Earth through the portal. Maybe he'd be angry or, even worse, sad. She cringed while her mind replayed the various scenarios over and over in her head. None of these outcomes ended positively. One thing for sure, he wouldn't be elated over the deception. Arista cursed under her breath, then turned to more immediate matters confronting her.

Vinique had promised to attend Arista's immersion. This assurance brought with it a peaceful resignation that Arista traveled in the path meant for her. Myriad emotions wrestled within her, all vying for the space at the top. Per Vinique's directions, the door to the basement lay just ahead. Arista slowed, and, just as her aunt had indicated, a light mist enveloped the space.

To passersby the condensation would appear to blend into the walls surrounding it. One would need to stop and wander into the foggy substance to realize it had a purpose—to conceal the door leading to the basement below. Arista extended her arms, groping for the doorknob in the deserted corridor. Her fingers met wood as they glided over markings of some kind etched in the door.

Adjusting her search downward, she located the doorknob, and pulling her key free with the other hand, she unlocked the door and gave the doorknob a quick twist. Unaccustomed to ancient doors she pushed lightly at first; then, as she heaved her weight into the mass of the door, it opened slowly, squeaking loudly in protest.

Arista squeezed through the opening she created, then fumbled along the wall, hoping for a light switch that would illuminate the darkness that stretched before her. *Thank goodness—there you are.* Flipping the switch, she peered deep into the enclosed space.

After shutting the door, a mustiness filled her nose that, accompanied by a damp chill which quickly permeated her clothing, sent a shiver down her spine. Was this really the place? Following Vinique's instructions as best she could, Arista inched down the steps. When she stepped beyond the last step, her foot slipped on the wet bumpiness of the cobblestone beneath her, and in the process of fumbling for a hold to grab, she hit another light switch, bathing the room in a low, warm light.

Arista gasped. Rows and rows of books filled shelf after shelf. This room contained more physical books than she'd ever seen in one place. But she continued, knowing this wasn't the room that held the grimoire. Farther ahead, hiding what should be the entrance to an inner chamber, a piece of wood lay ajar, not quite covering the hole behind it. *That must be it. Thank you, Vinique.*

On all fours, Arista crawled into the room and found the light switch. More books filled the space. A low hum buzzed around her. Arista turned in a circle in the middle of the floor, searching for its source. *What is it? Is someone here?* She stepped toward the books. The hum grew more intense. Then another step, followed by yet another. Tilting her head sideways, she read the book titles as she perused the shelves.

Soon the din hurt her ears. She paused. The book in front of Arista rocked under her touch, unsettling a light layer of dust that trickled slowly downward, landing on her shoes. The spine carried no markings, but she grabbed it and ran her fingers over the front cover. The sun was just like Vinique had described. *This is it!*

Arista hadn't had much experience with physical books, but it was plain this one was old. She settled on the floor. The book itself had been bound by hand, and a pentagram adorned the inside cover. Its pages consisted of thick yellowed paper. A crisp vibration trailed each turn of the page as the paper sliced through the air.

Arista raised her head and listened. The noise. It had stopped. She flipped through more pages; each appeared like the last— yellowed, dingy, and old. *Why are the pages blank?*

A hint of a whisper brushed by her ear. Arista lifted her head again. More whispers... *Higher, child. Lift your head higher.*

"Who's there? Great-Grandmother? Is it you?" Arista squinted as she examined the ceiling. The array of pictures there appeared to be swaying. "Are those figures moving?"

Indeed, they are.

"What are they saying?" Arista strained, arching her neck farther upward.

Listen ...

The maiden, the mother, the crone... The maiden, the mother, the crone... The maiden, the mother, the crone...

"What does it mean?"

Lift the book to me, child, so I may come to visit you in full form.

Arista rose, the tome splayed in front her.

That's it.

The pages flipped of their own accord, as if a strong wind had hit them by surprise. Then, without warning, a ball of light ignited from within its pages, rising to the ceiling.

Arista gasped. "Actual people are up there."

The chanting continued, growing louder and louder: *The maiden, the mother, the crone... The maiden, the mother, the crone... The maiden, the mother, the crone...*

The pages jerked straight up, as if at attention, then slumped back into place, revealing a blank page. The light that had dissipated above gathered and centered itself below. Arista closed her eyes, hoping the ball of fire wouldn't fall on her.

Instead the hot bright light landed on a page within the book, and a hissing sound rattled through its pages. A vapor rose from the book's creases, and soon the formless mass, pulling and twisting, took shape.

"Great-Grandmother?" Arista stared as her ancestor covered herself in a gown from the recesses of the room and then returned to Arista.

"My, it is good to see you, child." She shook her head. "Bad timing your mother taking off when she did. It's severely delayed your training."

Arista's head filled with questions. "Why do they continue to speak like that?"

The old woman turned skyward. "They're welcoming you. The coven. You represent the maiden. Whisterly represents the mother. And that would make me personify the crone of course."

"Oh, I see… No, maybe I don't…"

"There will be much more time for this later, as you begin learning your first element, Air. Your training will take a different path from your mother's, initially anyway. Her needs at the time of her immersion were different. Both she and Vinique have a full command of elemental magic. Eventually you will also."

"You speak of my mother as if she's still here."

The old woman croaked a laugh, and the gathering of women cackled in response. "Look around you. Our essence, and hers, is everywhere, including inside your being. We are all only energy. Even though you can't see her form as before, you think she's not among us?"

Arista scrunched her face. "Well, I… I'm not sure."

"I know something that will help with clarity—your immersion, the oneness with the grimoire."

Arista's gaze drifted to the tome, still exuding stray puffs of mist from its pages. "But Vinique said I would do that tomorrow."

"You are here now. What's the difference? Will you be more ready tomorrow?"

"I guess not." Arista met her great-grandmother's gaze and said again, this time more emphatically, "No. I'm ready now."

"Good. We'll begin. Stand beside me. Reach for me telepathically. I warn you though, when you do so, you will connect with the book also. Prepare. Take the knowledge in slowly. Push back when you need to in order to adjust the flow of information."

"All right." Arista sucked in a deep breath, then extended her thought waves to her great-grandmother.

"That's it! Now breathe. Push it back to me. Rest. Breathe. Start again… You've got it."

Arista's eyes widened with each ebb and flow, and when the transfer had completed, she stared at the old woman, incredulous. "I never knew I could contain so much and understand so little." A wry laugh escaped her.

"Extraordinarily well put, my Arista. Now lean over here. Next we'll join you by the power of blood magic, just as your mother, father, and aunt have done before you."

Arista raised her brow. "My father?"

"Indeed. He is joined as well." The woman pulled a small knife from the folds of her dress. "Give me your palm." Arista lay her clammy fingers within the open hand of her mentor. Raising Arista's hand high, the woman sliced downward diagonally into Arista's palm. Blood dripped onto the open page, turning it into a sea of red. "Now, do you pronounce your intent to join us of your own accord, confirming the action your parents performed before your birth?"

Arista nodded. "I do."

The woman bound Arista's hand. "You are one of the chosen to be among us, restricted by bloodline. Your lifeblood will mingle with our own, becoming one. Welcome to the coven, Arista."

Shouts and cheers rang out from the witches, closely gathered now around Arista. Their hands linked as they circled Arista and her great-grandmother.

"The maiden, the mother, the crone…"

"How do you feel, Arista?"

A smile lit Arista's face. "Awake and alive."

"The maiden, the mother, the crone…"

"And so you are, dear Arista."

"The maiden, the mother, the crone…"

Later Arista climbed the stairs, mulling over all she had experienced. She understood it much more clearly now. Whisterly hadn't hidden her identity as witch. She'd worn it plainly. Arista, at that time, just didn't have the eyes to see. It was as much as a part of her as being a woman, or a mother even, a fact, if one were tuned in to see it. Tonight, for the first time ever, her eyes wide open, Arista could see.

JACK LEANED BACK in his chair in his bedroom, the book borrowed from Harry forgotten beside him, his coffee growing cool on the nightstand. He'd leave today. He had fully prepared Daniel, while Jack's own travel bag sat empty on the floor. Reaching for his coffee, he mentally prepared a list of the items he might need, for an undetermined length of time, in an uncertain environment.

Would anyone welcome him besides Arista? Might the council shun him? Would he still carry the stigma of a killer, even though Whisterly and Vinique had cleared him years ago? These questions rumbled through his mind, delaying his packing, as he gulped down swallows of his lukewarm drink.

From the corner of his field of vision the rising sun grabbed his attention, and turning toward the window, the brightness momentarily blinded him. Jack shielded his eyes and looked away, willing the spots in front of him to disappear. He blinked once, twice... Jolted by a falling sensation, Jack grasped either side of him, digging into the moist dirt of the surrounding pit. He was back on Guadalcanal, in the Solomon Islands, again.

He peered high above, through the branches covering the only exit of his cage, one that he could never hope to reach. His uniform, open in the front, clung to the sweat-drenched filth that coated his body. The floor of his confinement trapped his feet as they mired deep in the accumulated human waste, rotten food, and tainted water that littered the small space.

How many days had he been in here? The rain and slimy mess had covered his rudimentary marks multiple times. No way now to be sure. One day became the next and the next, all mixing together, while he waited for the bits of food and water that wouldn't sustain him, the stench of which often brought it right back up, adding to the muck that he existed within.

All at once, voices above yelled in Japanese, spewing words in quick succession back and forth, followed closely by the rapid stutter of machine gun fire. His feet made a sucking noise as he tried to free them and move to the side, melding himself into the disgusting mess of his pen. Jack knew his heart would betray him, loud as it was. His breaths heaved as the firepower paused, the yelling replaced now by muffled words interspersed with gagging and coughing.

"Papa! You're not listening. Why aren't you answering me? Papa?"

Jack startled, then glanced at Daniel, willing himself to be present so he could hear the words his son worked so hard to say. "Sorry, Daniel. I didn't hear you."

"Why not? I was yelling."

Jack was sure that was true. After all, in his mind, he'd been back in the Pacific Theater again. It wasn't the first time that he'd blanked out like that. "Climb up here for a minute."

With a huff Daniel navigated to Jack's lap and sat, staring out the window.

"Look. You're almost too big to sit with me now." Daniel fidgeted while Jack hugged his son. With no way to know how long he'd be gone, it'd be difficult for Daniel to understand, even though this wasn't the first time Jack had discussed the trip with him. Jack pulled away and smoothed the hair back from Daniel's face. "What were you trying to tell me?"

Daniel shoved his catcher's mitt in Jack's face. "Will you come play catch with me?"

How had he missed seeing the glove when Daniel had crawled up here? "Maybe in a little while. I need to pack a few things first. Remember? You're going to stay with Uncle Harry and Aunt Maggie for a while."

Recognition dawned on his son's face. He nodded and hung his head. "Oh, yeah… I remember. We packed my things yesterday."

"Yep. And I need to pack mine." Jack pointed to his empty bag.

Daniel slid to the floor. "I guess that means no," he mumbled softly, his mouth drawing out the O.

Jack couldn't hold back the smile that covered his face. He leaned in close to his son's ear. "Go check on your room again, and, as long as it's in tip-top shape, I'm sure there'll be time for a pitch or two."

"Really?"

"Really. Now go."

Fast footsteps echoed down the hall and met with an abrupt end, followed by the not-so-subtle noise of many items apparently finding their proper place.

Jack grabbed Harry's wayward book, threw it in his bag, and focused on the task at hand. He picked up his Bible from his night-stand. It had only been "his" for two years now, after his mother had died. Before then, it had always been borrowed, since that day years ago when he'd left to go find work after the disappearance of his father. His mother continued to say over and over that the good book would bring him back to her.

And so it seemed it did—back from the mine disaster, back from Remeon, and back from war. "Let's see if it still works with you in heaven." He opened the worn cover, slid a picture of him and Daniel between its pages, and placed the Bible into his bag. From his dresser he gathered a few necessities, and—along with several pairs of pants, some shirts, and a few toiletry items—he stuffed them inside.

Digging to the back of his top drawer, he withdrew a small box. He pulled up the top and stared at the small perfect diamond ring. After the war he'd sworn he'd finally return to Whisterly and put the ring on her finger. *We were so close, baby!* He snapped the lid shut and shoved the ring into his front pocket.

Now it would have to do to let their daughter see the ring so she'd fully understand what they had meant to each other. Jack reached for the key that still hung from his neck, closed his eyes, and squeezed it tight between his fingers, remembering the night, the last time they were together, when Whisterly had given it to him. Then, from atop his dresser, he picked up his dog tags and placed them around his neck as well. If he could find a way, these would go to Simon. That was it. His life reduced to a travel bag, with the exception of one final addition, his Colt M1911 and extra ammo.

Jack stowed his Ka-Bar in his boot, zippered the bag, grabbed it and his jacket, and headed down the hall toward his son's room. At the far end of the hall, he spotted it. "Daniel, come on. We've got a few minutes yet." The door to his son's room inched open only partially, revealing the havoc inside. "Son, what about tip-top shape wasn't clear?"

Daniel's eyes brimmed with tears. "It's not here." He threw up his arms. "I've looked everywhere."

"What isn't?"

"My baseball, Papa."

A smirked crossed Jack's lips as he pointed down the hall. "You mean, that baseball?"

Daniel ran the short distance and picked up the ball, then retreated back to his room. Jack had the mitt in his hand; he checked the time. "Well, there's not time now to straighten this mess *and* play catch."

His son's eyes wouldn't meet his own. "Get your jacket and suitcase, and put them in the car, then meet me outside. And here. Catch." Jack threw the baseball glove to Daniel.

Daniel tackled Jack in a hug, barely hanging onto both ball and glove.

Jack tousled his son's hair as he bent over him. "Go."

He beamed at Jack, then turned and ran outside.

Jack took in the totality of his son's room. Not much was left untouched in his search for the ball. The bed that had been made earlier had the covers peeled back. Clothes tumbled from drawers. Toys cluttered the floor, and items normally stowed under the bed had been thrown to the opposite side of the room. He shook his head. "You must have really wanted to find that ball." Jack picked up one of the stray comic books at his feet and stowed it in his back pocket before flicking off the light switch and closing the door on the gigantic mess. "Time to play catch."

ARISTA CALLED THE council meeting to order. As the murmurs died down, Vinique nodded to her side. With an inclination of her head, Arista silently acknowledged that Vinique had finished her task, each members' thoughts now monitored. "Council members, we have a short agenda today but several updates to attend to. First, I appreciate those of you who've come forward with recommendations for future council members."

The small gathering reacted automatically, scanning their numbers.

"Officially nominations are open. You must submit these proposed members in writing to me and Vinique. After our initial screening your recommendation will either be denied or brought to the full council for discussion and a vote." Arista paused and glanced at each member in turn. "Our council is the smallest in many decades, yet we believe also the most loyal combination we've had over that same time span. Brevity isn't the goal in this search.

"Choosing the best among us to represent Remeon is the needed outcome. So send in your suggestions, starting the process, then a lengthy research phase will begin—if the individual passes the initial screening completed by me and Vinique. Kix, thank you for agreeing to guide this effort. Before our next meeting we will discuss any candidates brought forth."

"Understood, ma'am."

Arista inclined her head. "Next, the status of the cure for PR 251. Pawk, I believe you have an update."

"Yes, ma'am, I do."

"Proceed."

Pawk stood to address the council. "As we all have seen, I'm pleased to report great progress on this front. Currently we are hovering at approximately 33 percent capacity in the infirmary, down from our highest point of 98 percent, right before the introduction of the cure."

The council members clapped, followed by additional chatter.

"Great news," Arista interjected. "Everyone, let's allow him to continue."

"Yes, well. This drug concoction has allowed Remeonites to return to active life by the hundreds. Our initial test subjects who have been monitored along each stage now show no evidence of virus in their bodies. As they leave the infirmary, their holographic patterns are stored for possible future needs.

"Not only are our people returning to their authentic lives but resources are being freed also. The amount of investment we've put into this project has paid off for our people. Now we can direct some of this capital elsewhere as the need for medical research and holographic resources continue to decline. Unfortunately some bad news comes with the good."

Pawk angled his head and found the eyes of each member. "This cure came too late for some. The disease progression was too far advanced in about 20 percent of reported cases. For them, the medicine will not stop the advancement of the virus. More deaths will still occur but at a steadily declining rate. Results show the cure works on young and old alike.

"In cases of new births, a vaccine is given, regardless of PR 251 status. While the disease isn't eradicated yet, we are certainly on our way. We are still monitoring and compiling data, but our initial goal of sustaining life for our people while the cure came to fruition has been a success. And the future looks even brighter."

"Excellent. Regarding that extra capacity you mentioned, Aero will have a report to address this for our next meeting. It bears repeating, for the record, that the fight for the cure cost us many dear lives. Whisterly worked her entire life to achieve this goal, then was killed just short of being able to reap its benefits. If she were here, she'd praise each and every one of your efforts. I will relay that for her. Believe me when I say, she rejoices with us."

The gathering came to their feet and applauded, with Arista and Vinique standing with the group as well.

"Ma'am, there is more I'd like to share," Pawk added.

Arista nodded. "Please, continue."

"Yes. Thank you." Pawk glanced around the room before continuing, flicking through the digital device in his hand. "Our operatives have determined the Night Dwellers have not fared as well. The majority, if not all, of you are aware now that Janus, a traitor to the Day Watchers, who once served on this council, has died recently, losing his battle to PR 251. Simon, a cruel leader in the Night Dweller community, was instrumental in capturing Stephen, whose blood led us to a cure, as you know. But the Night Dweller community also tested Stephen and is developing its own medical intervention for the disease. As yet they've only procured a vaccine. And while this is helping, their people are still dying in large numbers."

Arista shifted in her seat at the mention of Stephen. Of those in the room, only Vinique knew of Simon's connection to Whisterly and Arista. Eventually, on her own timetable, Arista would reveal this information. But not now. She tuned back in to Pawk.

"We anticipate that Simon will be vaulted into the position of commander over the Night Dwellers." Low murmurs of conversation erupted as Pawk continued. "Janus had been grooming Simon for this position since the kid could walk. And, if our information holds true, we believe Simon to be evil and sadistic, to an even further degree than his predecessor.

"Stephen, our asset, almost lost his life while imprisoned there. With the vaccine now among their people, indeed a cure isn't far behind. It's only a matter of time until we'll see if they stick to their original threat and march on our compound—to use their words, to take back what is theirs." Pawk returned to his seat.

"Thank you, Pawk for that update. The military threat you speak of is very real. We are monitoring within the Night Dweller camp as we speak, gauging possible threats. Occasionally their members seek asylum within our walls, and after subjecting them to a thorough brain scan, we interview them for verifiable facts. At present they are no match for our military strength.

"Last on the agenda. The council has been informed that two individuals from Earth will arrive for a visit later today. Both men have bravely served our cause and ultimately led us to our success. Years ago the results utilized from Jack—and Harry, his companion—put us on the path to the cure, and Stephen's DNA provided the actual building blocks of the cure.

"Without their sacrifices, a remedy would have come years later, after more of our people had died. Let me remind you, we can never forget that humans have saved our race. Some of you may recall that Janus tried to frame Jack for Damond's murder. Jack was eventually acquitted of all charges. You, as council members, must commit to treating these men with respect and dignity.

"Since Stephen returned to Earth about six months ago, Remeonites have been educated regarding the impact that humans had in the cure. What began with Jack came full circle in Stephen. They deserve our deep gratitude. See that they have it from this group particularly. Do your part."

"Ma'am?"

"Yes. Aero?"

Aero paused, raising his arms toward the group. "I believe I speak for the group when I say we commend your words. I personally hope to shake their hands."

As the assent in the room escalated, the council members again rose to their feet. "Thank you, Aero. And now, if there is no additional business to consider today, we will adjourn."

Vinique approached Arista, while the members exited the chamber. "That went extremely well. Wouldn't you agree?"

Arista faced Vinique, her eyebrows raised. "I think that had to be the most positive council meeting I've ever attended."

"Well, we did clean house, so to speak." A sly smile framed Vinique's lips. "Effective, wouldn't you say?"

"Yes. At a very high cost. At least we know our remaining members are supportive of our strategic direction. Did you find anything to the contrary in your telepathic connections?"

Vinique shook her head. "No, I can confirm there is no ill will at this time." The pair sat isolated in the now-empty room. "How do you feel with your father and Stephen scheduled to arrive in mere hours?"

"Well," Arista sighed, "my nerves are about to get the best of me."

"You do have quite a bit to discuss, with both of them."

Arista met Vinique's gaze. "I know I do. My thoughts are keeping me up nights. And I will. In time."

A smile played at the corner of Vinique's mouth. "You do have a full plate. I look forward to helping you with your lessons."

Arista bounded forward and grabbed Vinique's arms, pulling her closer. "Vinique, it's like I can barely contain myself. I don't know where to begin, so I feel I need to jump in all at once. I'm behind and ahead of myself at the same time."

"I remember the feeling well, after my immersion. And what you said is a pretty accurate assessment. Prepare yourself for a wild ride."

"That's the thing. For the first time since my mother's death, I feel a real hope for the future. I never knew of the sisterhood until I visited the basement. Yet, since my immersion, it seems there was no beginning. It just is. I'm stunned at my opportunity to follow in my mother's and great-grandmother's footsteps."

Vinique nodded as she listened to Arista's words and swallowed a laugh. "Oh, you just have no idea. Your world is about to transform."

IT WAS PAST noon when Jack and Harry found the meeting spot per Arista's instruction. Neither had said a word since leaving Daniel. "Well, damn, that was hard."

Harry nodded his head. "We'll take good care of him." He chuckled. "Don't forget he's kinda half mine. We both swore the oath. It's only right for me to take over now and then. Now's the time."

Jack ran his hand through his hair, not trusting himself to speak.

"What is it, Jack?"

Jack remained silent a few minutes, then breathed in deeply and let out a long sigh. "Now that I'm really going, it's harder than I thought—" He paused and sniffed. "Harder than I thought it'd be to leave, not knowing when I'll be back."

Harry shrugged. "For what's it worth, I think you're doing the right thing, getting to know Arista again. God, Jack. You weren't sure you'd have this chance. And there's the possibility of seeing Simon also."

Jack's gaze found Harry's. "Here's the thing. I've got to see Simon. Open the line of communication—or try to. Then we'll see. That might take a few days, a week, or a year…"

"Jack," Harry interrupted, "do you trust me?"

"Only with my life."

Harry put his hand on Jack's shoulder. "If you mean that, then go. Take the time you need to sort this out. You've been through a lot, Jack, and it hurts like hell not being able to help you. It'll be rough, no doubt about it. But I don't know of anyone who's more prepared to fight for, or more committed to, his family than you."

Jack's laugh reached his eyes. "Yeah, you don't get around much."

"The hell I don't."

Jack reached for Harry and held tight; then, after a thump on his back, let go. "I don't tell you this enough… You're closer to me than a brother, and you *have* helped me."

Harry's eyes misted. "Just remember, you need me. I don't want to have to come kick some Remeonite ass to get you back here."

A crooked smile formed on Jack's lips, remembering those same words from Harry when the pair had parted on Remeon years ago. "You got that right. I do."

The two stood in silence.

"I feel Arista on the other side, initiating the portal. Bye, Harry. God willing, I'll see you soon."

Harry took a step back and saluted.

Jack straightened his stature and returned the salute. And, with Harry still poised at attention, Jack turned away and disappeared into the rush of wind through the portal opening.

CHAPTER 5

THOMAS WOKE EARLY. He still had packing to do, and even though his parents weren't happy about him leaving, he was sure his ma would fix a big breakfast. Thomas heard the soft, even breaths of Belle, still on top of the covers at the bottom of his bed. She'd slept in her clothes all night long. He readjusted the blanket covering her, then slid from his bed and stepped into his pants pooled on the floor.

Where's my travel bag? Thomas stood in front of his closet, which was more of a mess than he'd remembered. Choosing a long-sleeved shirt that buttoned down the front, he yanked it from its hanger, stretched one arm in, then the other. He wanted to look well-put-together to see Arista again and Jack, her father.

Continuing his search through the closet, Thomas's thoughts drifted back to his recent meeting with Jack. Now that he'd met the man, he realized his speculation about him had been completely wrong. Just being in his presence, Thomas had felt a strength, a source of intensity that he found difficult to describe.

Not only the fact that Jack had him sized up before he'd even crossed the threshold but how he used that information…it was cunning. Of course he's a soldier, but also something else was evident… Jack's kindness and empathy. He cared about people, even after seeing them at their worst—he'd led men to and through battle, for God's sake. Thomas straightened his slouch. *And he didn't shy away when I said I'd had polio... I want to be like him.* But how the hell did he have a kid like Simon? Simon had to be the complete opposite of Jack.

After Thomas had relayed his story about his time on Remeon, then Jack had summarized his experience. He felt sorry, mostly for Arista, for not knowing her dad, but even for Simon, a little bit, the pig.

That day, at Jack's place, the two of them experienced so much sorrow, as naturally happens with telepathy, their thoughts and feelings drifting back and forth. So much pain. Then Jack spoke about his time in the war and a little about his mentor, Sam. Thomas didn't say a word as Jack relayed his adventures, only nodded his head, taking it all in. Quite honestly, by the end of the afternoon, Thomas felt honored that Jack had even given him the time of day.

The only area of his life that Jack had skimmed over had to do with Daniel. The kid was eight; Jack had mentioned that much but really nothing else. Seeing the two of them together, the times they'd interacted that afternoon, clearly Jack loved the boy, absolutely no question.

But when Jack had described meeting Whisterly, his eyes had misted, and his face lit up. When he spoke about her, it was almost like being transported with him back to Remeon—it was that real. Now he had a kid with someone else? It didn't fit with everything else Thomas already knew to be true about the man. Much more existed behind Daniel's story.

An array of clothing choices littered the space around Thomas's feet. He squatted, chose a few, and threw them in his bag. After packing a few comic books, toiletries, and underwear, only one item remained—the gift he'd gotten for Arista—a crystal. Thomas had uncovered it by accident as he'd fallen and slid among a section of rock.

After the discovery he'd cleaned and shined it; then, using his savings, he got a jeweler's help to fashion the rock into a setting for a ring. It had turned out beautifully. Turning the rock over in his hand, Jack watched as it reflected the sunlight, throwing its deep dazzling brilliance throughout the room. Enclosing it again in its small box, he placed it in his bag.

"Hey, what was that?"

Thomas moved toward the bed, kicking his bag to the side. "You fell asleep in here last night, Belle."

"What's in that box?"

"Box?"

She giggled. "Stop it, Thomas. You can't fool me."

He let out a low growl. "Oh, all right... Come look." Thomas pulled the small box from his bag and lifted the lid.

"Aah. It's so pretty. It's for Arista, isn't it?" Belle couldn't sit still as the information registered, the movement causing her curls to bounce up and down.

"It is." He clicked the lid shut. "No talking with her about it, okay? It's a surprise. Promise?"

Belle tossed her head up and down, barely able to contain her excitement. "I won't tell. I swear!"

"Good girl." Thomas stowed the treasure safely in his bag again.

"Besides," she added, "I mostly talk to Vinique, hardly ever Arista."

From his position on his knees, Thomas lifted his chin toward his sister, bringing him almost face-to-face with her. "Really? What kind of things are you talking with her about?"

Belle turned her eyes upward in mock thought. "Well, Remeon things."

Thomas chuckled. "Funny... That doesn't sound like the truth." He reached over and grabbed Belle on both sides, eliciting a stream of laughter.

He brought her forward in a hug, and she collapsed on his neck, out of breath. "It mostly is, Thomas," she whispered in his ear. Her tone changed.

Thomas sat back and studied his sister. "Is it something I should know about? You'd tell me if it were something serious, Belle, right? We need to trust each other."

Bell nodded solemnly. "Yes, a course."

Not completely convinced, Thomas lingered another minute with thoughts of digging a little deeper.

"Oh, no you don't," Belle answered to Thomas's unspoken thoughts.

"Just be honest," Thomas added. "Now are you ready for breakfast? The smell of the food downstairs is making my mouth water from here." Thomas slid on his braces, clicking them into place.

"Sure." Belle trailed Thomas down the steps and spoke quietly to herself. "It's just…you don't need to know quite yet. Soon though, Thomas. Soon."

The lively conversation that had started around the breakfast table between Ma, Pa, Belle, and Thomas slowed. Almost all the food had been eaten. Mary had stopped by yesterday to say her goodbye, promising to move heaven and Earth if Thomas didn't return home in a reasonable amount of time. She didn't like goodbyes. And Thomas knew his illness still troubled her, just like with Belle… Mary didn't need to say it out loud. Thomas could interpret her facial gestures; he'd seen them so often—the intense gaze, the determined set of the jaw—from all of his family.

"Be safe, Thomas."

Thomas nodded. "I can take care of myself, Mary. Things will be okay."

She'd given him that big-sister look, the one that said she knew better, then had cried as Thomas held her.

From the looks around the table, any minute there would be tears here too. "Ma, thanks for breakfast. Nothing can come close to your biscuits and gravy."

"Not even on Remeon?" Ma asked.

Thomas and Belle shared a glance, then burst out laughing. "Especially not on Remeon."

The corner of Pa's mouth turned up slightly, looking like something between a grimace and a grin.

"Pa?"

James raised his eyebrows in question as he gulped down a large swallow of coffee. "Yes, son."

"Would you and Ma like to come with me to the portal? It's time for me to go."

Thomas watched as his parents' gazes locked. He glanced back and forth between them. *Well, for sure, that must be their own telepathic communication. Belle, look.*

They're sad, Thomas. Give them a minute.

Pa cleared his throat and shifted his chair back. When he spoke, his voice shook. "I think we will, yes."

James rose and crossed the short distance to Elizabeth. "Ready?"

She nodded slowly and placed her fingers into James's outstretched hand.

Thomas watched dumbfounded as they turned and left the house, dirty dishes still on the table and food on the stove.

Belle elbowed Thomas. "Come on. Let's go, silly. They don't know where to go. Remember?"

Thomas shook off his surprise at his parents' reaction. "Oh. Oh, yeah. Right. Let me grab my jacket."

Belle led the way to the creek, the same one she'd brought Thomas home through not that long ago. Thomas walked in line with his parents. But no one spoke.

"Here we are," Belle said, turning to scan the faces of her ma, pa, and brother behind her. "Thomas, show me your rock," she demanded.

Thomas fished through his pockets. When he pulled his hand free, it was full. In the middle of his palm lay the silver compass, the heart-shaped rock, and his flint.

The three stared at his birthday gifts.

He grinned into their surprised faces. "You didn't think I'd leave without them, did you? They're my link to you guys."

Belle and Ma closed in on either side of Thomas, and he squeezed them in, hugging them close.

Pa extended his arm. Thomas released Belle to grasp Pa's hand, and he pulled Thomas to him. "Stay safe, son. Come back to us, safe and whole."

Thomas searched Pa's eyes. "I will, and thanks, Pa."

"Look," Belle screamed. "It's starting!"

The wind picked up, and the trees swirled, bending, surrendering to the power of the wind.

"James, is it a storm?" Ma asked.

He examined the sky and shook his head. "Look. No clouds. I don't believe it is."

A void opened in front of Thomas. Belle ran to him. "I love you," she whispered. "Don't do anything stupid."

"Got it. That's not my plan. I love you too. Bye, Ma, Pa."

"You're going in there?"

Thomas could hear the desperation threading his ma's voice. "I am, and I'll be fine." Thomas took off his braces and shoved them in his bag, giving him a few additional minutes to prepare himself. Then he inhaled deeply and took several steps forward before the swirling winds surrounded him and pulled him toward the gushing waters of the falls in the distance.

"Doesn't it look like fun?" Belle asked.

Walking back and forth, pacing the ground, Pa stared at where their son had just been. Lifting his head, he caught Belle's excited gaze, and the lines in his forehead scrunched in confusion. "No, it definitely does not look fun."

AS JACK WATCHED the reunion of Thomas and Arista, his mind dialed back the years to his reuniting with Whisterly, a lifetime ago now, soon after the birth of their daughter. They had been so young and desperately in love. He remembered every curve and slope of her body and their unending hunger for each other. It hadn't waned, even after all this time. Keeping in touch via telepathy daily was one thing, but she'd never brought him back again to Remeon in full form. Knowing why didn't help. The risk didn't matter, not if it meant they could be together. All this time wasted. Time they could have been together. Now it was clear to see the years away weren't worth it—the cost too great. And now they would never be.

The roar of the waterfall pounded in his head. He slid to the ground, facing the rushing water below. The musty coolness of the rocks and moss tricked him, triggering his senses. If he closed his eyes, he could almost feel Whisterly beside him as they sat along the water bank with Arista between them, discussing a future that would never come. Their dance later that night, the beat of her heart, their oneness as they had merged. Maybe he should just stay here, where he could still feel his wife with him.

If they had chosen differently, would they all be alive, their family whole?

Just a few more minutes and then he'd face reality. He looked out over the water, framed by the magnificence of the huge trees, their roots clinging to the tall riverbank, long branches hovering over the water, teasing the watery oasis from their height above. The promise of the cool water below sounded like a good idea, submerging, instead of going through it into the portal.

Becoming a part of this place forever, with Whisterly here, where he could hold time captive, in a way felt right. He inched closer. It wouldn't take much…to sink between the choppy waves…a path to finally possess the peace he'd been seeking… *This is the only way to have her again now.*

He closed his eyes and scooted nearer the edge. Soft wisps of wind caressed his face, inviting him forward… *Wait… Do witches go to heaven?* Jack shook his head, thinking. *Hell, where do they go?*

Lost in his reverie, he didn't hear her the first time. Arista reached for Jack telepathically. He turned, giving the swirling waters another wistful glance. His daughter's gaze darted to the water, then to Jack in unspoken question as she extended an arm to him. He stood and dusted off his hands. Her long blond hair escaped from behind her shoulder, and those deep blue eyes that mirrored his own held him mesmerized.

But, up close, he could easily tell she was a smaller version of her mother—her mannerisms, stature, her command of herself, all screamed Whisterly. His heart ached, but he didn't want to scare her away. Arista leaned in, making the first move. Her head landed on Jack's shoulder, and his arms easily circled her. The pair swayed in silence. Jack stifled a rising sob, then tried to disguise it as a cough.

Clearing her throat, Arista pulled away. "What should I call you?"

Jack shrugged, then smiled. "I'll leave that up to you. You can call me Jack. My son, Daniel, calls me Papa."

Arista cocked her head, her eyes appraising him. "*Papa…* It fits you. I like it. May I call you that as well?"

Jack sucked in a breath, not trusting himself to speak initially. "Uh…sure. I'd like that."

Arista beamed back at him, and instantly Jack was taken years back, to the cabin behind him now, where he'd spent the night with Whisterly and Arista. He'd held his daughter in his arms, rocking her. That smile—it was just the same.

"Would you like to take a walk? Stephen went inside the cabin, to give us some time. I brought us some food; we can share a meal. Afterward, we'll head back to the compound."

"Sounds great." Jack and Arista set a slow pace parallel to the falls. "I'm not sure where to begin though. I should have this wonderful speech prepared, but I don't."

"We could join our consciousnesses, to bridge the gap, if you're all right with that."

"Okay." Jack led Arista to a large fallen log. As they sat facing each other, Jack lay his hands palms up, and Arista placed her hands on top of Jack's. Then, leaning in, their foreheads made contact. Jack gasped as the images passed through his thoughts: Whisterly with Arista as a young child; Arista's early education; training to fight; preparation for council leadership, all under Whisterly's tutelage.

The transition was clear, when Whisterly, ill from PR 251, her body thin and pale, suddenly appeared normal again. Her hologram had been activated. Toward the end, Jack witnessed Whisterly's funeral and Arista's eloquent eulogy, plus Arista's time with Thomas. These were visions he'd never thought he'd witness.

Finally he saw Arista's immersion, her journey as an apprentice witch, which had begun close to the same time table as her mother's. Jack sat up and cleared his throat, giving him time to rein in his emotions from the visions he'd witnessed—a gift from the time he'd lost.

Eventually gaining a semblance of control, he glanced up again. With her head hung low and shoulders shaking, Arista wouldn't meet Jack's gaze. Jack put his fingers under Arista's chin and lifted until they could look at one another, face-to-face. Her face contorted as she fell into his arms, and he rocked her until her crying stopped and her heaving breaths normalized.

She pulled away, as she whispered, "I'm sorry... I just didn't know it would be like that. So much...pain. And my mother coming to you at the end—how horrible for you."

"It was better than not knowing at all," Jack said, his voice hoarse. "Thinking back now, I realize it must have been quite a feat for her at the time, and I'm grateful to have had those last seconds with her. Horrible as they were, I could feel her love."

Arista nodded through a fresh burst of tears. "She must have loved you very much."

Jack cupped his daughter's cheek. "We loved each other deeply."

"I didn't know," Arista began, "about you, until I read it in her letters. I'm no longer mad at her, but I was at first."

Jack nodded. "Our lives were complicated. But I wanted nothing more than to be here with you, your mother, and even Simon."

"Simon?" Arista's voice croaked.

Jack's eyes narrowed. "He deserved a chance. Don't you think?"

"I think you need to hear about all he's done, then decide."

"He was torn from your mother, a ruthless hateful act." Jack gave Arista a searching glance. "I blame myself. I should have been there, and here for him."

Arista shook her head, her tears beginning anew. "Papa, you've had so much pain, being without us, the awful war, your captivity, the loss of the men you served with… The list goes on and on."

Jack's eyes misted. "You called me *Papa*."

Arista froze. "But you said it was okay… I'm—"

"*Shhh…* It is." Jack's voice broke as he battled a smile. "I don't think I've been this happy since I returned to Remeon when you were about a month old."

Arista's smile lit her face. "I can see why my mother fell in love with you, Mr. Jack Livingston. I'll bet, on Earth, you're one of a kind."

Jack chuckled. "I'm not sure anyone on Earth would agree with you."

"Your memories don't concur with your assessment."

"Well, maybe Harry would say I'm one of kind." Jack's lip tipped up in a crooked grin. "But then, he would fall in that same bucket."

Arista covered her father's hands with her own. "Seeing isn't enough. I want to hear about all of it—you and my mother, your work on that dam, the war, and Daniel. Please, Papa."

Jack squeezed Arista's hands. "How could I ever say no?"

"Hey, you two," Vinique called.

Jack turned toward her voice. "I didn't know she had come to meet us."

Arista giggled. "No way she would stay at the compound. Vinique insisted. I think she was almost as eager as me to see you."

"You know, even though she was just a young kid at the time, she was my best friend on Remeon. She stood up for me when many others didn't."

"Sounds like my aunt."

"Ah, so you found out about that also."

Arista nodded. "Only a few days ago. Right about the time of my immersion. It makes perfect sense though. She's like a missing piece to a puzzle that never quite fit together."

Jack waved. "I should go say hi."

"She's fixed the food we brought. I'll bet it's time to eat."

Jack leaned over and kissed Arista on the cheek. "To be continued then. Let's eat."

Jack and Arista walked to the cabin, her father's arm across Arista's shoulder. As they got closer, Vinique took off at a run and flung herself into Jack's arms. "It's so good to see you again, Jack. I've missed you."

"Wow, I'm almost speechless." Jack planted a kiss on Vinique's cheek as well.

Stephen appeared from behind Vinique. "Hello again, sir." He stretched out his arm to Jack.

"Stephen, it's *Jack*. Remember?" Jack shook Stephen's hand.

"Jack… Okay."

Vinique waved them toward the cabin. "Let's eat, everyone."

ARISTA TOOK IN the food spread before them. How could she ever eat? Her father was right beside her. Conversation flowed around her. She couldn't focus on any of it. Sitting back from the table, she glanced toward the man beside her. Jack's easy banter with Vinique relaxed him. Arista could tell. He leaned forward, engaged in deep conversation with her aunt, and his smile danced behind his eyes. Even if Jack didn't realize it, he commanded attention. She'd felt a similar draw herself during council meetings and while watching her mother preside over events in the past.

People would listen to him.

Jack leaned back and ran his fingers through his hair, then turned toward Arista. Concern etched his face. "Are you all right?" Jack placed a hand on Arista's shoulder.

"*Mmm.* I am." Arista cast her gaze to her lap. "I'm sorry. I didn't mean to make you uncomfortable."

The corner of his mouth turned up in a lopsided grin. "You didn't."

Her heart melted. "It's just that, now that you're here, I want to hear about it all. The little details *and* the big ones that I've experienced through our link. Does that make any sense? Because I feel like I'm rambling."

"No, you're not." He patted her hand, assuring her.

"Tell us a little more about your business," Vinique chimed in. "After that we should probably head back and get you settled. You mentioned wanting to visit the basement this evening. Is that still the case?"

Jack nodded and sat up a little straighter. "Yes. If there's time, I'd like that very much."

"If your house is any indication of what you've built, you must be making a killing, Jack." Stephen hesitated. "What I mean is, you must be doing really well."

"Well, I'm making out all right." Jack tilted his head as if considering and weighing his words. "After working on the Hoover Dam project, I found I enjoyed working with my hands. I worked my way up to supervisor while Harry and I were there, and it seemed I had a knack for construction. So, after the end of the war, I went into business for myself. Before hanging out my sign, I built my own house, with Harry's help of course."

Stephen scrunched his forehead. "So do you build, provide resources, draw up plans, supervise, what?"

"That sums it up fairly well. I draw up plans, estimate a cost, research building materials, hire a site manager—if it's a big job. Otherwise I do that piece myself also. And of course, I dig in on the manual labor, depending on the size of the project."

"Does it occupy all your time?" Arista asked.

"I'm betting so," Stephen added. "The woodwork is amazing."

"It keeps me pretty busy. Yes. And thanks for noticing, Stephen. You must have a keen eye for detail. I'm involved in two projects currently, with about five on a wait list for my services."

"Tell me what happens now that you're here, Papa—to your business, I mean."

Jack leaned forward and kissed Arista's forehead. "Ah, you warm my heart, little one."

"My mother used to call me that," she whispered.

Jack stared into Arista's eyes and squeezed her hand. "We both did. And to answer your question, my two jobs are on hold for the moment."

"Do you know how long you're staying, Jack?" Vinique asked.

Jack felt Arista squeeze his hand this time. "That depends on several factors. I'm not sure yet." He eyed Vinique. "Do I need to set a return date now?"

"No. Absolutely not. In fact I have quite a bit to discuss with you myself. That's a shame though for those waiting for their work to be completed back on Earth."

"My place is here for right now." Jack shrugged. "Besides, the two current contracts I'm working on are okay with the delay, for the short term anyway."

Stephen repositioned in his seat. "Sounds like you could use a partner."

"Isn't that the truth? I've been trying to convince Harry of that. And I think he might just be coming around."

"Oh, Jack, tell us about Harry." Vinique cleared their plates, then returned to the table.

A proud smirk crossed Jack's face. "He is doing well, and since we returned from the war, he's been recruiting for the marines. As I said, I'm trying to bring him into business with me. He'll be checking in with my clients while I'm here. And I'm hoping that will encourage him to become more involved after taking the reins for a bit, so to speak."

Vinique raised an eyebrow. "Did he mate with someone?"

"He did—a wonderful woman—name's Maggie. They're great together. She keeps Harry straight. And they are head over heels in love." Jack's smile lingered, lighting up his face. "I'm hoping they make me Uncle Jack soon."

The four quieted, lost in their own thoughts.

"Jack, I think we should head out." Vinique glanced at Stephen and Jack. "If you two don't mind, you'll be sharing living quarters for right now. Due to shifting our numbers from the infirmary back to new quarters, some rooms are being remodeled, while others are filled. I'm sure you get the idea."

Jack glanced at Stephen across the table. "Fine by me. Stephen?"

"Sure, no problem."

AFTER A QUICK ride to the compound in a vehicle that drove like a military jeep, Jack found himself on the way to the basement with Vinique. The Remeonites they passed followed the pair with their eyes as they traveled, and Jack picked up fragments of conversation as they walked. "Vinique?"

"Yes, Jack? Odd being back?"

"In so many ways, yes. But what can we expect from the Remeonite people? I feel a mixed response from what I can quickly pick up as we walk."

"Well, as a whole, Remeonites know that human testing led us to a cure, so there's been an enormous attitude shift. As is always the case, there are those who will shun you both. You must report any activity of this type to me. It will be dealt with, with expediency."

"Ah." Jack twisted his lips with a knowing nod. "So you're saying I shouldn't deal with behavior of that type on my own?"

"We are on new ground here, Jack." Vinique paused and faced him. "Let's not destroy it in its infancy. I'll need names to address and squelch their behavior before it gets a hold. Do you get my meaning?"

Jack's eye twitched. "Your meaning? Sure. Truly I can handle it on my own."

"I'll leave it to your discretion. Don't make me regret it."

"Understood."

"Almost there, Jack."

"I can tell. I remember the way. But what is that surrounding the door? It looks like fog of some type."

Vinique nodded. "Pretty incredible, isn't it? It's been there since Whisterly died. The door is behind there. I trust you still have your key? Whisterly mentioned to me years ago that she'd given you one."

Jack pulled his key free. "I do."

"Before you go down, I wanted to give you these."

Jack recognized his wedding gift to Whisterly before Vinique lifted Sam's dog tags from around her neck.

"Not sure what you want to do with them. Maybe give them to Arista for the time being? But I wanted you to have them, so you could decide."

"I see." The memories came flooding back—Sam… Whisterly—as Jack felt the bumpy coolness of the metal between his fingers. His gaze softened, and his voice came out gentle. "I'm not sure yet, but I'll hang on to them for now."

Vinique nodded. "Okay. Do you want company?"

Jack's throat constricted, and tears pricked at the back of his eyes. So he just shook head, not wanting to speak.

Vinique leaned toward Jack and wrapped him in a hug. "We need to have a longer conversation soon, Jack. Very soon," she whispered in his ear. Without another word she disappeared down the hallway.

Jack slid the key tentatively in the keyhole. It was his first time using it. Whisterly had given it to him during his last visit through the portal, when the world had shattered between them with news of her illness. The lock clicked open. Jack released a pent-up breath. *I'm in at least.*

He flipped on the light switch and strolled down the steps. Time seemed to slow as the memories hit him, and with each step, his body felt heavier than the last. At the bottom, his feet hit the slippery cobblestone. He easily traversed the space, remembering steadying his wife through here, tricky as it was at times. He found the gap leading to the small room where the grimoire had been kept, and to his trained eye, he could tell the ground had been recently disturbed—by Arista crawling through for her immersion most likely.

After removing the wooden plank covering the opening, he crawled inside, turned the light on and made himself trudge toward the book—the one they'd discovered together, the one marked by his family's blood. He couldn't bring himself to take this step on Earth, to face Whisterly's death. Now he knew why. *Here* would be his final goodbye.

The tome lay on a wooden stand, and as Jack approached, the low light that filtered through a maze of dust and books brightened. Jack's eyes flickered; then his gaze traveled to the ceiling, where the mural twisted and turned in strained movement. Soon the void in front of him filled with coven members. Jack eyed the old witches as they surrounded him. He picked out Whisterly's grandmother, Arista, who nodded but didn't speak. Jack had expected company; he wasn't sure how it would materialize.

He continued toward the book.

Even though he wasn't a witch or a warlock, Jack's blood was tied to the grimoire through Whisterly and their children. He dragged the book from its resting place and set it on the floor. The surrounding light was even brighter now and was more focused on him and the magical book. Jack kneeled and opened the cover, pausing at the familiar image of the pentagram which adorned the inside cover.

As he watched, the pages flipped silently, finally settling on a blank page. He released his grip on Sam's dog tags. They fell across the length of the paper, coming to rest in the crease, like a bookmark. Scanning the witches as they continued to close in, Jack reached for the knife in his boot. He raked it across his palm, lifted his hand high, and closed his eyes.

A hum began, low at first; then it grew a little louder. The rhythm soothed him, and the beat steadied his determination.

He squeezed his hand, and drops of blood fell to the open pages, streaking them red. Bending low, Jack folded his hands, while, at the same time, led by the old woman, the gathered coven laid hands on his head, back, and arms, forming an even tighter knot around him.

He wanted to tell Whisterly what life was like now without any hope of her in it. He wanted to tell her just one more time that he loved her and ached to feel her spirit safe again in his thoughts. *Want... want... want...* Instead he released these thoughts, and they simmered between him and Whisterly's sisters, before the coven who knit the bits into the fabric of their congregation.

The words he did say out loud came easily; he'd recited something similar at services for his fallen soldiers, even if the pain they produced this time when they left him tore his insides like a death wound. Because now it was his soul mate, and his heart was sliced open for all to see. But here they knew. And here he didn't hide his tears.

"God is our refuge and strength, a present help in trouble. Therefore we will not fear, though the earth be removed, and the mountains be carried into the midst of the sea, though the waters roar and be troubled, though the mountains shake with the swelling. God is in the midst of her; she shall not be moved. Be still, and know that I am God. The Lord of hosts is with us; the God of Jacob is our refuge."

Uncertain how long he remained, his grief laid bare, Jack swayed, buoyed and held upright by those gathered. Then the coven's touch that had wrapped around him like a blanket left him, and a new spirit filled Jack. The murmured whispers seeped into his thoughts, calming his psyche, and he slept.

CHAPTER 6

A RISTA WOKE EARLY, her apprehension and nerves getting the better of her. This morning would be her first official lesson, and she'd be by herself with her great-grandmother, as well as the coven. Would she measure up to those who'd come before, namely her mother? The paper rustled between her fingers. During the night Arista had delved into another one of the letters her mother had written her—the one she'd written about her initial experience with the magical book.

Over Arista's light breakfast of tea and toast, she reread about the encounter. These words written long ago would now apply to her. *Its force is alive within me now. At the same time, it's as if it's always been with me. How can I explain such an energy?*

Empowered as she communed with her mother's words, she could wait no longer. Arista dressed and headed to the basement. A short time later she plodded carefully down the twisted staircase, her footfalls unsure. Once on the cobblestone, her breath quickened. *Almost there...* Arista bent low when she reached the small opening. The wood had been set back, and a dim light shone from within. Was Vinique in here?

Pushing her way through, expecting to find her aunt, Arista blinked into the brightness. Before her, Jack slept, the magical book atop his chest with one arm thrown over it. In his other hand, he clutched a necklace of some kind. Arista crept forward, trying not to wake him. She leaned in for a closer look…

In an instant Jack startled awake, grabbed her shoulders, and pushed her to the ground.

Arista's breath left her when she thudded to the floor. She searched her father's eyes, which today held a frenzied kind of madness, instead of the laughter from yesterday. "Papa?"

Jack shook his head. "Arista? God, I'm sorry." He helped her to her feet. "Are you all right?"

She stared at him again, the corners of his eyes now wrinkled with concern as she caught her breath. There he was, the man she recognized from yesterday. "I'm fine, really."

"Since the war I've been jumpy, pretty much all the time, but especially when I sleep. I've warned my son never to sneak up on me at night." He paused and looked her in the eye. "Uh, not that you were sneaking. If anyone is an intruder here, it's me."

An easy smile rested on her face. "No, don't say that. You belong here." Her gaze slid to the ceiling and fell on him again. "I can feel it."

Jack brought his hand to her cheek. "Just then, you looked exactly like your mother."

Arista covered his hand with her own. His eyes sparkled with unshed tears. "You're welcome to stay. I'm not too sure what I'm doing anyway. Besides, you said you'd tell me about Daniel."

"And I will. I promise." Jack pulled the necklace, still speckled with blood, over his head and picked up the book, then handed it to Arista. "But for now I'll leave you to it." He turned to leave.

"Wait. Are you sure you're okay? Your hand looks like it might be bleeding."

Jack twisted his hand around, examining the dried blood. "Nah. It's fine. Don't worry about me." He flashed her a smile. "I'll see you later."

Arista listened to Jack's retreating footsteps and finally the opening and closing of the door above.

She sighed and returned her focus to the tome in her hands. "Where to begin…"

Close your eyes, feel the energy coursing through your veins, then draw on that power before opening the book's pages.

"Great-Grandmother?"

Yes, child. Do as you're told.

Arista silenced the noise within her head and called upon the same focus she had used during the process of intricate telepathy. Minutes later she opened the book.

That's it. Now call to me.

In an awe-filled wonder Arista watched the book elect a page for its magic, in order to bring forth the old woman. The ball of light, the mist as it oozed, hissing forth from the book's creases, then its skyward travel toward the mural, all culminated with her great-grandmother, who stood before her now.

A broad smile fixed on the woman's full lips. "Let's begin."

The book snapped to life again, the pages dancing before her eyes as if waiting for Arista to choose. Without warning, and as quickly as it had begun, the book settled, resting on a page which read Elemental Magic—Air. Arista's gaze flicked to her mentor.

"Yes." She nodded. "This is where you will begin. Your mother and Vinique command all the elemental forces: Air, Fire, Water, and Ground. You will concentrate on Air, master the magical use of this element, and move on to the next."

Arista cocked her head. "But how do I start?"

"Look within. You possess the ability. It resides within the knowledge you've already gained from the grimoire. You must call it forth at times of need. But first you'll need to study and research its power. Uses of its mastery consists of control over weather, including the ability to fight by harnessing the strength of the wind. Also, by wielding this elemental force you can literally steal the breath of another, killing them through suffocation, a deadly weapon for sure. Inexperience can bring you quite succinctly and unintentionally to your own death as well."

Arista stared wild-eyed at her ancestor.

"We will also manipulate this force in combination with the other three elements. When all are combined toward a singularly specific goal, new life at its truest, most basic form can be the result. Our works seek to climax in that most fruitful end. With the power of Vinique, yourself, the coven, and one other, we just might gain the control we need to…"

An understanding flashed in Arista's eyes. "You don't mean—"

A satisfied smile took over the older woman's face. "Now don't get ahead of yourself. But I will tell you all things are possible within the magic we possess. With the right knowledge, control, and harnessing our power, we can work toward any outcome. If we fail or if we win is up to us. It all commences here. She closed her eyes, muttered several words, puckered her lips, and blew forcefully.

Arista's feet left the floor as the ensuing wind pushed her against the wall, pasting her there, unable to move. She nodded to her great-granddaughter.

"See? Now that is what you'll do to me before leaving here today. Let's begin small at first. Transport the book using the air within and around you. Rein it in and channel it toward me."

Arista closed her eyes and focused within.

"That's right. See it in your mind. While conjuring the outcome in your head, speak the words written within the grimoire which give the words life, then manifest that to moving the book."

The minutes lingered. Deep within Arista's previously unused connections and pathways unleashed a new freedom as they sparked to life. She mimicked her great-grandmother and pushed the air through herself to the book. Hopeful, Arista flicked her eyes open in time to see its cover fly up, and the pages inside ruffle. Seconds later the subtle twist of air resettled, leaving the pages exposed. Arista rolled her eyes and huffed out a breath.

A hearty laugh erupted from the woman in front of her. "Not bad for a first attempt. Surely you understand the problem. Did you feel it when it happened?"

Arista nodded. "At the last minute, as I pushed out the air, I didn't believe it would happen. The motion stopped. The air, the power, the belief... I killed it."

"Good girl. Now fix it."

AFTER JACK LEFT Arista in the basement, he wandered through the hallways, piecing together the memories of his time here from before. Everything was familiar, yet different at the same time. It almost felt like, at any second, he would run into Whisterly, and they would pick up where they had left off before they'd had so many years pass between them.

In his private ceremony with the coven last night, he'd vowed to finally begin the process of releasing his wife. Before, the burden had been too massive to bear, the hurt crushing him at times. Now, even though the full brunt of his grief was still there, it was as if others were helping to ease the weight a bit. A small step, yes, but one in the right direction.

If he were to choose to live for his sons and daughter, he'd need to find a way. And, with the coven, he found an understanding deep within his soul, without having to explain a word. Today the pain was slightly different; maybe tomorrow would bring even further change.

Through the children, the dead live. He remembered finding that answer with Whisterly ages ago. And there was something else. He couldn't name it beyond *simply hope*. He'd felt it within each one of the members last night, and they somehow left something of it within him. How had they bestowed it upon him?

He approached the room that he shared with Stephen. *All his mind must be filled with... I remember.*

SIMON WOKE, LURCHING forward, his body covered in a cool sweat. He glanced at the woman by his side, remembering. Hastily he entered her thoughts. *Leave me now.* Disoriented, her eyes shot open, and she fumbled with her belongings, dressing quickly. Mere minutes later, and barely put together, she left his chambers without a word or a backward glance.

He threw the bedcovers forward and sighed, as he ran his fingers through his hair. This was the third night in a row he'd woken, yanked from a sound sleep by an unknown and unseen nagging force. A surge of raw power flowed through him, and he shivered.

Pacing the room, Simon reached out through his thoughts, attempting to isolate the source. The previous night's interruption had felt similar, but tonight the energy was stronger and more focused. Fifteen minutes passed, then thirty, before his only gain was revealed to him—now he knew this strange influence emanated from the depths within the compound.

He connected with it, wrestled it within his mind, attempting to hold the intrusion at bay. As he did, flashes of scenes formed in his head, bits and pieces that didn't quite seem to mesh together. He dropped into a chair, and his subconscious took over, mentally linking the images. Mesmerized, now the isolated parts replayed before him, and he watched like a bystander as the events unfolded.

In the recesses of his mind the brightness of the room made Simon squint. Several people gathered near the feet of a very pregnant woman. She didn't move. But those around her were busy at work. Someone brought forth a bundle, a baby, announcing it was a boy. Minutes later, another delivered, this one a girl.

The woman holding the first child moved to the side and removed her mask, cooing to the baby in her arms. She whispered to the squiggly mass, *Simon... I'll call him Simon.* Recognition dawned on him—Mila, a very young Mila, swayed with him in her arms. But the other woman, the birth mother, who was she? Simon clung to the fading picture. He needed to know now.

For some reason, here he was at the moment of his birth. He forced his gaze to the unconscious woman. The flurry of activity calmed. As the last person moved away from the sleeping woman, he could make out her face. Simon sucked in a deep breath and coughed it back out. Whisterly! His mother? And his sister, Arista, the second baby? He shook his head, fighting to rid himself of the images before him. "No!" These women he'd despised his whole existence were his mother and sister?

He struggled against the vision, fighting to break free. Instead the view before him shifted, then reformed, as a young man stormed into the same room Mila had just exited with newborn Simon in tow.

Simon probed as he watched the reunion. Clearly this person was his real father, and without a doubt, he cared for Whisterly and Arista, whom he swooned after. *Look who we made, Mrs. Livingston... Jack...* Jack. His father's name was Jack. Still the apparition gripped him. Disgust clawed at his insides. How could he be a product of hers?

He hadn't wanted to admit it. Through the fragment of thought ripped from Thomas before he'd left Remeon, Simon had first learned of his human father but had been blind to the rest. It rang true now, searing his insides like hot embers.

A musty wetness filled his nostrils as the hallucination faded from view, then reformed, continued at a different location. Simon wasn't alone. Beings surrounded him; they chanted and swayed in unison to a distant beat. Before him a book fell open, its pages twisting and turning of their own accord. A presence drew him forward, inciting a powerful urge he couldn't resist.

A cloaked figure approached, then grabbed his hand. Bearing a blade, the entity slashed Simon's palm before he could even protest, and holding his hand up high, dropped blood, darkening the page before him. The massive tome seemed to collide with his consciousness as the pages wrenched back and forth, parading to its own unique rhythm.

Simon gasped while wave after wave of raw power hit him repeatedly. And cowering to the onslaught, he slid down prone on the floor, unable to suck in a breath.

Minutes passed before Simon slowly lifted his head. Something had pushed its way inside him—had attacked and won. *How? My defenses are unmatched.* Peeling himself off the floor, a transformed hatred sparked from within. Residing deep in his core, a primal rage spewed forth in an agonized guttural wail. A mass appeared, organizing and assembling itself before him.

Instinctively Simon knew he had created this…thing…somehow… The spirit writhed as it drifted higher and higher out of reach. Simon recoiled, trying to ignore the sensation building in his gut. He was fundamentally changed. What had unleashed within him? And why?

Simon blinked, and his quarters reappeared. He heaved himself to a stand and trudged to the shower. Only seconds later he stumbled, hit a chair, and fell to his knees.

"Sir? Is everything okay in there? Do you need assistance?"

"No. Stay at your post," Simon hissed through his teeth. Regaining his footing, his bloodstained hand left several grisly prints, marking his path as he made his way to the shower again. Simon leaned against the stone while the water washed over him, and the clutter loosened in his mind, a seething rage simmering and threatening to consume him.

Janus or Mila should have told Simon. He'd not been adopted as a child. That had just been a made-up story. He'd been abducted. Even his parents hadn't realized it at the time, so it appeared, if this vision had been reality. *They had wanted me.*

Snippets of ancient conversations with Janus crept into Simon's thoughts. The punishing rants had happened often. These *conversations*, as Janus referred to them, were really warfare training, and had begun at an exceedingly young age. Janus would plunge into Simon's brain and tear around inside him until Simon had been mentally strong enough to push Janus out.

These exercises escalated in difficulty, but eventually, over a period of years, Janus could no longer break through. Then Simon realized his talent which he'd been uniquely prepared for—bending others to his will. After these sessions, Mila would build him up with promises of a future where he would be destined to steal back power from the Day Watchers. Then Janus would snap Simon back, reminding him of his place, ensuring him that he'd never be good enough.

The old man had led Simon toward a fate that Janus himself had predefined. Simon could bring any person to his knees in seconds, then either bend them to his will or kill the person, with simply a crushing, well-engineered thought. Those beneath him had been trained to carry out the same sentences.

Questions pooled at the back of his mind.

He'd trusted in his love for Mila all his life, the only mother he'd ever known—a small slice of goodness in his life that was never allowed to be. Janus had seen Mila as Simon's weakness. Once his younger brother had come along, Janus had isolated Simon, his days crammed full with mental and physical training and combat maneuvers.

Only on special occasions were the four of them together. And those special occasions were frequently tainted by beatings, which Mila endured, since she got to spend time with Simon. Eventually, just as Janus wished, Simon wouldn't attend the family gatherings, hoping that his mother wouldn't suffer. And, of course, she still did, only without Simon present. Both Mila and his younger brother, Willie, endured Janus's daily torment. His control had just been a fact of life.

Simon flung his hands down his face. The attack hadn't come from Whisterly this time. And it didn't have the signature he'd expect from his sister Arista or Vinique. He sunk to the floor of the shower, letting the force of the water rain down on his shoulders, easing the tension in his muscles.

He focused his thoughts and then projected them forward, searching, in an attempt to detect subtle changes in the masses of thought exchanges during the day. Simon's eyes jerked open, and a smile split his face. So, Stephen had returned, and he brought a friend—Jack. Neither of these human foreigners could have promulgated that attack, but Simon could plan one of his own regardless, against the traitor, Stephen. And whatever had befallen Simon today, was it due to Jack's return? That question needed an answer.

Simon towel-dried and peered at his reflection in the mirror. The sinking feeling from before returned. He got closer, rubbing off the condensation gathered on the mirror for a clearer view. Simon focused, then frowned. It was as if a stranger stared back at him, bearing his own face. The base of his spine quivered. Simon pulled his gaze from the being glaring at him, and with sunrise still hours away, he plodded back to bed. *Damn it to hells, maybe I dreamed this entire mess.*

An uneasy sleep came for Simon, while, at the same time, an unfamiliar fear clutched at the pit of his stomach.

THE COVEN RELEASED a collective shudder. They'd been powerless to prevent what had been set in motion so long ago by

Whisterly's and Jack's link with the grimoire. Simon, along with Arista, were initiated years ago when they were but yet in the womb, both promised to the service of the coven and both bound to one another. The magical book wrestled with its new member as Simon assembled, unaware, with the whole.

After seeking out Simon, the book had completed the immersion process. The crone drifted down, dissipating the intruder Simon and quelling the uneasiness among the coven. Untrained and ignorant regarding the ways of sorcery, Simon's needs as a fledgling warlock required attention, before he wrought havoc upon masses of people due to his lack of knowledge regarding the craft. Soon they would have much more to deal with than Simon's wraith unwittingly conjured.

ARISTA FLITTED AROUND her chambers. She was uncharacteristically a nervous wreck. *He's gonna be here any minute.* The paperwork that had gathered due to her absence yesterday still remained untouched. With the events of the last day still at the forefront of her mind, somehow these other minor work details seemed less important today.

The coffee's scent permeated the room. It wasn't quite done. Bubbling noises reached her ears from the kitchen. Arista breathed in through her nose. *Ah...* She didn't make her own coffee. In fact, in general she opted for tea, but Vinique had let Arista know that Jack loved the hot beverage. Her first unaided attempt had ended in a pasty burned mess. Vinique had encouraged Arista to reach for her own magical resources, and this second attempt appeared to come along nicely—it smelled better anyway.

Remeonites' "coffee" was different from Earth's version of the drink. The universal translator led Arista's efforts to the concoction she was preparing now. And by her standards the beverage was just okay.

Picking up the small stack of letters, she abandoned her desk and moved to her large sitting area. She thumbed through them, then lay the missives on the side table beside her. Jack should choose; she'd already decided. It really didn't matter to her which letter was read first. The words themselves—that was what mattered. But, before that, if he agreed, she wanted to hear about Daniel. Did her father have another love, one stronger than what he'd felt for Whisterly? Did he have a quick romance during the war, or was there some other explanation?

A short buzz sounded. "Mistress, your guest."

"Thank you. Send him in."

"Papa, thanks for coming."

Jack nodded. "I don't want to miss any time I can have with you."

"Please sit." Arista pointed him to a chair. "I've tried to make some coffee for you. I'm hoping you'll give it a try."

"It smells great. I'd love some."

"Should I add anything to it for you?"

Jack shook his head. "No, over time, I've learned to drink it black and strong."

Arista returned, carrying two steaming mugs of hot coffee. She set them both on the side table between them. "Okay. Give it a taste. I won't be offended if you hate it."

Jack picked up his cup. "You just don't know how much bad coffee I've had over the years. I'm sure it's great." He took a large swallow and nodded. His mouth ticked up. "It's really good, fittingly unlike any I've ever tasted before."

Arista breathed a sigh of relief. "I'm glad." She squirmed in her seat. "Papa, you're aware the official records show Damond as my father."

Arista watched while what looked like a mixture of hatred and disgust warred for dominance of Jack's face. "I am. Whisterly thought it best at the time. Back then they didn't need an excuse to kill me. Whisterly knew that. She wanted to protect me and her bloodline from scrutiny."

"We must be careful of our next steps. I'm not sure where all that stands—the council's knowledge mainly. But Vinique and I are looking into it."

Jack's jaw tightened, and a nerve pulsed at his temple. "I can see where all kinds of issues could arise, just by my presence here. So, yes, I agree."

"There's more. I can tell. Go ahead. Say it."

"Okay." Jack's lips turned into a thin line. "I need to see Simon, or try to at least."

Arista studied Jack over the rim of her cup, then placed it on the table again, thinking carefully before speaking. "He'll draw on your kindness, use you to his own advantage and to destroy the council. You know that, right?"

Jack reached for Arista's hand. "I have to try. He's part of me, just like you are."

She fought the disgust rising within her and averted her eyes. "We need to think about the best way to approach this. For now we'll keep our conversations, thoughts, well buried, so—"

"So they can't be pulled from me. Yes, I remember the deception well. Do what you must."

Arista's gaze met her father's, and his eyes softened. "Regret is a difficult companion."

Waves of sadness from years of hurt flowed through Arista from Jack, and her breath caught at the sheer weight of it. "We'll figure out a way. Just promise that you won't go without telling me."

"You have my word."

"Do you mind telling me a little bit about Daniel?"

Arista watched while light seemed to spark in Jack's eyes. "Sure. I guess what you really want to know is if he's related to you by blood?"

"Papa, you don't have to talk about him, if you'd rather not. I understand."

'No, I don't mind. But he's just an innocent bystander. I'd like to keep him out of the politics of Remeon. He's only a boy."

"I understand."

"I don't like to make a distinction between you and Daniel." Jack nodded as if in confirmation. "You're both mine, along with Simon. But Daniel is mine, born through an oath on the battlefield. His father was one of the men under my responsibility, and he died in my arms after leading a dangerous mission to rescue Harry and me." Jack paused, and his eyes glistened. "Harry and I would be dead if it weren't for Corporal Henry Johnson. I swore to him that day that I'd take care of his son, Daniel. Daniel's mother died in childbirth. The child deserved a chance at life, with somebody who cared." Jack studied his hands, then stood and turned away from Arista. "And my heart ached for a son, knowing that I'd let my flesh and blood just slip away from me."

Arista rose and went to her father. "I'm sorry, Papa, for all we've put you through. Daniel is a lucky little guy."

Jack laughed and faced his daughter again. "I don't know about that, but he does have someone. Me. And we have fun together. Everyone deserves someone who believes in them, no matter what. I am that for him."

"I'm sticking with my statement. He's one lucky little guy." Arista went to the kitchen to grab the pot of coffee. "How about a refill?"

Jack raised his cup. "Absolutely. Thanks."

Arista filled both of their mugs, then resettled in her seat. Her gaze drifted to Jack's letters.

"Those look familiar. They're the ones from me? I know Whisterly wrote you a ton of letters."

Those are from you. She communicated telepathically. *Pick one, will you? And read it to me.*

Jack reached for the stack and slowly sifted through them. He sat back in his chair, as if considering, weighing the options. Arista kept her eyes on him, watching his mind work through his facial expressions as he chose. "Well, if it's up to me, I've decided on this one." He lifted up the letter and replaced the remaining ones back on the table.

"I'm fine with whichever one you choose. Please read it. Out loud."

Jack nodded and ran his fingers through his hair. "Okay. Here goes."

"My dearest Arista. You'll know by now that I'm not a witch, warlock, or sorcerer of any kind. Before coming to Remeon, I'd never given the magical arts much thought at all, as a matter of fact. But, since visiting, I can confess that I feel the inner workings of magic throughout my life almost daily. You see, I was part of your mother's awakening to her true self. It was a journey we shared, and, as her skill level grew, I could feel the magic flow through her and embody Whisterly completely.

"At times her knowledge growth was alarming and even quite scary. Then I'd remind myself that this path was Whisterly's destiny, and she was uniquely qualified and destined to fill this role. I could see she was most alive within the powerful grip of sorcery. Whether dancing in invitation, learning a spell, or communing with the coven, it brought her pure joy to be herself.

"And I knew I couldn't compete for the place magic held in her heart, or pull it from her. Instead I was privileged to be a witness to the process, while our own love grew as well. So I encourage you to embrace this part of what is distinctively yours. Soon you'll see you can't separate Arista the witch from Arista the woman. You are one. That's as it should be.

"These yearnings to follow your true calling are coming. Don't try to change. Fulfill your destiny. Be who you were meant to be. You're a witch in the making. Be true to her. I love the you you're becoming, little one. Your father, Jack."

Tears sparkled in Jack's eyes when his face rose, seeking Arista's, and a lopsided smile drew his mouth up on one side. "I guess that was kinda odd, huh? Who knew I'd be here to read my own letter?"

Arista closed the short distance between them and threw her arms around Jack's neck. "I never knew how much I could miss what I've never had," she whispered.

The pair swayed silently; then Jack leaned back and ran his thumb against Arista's cheek, brushing away her tears. "And I never knew just how big that hole was in my heart, caused by leaving you behind, till yesterday."

"What will we do now, Papa? I don't ever want you to leave."

Jack kissed her forehead and tightened his embrace. "I don't know, little one."

CHAPTER 7

JACK RECLINED AGAINST the backboard of his bed, attempting to concentrate. He'd just gone over the same page in *Cannery Row* for the fifth time and still didn't know what he'd read. He glanced to the other side of the room at Stephen's empty bed and sighed. Even without trying, Jack had read Stephen's thoughts. It was still second nature to Jack, as was going about it gently and slowly so Stephen wouldn't realize. *And this is what I get—what I deserve—knowing now that he's with Arista.* Jack slammed the book shut. "Lights off."

This was unfamiliar territory. Stephen was nice enough. At least Jack had gotten to know him a little bit when he'd come all the way to Provo at Arista's urging. And God knows, Jack and Stephen had some of the most awful experiences in common: the testing here on Remeon, the life-altering mind control—Jack at the hand of Damond and Stephen under Simon's tutelage.

A low growl left Jack's throat. He didn't have any right to judge Arista and Stephen's relationship. Jack had only just stepped back into his daughter's life. Still it was hard not to. With the parallel experiences, Jack's mind automatically went to how close he and Whisterly became and how quickly it all came about. Jack huffed and flipped over in his bed, trying to focus his thoughts elsewhere. Tomorrow... he'd meet with Vinique. Her manner seemed...urgent almost.

The door clicked open, and Stephen blundered across the room, knocking into furniture along the way as he attempted to be quiet in the dark room.

Jack smirked. He could let Stephen continue to stumble, or make Stephen aware that he was awake. "Lights on."

"Oh. You're awake."

"For the moment. Yes."

"I'll hurry and change."

Jack shrugged. "No need to rush. How's Arista this evening?"

Stephen raised an eyebrow. "Good. She's good."

"Good. That's, uh… good… Listen, Stephen. Remind me sometime to give you a few pointers on protecting your thoughts. Honestly I wasn't trying to pull information from you. Being back here, it's a defensive mechanism almost."

Stephen chuckled and met Jack's gaze. "Arista's practiced with me, but sure. My skills obviously need work."

"Great. I'm happy to help." Jack turned over and resettled in the bed.

"Jack?"

"Yeah?"

"Arista is really excited that you're here. She talked nonstop about you tonight. Really…nonstop."

Jack turned and propped up on one elbow. "She did?" Jack fought the smile rising within him but lost out as it flashed across his face.

"Did she ever."

"I've missed her. More than I could have imagined." Jack's face turned solemn. "So much time. Gone." Jack's gaze met Stephen's. Stephen shifted his shoulders uneasily. "Thanks for letting me know. I'm turning in. Night."

"You bet. Night, Jack. Lights off."

Jack fell into a restless sleep. Often this happened. Speaking about an event gave it life. Resurrected it in his mind. Jack had worked to keep this one well below the surface, but it was a daily struggle. The scene started to unfold. The years turned back. If only he could freeze time and somehow change the outcome.

The Solomon Islands, the armpit of the Pacific Theater. Along with several others from his platoon, Jack and Harry had been captured behind enemy lines and thrown into individual dirt pits. Here he was again, mired in the muck of filth, rotten food, and his own waste. The stale air hovered in close around Jack, creating a constant thin coat of sweat and filth.

During the day, the sun bore through the wooden lattice rooftop, the only doorway into this cell, locked high above him. Any movement sent Jack's boots farther into the oozing mess underneath him, trapping him, and beginning another round of freeing his feet. Even with the drop in temperature, the nights were worse. Mosquitoes whined in his ears and feasted on his body, or what was left of it. Most of Jack's platoon already had malaria—Harry and Jack included. The symptoms came and went.

Often at night, alone with his thoughts, he shivered with chills caused by the insipid disease, his only relief the small bits of conversation he let flow to Whisterly. This most disgusting perspective of his life he had tried to shield from her. Yet she read his thoughts, sensed his suffering, and wept for him.

His time here neared two weeks, and one way or another, Jack knew his captivity would soon end. He marked the passing days with rocks, bits of bark, or bone fragments. The last of which littered the compact space, leaving no illusions as to the last occupant's fate. Food, when it came, was sparse and foul, and often found its way back up through his system. Water was even more infrequent and tainted.

When it rained Jack captured what water he could in a boot—a painstaking, laborious process, but quite possibly this action could have been what kept him alive.

During the long nights, when it was quiet, Jack and Harry tried communicating by a rudimentary version of Morse code. Telepathy, they found, required much more brain activity than they could spare in their weak, emaciated state. Communicating by this method was difficult but gave his mind something else to do beyond focusing on his imminent death.

Figuring out individual messages took time, as did tapping out the letters and spaces to form words, some letters distinguishable only after trying to fit them with specific words in the context of a sentence. The intricate work kept his brain functioning and alert— as he memorized the bits and pieces of possible messages, preparing for what came next—yet hope for their survival was just beyond their reach.

In the end it was just too difficult to create and decipher a message using this approach, so Harry and Jack gave up and went back to telepathy. Even though it was more mentally taxing, their efforts were accurate, unlike with their botched form of Morse code. When the latest stutter of machine gun fire rained on the enemy above, Jack said a silent prayer for his men and his own soul, should he die in this hellhole or the piece of dirt just above it. Certainly he wouldn't be much longer for this world here in this pit.

With each passing day more and more energy seeped from him, and his thoughts meandered, clumsy and unfocused. Simple tasks, at times, evaded him.

Breathe. Just breathe. I love you, Jack, Whisterly had whispered into his thoughts.

Individual bursts of artillery sounded above, and Jack's wooden lattice cage door tore from its hinges. *It's time.* A rope tumbled down into the pit. His ability to climb out of this cesspool was long gone. Jack knotted the rope around his waist and tugged, hoping enough manpower was above to pull him free. When his upward momentum jerked to a stop, Jack pasted himself against the slimy sludge of his prison while another barrage of fire cascaded from above.

As Jack broke the surface, his eyes scanned the Japanese camp. From what he could see, besides the small crew of Americans, only dead Japanese littered the ground. Corporal Henry Johnson came face-to-face with Jack, a canteen in hand. He shoved the water, a weapon, and a helmet into Jack's arms.

"Glad to have you back with us, sir."

Jack slammed Henry on the back and nodded as he sucked down a drink. "Thanks for coming back for us. Who else is left?"

Harry nudged Jack from behind. "Hey, I've got the rear."

"Thank God, Harry." Jack turned and, through the filth on his friend's face, spotted Harry's smile. He threw his hand into Harry's, while he assessed the manpower available. Jack motioned to the men behind him, then turned back to Henry. "Let's get the hell outta here, Corporal."

The small band of men clawed forward, each action painfully slow as they inched their way back toward freedom. A tremor shot down the length of Jack's spine just before his eyes darted toward the sky. The corporal was too far ahead, so in the instant he had, Jack threw himself on the men behind him, pressing them to the dirt as the latest slur of bullets covered their position. "All right. Let's go." Jack turned in search of Henry. "Corporal?"

"Here…sir. I'm…hit."

Jack followed the ragged voice with Harry close at his heels. After pulling Henry to the relative safety of the nearest tree, Jack examined the corporal's multiple wounds. Below the knee Henry's leg hung in tattered shreds, but that wasn't the wound that would kill him first. If only that, a tourniquet could have saved his life, followed by amputation. But he'd also caught bullets to the chest and gut; his life force quickly poured from him. Jack and Harry exchanged a glance.

"It's bad, isn't it? Give it to me straight."

Jack pressed his hand solidly onto Henry's shoulder and nodded. "It isn't good."

Harry added pressure to Henry's chest and stomach wounds, but he couldn't keep pace with the blood loss.

"I can't feel anything." The corporal's teeth chattered as his body shivered. "Only the cold, sir."

Jack nodded and moved closer, transferring what body heat he could. "It's okay. I'm here."

"Sir," Henry whispered through mangled breaths, "my son, Daniel, there's nobody for him. Please find him a home."

Jack removed Henry's helmet and scooted him to a more comfortable position. Then he hovered above Henry, meeting his gaze. "Your son will have a home with me. I give you my word."

Harry slid to Henry's other side. "You have my word as well. Daniel will be well taken care of."

Jack grasped Henry's hand and nodded. "Rest easy, solider. Job well done. Godspeed."

Henry nodded and spluttered blood from the side of his mouth. His gaze alternated, resting between Jack and Harry, and his raspy breaths slowed. Seconds later his arm went slack underneath Jack's, and Henry's gaze stared, fixed now at the sky above.

Jack closed the soldier's eyes, then bent his head and mumbled a silent prayer. Harry tapped Jack on his shoulder, the quick motion urging him forward. Turning to the remaining men, he communicated through hand signals, and they advanced forward once again.

Flinging himself forward, Jack startled awake, his breath coming in heaving bursts. In the momentary darkness and confusion, his mind sought Whisterly's. He slowed his labored breathing and fell back against the covers. Sleep wouldn't come for him again this night if Jack could help it.

VINIQUE HAD BEEN up since early morning, first meeting with Arista, then planning for her upcoming meeting with Jack. She flipped through the documentation regarding candidates for the council. After the conversation with Arista had steered off course, they'd tabled the discussion regarding new council members. They'd meet another time to go over each prospect in detail, giving them the proper scrutiny they deserved.

Her thoughts returned to Jack. First and foremost he was the key. After their discussion, Vinique would know if hope still existed.

"Ma'am, your visitor is here."

"Thank you. Send him in."

Vinique rounded from behind her desk and met Jack in the middle of the room, stretching out her arms to give him a hug.

"Nice quarters you have here. Looks similar to Whisterly's."

Vinique nodded and led him to a couch. "Almost identical, in fact, in the set up. How about some coffee? Arista mentioned that was a hit with you. Not sure if mine will be as good though. But I went ahead and got it started, just in case." She hovered by the kitchen.

"Sure. That sounds great. I'm not sleeping so good, so I could use it."

Vinique placed a steaming cup in Jack's hand then sat down beside him. "Is that good as it is?"

"It is. Thanks."

"So how is it being back, spending time with Arista?"

Jack swallowed a large gulp of coffee. "She's amazing. You, and Whisterly of course, have done a great job with her."

"She's her mother's daughter, no doubt about it. But her eyes are all you, Jack."

"I guess that's something." Jack shifted in his seat.

"What is it?"

"Being here, having all these feelings surface from so long ago, well, I see things in a different light now. It's hard, Vinique …hard to feel anger…toward Whisterly, for keeping me away, when, at the same time, I miss her so much that it tears me up inside."

Vinique squeezed Jack's hand. His gaze held a distant faraway look.

"Visiting the coven helped, in many ways. I wasn't real sure what to expect." Jack bowed his head before he continued. "It's different on Earth. Here, on Remeon, was the first time since losing Whisterly that I could share that pain in a real way and feel...understood." He paused, shaking his head. "I'm not even sure that makes any sense."

"It does, Jack. You don't really comprehend the power of the coven until you've experienced it. And I'm glad you found some peace."

Jack cleared his throat; then he lifted his head, seeking Vinique's eyes. "You're barring your thoughts from me. Why?"

Vinique sighed. "Because I don't want you to read thoughts from me before I can share them, the way I want to. That's why you're here."

"I'm guessing you're sending me back, huh?"

She shook her head. "No. No, I'm not. As a matter of fact it's quite the opposite."

Jack crossed his leg over one knee. "I'm all ears."

"Let me explain a little, if I may, some background."

"Please, feel free."

"During the years you were gone, Whisterly became an extremely powerful and accomplished witch. She taught me as well. And, along with the coven, Whisterly and I could perform feats of magic using all the elemental forces. Are you familiar with those?"

"Yes. I believe so. Ground, Fire, Water, and Air." He raised his eyebrows. "Right?"

"That's correct. Along with the capability to command these forces, she mastered the ability to jump her conscious mind from one body to another and even into a corpse."

"I remember one such experience with her. She wasn't so good at it then." Jack's voice darkened. "It was quite scary at the time, for both of us. I guess, back then, she was still somewhat of a novice." Jack rubbed his neck at the healed site of the bite Whisterly had inflicted. "We were lucky to make it out relatively unscathed."

"Be assured she did master this skill. And she had me practice until I mastered it as well." Vinique straightened and crossed toward the large window and gestured with her hands. "She didn't want to miss out on this—her legacy, a healed race. She was counting on the fact that she'd eventually leave the infirmary, healed. But if not"— Vinique turned back toward Jack—"she'd trained with her grandmother and the coven to perfect her ability to throw her consciousness into the body of another, if her body gave out before the cure were available."

"I'm not really sure what you're getting at. Whisterly was attacked and killed. She had very little time to *do* anything. Isn't that correct?"

Vinique nodded. "That's true. Her body died that day."

"Vinique, what are you trying to say?"

"When witches in our line die, Jack, a piece of their spirit always resides with the coven eventually. As part of the spirit world, Whisterly would continue to guide others in the craft and participate in rituals. I'll not pretend that I know how that process works, but Whisterly's grandmother could not locate her granddaughter's spirit after her death, and Whisterly has not joined the coven since her death."

Jack met Vinique at the window and took her by the arms. "What does that mean exactly?"

"Well, over the years, Whisterly and her grandmother trained for this possibility often. She knew it could be her last option for survival. If she had enough time and strength before she died...she could have done it. And if I know Whisterly, she would have already planned where her jump would lead."

"Are you saying Whisterly could still be *alive* somewhere?"

Vinique took Jack's hand in her own. "Now wait a minute, Jack. This is why I didn't tell you right away. Don't get your hopes up. *If* she made it into another body, and *if* her consciousness survived the transfer, at the very best she's lost within the host body, with nothing to anchor to. And that best-case scenario is still pretty bad."

"What can we *do*?" Jack's voice left him in a streaming hiss.

"Come over here, and sit down, take a deep breath, and let me finish. There's no quick, easy answer."

Jack sucked in air, his chest heaving, and sat down hard. "I'm waiting."

"It's a long shot, Jack, that we could even bring Whisterly back to herself in this new body, if in fact the transfer took place. We need to enhance our power for the task ahead. Toward that end, we've accelerated Arista's training, but we must wait until she's ready. And we need more strength still. I have another in mind who can help us… Once we have our combined forces fully prepared, we can proceed with our plan. But there's still a missing piece to the puzzle."

Jack huffed. "It sounds like a lot is missing in this puzzle."

"It's you, Jack."

Jack met Vinique's gaze. "Me? How?"

"Whisterly's true name. It's inside you."

Understanding flashed in his eyes. "That's right… She whispered it to me, the night we married."

Vinique nodded. "The only others who knew it, her parents, are dead. Calling Whisterly by her true name should bring her back to herself, in her new body."

"How do you get it from me?"

"Only by very powerful magic. And just to be absolutely clear, the chances are quite high the magic could kill you in the process of obtaining Whisterly's true name." Vinique's gaze lifted to Jack's. "Now do you understand my reluctance? I can't ask you to risk your life on a chance outcome."

"So be it. I would have given anything to have been here to protect her, and I wasn't." Jack's voice cracked. "So, if there's even the slightest possibility that I can help in bringing her back, just tell me what to do."

First one tear then another streaked down Jack's face, and Vinique gathered him into a hug. "You could be the one who saves her life," she whispered in his ear.

Jack sat back and wiped his face with the back of his hand. "You don't know which body she transferred into?"

"We believe there are five possibilities. Each one was in the infirmary the day Whisterly's body died. All five were on life support at the time and amazingly enough, two were not infected by PR 251 yet. Severe accidents had landed those two women in the infirmary. The other three have already been administered the cure. Brain scans we've reviewed of those five people show no change from the day before Whisterly died to the day of her death."

"Then how will you determine which one is the right one?"

"That's still an unknown. We are trying various methods."

Jack ran his fingers through his hair. "Let me go."

"Go where, Jack?"

"To visit them."

Vinique studied Jack. It was almost as if she could feel the anguish seeping from him. Through the contorted lines of his face, Jack's eyes held a yearning she couldn't put into words. "I'm not sure that's a good idea."

Jack's exasperated sigh echoed in the room. "Why not? Might be worth a try."

"We've already tried to connect with her spirit, Jack. Arista has spent hours reaching out to her mother. Without her true name, she's lost to herself and us."

Vinique watched as anger and possibly guilt warred on Jack's face. "Let me try. Please."

The lines in Vinique's forehead scrunched together. "Okay, Jack. You can go. But I'm coming with you. And not today."

"When then?"

"We'll go tomorrow. Come by here after the midday meal."

"I'll be here."

"Oh, and Jack—"

"I know. I can't talk about this, right?"

"No, you can't. But that's not what I was about to say. Join me for dinner will you? I'm pretty sure Arista and Stephen already made plans."

The grimace on Jack's face changed into the barest of grins. "I know what you're trying to do, Vinique."

"You do?"

Jack's grin grew. "Yes. I do. And thank you. You're a good friend. Sure, I accept."

"I'm not just a good friend, Jack. You're my sister's mate. We're family."

Jack nodded. "You're right, I guess. I hadn't thought of it that way. *Family.* I think I'll like having a little sister." The side of his mouth quirked up. "I'll see you later."

Vinique warmed up her coffee and walked back to her desk. Another important piece of that puzzle needed to be pushed into place today, or at least the fitting process begun. Some rules would need to be broken for this plan to work, but there wasn't another option, so it *had* to work. *We need her here as soon as possible.*

JACK BURST OUT the door from his meeting with Vinique. Surely any second his insides would explode. He replayed the conversation with Vinique over and over in his mind.

The possibility existed. Whisterly could be alive. Somewhere.

He walked the halls of the compound, and when he came upon an exit, he took it. *Could she really have found a way?* Jack felt his heart might burst if he didn't move, if he didn't *do* something. He took off his shirt and headed out at a fast run, going nowhere specific. His mind reeled. Did he dare get his hopes up only to be crushed again?

Through the steady *thud* of his feet hitting the ground, he heard his heart echoing in his ears. He had to run faster, crowding out everything else, until his only thought was the next step. Ahead the shooting range loomed. Another site where Damond had attacked him. *What a disgusting piece of shit.*

In a way, Jack wished Damond were still alive so Jack could kill him all over again. Only this time he'd strangle him and watch him die, slowly, as his breath oozed from him, bit by bit. Jack had killed men many different ways during the war. But God help him, none had been as satisfying as Damond—the first.

As he neared the shooting range, Jack eyed the activity. Old painful memories of the place surfaced, clouding his thoughts. He pushed them deeper. Not wanting to see or talk to anyone, he turned around and headed back toward the compound. Picking up the pace, he could see it wasn't far now. When he finally reached the spot, the glade where he and Whisterly had pledged themselves to each other, he slowed. His chest heaved, and his cheeks stung from the wind slapping his face.

Settling into a familiar place, by the water, he slid to the ground. Glancing around, he noticed the overgrown vegetation. The huge rocks they'd rested against were almost completely obscured. Had anyone been here since their visit so long ago? He leaned his head back and let the wind wash over him, drying the sweat from his body and cooling him down.

In their secret place, he let the words Vinique had spoken to him sink in. Truthfully it sounded like the plan might never work. He could die... Whisterly's new body could die... If this were a mission where he had command, he'd rate the probably of success on the low side.

But this wasn't some military strategy. And the forces he would rely on were not the marines but those he'd learned to trust years ago when Whisterly had proven herself to be a witch in the enchanted room of the ancient basement, where their family was bound together within the grimoire. There would be no turning back now.

But was she dead or alive? Seemed no one knew for sure. He'd only just let her go, didn't he?

That's all we've had all these years, baby, is hope. I'm still hanging on, and, by God, it sounds like you found a way. So I'm sure as hell not giving up on you. Besides, you need to be back so I can yell at you, in person. Real loud. Then, when I'm done, I'm going to love you like there's no tomorrow, 'cause I know just how high a probability that can be. Jack hung his head. *I just pray I get the chance.*

Jack groped for his shirt and then made his way toward the compound.

Jack! This is unbelievable, man. Only with you two could something like this come about.

Harry, sometimes I forget I've given you free reign in my head. I'm not sure what to make of it, well, except for the distinct possibility of dying.

Yeah, but you've been there before.

If this should all go south, Harry…

Jack, it won't. But, like I said before you left, you don't need to worry about a thing here. Besides missing your craziness, Daniel is doing great. Oh, and I miss you too.

Jack couldn't help the wide grin that settled on his face. Where would he be without Harry? *That's good to hear. Tell Daniel I love him, will ya?*

You bet. And, Jack, watch your back. That's usually my job.

That's true. But I need you right where you are.

Jack entered the compound and headed for his room and a shower. He had a promise to keep.

ARISTA PACED THE dimly lit room. Her great-grandmother had decided to add the study of Fire to Air. It was coming along but not fast enough for Arista. Above, the door creaked open and shut again, followed by muffled footfalls. Jack was here. Minutes later he crawled through the hole leading to the magical room.

"Arista, you are quite a vision... You…"

"Papa." She reached for Jack's arms as he folded her into a hug. "You were going to say I look like Mother, weren't you? But you stopped."

Jack nodded.

"It's wonderful, isn't it? The chance that we could have her back with us."

"Can you sit for a few minutes?"

"Sure. Let me grab us a few blankets to sit on."

Jack's chuckle made Arista's heart feel light. "What a great idea. The chill down here always seems to work its way into your bones."

"Mother kept a stack of them down here. She said she started doing it because she used to come down here with me when I was little, and she wanted me to be warm."

When Jack raised his eyes to meet Arista's, they were misty. The pair sat in silence a few minutes before both speaking at once. "You first, Arista."

"I didn't find out about the possibility of Mother… returning… until just before your arrival." Arista held up both her hands and shrugged. "With all this as well, it's overwhelming."

Jack reached for her hand. "I'm sorry I didn't go ahead and say what I was thinking. You'll always look like your mother. She was beautiful. Just like you. But I am saddened by the loss of her body that I knew." He took a shaky breath.

"Papa, you don't have to—"

"I do." He squeezed her hand. "I pray that Vinique's plan, and yours, works. And if it does…when it does, we'll have Whisterly back, in a different form. But you know the best thing about Remeon?"

Arista raised her eyebrows. "I'm not sure what you would say is the best thing about Remeon."

"Well, it's this. She'll be the same up here." Jack pointed to his head. "And that's what I miss the most, and what nobody else on Earth, except a very few, would ever understand. But here, on Remeon, it makes perfect sense."

Arista nodded, then leaned over and kissed Jack's cheek. "You're right, Papa. And we're all working very hard to bring her back."

Jack smiled. "We sure are."

"Mother's already done the hard part. She's given us a fighting chance."

"That's Whisterly at her heart, wouldn't you say, little one?"

Arista nodded. "You know her well, Papa. Now that I'm a blubbering mess, I'm not sure I can complete this task I wanted to show you."

"I'll bet you can. Give it a go."

Arista rose and stood in front of the grimoire. She closed her eyes. Jack watched as the book flew open in front of his daughter. She thrust her hands up, palms forward, and as she did, a spark ignited in the center of each hand.

Lifting them still higher lengthened the flames, and when she twisted her arms in front of her, the flames seemed to join to become one single source. Dancing and sputtering, the fire grew, until Arista separated her hands, coming away with two separate cords of light. Then, as her two hands came together, the flames shifted while she worked, molding them into one circle of fire. When she finished, she laid the small ball of light inside the tome.

Arista stepped back and closed her eyes once again. With a flick of her wrist, her fingers turned in the air. Suddenly the air shifted and gathered. While her fingers worked, the momentum continued, an unnatural hiss streaming through the air as it flowed faster throughout the small space. Still the round flame remained steady on the magical book.

Arista took a deep breath from the blustering wind, and it drew toward her. Stray books and forgotten items floated in the air. Jack's eyes widened, while the extra blankets beside him rose as well and pranced toward his daughter. Then Arista's mouth closed, and her arms fell to the side. The magical book shifted, swaying with the movement of the wind.

In one final action, her hands touched, and the gusts of wind snapped the great book closed, extinguishing the circle of fire. All the items hovering from the force of the wind plummeted to the ground with a clamor that left echoes ringing in their wake. Arista smiled and glanced at her father and, with a wave of her hand, parted the book's pages again. As they fluttered, small puffs of smoke rose from between them, attesting to the fire's demise.

Jack stood and came in for a closer look. He found no burn marks or blackened pages. In fact, if it weren't for the disarray in the room, one might never have known that flames had been set loose within its covers. Pride tugged at his chest. "Your talent is incredible, Arista."

Arista beamed back at him and giggled. "That's actually the first time I've gotten it right."

CHAPTER 8

VINIQUE PACED HER office. She'd need to bring her here, just like she had Stephen and Jack. That way there would be less scrutiny involved with her travel; furthermore, approval would not require the full council. This morning when Vinique had spoken again to Arista regarding this particular visitor, Arista had still been tentative, not fully committed. Still Arista hadn't experienced this little one's might to the extent Vinique had.

The night Whisterly had died had been painful in so many ways. Losing Arista in the battle to bring Stephen home had been one of them and a significant blow. Caught up in her own grief that horrible night, Arista couldn't continue in her efforts towards Stephen's rescue mission, understandably. And at the time, there had been no other way forward, only Belle and herself. Belle had proven her worth that day.

Belle's innate magical ability, for an Earthling, and as a child, well, it had been startling. And in order to amass the level of power needed to connect Whisterly to her true name, Belle needed to be here. Once she was back on planet, the coven would evaluate Belle; then more would be known. If Vinique's suspicions were correct, more was running through Belle's veins than human blood.

Funneling Belle's power through her holographic form during her previous visit had been an amazing feat. But for what Vinique, Arista, and Jack were to undertake now, they would need her here in flesh and blood. Holographic forms weren't made to withstand this type of activity long term. Her holographic form would quickly degrade, right when they were in dire need of her.

Stephen would be utilized to bring her through the portal, since the true love requirement had to be met to activate interplanetary travel. But Vinique wouldn't inform him—Arista would. That way the request would officially come from the council chair.

Belle dear?

Vinique, is it you?

It is. How are you today?

Good. How is Th—Stephen?

Your brother is well.

Ma and Pa miss him. I can tell even though they don't talk about it. I can feel their sadness when I see their faces.

Vinique kept her emotions in check. Belle would feel even the slightest twinge of concern from the telepathy link they shared.

I'm sure that's difficult for them. But surely you've been in contact with your brother since he's been back on Remeon. Have you let your parents know about his well-being?

We've only talked a little bit. He says he's busy most of the time.

Ah. I see.

I'm helping out a lot more now with his chores.

Belle wasn't going to make this easy…

We've talked a couple times now about your adventure, when you were here on Remeon before.

Uh-huh.

And our need to have you come back.

You said Miss Whisterly could maybe return.

Quite possibly, with your help.

I would love to see you, Arista, Stephen, and help Miss Whisterly if I can.

That's good to hear, Belle.

But why can't I tell Ma and Pa? I don't understand that part.

Your ma and pa love you very much, Belle. I'm sure they would feel frightened if they knew of your plans to visit again.

I think so too.

Do you believe that you'll be safe here?

With you and Arista and Stephen there, sure I do.

Well, that's good. But, if your parents knew beforehand, they might be so fearful they would keep you from coming.

Yeah. They might.

Maybe if they understood having you here was a matter of life and death, they could accept it better.

Maybe. But I don't think I could explain that part to them very well.

Tell me truthfully. Do you want to return to help bring Whisterly back? I won't lie and tell you that it will be fun and games because it will be a lot of work, like when we were working together to find your brother among the Night Dwellers. We desperately need your help. Still, even with that, it's okay to tell me no if you don't want to come.

Vinique, I want to come and help and learn more. Will you teach me more fun stuff?

You will, indeed, learn more and grow in your skill level.

What should I say to Ma and Pa, Vinique?

Why don't you write them a letter? Then talk it over with your brother. I'll help as well, if you'd like for me to.

Okay. When would I come?

As soon as possible. How does two days sound?

I guess I can have it done by then.

I'll need to speak with Stephen first, but after I do, why don't you talk with him, about the letter and to plan when you'll leave?

All right. I'll get started on the letter today.

Sounds good, Belle.

Vinique released a deep sigh. Inwardly she'd put the conversation in the win column, since they were one step closer to their goal, but she couldn't imagine being James and Elizabeth Stewart, waking up to find their daughter gone. They had already been through so much. Vinique shoved the emotion aside.

Without Belle, their chances were slim for success. With Belle, their likelihood of success increased exponentially. Ultimately this would become a win for Belle as well. Digging into her ancestry would reveal what else flowed through her besides human blood. She'd need that information going forward. Her future may lay beyond Earth.

Vinique smiled as she considered all that was to come—the important role that this Earthling would play. This was only the beginning for Belle.

Now Stephen.

Stephen, could you come to see me? And if Arista is with you, bring her as well.

Sure. Be right there, Vinique.

BELLE GLANCED AROUND the empty kitchen, thinking about the telepathic conversation she'd just had with Vinique. She took another large swallow of milk and picked up the cookie crumbs that had fallen on the table, then licked her fingers. Her mind whirled. Could she really leave without speaking to her ma and pa? Would they ever forgive her?

This time it would be by choice. They'd know from the letter she would leave them, explaining it all. Sometimes, when she looked deep into her ma's eyes, she knew that her mother was thinking about Remeon and her brother, mentally weighing the odds that he'd be coming back. During these times her ma looked lost...far away. It was almost like she had to let go of the present to picture Thomas in another place, far from Earth.

Then Ma would squeeze Belle's hand and ask how she knew what she'd been thinking at that particular moment. Belle would let her know how her face told the story. Pa's was different. When he thought of Thomas, a satisfied smile tugged at his lips. His face was proud, strong, knowing that Thomas was exploring, just like he'd always dreamed.

What would they think after I leave? Will they know that I'm following my own dreams also? That, even though I'm a girl, I want to do great things? And that sometimes doing the right thing didn't make everyone happy? We'd learned that already in this household for sure. Belle gulped down the last of her milk and reached for another cookie. They would know because she'd tell them in the letter she'd write.

Belle plodded up the stairs just as her ma came inside; Shep barked close on her heels. "Belle, how about some beans to go with the casserole for dinner?" She turned, headed back down the steps, and met her ma in the kitchen.

"Sounds good, Ma."

"Would you like to help me cook them? Go on and grab a jar from the cellar. You know they're your pa's favorite."

"Sure, but do I have time to work on something upstairs first?"

Ma paused, bent low, and searched her daughter's eyes. "*Work* on something? You're thinking about Thomas, aren't you? Is everything okay?"

Belle nodded.

Ma could sniff out a lie coming from miles away. "Is Thomas in trouble?"

"No, Ma. He's fine, honest."

Ma's gaze still held her own. "Just worried about him then?"

"Only a little. He's happy, Ma."

Ma turned her attention to the sink and began putting away the dishes in the drain. "Okay, go on. I'll call you when I need your help."

"Thanks, Ma." Belle turned to leave just as Pa came through the door. She ran to him and squeezed him around the waist.

Pa reached down, picked her up, and hugged her tight against his chest.

Belle breathed in, smelling the warmth of the sun still on his skin. "Pretty soon I'm gonna be too big to pick up," Belle announced.

Pa kissed her forehead and set Belle on her feet again. "I think you're right. Soon. You're growing like a weed."

Belle giggled and headed up the steps once again. When she got to Thomas's room, she ducked inside and quickly looked for the dictionary she'd need to write the letter. *I bet it's under the bed where he shoves everything.* Minutes later, dictionary in hand, she sat at her small desk, gazing out the window, thinking of the words she would write that might comfort and explain at the same time.

Ma and Pa,

You've told me as long as I can remember that this day would come. You say it so often—that someday I would need to spread my wings. Put others' needs before my own, and that's what I've done. I'm needed to help save someone on Remeon, so I must go. I'm learning and growing, just as you say I should, so don't be sad. I want to do this, and I will see you again soon. Ma and Pa, your love has made me strong. And just like you promised me, my dreams have come true. Even me, just me, can make a difference. Love, Belle.

THE NEXT DAY dragged by, waiting, while time crept toward the midday meal, and the somewhat morbid meeting Jack had arranged with Vinique. By the time Jack had woken, Stephen had already dressed and left. *He's probably already with Arista this morning.* Dreams had plagued Jack's sleep, but he'd expected as much— welcomed it even.

Long ago he learned to be open to what his psyche communicated to him, especially in matters involving Whisterly. No end existed to the avenues available through which she might reach him.

Jack had time to kill. While he stood in the shower, the force of the water pouring over his shoulders helped decrease the tension residing there. He turned, letting the water pound him in the face, while his thoughts roamed from Whisterly to Arista and Simon. Already gifted in the art of telepathy, Arista would soon be a powerful witch as well.

Hearing stories, not only from Stephen but others also, Simon's prowess in telepathy was seemingly unattainable, with the possible exceptions of Whisterly, Arista, and Vinique. Was it guaranteed that Simon would inherit Whisterly's innate skill? If so, had he discovered any of his latent powers of sorcery yet? If not, the lurking, undeveloped ability would be a danger to them all eventually.

Even in the steam rising from the shower, a chill pierced through him. Jack ran a hand down his face. He turned off the water and towel-dried, then dressed. *Have Vinique and Arista even considered the possible impact of Simon's abilities when he's had no one to lead him?* This question churned inside Jack as he left for the gathering area to eat, even though food didn't interest him in the least.

Jack desired little one-on-one interaction; so, instead of waiting to be served, he picked up a few items through the cafeteria-style line and scanned the area, searching for a seat. The shafts of sunlight spilling through the tall windows drew Jack toward the room's edge. He picked a seat along the end of the wall, where he could feel the radiant warmth of the sun while still able to survey those coming and going around him.

He prepared his mind defensively for the assault on his thoughts that he knew would come, then sat back and shoved the food down his throat while letting his mind drift. The branches above played games with the light, sending shadows across the room, meandering through his thoughts, tugging him away. Jack felt his insides being drawn back to the Solomon Islands again, this time a happier memory, before his capture, when the platoon enjoyed some rare moments of peace in the island jungle.

Jack basked in the memory and warmth, and when he heard the voice, he chastised himself for not feeling the man's approach.

"Jack, isn't it?"

Jack adjusted to face the man who'd come upon him from the outskirts of the room. He wore a pendant which Jack recalled identified him as a council member. Recognition flashed in Jack's mind as he rose to shake the man's hand. "Kix, yes. That's right. It's Jack."

In the awkward silence that followed, Kix peered around the perimeter of the space, as if looking for someone.

"Well, I'd ask you to join me, but I'll be leaving in just a few minutes myself." Jack recalled the council member's help at the shooting range when Damond had attacked him and Harry. Without his intervention, they both might have died. "It was a long time ago, but I never got the chance to properly thank you for stopping Damond from killing me and Harry."

"Ah, that. Well, I doubt he would have killed you."

Jack's mouth became a thin line. "No. I'm certain he would have."

"Interesting having you back here again." The man's eyebrows rose. "Hopefully you haven't experienced any harassment during your visit?"

Kix wanted more information. Jack could feel the slight hesitation. The change in his tone… The unspoken question… Well, too bad, not today. But examining his interest would be a good idea. "I need to be going. You caught me on the way out."

"Sure, Jack."

Without a backward glance, Jack bent his body around the nearest tree and left for the infirmary.

JACK RELEASED A pent-up breath. Vinique beat him to their prearranged meeting spot. "Are you ready to go in?"

His lips drew back in a grimace. "As ready as I'm gonna be."

"One of the five we've been monitoring died late yesterday. So there are four now." Jack's eyes darted toward Vinique's. "Nothing we can do about it. All five were receiving around-the-clock care and are under full time guard as well."

Jack rubbed the back of his neck and nodded.

"I've had the staff pull the doctor's notes since Whisterly's death for the remaining four. You're welcome to review them, although I'm not sure how much you'll understand. We don't ever allow outsiders to view this type of personal information. I'm sure you recognize that all you will see and hear needs to remain private."

"Absolutely."

"All right. Let's go in." Vinique intercepted the closest staff member and spoke under her breath, tilting her head back toward Jack. Minutes later she rejoined him.

"Is the staff aware of your interest in these four women and why?"

"No. Not specifically. Once we determined the five, now four, most likely possibilities for Whisterly's jump I made their care top priority with any updates as to changes in their medical condition reportable to the council chair. So the staff is aware we are following these four women's medical progress carefully. And, as I mentioned, they are closely guarded, so we are alerted to anything out of the ordinary. I don't want to give out any more detail than that. As to why you're here, the staff has been made aware that you're offering comfort to the infirmary's longest term visitors hoping to aid in healing efforts. Your visits are also covered with a spell. In their memories they will only remember a visitor offering kind words and reading to the ill." Vinique handed Jack four files. "Here's the medical documentation. You're welcome to sit by them as you read. Try to communicate—it's up to you how. I'll be right outside, tending to some other matters, if you need me."

"Vinique, thank you. I need this."

"Jack, this is Lily. She'll answer any questions you might have. And I'll see you a bit later." Vinique flashed a practiced smile at both of them, then left the room.

"Follow me, Jack. These four are now our longest term residents. We still have several hundred too sick to leave, in various stages of the disease, but everyone else has either been cured, died, or is now well enough to recuperate in their own chambers."

Jack nodded. "I see."

"And to add to the commotion, we are now redesignating some of this space, since our occupation rate has gone way down. So please pardon the mess."

Lily led Jack behind a curtain with four individual partitions. "Here we are. Feel free to take your time. I'll be at the desk if you need anything at all."

"Thank you for your help, Lily."

Jack noticed her shy smile as she winked at him. "Don't mention it."

The constant whirring and blinking of machinery gave Jack a sinking uneasiness that shot down to his core. From his experience here, being tested and abused, to his injuries earned in combat, he'd prefer never to set foot in a hospital again. Jack pushed the feeling aside; they'd still be there to deal with later.

He grabbed a chair and sat beside the first woman's bed, while reading her before and after charts. Just as Vinique had mentioned, even he could tell there had been no significant change. Jack made an attempt to connect with her, to no avail, as expected. A picture, presumably of the woman, stared back at him from behind a frame on a side table. Something tugged at Jack. Something he should do. *What is it?*

He moved on to the second woman and repeated the process. Just like the first, there was nothing of significance that happened medically to her the day of or after Whisterly's death. Jack picked up the picture beside this one's bed also. Wouldn't he feel something if Whisterly were lost inside one of these women?

Jack proceeded to the third. She had been on life support for the least amount of time. Still, there had been no changes in this woman's chart either the day of or after Whisterly's death. He called to her, and just like the previous two, this one elicited no response. The picture of her seemed more vivid, and she had striking blue eyes. He replaced the picture on the side table and continued on to the last woman. The nagging feeling in the back of his mind pulsed through him, stronger than ever as he pulled back the last curtain.

The process mimicked the other three—no significant medical change experienced the day of or after Whisterly's death. Her picture by the bed seemed so lifelike. But when he picked it up and attempted a connection, he only felt a deep nothingness inside. Jack released an irritated sigh. He had to be missing something. There were clues here. He just didn't know what to look for.

If none of the medical stats changed, there must be something else. *What else can I check? Inside, deep inside, one of these women possesses Whisterly's soul. Damn it! She trusted me to come through for her. She trusted in our love. I need to also.* Jack slumped in the chair and buried his head in his hands, remembering each of the women's pictures as they flashed before him in his mind, one after the other.

Then Whisterly's face beamed at him behind his closed eyes. *That's it!* Jack grabbed the photo of the fourth woman, walked to her side, and raised the woman's eyelid. Her eye color matched the photo. Both were brown. He replaced the picture and started back at number one. She had green eyes in her photo. Jack raised an eyelid of number one. Green. Still green. *Maybe this is a dumb idea.*

He pulled back the curtain from number two. Her picture showed blue eyes. He repeated the same process. *And she still has blue eyes. Of course she does.* Jack moved to the last woman and picked up the picture that held the vivid blue eyes. He gingerly raised an eyelid, then gasped, and ran to the other side to check her other eye as well, dropping the picture with a loud clatter.

Her eyes are gray! Just like Whisterly's! Before they were unmistakably bright blue! Whisterly, baby, you're in there!

"LEAVE. NOW!" SIMON ordered.

The young girl, Nela, drew herself to a stand. Whimpering from Simon's latest attack into her thoughts, she slowly crossed the floor, trembling as she moved one foot in front of the other. When she reached the door, Nela leaned her back against it, taking in deep gulps of air. From across the room Simon's cold stare met hers. Her eyes widened as their gazes locked, and she exited, tripping and falling on the other side of the door.

It had been two days since the strange nocturnal vision, and everything in Simon's life seemed off. And tonight his attempted thought transfer with Nela brought him no relief. Even his desire for female companionship had waned since that evening. The memory of the attack into his thoughts and the odd happenings afterward had kept him on edge.

Sleep. He craved sleep.

What came after the apparition, or nightmare—the noise that had filled his head that night—could not be classified as rest. Simon scoffed and trudged to the bathroom to prepare for bed and change. He hung his head over the sink; the monotonous pounding in his ears groaned on as if it would never end.

Throwing off his clothes, he gawked at the person in the mirror staring back at him. Dark circles loomed under his eyes, his face long and thin, his skin transparent under his fingers. Simon drew closer, then took a step back, and looked behind him. It was almost as if it wasn't him in the mirror. Was someone else here playing tricks and controlling his mind?

A long night stretched ahead of him with the opportunity of uninterrupted sleep, but instinctively he knew this process would repeat—the dreams and no rest. Jack, Stephen, and Arista, were they the reason for this assault?

Perhaps this mind game had been a new trick of the Day Watchers, and none of it was true after all. Simon needed more information. Maybe he could get Jack and Stephen to come to him. The Day Watchers wouldn't allow Arista to stray far from the compound.

Following the logic through though, if the source of his parentage were true, the Night Dwellers, the Day Watchers, the council—they all belonged to him anyway. He was the rightful heir, despite the Night Dwellers' plan already in place to return to the compound in victory over the Day Watchers with a healed community of Night Dwellers. Now, in addition to the help Simon hoped to gain from the inside, the law would be on his side as well. Mila and Janus had known this the whole time. *Hells, they should have told me.*

Simon paced, avoiding heading to bed where his mind would be locked in a prison for yet another night. Hours passed, and finally, dead on his feet, Simon grabbed a blanket and fell on the couch. His eyes ached and burned from lack of sleep, and his thoughts, typically clear and direct, jumbled together from lack of focus. *I need to go back.*

Fighting to search for the place his mind had traveled several nights before, Simon imagined the pieces he could remember, hoping his memory would kick in to fill out the rest. The musty, dank space, the cool dampness underneath him, the inhuman beings gathered around him, the illuminated book that sought his blood, all appeared before him. His eyelids drooped shut.

Jack.

The low hum of chanting voices met his ears, then louder it soared, and even louder until all other thoughts spilled from him. Initially Simon struggled to hear, the words sounding like tiny grunts and groans. Then the syllables smoothed, and the words, once again familiar, transformed as they fell from his lips with the crowd.

The maiden, the mother, the crone.

The maiden, the mother, the crone.

The maiden, the mother, the crone.

The maiden, the mother, the crone.

The maiden, the mother, the crone.

Simon hovered in the air, at once caught up and one with the mass of chanting voices. He tried to speak, but his voice didn't come. Reaching out to those forms around him brought no contact. The surroundings were the same, but his perspective was different. A commotion below caught his attention. The beings moved forward in unison toward a person below. Simon tumbled in among them and fell to the ground within their mass.

He peered at the person in the center of the circle. Jack, the human, Simon's father, lay prone before the gathering, mumbling something. Simon flung his arms out in frustration, and all motion stopped.

Scanning the area, he moved his right hand to the left, and the scene changed. Now Arista appeared below, and Jack stood along the perimeter of the room, watching. As before, Simon could manipulate his movement through the space. Arista spoke, sparking a light source, then next a strong wind.

Simon's mouth gaped open; what was she? With another movement of his hand, Arista faded, and the gathered beings from on high joined him below. Their faces and bodies were covered by cloaks, and their chanting began anew. The words came to Simon and somehow formed on his lips before they spewed forth from his mouth as he participated in the ritual taking place.

Simon raised his hand high once again, and the action froze. *I'm controlling this somehow? This is me?*

Amid the stock-still entities, one flowed toward Simon. He twisted to take a glimpse behind him, then turned forward once again.

"Yes, I see you, Simon. You don't belong here. Maybe once you would have—if fate had been different."

Simon's gaze drew him into the dark depths of the woman's eyes. They seemed to suck him in and hold him there, immobile. "Where am I? Where is here?"

"You have seen enough to answer your questions. Even now the explanation lies inside you."

Simon attempted to break the hold the woman had on him but found he couldn't tear himself away. "Why…why was I attacked?"

"Nothing could prevent the act set forth at your birth, confirmed through your heritage by birthright. But to continue on this path, there is much more you must present, and you are…unprepared and unworthy."

Simon attempted a telepathic hold on the woman but connected only with nothingness and space.

A groaning cackle filled the air. "You do not possess the power to control me."

He scrunched his forehead. "I don't understand. Someone brought me here before."

"You brought yourself here, Simon. And tonight that is all the information you will gain."

"Wait!" The old witch focused her gaze on Simon again, just as a shudder flowed through his spine.

"No. It is done."

The scene before him transformed into a murky haze, and another jolt passed through him. Simon pried his eyes open and found himself back on the couch in his quarters. A chill seeped into his bones, and his body trembled with uncontrollable spasms. He yanked the blanket up to his neck and curled himself into a ball. A yearning deep within his gut poured from him, like a sickness.

Where had he been? The compound? Or maybe another realm altogether? None of it made sense. He blinked, and sleep fought for control.

Snapping his eyes open again, Simon tried to piece together what he did know. He was different since the force had attacked him several days ago. Somehow he had been part of a group with Jack, Arista, and maybe even Whisterly. He'd been judged and found unworthy. His power of telepathy had failed him with that...being.

But some innate aptitude had gained him entrance. This proved his theory. If Jack were there and Arista—and they had been from the scenes Simon had visited—then that meant Simon and Whisterly were too—their bonds connected by birth. *She said the answers lay within me. Me?*

Simon's eyes closed, and the room came to life, swirling around him. The dream that descended upon him claimed him for the remainder of the night and the next morning, and when his personal guards were unable to wake him, he was rushed to the infirmary.

THE OLD WOMAN addressed the coven. *We knew this day would come eventually. Because Simon willed it to be, he has access to the grimoire. Soon he may understand his power, and it will be too late. He must be trained or exiled and torn from the tome. The initial choice was made for him years ago, and immersion followed at the proper time. Now Simon possesses the knowledge to one day become a warlock, being born of a witch. His power is strong, unbeknownst to him yet. As a child of Whisterly, his wisdom in the craft will grow, even without formal training.*

In the near future our ability to act will be limited. So, for now, until his future can be discussed in detail and agreed upon by the coven, Simon has been banned from visiting the magical tome and this sanctu-

ary which holds the powers intact. However, the measure is only tempo-rary, and Simon's capacity for magic, potentially great. We must not delay to make a formal decision. One day his influence could rival his mother's.

CHAPTER 9

JACK RETRIEVED THE box that Arista had given him from her desk. In it were all Whisterly's letters. Throughout her time with her daughter, Whisterly had written these forty-nine notes to Arista, then arranged them in numerical order. After Arista's initial shock regarding Simon and her parentage, she had decided to take her time opening the rest. *Fair enough. It's a lot to take in.* Arista had given Jack a quick summary of the first one. *But why was that letter she read only a partial truth? Maybe to soften the blow? To save it for later? For blackmail?*

Shortly after Jack had returned to Earth the last time, Whisterly had learned of Simon's kidnapping at birth, while Whisterly was still drugged and going through childbirth. Jack had wanted to come back to Remeon right then to fight for his son's return. But considering the bigger picture, Whisterly had wanted him to remain on Earth.

Jack scoffed and threw up his arms, the irritation still affecting him, even after all the time that had passed. *What is more important than protecting your children? Nothing. Absolutely nothing.*

Afterward they'd argued extensively for days. Jack had to seethe silently. Whisterly hurt; he hurt. And, in the end, to maintain a relationship, even a telepathic one, Jack had backed off. Some of her reasons made sense, at the time. Janus had accused Jack of murder before departing, and forming the Night Dwellers. That charge had taken ages to put to rest, but even after that, Whisterly stood her ground regarding Simon. *She knew me too well. I'd have gone after him. Hell yeah! I would have. But, if I had gotten Simon back, his and Arista's parentage would have been revealed. And Whisterly's reign on the council? Well, who knew what course that would have taken.*

The exodus of some of her citizens, the abduction of her newborn child, the loss of her parents, her own illness, blackmail. God, she was strong; he knew it to be true, and to bear all that at such a young age—it must have been horrible.

But power or your children? To Jack the choice was simple.

He pushed the box aside and leaned his head back against the wall, punctuating his feelings with his fists, balled at his side. Memories of his own father flooded Jack's thoughts. It had been so long since he'd even allowed himself to reflect on the man who had been his biological father. He'd been a coward, abandoning his family to take care of himself.

And, in a way, in his darkest thoughts, Jack felt as if he'd been forced to do the same. Even making a decision in the name of love didn't fix this. The ugliness still gnawed at his soul. He'd failed to protect his family before he'd even gotten started at this father thing.

And it was still a deeper mess than that... Jack was no stranger to the helplessness that curdled in his gut, that then settled and festered there since he'd left his wife and children on Remeon all those years ago.

He'd ignored it. Hidden from it. Run from it. Fought against it. But it was still there, day after day, waiting for him.

They'd created Simon, he and Whisterly, but along with Mila's and Janus's treachery, Jack and Whisterly were also to blame.

A low growl formed in the back of his throat. At least no one was here with him now. All he could do at this point was to read the words of a young council chair witch, in love and overwhelmed with the weight of the world on her shoulders. Jack sunk his head in hands and exhaled a deep breath.

Letters one and two first, just like Arista.

He picked the two letters from the carefully sorted stack. But before he opened them, he closed his eyes and let himself drift back in time to his last visit on Remeon, to those precious moments Jack and Whisterly had had together. Jack ran his hand through his hair, and as he pulled the first letter free, the years melted away. He imagined his young wife writing to their daughter for the first time.

Tears bit the back of his eyes as he read, imagining her alone and in charge of the council with her mentors dead, and having just been betrayed by Janus. He let the tears come. It made the reading of these first letters easier. After finishing, he glanced at the neatly arrayed stack remaining. The final one would tell him the most about her state of mind close to the end. His next letter needed to be her last.

Jack's fingers flipped to the back of the stack, letter forty-nine. He shifted the envelope back and forth between his forefinger and this thumb, undecided. Originally he'd planned to read them in order. But this last one would have been written closer to Whisterly's death. The thoughts conveyed to her daughter would likely reflect a huge change from the initial writings of letters one and two that he'd just read. He hesitated a moment longer, then plunged his fingers into the envelope and grabbed the missive.

As I watch you, Arista, I see my mistakes more clearly than I ever have before. Blinded by my duty, I let it dictate my life, and I've raised you to follow in my footsteps. But now, living with the daily pain of the suffering I've caused over the years, if I had it to do over again, would I make the same decisions or make choices which would have kept your father at my side?

With so many moving parts, that's difficult to answer, even now. Did the good decisions outweigh the bad? I still don't know. My only certainty is this: I've missed Jack, the love of my life, each and every day.

If you've read these letters in order, you already know your father was human. He was one of the first humans to be tested. His results helped immensely in our fight for the cure. To be clear, those first sets of test were grueling, but your father didn't die. I've buried the truth, never wanting your parentage to be in question. Records document that your father is Damond, just as you've been told, but Jack Livingston is your father.

All I've done since your birth, and since Jack's departure from Remeon, was to protect him, and you, in the hope that someday we'd be reunited again.

You'll recognize how high the costs have been and even might question some of the decisions I've made. But, for the chance for us to be together, and eventually maybe even Simon too, my heart believed it to be the right direction. I understand it may be too late for your brother. But maintaining him in the environment where he was raised from birth seemed to be the right decision at the time. I'd even convinced myself that keeping Simon with the Night Dwellers might be advantageous—for the greater good. Even to the point of envisioning the Night Dwellers as a kind of foster family... With my blood pumping through his veins he would surely find his way back to us and council leadership, ultimately bringing the two factions together again. Both you and Simon were destined to become great leaders. Or so I thought.

Fighting for Simon's return initially threatened everything I was trying to keep together and our eventual reunion with Jack. There was so much at stake. Your future and the healing of our race had to take precedence until I could bring Jack back, who would help with Simon, if that's even an option at this point.

It's so much more complicated, but that's the gist of it. Telepathy is easy for you; you excel naturally, and you'll find witchcraft to be second nature, similar to breathing. It's who you are. But the hard stuff—love, children, family—so often there are no right answers. We're blindly reaching for the truth and the way as we render decisions as best we can.

Consider carefully and entertain additional counsel before revealing the contents of this letter. Many realities could change with the release of these truths. Look at all the humans have done for Remeonites. Even now as I write this, our scientists are close to confirming that humans are the missing link to the cure for PR 251. We must consider the needs of other races now, besides ourselves. It is past time to do so.

Be kind to yourself, my sweet Arista. Enjoy the love in your life. Treat the people of Remeon with the utmost of care. Their lives depend on your guidance and your assessment of the future. Use the knowledge of the craft. Weave it into all you do. You'll reap the rewards for your lifetime and your children's.

I'll share more in my next letter.

All my love,
Mother

After rereading letter forty-nine, Jack wiped his face with the heel of his palm, then stowed Whisterly's last installment in the envelope, careful not to smear the words. At the point this information got out, the council would be in an uproar. When all these decisions had been set in motion, could they have predicted the outcome? *They shouldn't have forced their daughter to conceive an heir. It was Whisterly's parents' fault. Of course it was.*

In spite of himself, Jack smirked, the tears pooling in his eyes again. One thing had led to another, setting up a chain reaction, and here they were, still dealing with the mess of a prior generation. Just like Jack was still dealing with the ghost of his father. And as long as Jack remained alive, he would fight that internal battle. *Is that all we do in this life? Labor on the decisions that have come before, no matter what we do, destined to repeat our ancestor's history?*

Jack contemplated reading another letter, picking back up at installment number three. But he hadn't counted on the energy it would take to relive all these experiences. Better to wait; besides, at the very least Arista needed to be aware of the contents of this last letter, even if she didn't act on it right away. Vinique surely knew everything it contained. She'd been right there the whole time, living it with Whisterly.

Jack, sorry to interrupt. You, me, and Arista need to talk. Simon has found his way into the grimoire. He doesn't realize it yet, but he's gone through the immersion process. He's officially an apprentice warlock but banned by the coven. Our schedule just got another bump forward.

Vinique, just tell me when and where.

ARISTA WATCHED STEPHEN from the kitchen in her quarters while she refilled their coffee cups, studying him from a distance. Having him back had been like a dream come true, sharing early-morning breakfasts and late-night dinners. Managing to find time alone together, considering her council responsibilities and time with Jack as well, had been challenging but worth it.

Stephen seemed to be adapting also. Their discussions about Earth and Remeon had contained no depth as yet. She needed to dig a little deeper to see how much trouble she was in. Vinique had warned her to talk to Stephen about the somewhat rash decision that Arista had made independently, just before he'd left for Earth, but to date she had not. The secret was eating away at her. She needed to tell him.

"Here we are. More coffee." Arista placed the cups on the table in front of the couch the two shared.

Stephen leaned forward, grabbed his cup, and took a deep drink. "That's so good. Coffee tastes different here though. Maybe the process for growing the beans is different, creating a unique blend. Makes sense I guess."

She shrugged, taking small sips, eyeing him over the rim of her cup. "I'd never really had much interest in it until I found out you and Papa liked it so much." The grin that settled on Stephen's face made Arista's heart flutter. How did he have such power over her? In the short time he'd been on Earth, it seemed Stephen had become even more handsome and confident, if that was possible.

"I know I've been taking up all your time, but would you like to spend the day together?"

Arista's face lit with a smile she couldn't hold back.

Stephen inched closer and brushed his lips against hers, sending her heart into a beating frenzy. "Is that a yes?" he whispered.

"*Hmmm.* I do have some council business I must attend to…"

"Wait… I must not have been convincing enough. I can do better. Let me try again." Stephen cupped her cheek, then kissed her mouth, nudging her toward the arm of the couch as he leaned into her, pressing their bodies together.

"You're making me crazy," she muttered into his ear. "I can't focus."

"Let's see about that." He arched one eyebrow. "What's your answer?" His fingers rested on her waist as he kissed her nose, then met her lips again. A groan escaped him when she buried her fingers in his hair. And when she gasped for a breath, he lowered his mouth to hers again, deepening their kiss. Her fingernails slid down his arms and she felt his body shiver. "Now who's driving who crazy?"

Arista smiled. "Me?"

Stephen maneuvered Arista into a sitting position, then dotted her neck with soft kisses. "*Mmm.*"

"You can join me, if you'd like. I need to spend some time training with my great-grandmother and then a council meeting briefing. After that, I'm all yours."

He chuckled. "Sounds like I'm last on your list, but I guess that will have to do."

The lines in her forehead deepened. "That's not true. All I ever think about is making a life with you."

Stephen's eyes found hers. "You don't think I spend almost every waking minute with the same thoughts?" He took her hands. "I want you so much it scares me sometimes. Then I realize how stupid I must seem to you, a human believing there is any chance at all for us."

"Of course there's a chance. I want to be with you too. Maybe we can make it work. My parents did."

A wry smile crossed his lips. "And look how well that worked out for them."

Arista wriggled free.

"Sorry. That didn't come out so great."

Arista stared at Stephen from the short distance between them.

"Stop that, Arista. Let's not fight."

"I need to discuss something with you." Arista reached for her lukewarm drink and absentmindedly took a sip.

Stephen closed the gap between them and blew out a breath. "Okay. I've sensed that. I figured you'd tell me when you were ready."

"I'm not sure that I am...ready." Arista walked to the large window behind her desk.

Stephen followed her. "What is it?" He squeezed her shoulders.

Her chest heaved, her focus out the window. "When Remeonites mate, it's for life. Did you know that, Stephen?"

"Now I do."

"Even if one of them dies, the survivor cannot mate again. Our bodies only mate once. And the experience is incredible when two bodies are telepathically immersed and beat as one."

"It sounds like it. Maybe that could be us, one day, if that's what you want. Immersion sounds...interesting."

"What I want is to make my own decision, Stephen, not be forced as my mother was and her mother before her and so on. Why would a council chair not make her own choice?"

Stephen kissed the back of her neck. When he reached for her hand, she turned to face him. "I guess I'm missing what the problem is here. What's wrong?"

"You remember going home through the portal, when you were here before?"

He nodded. "Well, of course I remember. I was pretty scared at the time—that waterfall—man..."

"That's it."

"Whatever you did right before I passed through was pretty incredible. It felt like our hearts were beating together... Whoa... Wait a minute... Do you mean..."

Arista eyes prickled. She blinked, trying to stop the tears before they started. "Stephen, that was the mating ceremony, a shortened version, but the mating ceremony all the same."

"You mean, we're mated, for life?"

"I am. As a human, you are free to do as you wish."

"What? Wait. I don't understand. Why were we mated then?"

"Because I decided to mate before you left," she whispered.

Stephen's eyes widened. "Arista, I love you, but why wouldn't you talk to me first?"

"We didn't have much time. Remember? You needed to get off-world, fast."

He shook his head. "This isn't how I wanted this to go for us. I wanted to ask you to be my wife."

"I was afraid to wait. I didn't want to be forced to mate for the sake of an heir, like my mother was."

Stephen looked into her eyes. "I'm sure you don't want this yet either. There must be a way to undo this. Whatever this is that you've done. And when we're ready, we'll do it the right way."

Tears streamed down her face. "What? What do you mean, the right way?"

"What about a courtship, a marriage—my family's never even met you."

She wiped her eyes. "You're not on Earth. Remember?"

Stephen turned and paced. "How stupid of me. How could I ever forget? Do you want to lock me in my room too? Or maybe ship me off to Simon for more tests?" Stephen stretched out his arms. "Why wouldn't you just take a few seconds and talk to me?"

"I was afraid, Stephen," she repeated, her voice low.

A knock sounded, and Arista's guard motioned Jack through the door. "Thank you, she's expecting me."

"I can see you're on her schedule for today," the guard replied.

Arista's gaze shot to her father. "Oh, Papa, I forgot."

Jack froze midstride as the door closed. His daughter's features, normally full of the grace and beauty which so mirrored her mother's, were contorted... How could the face he'd known for such a short time be marked with so much grief and pain? And Stephen's... with one glance, Jack felt the betrayal that sparked a madness in Stephen's eyes. *What happened here?*

Jack reached for his daughter. "Arista, are you all right?"

"Stephen was just leaving."

A glare flew between Arista and Stephen.

Jack was glad he hadn't been standing between them. And considering his daughter's powers, Stephen was fortunate to still be upright.

"Just for the record, Arista, I would have said, *Hell yeah.* That is, if I'd had a chance." Stephen inclined his head toward Jack, then left without another word.

In her next breath Arista flung herself into Jack's arms. "Hells. What a mess I've made of things."

Over the next few minutes Jack listened, becoming more uneasy as Arista explained. "After what my mother went through, I wanted to ensure I wouldn't be destined to repeat all her pain and suffering."

"But your mother would never have forced you to mate."

"Maybe not but, after her death, the council could have. I didn't want to take that chance."

Jack patted her hand. "I'm afraid I do see Stephen's point. That's just not how things are done on Earth. When a couple wants to marry, generally the man asks the woman first, but also they make plans, often for months in advance." Jack raised his gaze to meet his daughter's. "Even here on Remeon, who wouldn't want to know they are mating ahead of time? I'm sure the initial shock will wear off for him soon. It's clear as day that he loves you."

"I don't know about that now."

"Give him a little time. Few men I know appreciate their decisions being made for them, especially life-defining ones, like marriage."

"I guess you and my mother talked about it before, you, uh… mated."

Jack's throat constricted. "Uh. Yes. We did, for quite a while as a matter of fact. I wanted her to find love again, to mate again, if I should die." He paused and took in a breath. "I didn't want her to be stuck in a decision made in haste, even if I wasn't bound by the same agreement. It didn't seem right. The Remeonite mating decision is so…final."

"But you ended up mated."

Jack nodded. "Looking back, I wouldn't change it. Our commitment to each other has remained, even with our unusual relationship."

"I won't pretend that I didn't know what I was doing. But I did act out of love, if not fear as well. Now who knows if he'll forgive me." Arista laid her head on Jack's shoulder.

Jack squeezed her arm. "I wish I could be here for you always."

She sniffed. "Me too, Papa."

"We're meeting with Vinique in just a little while. Will you be ready?"

Arista stretched. "Sure. Give me just a minute. I'll be right back."

"COME ON IN and have a seat." Vinique arranged another chair around her desk as Jack and Arista came in and sat down.

"Will someone else be joining us?" Arista asked, glancing at the extra chair. "Didn't we already discuss who needed to be here?"

Vinique nodded. "We did. I thought it might be a good idea to involve Stephen, since we will be bringing his little sister to Remeon tomorrow."

"Yes." Arista cleared her throat. "Of course. He'll need to meet her at the portal. Thanks for arranging that."

"Nice to see the pieces coming together." Vinique scanned the agenda. "We'll discuss that part first. Then Stephen can take off." A buzz sounded.

"He's here." Vinique met Stephen in the middle of the room. "Have a seat. Thanks for coming."

"Sure." Stephen averted his eyes and took the open seat next to Jack.

"Stephen, when I last communicated with Belle, she was planning to contact you about her upcoming visit. Did she reach out to you?"

"Yes, ma'am. Yesterday. She's excited to help but not sure how to handle Ma and Pa. Honestly I don't know if they'll let her come. She's just a kid."

Vinique set down her agenda and leaned forward in her chair. "She may be young, but she's talented. Remember she was instrumental in us finding you in the Night Dwellers' cave. Without her help we might have arrived too late." Vinique's gaze darted to Arista. "Considering all that happened that day, including the loss of Whisterly, we were fortunate to even carry out the mission."

Stephen eyed the small group. "But, Vinique, do you know how Belle was able to help without being a witch from Remeon?"

"We recognized her extraordinary ability when she first arrived here. She's gifted in the art of telepathy, no doubt. But there's more, so much more. A power exists inside her, almost as if she'd been born of the bloodline of a witch."

Stephen shook his head and shrugged. "Not sure how that could be."

"We'll find out more once she's here and has visited the coven. What advice did you give her regarding her trip to Remeon?"

"To talk to our ma. She's more likely to understand than Pa and to be more open to the idea."

"Well, without her, our chance of success goes down, even if all the other variables come together. So hopefully, your mother allows Belle to make this trip."

"My parents aren't opened-minded about anything out of the ordinary. But I hope so too though."

"Assuming all goes as planned, we'll need you at the portal to anchor your sister for arrival."

"Of course."

"And I thought she might stay with Arista. What do you both think? We can certainly find somewhere else, if needed. But, since Belle knows you already, she'll be more comfortable around you, Arista."

Arista and Stephen shared a glance. "No problem at all. I'd love to have her."

"Good. Glad that's settled." Vinique's gaze rested on Stephen. "Thank you for coming. You're free to go."

"You bet."

Arista turned and stared wistfully at Stephen's retreating back.

"All right. Let's continue. Arista and I have spoken about this next piece, Jack, but I doubt you're aware." Vinique raised her eyebrows in question, glancing in Arista's direction.

Arista shook her head.

"Okay." Vinique's focus turned toward Jack. "We had not expected or anticipated this latest development with Simon."

Jack shifted in his seat. "I'm listening."

"Simon has been immersed. He's now an apprentice warlock and most likely has no idea what's happened to him."

Jack squeezed Arista's hand. "And how did that happen exactly?"

"Arista, would you like to take that question?"

"Sure. Our best guess is the grimoire sought him, Papa. Remember about Mother's blood sacrifice after she became pregnant with us? She'd been searching for an answer to questions to further her studies of witchcraft. At that time, both Simon and I were bound to the book."

Jack battled a smile. "Now that you mention it, I do remember. We talked about her grandmother's words later, and that was the night she told me she was pregnant. I'd gone to the basement to get her."

Arista caught the faraway look in his eye. "While Simon might not know what this means yet, we do. He's got developing powers that he doesn't have any idea how to use."

"Simon also may have gained knowledge, information about you, Jack, from his initial experience with the grimoire," Vinique interjected. "Up until this point he'd believed himself to be adopted by Mila. Now it's possible that he's aware who his actual parents and sister are. In fact, going forward, we should assume he possesses that knowledge."

"I see."

"Temporarily he's been banned by the coven. It's clear his innate knowledge is deep. On his own he initiated contact, after his immersion occurred. I would suspect in order to gain a clearer understanding of what happened to him. Without direction from the coven or specific knowledge from the grimoire yet, he connected directly and obtained information. We should assume he plans to use it to his greatest advantage."

Jack cocked his head. "Is it possible… I mean, do you think that this new information could change him, for the better?"

Arista's jaw dropped. "I know you want to find some…good in him, Papa. But he's proven himself to be just like Janus, over and over again—pure evil. We need to look for additional ways to protect ourselves and find a way to ban him for good, so he can draw no more power from the tome."

"There's got to be something I can do," Jack insisted, the frustration apparent in his voice.

"Papa, even though Simon can't send his apparition into the basement for now, he's still gained all the knowledge from the grimoire. You'll be no match for his power."

Jack's frown deepened. "Maybe not. But I'm not walking away from him either."

"The coven, along with Vinique and me, are dredging up what we can to determine our options. But, for now, he's to be considered a dangerous loose end, even if we are biologically connected."

"Let's move on to some more exciting news," Vinique continued. "Jack, your visit to the infirmary is the best lead we've had as to which of the four young women could possibly house Whisterly's consciousness. It was a stroke of genius, how a picture could prompt you to check their eye color…brilliant!"

Jack stifled a laugh. "Hardly brilliant. Staring at one of their pictures just made me remember Whisterly's eyes. I recall hearing that your eyes are the window to your soul." Jack shrugged. "So I thought I'd give it a shot."

"Maybe we'll find further corroborating links when we step back and focus on other characteristics and not just matching medical statistics."

"I didn't think to ask about her family while I was there. I figured somebody must be visiting each of them, since their pictures were close by."

"Sadly her family had been decimated by PR 251. Her mate died months before the cure became available."

"Can you tell me her name? After all that data I reviewed, I don't recall seeing her name."

"Sure, Jack. Yara is her name."

"I'd like to continue to visit her."

Vinique eyed the pair across her desk. "That can be arranged, for you and Arista both."

"Thank you," Jack said with a tension easing sigh.

"Last topic. Belle's training… Oh, Jack, you're free to leave if you'd like. This piece is mostly for Arista and me to discuss."

"No. If it's all the same to you, I think I'll stay. I experienced Arista's training firsthand the other day." A grin stretched Jack's mouth. "Wind and Fire are definitely coming along."

"Now for the other two," Vinique said with a sideways glance to Arista. "We're counting on her to continue at this pace."

An easy smile fell on Arista's lips. "I'm ready."

"For Belle's elemental training, my thoughts are to begin with Ground, the magic within Remeon—its essence. See if she can harness its power and then move on to Water. And Arista, since you're just beginning with these two as well, maybe you can train together."

"I was hoping to train with her. Vinique, will Belle be immersed?"

Vinique shook her head. "She's not of our bloodline, but, if we're right about Belle, she already possesses the knowledge through her own bloodline, even if not directly through her parents. She'll be fully tested when she arrives."

"I assume you and the coven have a plan," Jack said. "That using all these…elements will lead to an outcome that we need. How does that help us with Whisterly's true name?" Jack's gaze shifted between the two women, who shared a glance between themselves. "What? Is it a secret?"

"Well, no. That piece will involve you directly though. Working together, using elemental magic, we will create a potion. After you drink this potion, assuming we've done everything correctly, Whisterly's true name will be unlocked, and we can obtain it from you."

"All right, and what if things don't go as planned, or everything isn't completed correctly?"

"Were hoping it doesn't come to that. However, if that happens, death for the person drinking the potion is a likely result."

"*Mmm-hmm.* Just tell me what I can do to help."

Arista leaned over and kissed Jack's cheek. "We will get this right, Papa."

"Just remember. Whisterly is counting on all of you to get this thing outta my head. No price is too high for me to pay. You make it, and I'll drink it."

CHAPTER 10

JACK SHUT THE door to Vinique's quarters behind him, his body tense and his head full of all the possible outcomes surrounding his family. Only a few offered an opportunity where all four of them came out whole on the other side of this event. Yesterday Arista had mentioned their new holographic entertainment area. While he didn't particularly care about plays, book discussions, or in-depth learning opportunities at the moment, one of the other potential uses did interest him, and he planned to give it a try today—training.

With use of holographic forms declining, an array of new options had opened up for the people. And it was just the beginning. The excess resource capacity that Remeonites possessed now, due to their healing of the PR 251 disease, had easily transferred over to this particular new form of leisure activity. And, while Arista had warned of issues others had found while working out the kinks in this new venue, Jack didn't mind putting it to the test; in fact, he was intrigued.

"Jack... Jack, hold up a minute, would ya?"

Jack turned to see Stephen jogging down the hall toward him, despite his brace, making seamless progress. "Sure. What's on your mind?"

Stephen followed Jack's glance toward his brace. "No, my legs are fine. I wear them occasionally, sometimes only one, especially if I'm planning physical activity. It just depends on the day."

Jack nodded. "I seem to remember you saying that before."

"Do you have a few minutes?" Stephen stared at the floor between them, then met Jack's eyes. "To talk."

"All right." Jack mentally judged the distance back to their room, then glanced toward the gathering area.

Stephen read Jack's thoughts and nodded in agreement, and they walked the short distance in silence to the hub of social activity in the compound—the gathering area.

As he navigated through the maze of small trees, large branches, and enormous planters full of vegetation Jack didn't recognize, his thoughts focused on his daughter. *I really don't want to get in the middle of this.* Jack moved toward the periphery, knowing from years of experience that he'd feel less trapped if he could easily see an exit route. The light spilling from the tall windows, bathing the space in warmth, and the deep earthy smell emanating from the plant life helped to put him at ease though, and when Jack turned to Stephen again, Jack felt some of the tension roll off his shoulders. "How's this?"

Stephen barely looked up. "Fine."

"Just so you're aware, we're sitting ducks here. Put those telepathy skills to work and protect your thoughts. All right?"

"Right. Okay… Got it."

Jack took a seat and motioned to Stephen to do the same. "Now, what can I do for you?"

"Well"—Stephen cleared his throat, glanced down at his hands, then met Jack's gaze—"I'd like to talk to you about Arista and me. That is, if you don't mind."

"No, I don't mind, but I'm not going to speak about things that are better left for her to say, if you understand my meaning."

Stephen nodded. "I think I do."

Jack engaged the server as she walked by, raising his eyebrows in question to Stephen, then confirmed his order. "Make it two."

Stephen eyed the server until she was out of sight then inclined his head to Jack, "Arista spoke with you, didn't she, about our argument?"

"Yes. She did."

Stephen's brows furrowed. "This is difficult for me, but I'd like to be open with you, rather than not."

"Sounds like a good start."

"Well, the conversation we had surprised me—no, shocked me really." Stephen released a deep breath. "And it's not that I don't love her, 'cause I do."

Jack watched a deep crimson color creep up Stephen's neck and bloom on his face. *Damn, this is gonna be really hard.* Jack had lost count of the number of times he'd talked with individual soldiers who reported to him on matters of the heart. And given the circumstances back then, and the fact a war had been going on at the time, only a few of the scenarios had had happy outcomes.

But this was Arista they were discussing and Stephen, a potential son-in-law. After reconnecting with his daughter only days earlier, Jack felt completely unprepared for this conversation. "The fact that you care deeply for her is evident."

"Yes." Stephen gulped another breath. "It's just, marriage, or mating…I'd not given much thought to that just yet. I want it, but in the future."

"Sure." Jack nodded. "I understand."

Receiving affirmation, Stephen continued. "It's been drilled into me for as long as I can remember that I need to be productive, support myself, before taking responsibility for another. And a mate, a wife, would be my responsibility." Stephen's gaze met Jack's, as if wanting confirmation.

"Typically, if we were on Earth, I'd agree with you. A man needs to be self-sufficient before taking a wife." Laughter rose in his throat. "I've not been a shining example of that edict myself with Whisterly. But we're not on Earth. And Arista, like her mother before her, can and will take care of herself. Quite honestly she doesn't need you for that."

Stephen sat back, eyes wide, but paused and nodded slowly, considering Jack's words.

"And you, as a human, are not bound by the Remeon mating ceremony. Only Arista is."

Stephen squirmed in his seat. "But if we're a couple and love each other, we should be making decisions like this together. I don't want an out because I'm human."

"I can't really argue that point. I agree with you there."

"Okay. But what should I do? I feel like something is broken between us now, and I don't know how to fix it."

Jack shrugged. "I'm not sure I can help you with that question either. Ultimately only you two can decide your next steps. But I am sure of one thing. You won't know for certain going into a mating if you or she has the stuff to make it work. Only time will tell that. All you can do is be certain you have the right ingredients going in."

Stephen hung his head. "I don't know if talking with you was a good idea."

Jack couldn't help the small burst of laughter that escaped him. "Why do you say that? I hope I haven't made the situation worse."

"No, it's not that. *Shit*. You've probably already read my thoughts so—"

"No. I haven't."

"Well, I thought being here with you, on Remeon," Stephen swallowed hard and began again, "that I might have a chance to impress you. So that eventually you might not see me being a potential son-in-law as a bad thing." Stephen paused, appearing to gauge Jack's reaction. "Actually I'm sure now this was a bad idea." Stephen pushed back from the table.

"Wait, Stephen. Don't go. Please. What is it?"

Stephen sat perched with his head bowed in his hands. Then he raised his head to face Jack, heaving a deep breath. "I doubt you think I've got the *right ingredients* you spoke of, huh?"

"What? I must have missed something."

"Potential cripple isn't one of the things to tick off that list. Is it?"

Jack leaned in closer to Stephen. "Maybe you should try to read my thoughts before you go putting words in my mouth. Some of the bravest, most capable men I've had the privilege to know have been crippled, deformed, or maimed in some manner or another. And I don't know that I've known you long enough to judge your character.

"But it's not my opinion that matters. It's Arista's. She's the one you need to impress. I do trust her judgment, and she loves you. If you love her, then you'll figure out a way forward. On the other hand, if all this is too much to handle, then let her know now and leave. No one would blame you for that."

Stephen averted his eyes. "My love for her isn't in question, just so you know. So I'll sort through it all. Whatever I have to do, I want a life with her, if she'll have me."

"Now you're talking. Let her know that. Muddle through it together."

"And, Jack, I won't be a cripple."

Jack focused on Stephen. This last bit wouldn't be fixed with talk. "Look. I didn't even see our drinks arrive. How long have they been here?"

Stephen shrugged.

"Let's drink up. Then I had plans—"

"Sorry. I won't keep you any longer."

"I was trying to ask if you'd like to join me at the holographic entertainment center."

"Me? Really?"

A smile fell across Jack's face. "Yes. Really. If you want to, that is. I'm planning on some training maneuvers, drills. If that type of thing interests you, you're welcome to come along."

A fire lit behind Stephen's eyes. "Would I ever... Could you, I mean, would you mind showing me a thing or two?"

Jack tossed back the remainder of his drink. "Sure thing. If you're done with your drink, let's head out."

"I'm ready. What is a holographic entertainment center anyway?"

The pair talked as they walked. "I'm not real sure myself. My understanding is, through a mind link, a holographic environment is set for a training, in my case. For others it might entail acting out a book, reliving an experience, or visiting a faraway place. The opportunities are endless."

"Sounds pretty incredible. What type of training environment did you tell it to set up?"

"I haven't yet. Waiting to see how it all works when we get there."

"That must be it up ahead. See?"

"Things have definitely changed since I've last been by here." Jack smiled warmly to the woman behind the front desk. "You must be who I spoke with telepathically this morning when I made the appointment."

"I am. You're Jack?"

"Yes. And this is Stephen."

"As I explained this morning, after signing the paperwork, you'll be all set." The woman flashed a perfect smile. "While inherently there is no danger from the experience itself, you could fall and hurt yourself, or another unforeseen mishap might occur. So, in order to protect us, you must sign before experiencing the holographic suite."

The X flashed bright red in front of him. "I guess that makes sense." He scribbled a signature with his finger on the glowing screen.

"Now you, Stephen, if you're participating today, you sign as well."

"I am."

"My name is Sasha, if you need anything. To begin, go inside, place your palm where indicated. Your thoughts will create the setting for your adventure. From there, progress will continue per the ongoing reactions to the stimuli produced."

"Interesting. Just one question. How do I stop it? When the need arises."

"Speak or think, *Halt, Stop*, or *End*. If you have any problems, link directly with me, and I will assist you."

Jack nodded.

Sasha shot them a grin as she showed them the way forward. "If no further questions, you may begin."

The doors slid open, and Jack entered, followed by Stephen. A few seconds later Jack found the spot to place his palm. "Well, here we go."

The silver metallic background that had been in front of them initially flashed black before twisting into an assortment of bright colors—green, yellow, and red—followed by a substantial increase in temperature throughout the chamber.

"Are we back in the gathering place? I can't see for all the trees and the sun in my eyes. And man, is it hot." Stephen yanked at his collar.

"My God… No. That's not where we are. I'd never forget this hellhole. Son of a bitch. Can't imagine why, of all the places I've been, that this one would get pulled from my thoughts." A line of sweat broke out on Jack's forehead.

Birds screeched in the distance, catching Stephen's attention. "Should we continue with it, Jack? I mean, if you want something else, you can change it with a thought, right?"

"I think I'll let this play out a little while." His jaw tightened. "Feel free to leave if you'd like. I understand why you might not want to play around in my nightmare."

Stephen's eyes darted around, lighting on anything that moved. "No, I...I guess I'll stick it out here. I mean, there's no real danger..."

"Okay. Stay close and follow my lead." Jack tore a long piece of fabric from his shirt and tied it around his forehead, indicating for Stephen to do the same, then, ducking under the nearest branch, disappeared from view.

Stephen quickly followed and almost rammed himself into Jack's back. "Who are they?" Stephen asked, his mouth agape.

A long line of men stood at parade rest in their dress blues. Jack scanned their faces. "I don't know. These aren't men who served under my command." He squinted, studying them closer. "Still, some look very familiar."

Distracted, Stephen didn't see Jack at first, assessing the fire power available to them off to the side of the main venue.

Jack's eyes gleamed as he scrutinized the Thompson submachine gun. *If I could have had my hands on one of these... things might have turned out differently.*

"What are we doing here?" Stephen's gaze roamed over the available weaponry.

"What do you think? You hunt, right?"

"Well... sure..."

Jack wasn't really listening to him. Instead, he eyed the weapons in the shiny array with what seemed like an almost loving admiration.

"Think of this outing like that. Choose your madness. Be sure you're comfortable with the weapon before selecting it. I hear you're good with a blade, so grab one of those," Jack encouraged, pointing to the cluster of knives perched on the wall, "and plenty of ammunition."

"GOT IT." STEPHEN watched Jack disappear again, the Tommy gun perched on his shoulder and an M1911 pistol concealed in his waistband. Outfitted further with a blade hidden in each boot, Jack was a force to be reckoned with. With the drum magazine on the Tommy gun alone, fifty men could be taken out. Jack's intentions were clear.

Aiming to even up a score that had already been settled would take some doing. But with the expression that haunted Jack's features just now, Stephen was confident of the soldier's goal. To see the man's steely exterior crack just a bit from the echo of his past drove sheer terror through Stephen.

Grabbing a M1911 pistol as well, followed by a M1918 Browning Automatic, Stephen paused. "How hard could it be to shoot one of these?" Finally he slid one of the Ka-Bar knives from its sheath, examined it, and hid it in his boot. "What in God's name have I gotten myself into?"

Following Jack's path, Stephen trailed down the long line of soldiers, then ambled toward the tree line and ducked into the jungle. Straight ahead Stephen spotted Jack, with what looked like a Japanese soldier caught in his arms. Creeping closer, Stephen heard the gurgling sound emanating from the man as Jack slid his blade across the enemy's throat.

Jack dropped the corpse and ducked as he wiped the blade clean on his pant leg and guided the weapon into his boot again.

Stephen came upon the doomed man and blinked, watching in amazement as the fallen man dissipated into sparks of light. Stephen hesitated, witnessing the strange transformation, reluctant to call for Jack, who had once again vanished from sight. *Well, I guess it makes sense if this isn't actually real.*

Stephen trekked on, tracking Jack from the fallen vegetation at his feet and the torn branches at his side. This definitely wasn't a covert op… A rumbling above interrupted Stephen's thoughts. He examined the sky. Was that the sky? Really? Suddenly the stutter of machine gun fire rained down on his position. Stephen froze in place momentarily, then threw himself to the dirt and scuttled to the relative safety of the nearest tree. He heaved deep breaths; the only other sound he heard coming from his chest in loud rapid *thud*s. *I'm really gonna die in here.*

Before he could will himself to rise from the near miss of machine gun fire, someone pounced from above onto his back. Stephen sucked in a breath, then instinct led him to slam the perpetrator pinned to his back against the tree. Stephen twisted from his grasp; he could tell the man weighed nothing—wasn't even wearing a helmet.

The weapon on his back and in his waistband did him no good, but Stephen already had his knife in hand, and he didn't hesitate, shoving its point through his enemy's throat in one swift motion. The dying man struggled to form a word, to no avail. Blood bubbled from his lips and flowed freely from the wound Stephen had inflicted. As the raspy bits of air the man fought for stopped, Stephen saw the dead form disintegrate, just like Jack's kill before.

A hand landed on Stephen's shoulder, and he turned in the middle of cleaning his knife, prepared to strike once again. Jack caught Stephen's hand midair and disarmed him before Stephen could think to drop the knife.

A sheen of sweat covered Jack's skin, his bloodied clothing attesting to his activities, along with the frenzied look reflected in his eyes.

"Jack, are you actually enjoying this?"

Fear rippled through Stephen with the realization that he couldn't physically match Jack's pace. He was clearly a killing machine, with no end to the wrath he could unleash to atone for past losses.

A knowing glance flickered across Jack's face. "In some ways, yes." Jack sighed and wiped sweat from his forehead with his sleeve. "But, in others, it just reminds me of what this place turned me into, to survive. The activities that took place in the Pacific Theater left too many good men dead, decimating their families. But I don't think I can ever kill enough to make amends." He slapped his hand to his cheek, killing a mosquito. "And these pesky buggers... What could the creator have been thinking with these blood-sucking disease-carriers?" A hearty laugh escaped his lips. "You've done well, Stephen. Are you winded yet?"

Relief flooded him. There was some of the Jack Stephen thought he knew. "Winded? Hell yeah. Among other things. I'm just glad I didn't piss myself when the man came at me from the tree."

Jack shifted the Tommy gun to his shoulder, then reached for Stephen's arm, and as they clasped hands, Stephen felt an odd sense of peace flowing from Jack to him. Not a reconciliation exactly but maybe the beginnings of one.

"I can't say I won't be back here. Lord knows I'm here often enough in my head, but what would you say to some sparring practice instead? I have a feeling that's what you had in mind anyway."

"Sure."

"Halt."

The scene before the pair shifted, leaving behind lush greenery, blue sky, and humidity juxtaposed to the starvation, disease, and death of the Solomon Islands. In its place a darkened room, filled with the musty smell of unwashed bodies and fresh sweat, appeared before them. Stephen's mouth raised in a half smile. "Already this is much better than where we were. At least I can see the people coming at me this time. But where is *here*?"

"A hole in the wall in Germany that I used to frequent, when I was stationed there. We had nightly boxing contests, sometimes even with a cash prize." Jack huffed. "Most of the time I lost. I went up against some beasts. But I sure as hell learned a lot."

"Okay. I'm game."

"I don't think we'll need any gear beyond a helmet. But before we begin, you'll need to take off your metal brace. I'd prefer not to have that breaking my bones."

Stephen shrugged and pulled off the brace attached to his leg. "Using just that approach, I almost escaped the Night Dwellers' cave. They mistook me for a lame misfit. It cost them. But not dearly enough."

"One of the first lessons everyone should learn—never underestimate your opponent. At best you'll lose, and in the worst case, it could cost you your life." Jack threw Stephen a helmet, then held up the rope on the side of the ring for Stephen to slip through. "Lean back and watch the pair in the ring beside us for a few minutes. Notice how their fists are up, always protecting their face… And their feet…See how they're constantly moving? It's almost like a dance. You'll need to master these two basics before anything else. So, besides basic blocks, that's all we'll work on today."

Stephen faced Jack in the ring, helmet on, arms raised and fists clenched in front of him.

"Oh, and don't forget telepathy. You and I have that advantage. We can read each other's thoughts, so we know what our adversary's plans are in the making. While you're on Remeon, use this to your advantage. Normally, on Earth, it's not an issue. Between us, it is. Some of your mental strength and stamina will need to go toward protecting these thoughts. If you don't prepare in advance, you'll lose every time here on planet. Remeonites naturally excel at this. We do not. You'll need to stand out in other ways, like strength and strategy."

Stephen nodded. "Understood."

Jack began to move. Stephen watched as his opponent in the ring tapped out a rhythm, his feet shifting quietly and steadily on the floor. "Come on now, Stephen. Just like the pair you were watching before. A moving target is harder to hit…That's it. You're getting the hang of it. Now throw a punch."

Stephen led with his right fist and was instantly blocked with Jack's left arm and thrown off balance.

"Again, with more force this time. You're trying too hard. I bet you pommeled that guard harder than that."

Stephen nodded, this time throwing a punch with his right, followed by another with his left, both efficiently blocked by Jack.

"Better. Not a bad right hook. Keep 'em coming, and don't slow down."

An answering grin slid across Stephen's face. "This is kinda fun. I plan to land a punch by pretending you're Simon, so look out."

Jack chuckled. "Well, all right then, let's have it."

The two sparred for several hours, with drills woven in between, until Stephen's muscles screamed with overuse.

"If you don't mind, I think I've had enough for one day," Stephen said, wiping his forehead with his arm.

Jack glanced at Stephen's hands that he'd taped, now bloody and raw from drills. "Yep. Looks like you have."

Stephen lowered himself onto a bench. "I wonder if this place has holographic showers."

Jack's gaze met Stephen's. "You've dealt with a lot today. I'm proud of you. Keep it up."

"What?" Stephen leaned in closer, unsure of the words he thought he'd heard.

"You've done well. Now let's head out. I'm beat too." Jack slapped Stephen on the back.

"Gosh. I'm honored. That means a lot coming from you."

"Halt." The intricate facade fabricated around them faded, replaced once again with the silver metallic default framework.

Anytime, Stephen. I'm flesh and blood, just like you, and you held your own today.

Sasha greeted them as they exited. "Well, how was it?"

Jack shook his head and laughed. "Pretty incredible—the details amazingly accurate." He paused. "Except one thing. At the beginning, the line of soldiers, who were they? Can't say I recognized them. All the set up came from my thoughts, right?"

"Yes. Let me take a look. Since you've completed your session, I should be able to track the source. Give me just a minute."

"Sure."

"I've verified now that those men are the representations of those who have been inspired by you, your service, to join the marines."

"What? I don't recollect that information."

"Well, it's been collecting over time in your memory. Think back to past conversations, newspaper clippings, presentations over the years, sons born of the men you served with. Looks like those are the source materials. It would be difficult, no doubt, to recall all at once, as was exhibited here in your exercise."

Jack bent his head. Stephen could see a glistening in Jack's eyes. "Wow, Jack. Of course you're a hero, plain as day, but to see it like this..."

Jack met Stephen's gaze as a grimace thinned his lips, and he appeared to fight against tears. "I had no idea of the number...all those men..." Jack whispered.

"Thank you, Sasha," Stephen called back as they left the facility.

With tattered clothing, exhaustion lining their faces and hampering their gait, they strode down the halls of the compound. Neither noticed the stares or the number of Remeonites who cleared a path for the two.

That was one hell of an experience, Jack. I think I could go a while without heading back to the Solomon Islands though.

I'd have to agree with you there. Like none other. Can't you just imagine all the potential uses of a place like that though?

I wonder if an experience there could be real, with actual lasting consequences. I mean here on Remeon just about anything is possible, right?

Huh... Now there's a thought.

ARISTA FOUND IT difficult to concentrate on her lessons. At the moment she placed a higher priority on information from her father and Stephen, and she hadn't heard from either of them in several hours. Magic spells containing the elements filled her brain, but when she tried to get them out in the right order, her thoughts scattered. *Maybe I should just stop. Nothing is clicking for me today.*

Ah, child. You have control. And your thoughts are not truly with your task, are they?

Arista let out a small huff and continued to glide her fingers through the grimoire, waiting for it to choose her next stop. This is how it would normally happen—information provided at the moment of her need. The pages of the tome flipped past her faster, gaining speed. Evident was the fact, as expected, that the book was leading her now. She exhaled in relief when the pages eased to a standstill, its last flutter falling to a heading which read The Work of Water. *Ah, so here I will expend my efforts.*

This sounds like a good idea and notably part of the groundwork of our plan.

Stay a while, keep your presence here, will you, Great-Grandmother? Tell me what you know of this topic. Hearing and reading will improve my focus.

Certainly. But only you can take charge of your focus. Either be fully here or come back when you can. Half-hearted efforts will not help us when the time comes. Whisterly's and Jack's lives are forfeited if we fail. And should only one us not complete our part, it will be for naught. The price is too high for anything but your best.

Silently, Arista bowed.

Now, if you are mentally prepared this time, begin.

A large clear bowl containing water appeared on the podium which normally held the grimoire.

Good… As with the other elements you've studied, you must create a bond with the substance. Otherwise you can't command its use. Seek to be a part of the liquid. Then, when necessary, you can reconnect. Try it now.

Arista closed her eyes, allowing her singular focus to be the contents of the container before her. Her magic's precision had to be exact. For her, at this moment, nothing else existed but her and the water she sought to control with her power. "Aqua," she murmured.

Arista bid the water to her. As she did so, a trail of the substance floated to her and splashed in her face. Drops fell down, past her eyes, to her cheeks, in her mouth, then meandered the path of her neck, wetting her clothes. She brought her hands to her face, wiping away the dampness, collecting the remnants on her fingers.

Focusing, Arista cast another spell, flicking the remaining drops back toward the open container which still held a portion of the water.

Clear ice crystals sparkled as they transformed from the water drops and slid with audible plops into the basin, creating a small oasis of ice water. Arista giggled as she twirled her finger around faster and faster, until the water and ice mixture rose from the basin in a miniature water spout.

That's it. You've got it.

Next she moved her hands in tandem, one above the other in a circular motion, and as she did so, the water splashed into the container, eventually rising to form little puffs of clouds, which then loosed rain down to the bowl below. Finally she raised her hands, levitating the liquid, then pushed the water to the left and the right, using opposite hand motions. With a splash, water hit the sides of the walls, then trickled down to the floor below.

She blew air from her mouth, and when it left her, she swirled it between her fingers, creating a disturbance that unsettled the grimoire and toppled the glass bowl but dried the floor and the walls of her study space.

Well done, child. Now that is the mark of a witch.

Remarkable. I could feel myself within the water's essence—even track the pulse of the water within my own body.

I'd say you've made significant progress today, worthy of your status as council chair. If the next part of our plan comes together as scheduled, you can wait a few days to train on your last element.

You mean, until Belle comes here to Remeon.

Indeed, I do. I have a suspicion about the source of her power, given all I've heard from you, Vinique, and Whisterly, regarding the strength of her aura and her telepathic abilities.

Whisterly spoke to you of Belle?

Yes, when Belle was brought to Remeon in holographic form, her skill had been apparent. Whisterly marveled at her expertise, coming from Earth, apparently with normal parents. But we believed even then there was much more to this little girl.

Arista connected with a stray drop of water at her feet, balancing it on one finger as she wrenched it round and round with the motion of her other hand. *I agree.*

Soon now we'll settle on an element for each of you, with the power of the coven contributing to all four realms of elemental magic.

Arista brushed the remaining droplets of water from her fingers. *It's all coming together so fast now. It's really happening.*

Slow down. As I said before, there's much left to accomplish. We are far from finished.

But look how far we've come. Arista paused, her minding working. *How exactly will these elements all combine to produce that which we need?*

Eager now for more? A jovial laugh reverberated through the room. *Each of us will work with an element, the outcome of which will come together to produce the substance we need to pull Whisterly's true name from Jack. Right now, her true name, that one isolated memory, is combined and coalesced with so many other memories that there is no way to break it down and segregate it, let alone take that one strand of truth we need from Jack.*

If Jack survives ingesting the substance, and we have done our work correctly, our chances to anchor Whisterly with her true name rise substantially. Once she is called from within, using her true name, our work is done. Whisterly must answer that call. We can do nothing from here but speak to her, hoping to draw her toward us and the life she remembers. If it has been too long, or if she is resigned, maybe even happy in the world she inhabits, then she'll not return to us.

No! She'd didn't want to leave her family or her people.

Definitely not. But, as to her existence now, we cannot say. As far back as I can remember, no one has ever returned to a habitable life-form in this manner. No one has ever completed the feat of transferring their consciousness, as your mother has done. From all recent history her power is unparalleled. But she didn't know what she'd encounter, and, if she returns, she might not be able to tell us of her existence after her body's death.

In all likelihood, where her spirit reigns, it will fight to hold her there. But the coven will battle for Whisterly's return. Through our alliances with you, Vinique, and Belle, we will evoke a force unmatched. We must be stronger collectively to overcome. Do you understand?

I'm not sure.

An honest answer. However, your conviction to our process and the part you control must receive your full faith and confidence. You've seen that power today in what you accomplished in only a short while. Doubts will cleave through our magic if anyone's commitment wavers. If that should happen, then our spells will falter, and Whisterly will be lost to us forever.

Determination battling within, Arista gritted her teeth and steeled her stance, her resolve strengthening. *You have my word and all my energy, Great-Grandmother. Through the combined efforts of the coven and the gifts of our magic, Whisterly will find her way back to us.*

A cackling wicked laugh filled the chamber. *I will hold you true to your pledge. With the intensity of the power we possess, Whisterly will be with us again. We will succeed.*

"ARISTA? IS IT okay if I come in?"

She communicated to her guards, allowing Stephen entrance. "Yes. Come in. Have a seat, if you'd like to."

Stephen sat on the couch, willing Arista to sit beside him. When she did, he released a pent-up breath. "I'm not real sure how to start what I have to say."

Arista didn't meet his eyes. "Just start anywhere. You blocked me from your thoughts, so I think I've got a pretty good idea how this will go."

Stephen nodded. "I did. I was confused, hurt. I even felt betrayed, I think. But I haven't stopped loving you."

He heard Arista gasp and used the opportunity to scoot along the couch, decreasing some of the distance between them. Taking a deep breath, he lifted his head to stare into her deep blue eyes. "Believe me, love. Since we met, I knew I was outta your league. When you said you loved me, I don't know that I really accepted it as truth, as real." Stephen reached over and squeezed her hand. "I know you're powerful, a council leader, and now a witch. And what am I?" He shrugged, then chuckled. "Well, honestly, I'm not sure myself just yet."

Arista opened her mouth to speak.

"Please, let me finish," he interrupted with another squeeze of her hand. "I remembered the portal wouldn't initialize without the certainty of our love, so that fact gave me some comfort. But as for us as a couple, I didn't see how we could ever happen—with you here, me on Earth—even as much as I wanted to be with you. Still, I wanted to make something of myself, then ask you to marry me, and pray that you'd agree. Well, that was my initial plan anyway."

Stephen lifted her hand to his mouth and kissed her fingers. "I didn't know what to make of it when you said we were mated, married basically, taking away my plans for us. I still have so far to go." He shook his head. "On Earth, generally the man asks the woman, when he's ready and can support a family. And even though I understand you don't need me to provide for you, I want to be able to. Hell, I don't even have a real job yet. I have millions of questions. Would I stay here? Would you come to Earth?" He hesitated, met her gaze, and saw tears glistening in her eyes. "Could I really make you happy for a lifetime, however long that is for us?"

A smirk crossed his face. "My pa may actually kill me, if my ma doesn't beat him to it first." Stephen fell to his knees at Arista's feet, reached into his pocket, and pulled out a small box, then opened it before her. "Will you marry me, Arista? Whether now or in the future, I want us to face whatever comes together, for better or worse, here, on Earth, or both. I want to protect you and provide for you, but mostly I want to love you."

He paused. "So that's what I've been thinking about since I blocked you from my thoughts. They've been a jumbled mess, and I wanted to be clear-headed before talking to you again. You're welcome back into my thoughts. But, for now, it'd just be good if you'd say something…anything."

Tears fell down her face. "So this means you still want me?"

Stephen rose from his knees and gathered her into his arms. "Yes. Constantly. Only every minute of every day." He wiped her cheeks with his thumbs. "You're trembling, love. I'm not sure if that's a good or a bad thing though, since you haven't given me an answer."

"Yes, Stephen. Yes! It's beautiful! Will you put it on my finger? I thought I'd messed everything up for good."

Arista held her breath while Stephen slid the ring into place.

Their gazes locked.

"You couldn't—ever." Stephen pressed his lips against hers, lightly grazing them, then tasting her softly, deepened the kiss. "God, I've missed this," he murmured against her mouth.

"*Mmm-hmm...* So we can be together soon? Married?" she asked, drawing back slightly from him.

Stephen nodded and repositioned himself on the couch. "Yes. Eventually. I wanted to let you know how I felt today, as quickly as possible, to hopefully end the silence between us." Stephen picked up her hands and rubbed her fingers with his thumbs, watching the sparkle of the crystal shift where the light hit it. "But, for a marriage, I think it best for us to wait till I'm older, at least seventeen. I know it doesn't much matter here on Remeon, since we've already been mated, but it makes a difference on Earth. I want everyone there to take me seriously. And I'd like for my family to be happy for us, but if they aren't, we will be officially married anyway, if you'll still have me."

"I'm sorry, Stephen, for starting this mess. I've muddled everything horribly."

"*Shhh.* No more *I'm sorry.* You're mine, and I'm yours." He buried his fingers in her hair, tilting her chin toward him, kissed her lips, then left a trail of soft kisses along her jaw. She shivered. "I love you," he whispered into her ear. "And I'm not going to let you forget it."

CHAPTER 11

BELLE'S EYES OPENED. She glanced outside her window. Blinking, she remembered not closing it last night. Now regretting that decision in the chill of the early morning, she huddled down deeper into the covers, relishing the warmth for a few more minutes. A scent of winter, its reach fresh and cold, drifted into the room on the morning breeze. That along with the frozen bits of decaying leaves mingling with the musty earthiness of the soil and the crispness of the air itself, announced with its presence that the growing season had long passed. How long would she be away from this, her life on the farm?

Belle slid from the bed, letting her toes linger briefly as they crossed the sheets. The compound had none of the small comforts of her room: her special blankets, treasured books, her own reading chair. She inched to her window on bare feet and pushed it shut. With a shiver, she wiggled into the clothes she'd laid out the night before, then hurried down the hall to the bathroom, her full bladder trumping all else at the moment.

As she reentered her bedroom, she scanned the walls and furniture, trying to think of anything else she might need but had forgotten to pack. She reached for the reddish rock on her nightstand. Turning it over in her palm, her thoughts turned to Thomas, who held its twin. He'd truly loved the gift she'd given him on his last birthday. It seemed so long ago, before...before their family had been changed forever by sickness and kidnapping. Before she and her brother had been awakened to life elsewhere in the universe. Before her world had cleaved itself apart, with no room for the farm and her sedate life there.

The letter she'd written lay isolated on her cleared desk. *Should I read it once more? Do I have every word perfect?* She dragged her feet as she moved toward the letter. *Will they ever forgive me?*

The darkness in the room lessened, drawing Belle's gaze back to the window. Sure enough it'd soon be sunup. Before that time, Pa would be up, downstairs, preparing for his chores, chores he'd expected her help with. Retrieving the letter, she slipped it between her teeth, then stumbled once before falling to her knees and peering under the bed for the bag she'd packed. Her arm couldn't reach it, so Belle glided farther under the bed until she disappeared completely, then finally grasped her satchel and pulled it to freedom.

A small sigh escaped her lips while she yanked her boots over her socks and donned a jacket. Then, picking up her bag, she plodded slowly down the staircase, carefully avoiding the creaking steps, like Thomas had advised her yesterday when she'd been practicing her route.

The house was still in semidarkness, but Shep lifted his head and wagged his tail as she hurried through the kitchen. The letter had moistened in her mouth, sticking to her lips. She took it out now and lay it on the table. Written boldly on the front were the words *Ma and Pa.*

Patting Shep she murmured, "*Shh*, boy. Go back to sleep. Pa will let you out soon." Belle extended her arm into the scraps bucket and pulled out a bone she'd placed there last night. After putting it in Shep's mouth, she leaned down, surrounding him in a quick hug. "Be a good boy. See you later."

She tiptoed through the family room and could see her parents' door still closed and heard no movement. *Thank goodness. Bye, Ma, Pa.*

As she pulled the front door opened slowly, a creak sounded. When the space was wide enough for her to squeeze out, she stood up straight and eked past, making sure her suitcase cleared before closing the door once again. She huffed and took a step forward, shivering in the brisk air. Relief flooded through her just the same. She'd made it. Inside, Pa would be rising any time now.

I'll be there soon, Thom—

"A little early yet, isn't it?"

Belle froze.

"For morning chores, that is."

"Pa?" Belle turned toward his voice. Even in the early light she could see his eyebrows raised in question.

"Belle?"

"Pa, I… I don't know what to say."

"What did you do to quiet Shep?"

She shrugged. "Just gave him a bone."

He pointed to the porch chair beside him, the same one she sat in when she shucked corn or ate ice cream with Thomas during the summer months. "Have a seat, and let's go with the truth."

Pa held the chair steady as she climbed into the rocker, her small bag abandoned for the moment. "I'm going back, Pa," Belle began, her voice shaky, "to Remeon."

"By yourself? Without a word?"

A momentary sliver of panic shot up her spine as the tone in Pa's voice hardened.

"Is Thomas behind this?"

Belle shook her head. "No, Pa. The leaders there—remember the ones Thomas talked to you about? They've asked me to come back, to help someone important. And I left you and Ma a note. It's inside."

Pa nodded. "I remember about the leaders. But I don't understand what a nine-year-old girl could do that they couldn't do by themselves."

"I'm different there, Pa—special. I can do things others can't, more than telepathy, even more advanced than their own people."

"Damn it, Belle! You're special here too. Are we just supposed to give you up to God-knows-what?"

Belle lifted her eyes and met her father's gaze, clear now in the advancing light. "I'm sorry, Pa. It's hard to understand. I know." She bowed her head, her thoughts roaming to her next move and to Thomas, who waited for her. "It's hard for me too. But she'll die if I don't help."

Pa heaved a sigh and ran a hand through his hair. "Who will die?"

"Whisterly."

"Didn't Thomas say she'd already died?"

"They thought so. But turns out she might not be. This is the only chance to have her back with them, if it works."

"Sounds like a lot of nonsense, Belle."

"You said months ago that you'd have done anything to get us back to you, Pa."

He nodded, then whispered, "That's true. I would have."

"They're no different really, Pa. They love her and want her back."

"And, if I forbid you to go…you'll just defy me? Is that it?"

"I guess for now, I'd go back to my room, Pa. But I'd try again. I can't just let her die if I can do something to help."

Pa stretched out his hand. "Come here, Belle." He helped her down, then navigated her to his chair, settling her on his lap. She laid her head against his chest, and her arms circled his waist. The chair moved back and forth in a silent rhythm, neither speaking.

After a few minutes his voice rang out clear and steady. "It's my job to protect you, Belle. And it will be until the day I die. Anything that could possibly hurt you, my duty is to stop it. Do you understand?"

She nodded against his chest and sniffed.

"But it's also my job to raise you to love God and your neighbors. It's hard to deny you when that's exactly what you're doing.

Sounds like a selfless act on your part, and it's not the first time either." He set his foot down flat, pausing the motion of the rocker. "Were you going through the portal...the same as Thomas? Was that your plan?"

Belle lifted her head. "Yes, Pa. He's meeting me so I can get to the other side. His love for me helps to activate the portal."

"*Hmph.*" Pa kissed her forehead and slid her to her feet. "Go get that note. I don't want your ma finding it before I get back. I'd rather talk to her first. Then we'll read it together. Lord knows she might not ever talk to me again after today. God forgive me."

"Back from where, Pa? You're letting me go?"

"I guess it's either that or guard you night and day. Shep failed. And I've got a farm to run." A corner of his mouth tugged upward just slightly. "Besides, you do make a pretty good case for yourself. So, yes, I'm taking you to the, uh...portal myself."

She gasped. "Oh, Pa! Be right back."

"Bring Shep too, worthless mutt."

After pushing the door closed behind Shep, Belle handed Pa the letter. He glanced at the wording on the outside, then folded it neatly and stowed it in his pocket. Belle searched his face. The deep lines in his forehead from only moments ago had smoothed, and the twinkle in his eye that she recognized from time to time was there now. Was it for her? Or was he thinking of talking to Ma?

He reached for her hand. "Ready?"

She put her hand in his. "Yes, Pa."

With his other hand, he picked up her satchel, then called to Shep, "Heel, boy."

Thomas, I'm coming.

I'm ready for you, Belle. Let me know when you're there, and Arista and Vinique will open the portal from this side.

When they reached the now-familiar creek, Pa stopped and stooped to one knee. "This is the place where Thomas went through."

"Yep." Belle fingered the rock in her pocket.

"What do you have there?"

She yanked the treasure from its hiding place. "My half of the rock I gave Thomas. Remember?"

He kissed her cheek and smoothed her hair with his hand. "I remember," he said in a raspy tone. "Be safe, sweetheart."

Belle tackled her father in a hug as the wind picked up and the vortex opened. "I will. Thanks, Pa." He turned her bag loose as her fingers closed around the handle.

"Incredible," he mumbled, watching the spectacle before him, Belle now heading toward the disturbance. "We love you, Belle." His voice broke. "Tell Thomas he'd better take care of you."

She looked over her shoulder and flashed a smile. "He knows, Pa. But it might be me taking care of him."

A ghost of a smile crossed his lips as he watched her disappear. "I just bet so."

STEPHEN WAS THE first to greet Belle when she emerged, beaming on the other side of the portal. She giggled as he reached for her, hugging tightly. "Oh, my goodness! You didn't tell me how fun it would be, coming through."

He scrunched his face as he stared at her. "Maybe that's because I didn't want to scare you. The first time I went in the portal, I thought I was gonna throw up."

"Really?" She cocked her head. "I can't wait to do it again."

Arista watched the reunion of brother and sister, lagging behind Stephen. She poked her head out, then extended her arms toward Belle. "Welcome back." The rush of water filled Arista's ears, soothing her. Matched by the graceful arch of the trees, the combination lent her solitude and strength. The secluded oasis was nothing short of magical. One glimpse of the siblings reminded her that Stephen didn't feel the same. "Come on. Let's move a little farther from the water's edge."

Belle grasped her hand but turned back to stare at the water surrounded by the intricate rock formation with its companion of looming trees. "It's beautiful. I love it here."

Arista and Stephen shared a glance. "Isn't it? It's one of my favorite places."

Stephen rolled his eyes.

"Belle, good to see you again." Vinique stretched her arms out in time for Belle to throw herself into them. Taking her by the shoulders, Vinique studied Belle's face. "How did it go with your parents?"

"Well, I decided to leave them a note."

"When I read your thoughts, just before you came through the portal," Stephen said, "I was shocked by Pa's response." He patted his sister's back. "You did a good job, Belle."

"Thanks, Tho—uh, Stephen."

"Wait. What happened?" Vinique led them to a table set back a little from the water but still giving the small group a perfect view. "Have a seat."

"Well, I wrote the note like I said, packed up, and woke up this morning to sneak out."

"So you'd decided not to tell them first?" Arista asked.

Belle bobbed her head. "I thought it was a better idea to write it out in a letter. If I sat down with both of them staring at me, I was scared I'd forget everything. Then they wouldn't let me come. So this morning I left the note where I knew they'd find it and tried to leave before Pa got up for chores."

"And?" Vinique encouraged.

"He was waiting for me on the porch right as I came out."

Stephen's face broke into a broad grin. "Amazing how he does stuff like that. You'd think he has telepathy too."

Belle narrowed her eyes, focusing on her brother. "It wasn't funny. But our talk did go better than I expected it would." Three pairs of eyes stared back at her. She continued. "I hadn't even given him a chance, and he listened, really heard what I had to say. When he understood that I'd be helping someone and that it could mean the difference between life and death, he agreed."

Vinique lay her hand atop Belle's. "I'm glad it went well. So he saw you off?"

"Yes. He walked me to the portal and watched me leave."

"He sounds like an extraordinary human."

"He is that," Stephen chimed in. "He'll need that to tell Ma."

Vinique cocked her head. "Sounds like it will be fine."

"Belle, we couldn't undergo this effort without you." Arista cleared her throat. "Are you ready to hear a little about what's ahead?"

Belle nodded, the eagerness apparent on her face.

"We're going to train you in the art of witchcraft, starting tomorrow."

Nobody spoke as all eyes rested on Belle.

"*Www*witchcraft?" Her eyes bulged as she sucked in a breath. "But how?"

Stephen squeezed in beside his sister. "It's all right. Really it is. Arista and Vinique are witches. And so was Whisterly."

But, Stephen, isn't it bad?

No. I don't believe it is. You'll have a chance to see. Trust me.

"I never knew you all were witches."

"It's part of who we are, born of our blood," Arista explained. "We must only acknowledge and accept its power, then train of course, so we know how to control its use."

Belle sat transfixed but appeared to be listening.

"Do you understand, Belle?"

"I guess so. You think I can help...? Even though I'm not a witch?" She scrutinized the group. "I'm not, am I?"

Stephen? Am I? Pa would kill me for sure.

Calm down. Just listen.

"No, we don't believe you are a witch," Arista continued. "But you are special. Different from other humans, with powers of your own." Stephen squeezed his sister's hand. "Those are the powers we seek to develop in the hope they will assist us in bringing Whisterly back."

"Oh." Belle's gaze darted between the three of them. "How will you do that?"

"Well, first you'll be evaluated by our coven. They'll help us determine your potential more specifically."

"The coven? That's a group of witches, right?"

"That's right, Belle."

"Then what?"

"Training of course. For the most part you'll work with me." Arista walked to Belle and squatted by her side. "This is all new to me too. I only found out a short time ago that I was a witch, like my mother and my aunt before me."

"Oh. Okay."

"We've all experienced the power within you, Belle. We know it's there. Whisterly knew it too. This is a chance to find out more, to develop in ways you could not on Earth."

Belle turned toward her brother. "You believe this too?"

He gave her an easy smile. "Without your help, Vinique and Arista said they'd never have found me in the Night Dwellers' cave. It was your bond that allowed our telepathic link. Simply put, I'm alive because of you. So, yeah, I believe it."

Belle threw her arms around his neck and squeezed.

"Okay. Don't get carried away. You're gonna choke me."

She rounded on the two women. "I'll do whatever I can to help. When do we start?"

"As soon as we get you back and settled. How's that sound?" Arista patted Belle on the back. "Unless you're tired. We can wait a day, if you'd rather."

"No. I'm not tired."

The eager innocence Arista sensed flowing through Belle's thoughts startled her. *Gods, we've got her. We can do this.*

The four piled into the waiting vehicle for the short drive back to the compound, with Stephen at the helm.

He parked and helped Belle out. "Can you manage your bag, little bit?"

"Of course." Belle flung it over her shoulder. "Let's go in." Arista watched Belle's expression as her eyes seemed to drink in everything around her. "The place is different somehow."

"Do you think so? Not much has changed." *Stephen, someone needs to tell her how, when she was here before, she wasn't in full form. I'm pretty sure that's the difference she's perceiving. Would you like me to do it? You know her best.*

Stephen glanced at his sister, her mouth agape and her eyes darting from one thing to the next. *No. I'll talk to her about it later. Let's give her a little time to adjust first.*

"I'll leave you all to get Belle settled. We'll meet up tonight as planned." Vinique stooped to Belle's level and squeezed her hand. "I'll see you later on."

"Okay. See you then."

"Belle, I thought you might like to share my quarters. I've got plenty of room available. What do you think?"

Stephen pinned Arista with a steady glare. *That's a really bad idea.*

Do you have a better plan? She needs someone available to her to answer her questions. The training won't be easy. I want to do what I can for her.

He huffed. *I guess not... It's just... It's not very good for us. Where else can we spend time together, truly alone?*

Arista met his gaze, and the longing she saw in his eyes shot to her core, warming her insides. *We're resourceful. Don't worry.*

Well, it's not like I can tell your father to get lost so I can ravage his daughter, now is it?

The corners of her mouth lifted. *No, I wouldn't suggest that. But he does know we're mated. Us spending time together would be expected in his eyes. Besides, you're the one who said that maybe we shouldn't be in such a hurry to let everyone know…of our situation. The more I think about it, the more I agree. No one else needs to know just yet. Vinique and Papa will keep it to themselves, and I've already protected your knowledge of our mating. We have time now to explore, just us. Plus I'd like to get to know your sister better. We are family after all.*

Stephen shrugged. *Sounds like you've decided.*

I promise. You'll have all the access to me you could ever want. We'll just need to plan it.

The grimace that had settled on his face turned into the ghost of a smile. *That's not possible. I'll not be satisfied with less than full-time access to you. What do you think a mating means?*

Eventually that will happen.

The three entered Arista's chambers. "Belle, I'll have your room made up for you right away. It's just through those doors. Go ahead and take a look."

Belle shrieked as she plunged herself into her new living space.

Stephen tugged Arista toward him, groping at her gown as he meshed their bodies together, claiming her mouth in a quick deep kiss. Then, just as suddenly, he gazed into her eyes and let her go, leaving her breathless, and followed his sister into her new room.

SIMON TRIED TO tune back into the conversation with Travis even though his head throbbed, and it hurt to hold open his eyes. The haze of the infirmary still clung to him, the retched stench of sickness like a barrier to the outside healthy world. Two whole days they'd kept him there, not knowing what to do to help him apparently.

Literally out of his mind, Simon remembered little of the ordeal, except coming to with tubes sticking out of him. *No one here could possibly know what's the matter with me. And for now, that will remain the case.*

"Keep me apprised of any happenings of importance." Simon's forehead wrinkled. "You do know what *items of importance* would entail?"

"Of course, Commander. I am your second. You've trained me well."

After a quick scan of Travis's thoughts, Simon nodded, satisfied. "I'll be deep in…study, as I recuperate further. But let me know if you encounter anything amiss, anything at all that you find unusual or out of place."

Travis scrunched his face. "Absolutely. But what are you not telling me? Are you sensing danger?"

"Perhaps." Simon swiveled in his chair away from his second and massaged above his eyes, the pain returning with a renewed intensity. "We'll meet again tomorrow," he continued. "Until then, don't disturb me unless absolutely necessary."

Travis nodded to Simon's back. "Certainly. Let me know if there is anything else I can do for you."

The door slid closed behind Travis. Simon plodded to the relative comfort of the couch and pulled a blanket over his face. He sighed, feeling the tension leave him as the artificial light and stray noises faded. Turning his focus inward, he searched for that piece of him recently integrated and connected with it.

Unlike the first time, when he'd collided with an unknown source of information, he was prepared this time. He pushed back, and easily determining what appeared to be the starting point, he accessed a database, now fully lodged inside him. Moving efficiently within the data via his thoughts, he found, quite by accident, that hand motions also performed the same function. He soaked in the words as he read them. When he found some sections locked to him, he proceeded forward—however he could to the next available segment. *Gods, is all this stuff what I think it is?*

As Simon read, the sluggishness left him, and the pounding behind his eyes lessened. Somewhat energized, he attempted the connection he had formed previously. Now, with the benefit of more knowledge on his side, he knew what the old woman and the others were—witches. And being born of the same line, that made him… What?

The place of his prior visions formed in his mind, but the darkness only swirled before him and didn't take shape. It was as the old woman had said, she'd thrown him out. How would he gain entrance now? The words he'd read implied that hands-on teaching was the best mechanism for learning this craft.

Would his exile be permanent? In his short time poring over the details newly lodged in his head, he'd gained most of his strength back. But he wasn't the same, and clearly he never would be again.

Now he wasn't fighting the force within him though. Through the steps taken today, it had become a part of him. And, unlike anything else in his life, even Mila's guiding presence, the "rightness" of the power developing inside his core couldn't be denied. The murkiness before him still flowed, shifting, changing. Could he travel elsewhere with these newly developing skills?

As he did most evenings, he searched the thought patterns for the day, determining any unusual changes or patterns that might be useful to him. Frequently his ability to retrieve this data reached into the compound. The strength of his power ebbed and flowed daily, but with this new capability…just maybe he could access more than before. His fingers manipulated the field before him, alternating by expanding and contrasting the squiggly matter, practicing what his mind led him to carry out.

Belle? Simon's search paused. *Mary Belle…* She's back from Earth as well. Her true name had been betrayed by Thomas before his quick departure. Now it was Simon's to use as he pleased. *Jack, Thomas, and Belle, all back on Remeon, despite the personal danger to all three.*

Using telepathy, he determined Belle's location. Notably, her skills at protecting her thoughts had improved, or more likely, someone else was aiding her. Simon homed in on Belle and, peering through the mass before him, forms settled within the substance— Belle and Stephen. *Ah! Look what I've done. This skill will prove extremely useful.* The grimace that had been his permanent companion for the past several days lifted to form a wry grin.

After watching their interaction for a few moments, Simon pulled away. Hopefully any time now, he could visualize who he wanted to see and be taken there via his mind...

"Stephen! Something's not right." Belle's forehead crinkled together, her gaze scanning the room, then, appearing to see him, looked right at Simon.

She prowled the circumference of her new quarters. "He's here somehow."

"Who's here, Belle?"

"Simon."

"Simon? How can you tell?"

"*Shh.*"

Simon looked on as Belle closed her eyes.

As she did so, their image disintegrated from Simon's view. *Humph. Interesting. How did she do that? I'll need to investigate her skill level further.*

The darkness spun before Simon yet again, as if waiting for a new destination or subject. *Where to now?* The dizzying blur of opportunities seemed to parade before his mind's eye. The options were endless, but with all the knowledge he'd gained recently, his interests lay toward Jack—finding out more about his father.

Whisterly was lost to him. He would not mourn her loss, even now, knowing that she was his birth mother. But his father, here from Earth? Who knew when the possibility might present itself again? A searing ache rose from his stomach. His concentration waned, and the field before him dissolved.

The fading mist didn't matter though because Simon didn't want to see a vision of Jack again; Simon wanted to know Jack's thoughts. Simon wanted to meet his father—to ask him why his own son wasn't worth his time. But reading the thoughts of someone in the compound would be tricky. Typically a close family member would hold their loved one's true name—hidden deep, safe within their own thoughts, in case of a dire circumstance. *Hells, that won't stop me. I can just give it a go. Whatever this is that's changing me, it's making me stronger. And I've got to know more.*

Simon had food brought in and found that his appetite had returned. For the first time in many days, he felt like his old self again, except better. The more he accepted and integrated with this new information source, the more it flourished within him. He'd been going at it all wrong. Fighting against it was the worst approach.

Simon had a sense of the raw power within him and also the realization that he didn't possess the knowledge yet to utilize this new aptitude to its fullest extent. Those beings that he'd seen, gathered together in his vision, wouldn't train him, not yet, maybe not ever. But someone would. Simon could almost always offer what another needed or desired in return. If not that, then he could convince them in his own special way to help him. He'd not *ever* failed with that approach.

Fully sated with food, Simon required sleep. So, with a plan in place now to reach out to his father upon waking, he slept. Waking dreams and visions crept into his slumber, but instead of making him more tired, he was energized by their presence. The information he'd processed during his conscious hours became more solidified, almost as if the time he spent in a trance, dreamlike state were a necessary ingredient for his new learning to solidify.

After sleeping deeper than he could ever remember, he woke, showered, and dressed. Immediately he was able to process another section of the data which had been closed to him yesterday.

Would his new abilities help him penetrate the compound to reach Jack? It was time to find out.

Simon closed his eyes and focused on the more recent vision of Jack, the one where he'd bowed down to those flying beings. As Simon let the scene wash over him, he could make out some of the words that Jack had spoken—words filled with sorrow and emotion, Simon could tell now.

Next he sought out the birth that he'd witnessed, his own. Using his hands, he pushed backward and found the place in time again, right after he had been born, then Arista, he'd been taken by Mila and Janus, before Jack joined Whisterly. The scene replayed. Simon hadn't been mistaken. At that point his parents hadn't known they'd had a son. But later they did.

He used these visions to help anchor himself to Jack, to pull Jack's thoughts to his own. If Simon were right, Jack's common name and his true name were one and the same. Only Jack's personal defenses would keep Simon at bay. *Ah…found you. Let's see what you're made of.*

And reaching out, he began the telepathic connection with his name.

Jack.

CHAPTER 12

ARISTA LED THE small group toward the basement, lost in thought. It could potentially be a big day for Belle, but all Arista could think about was Stephen and the way he'd left her yesterday. Vinique and Belle chatted softly behind her while they walked slowly, Vinique pointing out various places to Belle as they progressed toward the basement.

"Do you remember the gathering place, Belle?"

"Sure do. My brother said I'd have some more things to choose from…to eat, since my body is really here this time, and I could eat more than just those small squares."

Arista heard Vinique laugh. "That's right. It's different for you this time. I'm glad Stephen explained it to you."

"Is it true my power will be different too?" Belle looked up at Vinique, excitement sparkling in her eyes.

"I believe it will be, yes. The form you had before couldn't handle the stress of strong magic. Everything has changed for you this visit. We'll know more when we try it out."

With the voices fading behind her, Arista let herself dissolve deeper in thought. *So he did talk to Belle about it. Good. One less item for me to discuss with her.* Her fingers drifted to her lips as she remembered Stephen's kiss from last night. The intensity. Her insides warmed still, even thinking about it now. But how could he just walk away like that, after that kiss?

Simon's interruption that Belle had handled so swiftly had taken up the remainder of their time together yesterday. And like Vinique had alluded to, Simon had been through his own awakening, claimed by the grimoire and due to his blood connection and age, not derived of his own making. The implications were serious. The ability to see into Belle's current environment showed clearly that Simon's skills were advancing somewhat, even without training.

Belle's own instinctive ability to mentally throw him out attested to her potential usefulness in what lay ahead. The end to the evening had been unsettling, and Stephen had barely said "Good night" when they'd parted. That along with his hasty "Good morning" left Arista feeling disjointed—probably exactly what Stephen's intent had been with his searing kiss.

Like everyone else, with the dissemination of the cure, Arista's daily medication had changed. No longer would Remeonites need to solely depend on life created in the laboratory. Once again individuals could choose to procreate of their own choosing and timing. The council had agreed on this point unanimously. And eventually their numbers would increase, achieving what their ancestors had wanted for so long.

But, so conditioned as they had been for generations to avoid this "barbaric" physical form of breeding, many chose to make no changes to their daily elixir, except those necessary for the cure and vaccination against PR 251. At least for the time being, Arista had chosen to let her body work as intended. Maybe she needed to rethink that… She'd read all the material herself. The council desired and expected the birthrate to soar, adding to their dwindling numbers of births. It would be a welcome trend. *I'm not sure I want to be adding to our numbers personally, just yet.*

She and Stephen had not specifically discussed children, having only recently both accepted their mutual desire for a life together. They still had much to work through as they learned to be a couple. And even though they were formally mated, Arista didn't have a longing to follow in her mother's footsteps and have a child so early in life. Arista doubted, if not forced, that her mother would have made that decision independently.

As Arista had discussed with Stephen, her decision to perform the mating ceremony had a lot to do with having a voice to drive her own future path for her mate and possibly children. She and Stephen would need to talk more about their future soon. The changes within her were likely due to the alterations in the mixtures and dosages of her medication. It made sense.

Arista felt heat rising to her cheeks. Did Stephen want human coupling now? Did she? Maybe he did and that was the source of his anger regarding Belle's living quarters. *Hells, is loving someone always this difficult?*

The mist-like vapor hung about the basement door, effectively hiding the opening to those who knew nothing of its presence. Arista ducked into the familiar cover, followed by Vinique and a loudly questioning Belle. "*Shh.* Just a minute, Belle, and we'll be inside." The trio slipped behind the ancient door. Arista heard the loud groan as Vinique pulled it closed.

"Can I talk now?" Belle loud-whispered.

Vinique smiled. "Yes, Belle dear."

"Will my brother be coming too?"

Arista heard the quiver in Belle's voice. "No. Remember how we talked about this last night before you went to sleep? It'll just be us. Better to focus that way. You said you were ready to learn." Arista turned and extended her arm toward Belle. "Here. Take my hand. It's a little slippery at this point coming off the stairs."

"I am ready."

Arista and Vinique shared a glance. "Well, all right then. Follow me and take the bumpy path slowly," Arista added.

When they reached the hidden opening, Arista stooped, loosened the board, and squeezed herself through.

"Go on in," Vinique encouraged from behind Belle. "It will be easy for you."

Arista helped Belle to her feet, watching her wide-eyed expression. "Well, what do you think?"

Belle stumbled as she moved toward the center of the room. "It's perfect," she called to them. She bent down, closed her eyes, and felt the damp soil beneath her fingertips. Arista and Vinique watched as a tremor visibly took hold of Belle's body. A hum emanated through the room.

Arista inched toward Belle, who appeared to be in a trance of some sort. "Belle? Are you okay?"

A smile lit her face, and Belle nodded. "Yes. They're speaking to me."

"Who is?"

Belle took in her surroundings, pausing when she came to the mural-covered ceiling for a deeper look. "The little people. They're here on Remeon too. Can't you hear them?"

"Great-Grandmother, join us, will you?" Arista asked.

Belle walked toward the grimoire. When she got there, she stood on tiptoe, unable to reach the tome.

"Here. Let me." Vinique grabbed the book and placed it in Belle's waiting arms.

Belle sunk to her knees and opened the cover. Her fingers slowly traced the pentagram within.

Vinique joined her, whispering a spell that split open the pages and sent a sliver of light skyward. Joined at the ceiling in a ball of light, it sparked back toward the trio. Vinique pulled Belle from the magical book just as the light beam hit the open page. Belle's mouth gaped open when the mist rising from its creases slowly twisted into a humanlike form.

"Oh. Hello," Belle said, smiling, entranced with the newcomer.

The old witch grabbed a garment and strode in front of the three women.

"Hello, Belle. We've been anxious for you to join us."

"I'm quite happy to be here." Belle beamed. "Thank you, Miss…"

"My name's Arista, just like this young witch before you. She's my namesake."

Belle looked back and forth between the two. "I see… I think."

"That's not as important as what's ahead. Right, child?"

Belle stole a glimpse at Vinique and Arista. "Well, I guess so."

Arista picked up the book and placed it back on its stand. "So what's next, Great-Grandmother? You saw what she did and her connection with the little people?"

"Indeed I did, Arista. This little one here is very powerful. But you don't have to be a witch to have impressive powers."

"Tell us, Great-Grandmother." A quiet solemnness filled the room.

"Belle, tell me. You've felt this before? You've been able to make a connection with the little people on Earth?"

Belle glanced about the circle of women.

Arista took her hand. "It's all right, Belle. You're safe here."

Belle's gaze flicked back and forth among the three. "Yes. I just never told anyone. In the forest at home, they would call to me. We'd play and talk. When others came around, they would disappear. They don't like to be around people. They're shy."

Arista nodded, and Vinique raised one brow.

"Very interesting. Based on her past help in searching for her brother," the old witch added, "I believe that Belle has some Elven blood in her, closely aligned with and perhaps a mixture of the Fae as well. It's difficult to know the concentration exactly, but she's shown her ability to ward off evil through her dealings with Simon, and she already possesses a connection to the element Ground on her home planet. This will prove to be her strongest association with us as witches.

"Some elves are incredibly kind creatures and control their magic for benevolent purposes. Belle's power comes from her blood, and likely her magical abilities will continue to grow as she does. We'll know more as we work with her." The old woman turned her attention back to the child. "Belle, what else can you do, with your powers on Earth?"

Belle's forehead drew together in pensive thought. "Well, on the farm, the animals would do my bidding easily. It was like they understood my words, even my thoughts."

The old witch nodded. "Go on."

"And while speaking with the little people in the forest, we brought rain and storms when the dry ground needed it. Sometimes the storms protected me. When I was lost, they lit my way home or kept dangerous animals from me."

The old witch laughed. "That was all you, Belle. Let's see some more of what you can do. From what we've witnessed so far it's highly likely you'll be able to harness power from within using yourself as a conduit for the essence of Remeon through its soil, plant life, animal population and its life giving sustenance which unites and flows through us all. Arista, you'll work with the element Ground today also. Step up and find your place in the grimoire." The crone's cackle continued as she addressed her namesake. "I'd say you have some catching up to do, Great-Granddaughter."

Arista's face broke into a smile as she stood before the magical book. The pages flipped, slicing through air while their speed increased, the chosen page still a mystery. She glanced at Belle, who had once again squatted to the ground, her head hung low, her communion with the core of Remeon beginning anew. "I'm ready." Arista beamed a wide smile toward Belle. "Let's begin."

THE SUN STREAMED in through the window, stretching its long fingers across the desk, spilling into the room. Jack lifted his face to its warmth, instantly remembering another morning, waking up with the sun shining down on him while on Remeon with Whisterly by his side, the morning after their wedding. He leaned back, recalling those stolen precious moments.

Time.

He wanted more of it with her. Not just a recollection of what had been.

Jack stretched, arching back in the chair that barely accommodated his frame. Sitting still at the desk, reading a book for so long, had begun to put one arm to sleep. He yawned, moving his arm back and forth to restore the blood flow. Arista had found him a book on Remeonite history in the basement, so it was extremely old. This particular book couldn't be found in the digitized collection. He couldn't help but wonder if it had been excluded on purpose.

Arista had submitted the book to be created in holoform and in English, so he could read it. Then later she had highlighted a couple places where the events that had happened were those orchestrated by witchcraft. Even though they weren't noted as such in the book specifically, for obvious reasons, with Jack's knowledge of the craft, the influence was clear. Whisterly had brought the book to Arista's attention years ago, apparently as part of her studies. Only now, awakened as a witch, did Arista fully comprehend its meaning.

Eager to dig in on choice bits of his family's history, he'd pored over its pages. Fascinated, Jack had read most of the morning. He'd found paper to add his own scribbled notes, creating a time line of events that occurred as the result of witchcraft, so he could keep it. Whisterly, Arista, Vinique, and their ancestral bloodline were truly a monumental part of Remeonite history.

Food. That might help my focus. He slid back his chair.

Jack.

He froze and a chill shot up his spine. Instinctively he knew who the communication was from, its signature unique but at the same time familiar. When he'd communicated with Arista via telepathy for the first time, he'd noticed the similarity in pattern to Whisterly's. Was it a familial thing? Or just instinctual? He didn't know enough about telepathy to know the answer.

But he knew his family when they contacted him. And despite his simultaneous urges to push Simon away and draw him close, Jack wavered, undecided on his next step.

Jack.

He felt the call again, this one a much more intrusive attempt. One that he halted.

After the attack by Damond years ago, and Whisterly's subsequent healing of Jack, they'd eventually worked together on methods to protect him—approaches that didn't require witchcraft but training instead. So Jack had learned, vowing he'd not be caught defenseless by invasive telepathy again.

Not only did that mental attack by Damond almost cost Jack his life but ultimately it could have meant the death of his family—both Whisterly and their twin children she'd been carrying at the time—since ultimately she'd fought to heal Jack so close to giving birth.

So much time had passed. And Jack already knew firsthand what those years could do—years lacking love in one's life. Worry creased his face as Jack rehashed the memories. What he did now would have a lasting impact, but he'd returned to Remeon not only to connect with his daughter but also with his son as well, whatever the costs.

This wasn't how he'd wanted their first contact to go. It should be face-to-face. He steeled himself with a mental preparation not unlike battle. If he was to repair what had been done long ago, it had to start somewhere. If nothing else…he could begin communication.

His lips pressed together in a straight line. His defenses held against Simon. Yet Jack hesitated. He could choose to wait, but deep down, he knew his heart wouldn't let him, despite what he knew about the man, Simon. How could he be anything but what he was? Lying, deceitfulness, sickness, and pain were all he knew. True love had never touched him, except in his initial creation.

Jack's life had been anything but easy. But he'd had the love of his mother, and later Sam, the person who had shaped him into the man Jack would become. Whisterly was the one true love he'd have in this world, and their love had culminated in the birth of Arista and Simon.

Simon needed Jack, just as Jack had needed Sam, someone who could show him what it meant to be a man, loving and true. Hopefully it wasn't too late. Jack checked the protections he had in place for a third time, assuring himself that Simon wouldn't pull anything from him but information Jack wanted him to have. Whisterly, Arista, Daniel, and Stephen needed Jack's protection. Jack would not be an avenue to betray his family, if Simon was seeking that.

Jack would have to be cautious. He'd have to treat Simon like an enemy—his own son. A deep ache screamed to life within him, one whose echoes began years ago when he'd first learned of the abduction of their son.

Simon. I'm here. Jack could hear Simon's chuckle flowing through his thoughts. Jack waited. He wouldn't be provoked by a child, especially not his own child.

And so you are. I'm deeply moved.

Once again Jack marveled at this form of communication. He wished he could use it with people on Earth, humans. Even without physical cues, through telepathy, Jack had learned to pick out sarcasm. Clearly Simon believed he had the upper hand here.

I was hoping we'd have the chance to communicate, even if for nothing more than to set the record straight.

Big of you, Jack. After all this time? And now it's time to set the record straight? Enlighten me. Please.

You were only a baby, Simon. It wasn't your fault.

You're right there. It was yours.

All right. It was mine.

How could you leave an innocent child in the hands of Janus?

I think you know the answer to that, Simon. I didn't even know of your existence.

What kind of father are you?

Jack winced. And felt sure that the emotion would get translated to Simon through their bond. Jack sucked in a breath and reined in the years of remorse and sadness pulsing through him, yearning to be set free.

That's a good question, Simon. I'd hoped, during all these years that have passed, that you'd have an opportunity to find out.

I don't need a father now. But I did long ago.

I can't do anything about the past. Maybe we can get to know each other now. I don't expect you to treat me as your father.

Jack heard a stifled breath between them and took the opportunity to dig deeper into Simon's consciousness. Pictures of beatings at the hands of Janus flashed to life before him. He'd expected this and worse. It didn't make the fact any easier that his child had suffered at the hands of that animal. In Jack's dreams he'd seen Simon killed multiple ways, many times in his recurring nightmares.

Keep your distance, Jack. I don't want you in my head!

Jack fought to keep the emotion out of his response. It wouldn't help either of them. *I'm sorry you suffered at Janus's hand. He was cruel. You didn't deserve it.*

You got that right. But I did persevere. I'm stronger than I've ever been. Thanks to Mother...

Jack thought this might come up as well and maintained his even tone. He'd not jeopardize her return, for anyone.

Oh?

Innocence doesn't sound good on you, Jack. I don't need you. Soon I'll get to the bottom of this on my own.

I hope someday you'll consider a relationship between us, Simon.

I've got more power than I know what to do with. And I'm learning, fast. As promised, I'll be at the Day Watchers' doorstep, ready to take what's mine. You, Arista, and Vinique can't stop me, not to mention Stephen and Belle.

Jack heard a sinister cackle creep into his thoughts. The last time he'd been in the presence of thoughts this dark had been during Damond's attack. Jack felt bile rise in his throat and hoped he wouldn't be sick. How naive he'd been to think he could spark some good in his son.

In his desperation he'd wished that Simon had missed him, even if only a little bit, so there would be a chance, a small chance for a reconciliation. But can someone miss what they've never had? Jack recognized the sound of a hearty laugh.

You're slipping, Jack. A reconciliation? Really? You made your choice when you left your defenseless children.

Jack pushed back at the rising pool of anger bubbling up inside him. *No. Like you, Simon, I had no choice.*

Too bad you can't take that up with Whisterly now, isn't it? What kind of man allows his mate to make his decisions for him?

Time and space paused. Afraid of what he might do or say in his next breath, Jack remained silent and counted in his head, hoping his sanity would return before he spewed the words that were crawling up his throat to this being who inconceivably was his own flesh and blood. Jack had known total rejection would be a possibility. He knew of his son's evil traits. Still, Jack had hoped that he could make a difference.

Behind his closed eyes, he heard the shadow of Whisterly's voice. *Just breathe. That's it. In and out. In and out.* Jack felt the memories of her spirit cleanse him, and he knew what he had to do for now.

Let go.

Maybe over time, there would be another opportunity. He couldn't tell if sweat or tears ran down his face, since he was experiencing both. Jack shook with the effort of the communication forming in his mind. *Simon, you were stolen from us. Put the blame where it belongs, on Mila and Janus. We'll meet face-to-face one day soon. I look forward to it.*

Jack thrust Simon from his thoughts and made iron-clad sure he wouldn't claw his way back in. Jack stood and leaned on the back of the chair, while anger licked at his senses, then heaving a breath, picked up the chair and slammed it against the wall.

Swiping at his forehead and cheeks, he left his quarters. He only hoped that a holographic bay were open now. Later, he'd regret killing some Remeonite who got in his way.

ARISTA MANEUVERED HER way through the hallways, anxious to get off her feet. The council meeting this morning had gone better than expected. Three new members had been approved by the full body. Now the much-needed new blood may offer changed perspectives on issues of concern. They'd each handled the myriad questions well, especially those on human-Remeonite relations.

With all the focus recently on humans, considering their positive impact in healing Remeonites of PR 251, now was the time to take advantage of that human-Remeonite goodwill and stoke those fires while they were hot. Other questions surrounded that topic, like excess holographic capacity, preparing for rising birth rates in the future, and individual procreation—all worthwhile subjects for debate.

After the cure, now each Remeonite submitted to two consecutive tests, three months apart, affirming their disease-free status, before they were cleared to procreate individually. Of course this would be a long road. As a people, Remeonites were much more comfortable with the process of creating life in a laboratory. This more clinical approach allowed for ease of testing for genetic defects, determining a PR 251 prediagnosis, and detection of other abnormalities.

Over time, with increased individual conception on Remeon these types of decisions, based on results of genetic testing, could become less clinically centered in a lab setting and more personal, possibly creating long term shifts in Remeon's societal norms and culture. Education would be key here, along with corresponding alterations in one's daily medication. Natural urges to procreate had been all but eradicated through medication in order to stop the spread of PR 251, the stigma attached to the physical act deemed barbaric for centuries now.

These concepts would take reeducation and time, maybe even over generations, plus the energy and willingness to adapt. Only time would tell as the younger members of their society started to explore the truth of their sexuality and the needs of their own bodies, now so long ignored. Some doctors even wondered if the ability to procreate naturally had been bred out of their society as the years had passed.

I guess my mother blew that theory. Here I am as proof.

Arista found herself at the forefront, offering to adjust her medication early, since there would be no need to test her with subsequent intervals of waiting. Her immunity was well documented. The changes in her psyche and body so far had been monumental in her own mind. Arista wished her mother were here to discuss such matters.

Instead she would talk to Vinique about it eventually, but her mother's situation had been, at the very least, unique, actually mating and producing offspring successfully with a human. Someday Arista may consider this same course of action, if Stephen wanted to pursue human coupling and children. But for now, could her medication be adjusted to prevent pregnancy? Would she dare to ask in the situation they were in now, as a people?

Being so close to Stephen and Belle, and especially Jack, Arista was struck by their differences. Humans' interdependence on emotional fulfillment tended to make them more vulnerable, yet somehow stronger at the same time. How could that be? Whatever it was, she wanted more of it. Why, just this morning, she'd woken to find Belle's warm little body snug against hers. She'd not bathed the night before, as evidenced by the little tracks of dried tears apparent on her dirt-smudged cheeks. Their conversations from yesterday lingered in her mind.

"Belle, is everything all right?"

Her eyes, still bleary with sleep, had opened, half lidded, then closed. As a peaceful smile settled on Belle's face, she murmured, "Now it is," and had drifted back into an immediate slumber. Her need of bodily contact satisfied, this little one could be at rest. Would it be as simple with Stephen?

True to her word of finding them time alone, this morning, before her council meeting, she'd arranged a walk with Stephen, outside, beyond the compound walls. As they strolled in silence, their fingertips brushed, just barely making contact. Via their telepathic link Arista could tell Stephen was still brooding over her decision to bring Belle into her quarters. Arista turned and checked their distance to the compound, then veered onto a side path with plenty of cover. "Would you like to sit for a little while?"

"Sure. If you have time."

"You seem quiet this morning." Arista squeezed his hand.

Stephen shrugged and kicked a rock at his feet. "I guess."

"Well, it would be much easier to talk about it, instead of me probing your mind, right? But I guess I'll resort to that if I have to."

He moved his hand to her neck, gently massaging with his thumb.

"*Mmm.*" She closed her eyes. "That feels nice."

His fingers slid up her nape and into her hair, while he eased her forward. His mouth covered hers in a slow, gentle kiss. When they parted, Stephen drew her toward him again, hugging Arista close. They swayed back and forth.

"What is it?" she whispered in his ear.

He leaned back slightly, peering into the depths of her eyes. "I'd say I'm losing you, but I'm not even sure I had you to start with."

Arista pulled back so she could see his expression. "What do you mean? We're mated."

Stephen nodded. "Which you admitted you did out of desperation so you wouldn't be forced to mate another. I was a safe choice, on my way back to Earth."

"What do you mean, *safe*? I love you."

He lowered his gaze to meet hers. "Your decisions say otherwise." Stephen cleared his throat. "I'm considering going back to Earth for a while. But with Belle here, that presents a problem going by portal, doesn't it?"

"She's your sister." The tone of Arista's voice sharpened. "What would you have me do with her? She's only a child. She was so lonely and scared last night that she crawled into bed with me."

"Did she? I'll talk to her. Reassure her."

"We need her," Arista continued, her voice more steady. "And besides that, I love her too. I want Belle to feel at home with me."

Stephen ran a hand through his hair. "That's part of what I'm talking about. Belle seems to have a place here, a purpose. I'm not sure I do."

Arista lips twisted into a crooked smile. "*You*? The person ultimately responsible for curing our people? I disagree."

"*Now*. Right now. Why am I here? I'm not talking about the past."

"I thought I was clear when we discussed this, Stephen. I want to make a life with you. We're mated here on Remeon, and we can marry as your customs dictate on Earth. But tell me what *you* want. You don't seem as sure as when we've had our previous conversations and when you gave me this." She held up her hand. "Do you want it back?"

Stephen lifted his eyes to meet hers, ignoring her question. "What I want hasn't changed since I first laid eyes on you. Strange, isn't it? I knew then you were outta my league. I guess now I'm just really dense."

Tears pooled in her eyes. "That's not true."

"I'm not convinced."

She sniffed. "Would it help if I told you that I couldn't sleep at night, wondering if you want human coupling now, but I'm too afraid to ask or let you read those thoughts? I mean, what if you said no? Maybe it's my medication changes, but it's all I think about."

She raised both hands in frustration. "What's wrong with me anyway? I'm supposed to be a council leader, yet I can't even discern my own emotions. And what if we did?" Her eyes sought his, and she could feel the heat as her face colored. "You know... And I got pregnant. I don't want a child right now. My life is full of stuff I have to figure out soon. But you and I—I thought we had us covered."

Stephen's mouth hung open, surprise registering on his face. He reached for her and pressed her body tightly against his. "I'd say that helps," he said, his voice low, almost a growl. "At least I know I'm not the only one not sleeping here. And that you didn't ask my sister to stay with you to avoid me."

"What?" Her gaze raked over his. "Why would you say such a thing? Answer me! Is the human-style mating what you want? Now? I don't know what I'm doing, but I think my body does. Let's get it over with. Maybe then you'll be convinced." Arista squirmed in his embrace in an attempt to free herself.

Stephen held firm, easily overpowering her then changed his tone, similar to the voice he used when he dealt with skittish animals on the farm back home. "*Shhh.* Just be still a minute. And for God's sake, don't zap me with some spell and turn me into a bug or something." He heard a small giggle escape her lips.

"I was thinking more along the lines of a toad. But I'm not sure I know how to do that yet."

He kissed her temple. "Well, that's good to know at least. And that question you were asking? Of course I think about it...all the time. How could I not? You make me crazy with wanting you," he whispered in her ear.

She took his face in her hands. "Then let's do it."

He kissed her softly, then more urgently as she leaned into him, releasing the tension in her body. "No, as much as I want to, not like this, love. I don't want to *just get it over with*. It means the world to me just to know you feel the same, that you want me as much as I want you."

She nodded and leaned her forehead against his, giving them both time to catch their breath. "I do... So when then?"

"We need to plan our marriage ceremony." He laced his fingers with hers. "Maybe it will be on Earth, maybe here."

One of her eyebrows rose. "Ah. Okay. I'd love to visit Earth. You said that was important to your family. And the other event?"

Stephen's hands squeezed her shoulders, then slid down her arms, his mouth pressing kisses against her neck. "We need to plan that also, if you don't completely undo me before then."

CHAPTER 13

AFTER AN EXHAUSTING session at the holographic suite, thankfully Jack felt more like himself. Beating down the sadness, the loss, and the loneliness seemed to be a full-time job—and that was only keeping it at bay. The hole in his heart knew no depth, and his loss of Whisterly was mourned at his very core. Even though he'd felt the beginning of healing when he'd mourned with the coven, it hadn't been enough. He had a long way to go. Physically spent from his recent activity, his thoughts turned inward to Whisterly. He needed to visit Yara, the one who, they hoped, held Whisterly's consciousness.

Back at his quarters, he stripped down. The closeness of his small shower smelled musty and reeked of his sweat. Furthermore, the enclosure didn't quite fit the dimensions of his body. Still, it got the job done. He leaned his head against the tile and let the steaming water trickle over his arms, back, and legs, easing the tension in his muscles where it hit him.

The nagging thoughts returned, but clear-headed, his mind worked to process them better. When would he plan to meet Simon and how? The first meeting would likely not go well. Frankly Jack would be satisfied initially with just laying eyes on Simon. My God, his son was practically an adult, with powers stronger than Jack could imagine.

Being back on Remeon put everything in perspective in a way it hadn't been on Earth. Jack had already reconciled himself to dying on this trip. He believed in his heart he should have never left Remeon after that last time through the portal. But would he have died at the hands of the council due to Damond's murder as Whisterly had predicted? Or possibly later during an attempt to regain his son from the Night Dweller community?

Back then, at seventeen, Jack didn't have the skills or training to pull off an op like that. He had yet to serve in combat. And what if he'd taken Whisterly with him back to Earth? In those last few seconds before he'd returned to his own planet, she'd asked to go with him. Her and Arista. But Whisterly wouldn't have made it, not with her PR 251 diagnosis and no doctor with enough knowledge of the disease to treat her on Earth. Maybe she would have died in his arms instead of here on Remeon in the infirmary. But, without treatment from her own doctors, she'd have died long ago. Would he trade those years of her life, even though separated from her?

Remaining here, she could practice and fine-tune her craft, perfect the skills that enabled her to find an outcome that would give her life and them a chance to be together. Had she been right all along in her stance? Thoughts churned in his head. Even the betrayal by her council member she'd anticipated and had a contingency planned. She was a warrior through and through, always finding a path toward life. If this transference of Whisterly's spirit worked, he couldn't wait to spend the rest of his life making her happy.

His hand ran across the mirror, clearing the condensation enough to see his face. The wrinkles in his forehead deepened. He'd aged. Yara's body looked roughly to be that of a woman in her thirties from Earth. But time had not hit her body as it had his. He sighed, his lips twisting into a grimace. If growing old together was the most difficult issue he and Whisterly had to deal with, then their lives would be a fairy tale.

They were far from that at present. Arista and Simon were growing in their craft. Belle was pinch-hitting for an adult witch, and Whisterly's consciousness was currently dormant in the body of another. Plans to merge Yara's body with Whisterly's consciousness would most likely result in either Jack's death or Whisterly's or both. Odds were not currently in their favor to come out of this alive. Still, he needed to be close to her now, as close as possible.

After changing into clean clothes, Jack headed for the infirmary. The staff there knew Jack and waved him past the front desk. He ducked behind the curtain and greeted Whisterly per his usual pattern. After all, Yara was brain-dead. Any presence within her body would be Whisterly's consciousness, not Yara's. That was how Jack saw the situation anyway. His gaze shifted to Yara's shoulder length hair—blond instead of Whisterly's silver hair color he'd remembered—to Jack it didn't matter. Whisterly was here, now, inside of Yara. Everything else paled in comparison, including physical details.

He pulled out a notebook and noted her stats as he did with each visit. Then carefully, holding his breath, he checked her eyes. Still gray. Thank God. Releasing his pent-up breath, he lowered himself into the chair by her bed, kept company by the reassuring repetitive beep that let him know Yara's heart still beat.

Whisterly...baby, I talked to Simon today. It didn't go so well... I haven't given up, not by a long shot. He's a warlock, just as you predicted, and struggling with what he doesn't know. Along with a father to guide him and a teacher, a mother is what he needs. Jack squeezed the limp hand that lay outside the cover. Even though there was no response, her hand was warm, alive.

Lifting her fingers to his lips, he hesitated, then kissed them and held her hand to his cheek. He glanced at her with a crooked smile as he laid down her hand. *We're getting you outta here—soon. Count on it.*

Digging in his pocket, he pulled out the device Arista had given him, the one that held the book he'd started, got comfortable in his chair, and set to reading out loud, wanting to include her in the activity. He focused first on the pages Arista had pointed out to him, those which held the historical information Whisterly had taught her daughter.

Disguised behind historical facts, one would need to be a witch, or knowledgeable of their activities, in order to catch the significance of what he read. He varied his voice in pitch and tone, keeping an eye on Yara's heart rate. When he talked to her or read, it jumped from previous levels during the day. That had to mean something...

Speaking as animatedly as possible—for reciting Remeonite history, that is—he continued. It felt good to be here, where he believed Whisterly's consciousness lingered. Being without her for so long, it was like a lifeline he could cling to as he waited for the next steps in the coven's plan.

For now he held tight to the hope of the future, before the wrenching of Whisterly's true name from his brain and the unthinkable task of somehow melding that part of her into a new body. He shuddered. For now he chose to see them both whole and on the other side. Jack laced their fingers together. *We're going to make it, baby.*

Without warning, a series of beeps rang out, more intense and faster than the normal stats that flowed on the screen. He stood up, staring at the screen flashing red before him. The sedate lines that he'd been following along on the console now gyrated in peaks and valleys as they stuttered across the display. He grabbed her hand. "Don't you dare die on me, damn it! Do you hear me?"

"Jack. Step back." A nurse pulled him away, while several other medical personnel set to work on Yara.

"I'm not leaving." His face contorted. "What's wrong? What's happened to her?"

The partition flew back as the nurse continued to push Jack farther and farther from the bed, clearing a space for the extra equipment that whirled in behind her. "We don't know yet for sure, but it appears that the medications that have been holding her stable are not working anymore."

Jack's wild-eyed gaze met the nurse's. "Well then, get different medication."

"It's not that simple. Her body is dying."

"What…? How?"

A hand rested on his shoulder. Her soft voice drifted into his thoughts. *Papa.*

Jack turned. *Arista, we're losing her.* He pulled his daughter into his arms, fighting down the tide of emotions rising within him.

Come with me. Arista led Jack from the infirmary and out the closest exit.

"What are you doing? We need to be in there." Jack sucked in a deep breath, battling for control. "What if…"

She held his hands in hers. "Yara's body is dying, just as the nurse said, but I'm making it look worse on the equipment than it is."

Jack's shoulders slumped, and the folds in his forehead deepened. "What in God's name are you talking about?"

"Papa, they need to believe that she is clinically dead before they will release the body to the morgue."

"What!"

Her voice gentled. "It's easier this way with a slight bit of magic. We need to perform the reintegration now, before her body dies. Hopefully Whisterly's consciousness actively inside Yara will stabilize her body. But we need Yara's body to find out. It will be much simpler to steal her from the morgue than from the infirmary. We need to move her to the basement. We can't wait any longer." Arista paused, staring deep into her father's eyes. "Tonight. We'll do it tonight."

Jack blinked, and his brows knit together. "I see. I think." He swiped a hand down his face. "Did you know this would happen? Did you cause it?"

"No, of course not. We're not ready. More time would be better. But it has to be now, while she still lives. Whisterly isn't anchored to anybody now. If Yara's body were to die, Whisterly wouldn't know she'd have to leave the host, even if she could. Then all of Whisterly's work, her trials—they would have been for nothing."

Jack nodded slowly. "We won't let that happen. What next?"

"Well, they'll pronounce her dead soon and move her to the morgue. Let's not be here for that. Vinique has already planned how to get Yara to the basement tonight. We'll combine our powers, and under the disguise of magic, we will get her through the door. Could use your help to get her down the steps though."

"Anything. I'll do anything."

"I'll contact you when it's time. Belle will already be with me. You bring Stephen with you as well."

Jack gave her a questioning glance.

"He insisted, Papa. He wants to be there for his sister…and me."

Jack leaned forward and kissed her forehead. "Understood. I'll be waiting to hear from you."

"Keep believing, Papa."

He squeezed her hand. "It's what I do where your mother is concerned. Always."

ARISTA STRUGGLED TO relax as she neared the mist by the basement door. Disguised as two nurses transporting a patient in a wheelchair, Arista and Vinique would appear as such to anyone they passed. Yara, still alive, her head leaning to one side, looked to be asleep, not unconscious, as was her current state. Arista peered behind the door, relived to see Jack and Stephen who together carried Yara down the steps while Vinique handled the wheelchair.

Arista hurried behind the small caravan. Time wasn't on their side. Magic could keep Yara alive only so long, and that time frame was uncertain at best. And with no knowledge how long it would take to mix the potion, give it to Jack, retrieve Whisterly's true name from him, and integrate that name with Yara's body, Arista was understandably on edge.

Jack and Stephen settled Yara on a slab of raised rock, just in front of the grimoire. The candles burning throughout the space cast an eerie glow on her face. In the semidarkness, shadows swayed along the walls, their movements imitating the living, breathing actions of real life, which the coven, hidden within the mural above, no longer possessed.

Belle, already perched to one side of Yara, reached out to her brother, who gathered her into a quick hug, then, with a whispered word in her ear, moved off to the edge of the room.

Once Arista saw Vinique coming toward her, she opened the tome in preparation to summon her great-grandmother and the waiting coven.

Whatever happens, Arista, know you've done well. Your mother would be proud.

She turned and winked at her father. *She can tell me herself.*

With Vinique at her side, Arista closed her eyes, waving the pages forward with a hand motion. As the pages saluted in their ritual dance, Arista stretched her arms high toward the witches of the coven. Faint murmurings of the collective floated down to Arista when the balls of light forming at her fingertips shot to the ceiling.

And they are almost as eager as we are, Vinique. Acknowledging Arista's telepathic communication with a nod, Vinique looked skyward.

The pages slowed, then fluttered to a stop, awaiting the flame hurling toward its worn bindings. The ball of light made impact, shifting the book back and forth. The characteristic hissing rose from the book's creases to create a mist, its shape quickly taking on that of the crone.

Belle patiently waited for the old witch, gown in hand.

"Why thank you, dear."

Belle nodded, then lowered her eyes.

"Shall we get started?"

Cackles emanated from the witches up on high, and they descended upon the small group.

A shudder shot down Arista's spine. "Here we go."

Vinique lay a hand on her niece's shoulder, buoying her strength.

"Jack, come forward."

He closed his eyes and bowed his head, Arista guessed in prayer to his God. Seconds later he fell in line with Arista and Vinique.

"Hand me your blade, Arista."

She pulled the knife from its sheath and handed it to the old woman, who grasped Jack's hand, lifting it high over the magical tome.

Skin split apart as the knife slid across Jack's palm. Drops of blood spilled on the page; then one, two separate drips plopped into a small cauldron. The blood absorbed quickly, the page now exhibiting a reddish hue.

"You next, Arista." The crone clasped her great-grandchild's hand and, repeating the process, added drops to both the book and the waiting kettle.

"Vinique, your blood will substitute for Whisterly's as her half-sister."

She nodded, and her blood joined the other two, cast upon the book and dropped into the mixture.

The old witch lifted her arms and closed her eyes. "Now we call upon the one joined to the book not among us but bound just the same. His spirit, though not physically present, will support our efforts through no will of its own. Come to me now." Pausing, the crone shuddered through a soft sigh. "Each of you must bring to the table your addition through your capabilities, and I'll add the final element." The ancient witch nodded to Belle. "Come forward, child."

Belle approached the grimoire, the open page now a deep crimson color from the blood it had claimed. She averted her eyes and bent low, her fingers gliding over the floor's surface. A tremor shook the damp musty room. In Belle's fists, she had gathered bits of clumped soil. She gripped the substance tight, sending pieces of its essence into the cauldron. A sizzling sound lifted from the kettle that held the blood as the two ingredients melded together, forming a sticky paste.

"Vinique, your turn."

Vinique's long fingers grasped what appeared to be only air. But she held her closed fist over the kettle, and water dripped from her hands as a series of muttered words left her lips. The dark mixture swirled in the pot, finally settling to a calm surface once again.

Arista approached, cupped her hands around her mouth, and blew into the container. The contents heaved and swirled, lifting as a precarious mass from the kettle. Bits and pieces recognizable at first meshed into something new while Arista continued to blow, the wind growing in strength as the gathering of witches fought to stand their ground against its force. The wind died and a smooth mixture floated back into the pot.

The crone's lips lifted, a grin stretching her mouth. "Now the final ingredient." The coven huddled around the group, and their voices soared:

The maiden, the mother, the crone.
The maiden, the mother, the crone.
The maiden, the mother, the crone.
The maiden, the mother, the crone.

The maiden, the mother, the crone.

She squatted, her fingers scaling underneath the cauldron. Instantly sparks ignited fire within the grates below the pot. Waving her hand rapidly, the old woman encouraged the flames, and soon the concoction bubbled, spitting globs of hot liquid fizzling to the ground.

The hum of the coven droned on. One among them drew her hooded form forward and presented a small container. Not metal, wood, or glass, its sides deviated from one another, the essence of the thing appearing to ripple with movement. Puffs of smoke clung to the rim, making the true height and depth difficult to determine. Spindly fingers passed the cup born of the coven to the crone.

"Well done."

The chanting continued.

"Jack, come, listen. We must proceed. The body weakens each minute we delay."

He separated from Arista and Vinique.

Standing before the old woman, Arista could see sweat dripping down his neck, moistening his shirt where his muscles stretched. Drawing a deep breath, Arista held it. Musty earth mixed with the metallic smell of fresh blood—the combination the affirmation of life beginning or life ending. The thick liquid paraded into the cup at the crone's coaxing. Arista released her breath and reached for Vinique and Belle, who stood on either side. The three joined hands, and as they swayed, they chanted in unison with their sisters, the coven.

At the edge of the room a flicker of movement caught Arista's eye. Stephen sat, glued to the perimeter, his eyes fixated on her. She drew herself fully back with the group and let her eyes drift shut while the chanting and movement carried her within the coven.

"Jack, take this and drink. You must ingest it all. Take it in all at once. You'll not want to go back to finish the remainder, so leave none. You won't feel like yourself, which is as it should be. Our combined power will enter your subconsciousness. This substance will dull the resulting intrusion and pain as we search for authenticity in your matter which will guide us to Whisterly's true name.

"In addition, this solution dilutes any material to its most basic form, making her true name easier to locate. Death is a possible outcome, since this liquid could fundamentally change you as well, but the quicker we can get in and out, the better your prognosis will be." A deep raspy breath shook her chest. "Should you come through unscathed, you may see healing powers of your own from this elixir. Time will tell."

He nodded, a grimace crossing his face. "You've been in my head before and restored my life. It's yours to take. Use it and bring Whisterly back."

The old witch dipped her chin. "Belle will lend you aid, should you require it. Arista, Vinique, and I must work swiftly to integrate Whisterly's consciousness into Yara's body. Should we fail, we will, of course, lose them both."

Tears flowed down Arista's cheeks as they moved back and forth. She gripped the hands of the women tighter.

"Understood."

"Very well. Let's begin."

Jack took the chalice and found his fingers sinking deep into the sides. His attempt to gain a better hold with his other hand left both of his hands stuck to the thing. The liquid gurgled and hissed as he lifted the cup to his mouth. The stench hit Jack next, making him gag without even tasting the first drop. The liquid rose slowly from the bottom to meet his lips. Jack tossed his head back, allowing the mixture to coat his throat.

Once empty, the cup dissipated, turning to sparkling fragments in front of him. His body pulsed and throbbed, fighting the concoction as it worked its way down. He took a step, then one more, his mouth gaping open for the air that wouldn't flow. Falling to his knees, he caught sight of Belle from the corner of his eye, just before his eyelids drooped shut, and blackness surrounded him.

He didn't see Belle while she lay her hands on his chest, encouraging the muscle within him, steadying his heart from beat to beat.

Cradled in shadows, the coven joined their consciousnesses, surrounded Jack, then, as one accord, plunged into his head.

THE INTRUSION BIT into his brain. Remnants of Damond's attack from years ago floated into his conscious thought. With the limited capacity he possessed, he focused on doing nothing, giving the coven the access and time they needed. He made no attempt to block or thwart their intervention, even though it was instinctual by now to do so.

He didn't have the energy anyway. He'd faced many injuries in battle through the years, but nothing had compared with that particularly invasive mental assault from Damond. A calmness flowed through him next as he reached out to Arista and Vinique. Although he felt the touch of the entire coven, Arista and Vinique centered and focused him.

He drew a deep breath, then exhaled, letting the air escape through him, trying to relax as they delved deeper into the recesses of his mind. He trusted them. Synonymous with Whisterly, he'd accepted long ago that he couldn't have one without the rest: Arista, Vinique, and the coven. After the attack that had almost killed him long ago, it was the power of this group and Whisterly who'd healed him. His life was theirs to take, and he'd gladly give it up to bring Whisterly back.

Prickling sensations meandered their way through his brain, first one path, then another, while the search progressed. The pricks intensified, coming together in one spot as a searing pain. The chanting became indecipherable as the words blended together in a low hum. The pitch and tone from the gathering steadily grew louder and louder, the agony inside him mounting with it.

Evidently the search had ended, and the excavation had begun. Little bursts exploded inside his head. Clawing and tearing echoed within him, while pieces of his brain were dislodged in sickeningly visceral splatters of matter.

A scream left him, and sweat trickled down the side of his face, mingling with tears he didn't remember shedding. *Just take it. Take it now!*

Hands touched his shoulders, and another set slid down the sides of his cheeks.

"Almost done, Papa. Hold on. It's working."

Jack tried to speak, but his lips and tongue wouldn't work together to do so. Belle's petite hands were on him again. A sharp pain seared through his chest. "Come back to us, Mr. Jack. Miss Whisterly needs you."

Warmth seized his insides, pushing out the icy chill fingering down his spine. He gasped, taking in air deprived from his body. "Whisterly," he mumbled.

Arista stared deep into his eyes. "We're working on her, but I had to check on you." Belle and Arista shared a glance. "We almost lost you."

Jack rose, stumbling to his feet.

"Take your time," Belle said, reaching out a hand for support.

He fell against the nearest wall and swiped at his face. The commotion in the front of the room caught his gaze. "Go." Jack tipped his head forward. "I'm right behind you. The coven needs you now."

"But we need *you*," Arista whispered in Jack's ear. She nodded at Belle, then taking her hand, led her to the cluster of cloaked women where Yara lay.

Still feeling unsteady on his feet, Jack plodded along the wall, turned toward the center of the room, and wove his way into the group circling Yara. Candles fluttered around the unconscious woman as the gathering swayed in unison and chanted just under their breath. Jack stood behind this first circle, but since he was head and shoulders above the rest, he could see clearly. His hand skirted one of the hooded figures, who turned to stare at him.

Jack startled. The covering fell back, revealing patches of stringy white hair, still clinging to her scalp in places, while others were bare. Sunken eyes glared back at him, while her thin wrinkled lips continued to work, barely covering the three or four teeth in her mouth. Sagging skin covered bones that jutted from her face.

Flashes of memory returned to him—Whisterly haunting him when the corpse had taken over her body. A tremor seized him. If it hadn't been for practice like that particular event Whisterly would never have gained the experience necessary to jump into Yara's body.

Keeping his face neutral, Jack acknowledged the chanting members, then focused his attention once again on Yara. Her chest rose and fell rhythmically. The skin on her face and hands glowed. Warmth seemed to emanate from her. Maybe it was only the candles, or the connection to the group, but the pale, sickly version of the woman from the hospital appeared to be gone, at least for now.

Jack maneuvered through the tight ring of the coven, closing his eyes. *God, please bring Whisterly back to me.*

When Jack opened his eyes again, Arista somehow had the grimoire; she held it high in front of her. The open page gleamed. The old woman stood behind her; Vinique and Belle anchored the places to her left and to her right.

"Now, child, before it's too late."

Arista uncorked a small bottle and poured a reddish paste onto the page. Jack swallowed hard, swiping at a wetness dripping from his ear. A glimpse of his hand revealed his own blood, thick and sticky on his palm. He lifted his gaze to Arista, who now fanned a growing flame leaping higher and higher from the quickly disintegrating paper. The book slammed shut. It sizzled from within, and when Arista beckoned to it once again, the pages flipped to the ruined paper, and a vapor lifted above smoky ashes.

Joined by her great-grandmother, Vinique, Belle, and the coven, Arista blew the mist cloud toward Yara. Jack knelt and grasped Yara's hand. His hand smeared hers with blood, but her hand was warm. Jack moved his fingers toward her wrist, and comforted by a strong steady pulse, drew her fingers toward his lips and kissed them. The strange haze advanced farther, the chanting growing louder and louder as the mist inched toward the small space between Yara's lips.

Urged by the gathered, the magical vapor glided inside Yara. The women had closed their eyes, their chanting lowered to a murmur, while the small mass of bodies continued their rhythmic back and forth movement.

A sudden silence rippled through the air, as if in answer to the disappearing drifting mist.

Jack watched for signs of activity. Vacillating between Arista and Whisterly, he let his thoughts flow. *Did it work? When will we know?*

The crone nodded slowly, her mouth set in a straight line. "We will know very soon, Jack. We've done what we can."

Concern etched Jack's face, his gaze sweeping back to Whisterly. *Whisterly, baby, are you there? Speak to me, anything... Let us know you're there.* He kissed her hand and cupped it against his cheek. *I know you're in there somewhere. You don't give up on a fight. Ever. Damn it. Don't start now.*

Jack lifted his face toward Arista, which mirrored his own, tears flowing down her cheeks. "No, no, no, NO!" He stood and leaned over Whisterly, lightly grazing her lips with his. *Baby, I need you.*

From the depths of his brain, a crackling din ruptured through, her thoughts filling the voided space. His head still ached from the earlier invasion, but this time he welcomed the intrusion. "Oh, God."

Sinking to his knees, Jack cradled his forehead, gasping and panting for breath. "I can feel her...inside... It's really her!"

Arista nodded her agreement and ran to her father. He climbed to his feet. They both looked on with bated breath.

Whisterly's eyelids flickered open. "Jack..." She drew in a breath, and the room exploded into a cheer.

His heartbeat stuttered as her gray eyes found his. "It's really you."

A hoarse voice pushed through her throat. "Or rather some version of me. I do seem to remember I was in the process of dying." She reached out a shaky hand and lightly stroked Jack's face: his cheeks, eyes, and mouth. At the trail of blood from his ear, she stopped. She held his gaze. "It worked after all this time. My only hope was that you'd return. And you're here."

Jack nodded, a grin settling on his face. "Take it slow. You probably shouldn't talk so much at first."

Right. Arista?

Here, right here. Arista hugged her mother tight.

You look amazing, little one. She squeezed her daughter's hand. *Wait... Both of you? Jack and Arista? Together?* She glanced from one to the other, and they nodded as Jack kissed Arista's forehead. *I've dreamed of this for so long.*

We've so much to catch up on, Mother.

Whisterly's eyes glistened. *And I want to hear it all, but first I'd like to sit up.*

"Why don't you wait just a bit longer, child. Let the coven visit with you a few moments before they ascend. Arista and Jack aren't going anywhere."

Grandmother, I owe you and the coven my eternal gratitude.

The old woman cackled. "You do, but without Jack, who held your true name inside, along with the magical gifts of Arista, Vinique, and Belle, we would have failed."

Whisterly struggled up to one arm. Jack came up behind, supporting her. Her gaze scanned the circle, lingering on each coven member. "Please," she began, speaking softly, "come."

With Jack at her back and Arista on one side, Whisterly's sisters in the craft paraded their hooded figures by the mother, each speaking to her in turn. After the crowd cleared, Vinique appeared, holding Belle's hand.

"My sister, thank you. And Belle. I'm not surprised to see you here."

Belle managed a curtsy of sorts. "I'm so glad to be back, Miss Whisterly."

Whisterly smiled, making her eyes dance. "Belle, dear, you took the words right out of my mouth."

"My brother, Stephen, is here as well."

"Stephen… Belle, he did, didn't he bring the cure to Remeonites?"

Arista drew Stephen by her side. "He did, indeed, Mother, just as you envisioned."

Stephen bent slightly at the waist in a half bow. "So glad to see you again, ma'am."

"As we've said," Arista stated in a subdued tone, "we've lots to speak about, after you've regained some of your strength."

"Here, child, drink this, slowly. It will give you energy for the trip up above and to begin your new body's recovery."

"As you wish, Grandmother."

Jack lifted his chin to the wheelchair. "Just for this first journey."

She shook her head. "With your help, let me try to walk to the stairs."

CHAPTER 14

WHISTERLY LEANED HEAVILY on Jack, her arm around his neck and his securely anchored about her waist. They trudged along the cobblestones slowly, making progress nonetheless. At the steps Whisterly paused, her eyes scouring the insurmountable obstacle.

"Hold on tight," Jack said, kissing her cheek as he swept her off her feet and into his arms.

Stephen trailed behind with the wheelchair. And with the same action as before, but in reverse, Vinique and Arista disguised themselves once again as nurses transporting a patient. But the woman in the chair this time had undergone a significant transformation—she'd gone in as Yara and had come out as Whisterly, at least on the inside.

The trio made their way through the halls, with Jack following at a discrete distance. Vinique rolled her sister into the empty apartment, then helped her to her feet.

"Well, what do you think?" Vinique did a quick twirl and pointed to the view behind her. "We've been working on these rooms for a while. I'd held this space back in hope of your eventual return." Vinique paused, a brief shadow appearing to cross her face. She cleared her throat and continued. "As the healed leave the infirmary, more and more room has been allocated to living quarters, less to the sick. And with less holographic beings in use, we have additional technology for recreational use. You'll have that at your disposal as well. We've set up a display you can test later. See if you like it when you have some time to play with it. Maybe Jack can help too."

Whisterly rose and, more sure on her feet this time, crossed to the window. The window seat boasted several pillows and a blanket. She imagined herself curled up there, next to Jack, while they dreamed of a future they could finally plan. "It's absolutely breathtaking, Vinique. Almost sunrise by the looks of it. Thank you. I'll look forward to the new technology you spoke of."

"And this space is only a door away from me," Arista chimed in, moving to her mother's side. "Want to see the rest?"

"Absolutely." Whisterly allowed herself to be led through the newly decorated rooms, ending in the bedroom.

"Plenty of room in here for you…and Papa." Arista reached for her mother; the pair embraced in a silent sway.

"I'm so glad you found each other," Whisterly said as they parted.

"Me too, Mother. He's wonderful."

Whisterly's breath hitched, followed by a short gasp.

"What is it, Mother?"

A spasm shot up her spine.

Vinique and Arista supported her by the elbow, each on opposite sides.

Whisterly stared at her reflection in the mirror, then turned to face the woman she saw. "It's just going to be hard to get used to, adjusting to how I see myself, not to mention for others…you both…and Jack for starters. Oh, and explaining this, *um*…strange occurrence—that will be interesting."

"We feel you inside, sister, where you've always been, in our thoughts. And in that way, you're exactly the same." Vinique shrugged. "For the rest. It will take some time. We'll take it as it comes. And, when you're ready here in the next few days, we can talk about council impacts."

"Mother, I couldn't bring myself to throw away your things, so your clothes are hanging in the wardrobe. For now, pick out something, and I'll help you dress. Let's get you out of this hospital garb. Going forward, now that I think about it, you'll probably want new clothes."

Jack poked his head in the room. "Everything okay in here? I've brought some food." The three looked at him in silence. "What… It's almost breakfast time, right?"

"Yes, well, I could eat a bite." Arista flashed a smile for her father. "We'll be right out."

Jack laid out the food in the dining room, glancing up when the threesome entered. He swallowed hard, and Whisterly watched as multiple emotions appeared at war for control of his face.

Different, I know, huh? Yara's face, my clothes, my thoughts.

Jack shook his head and continued the silent communication even though they were at arm's length of each other. *Not at all. Yara no longer exists.*

The conversation surrounding the meal quickly disintegrated into small talk, barely worth the breath it took for the effort, the evening's activity taking a personal toll on each of them.

"Thanks, Papa. The food was just what I needed. I'm exhausted though now, and I'm headed for bed. I encourage you both to do the same." Arista raised her eyebrows. "You look awful, by the way, Papa. Rest up."

"I second that. Right behind you, Arista." Vinique kissed her sister on the temple, then stood. "Today's magic has drained me completely."

Within the span of a few minutes, the couple was alone. A slow smile crept onto Jack's face. "All alone. What shall we do?"

"I have a few thoughts on the subject."

"Do you now?" His smile lingered, reaching his eyes as he led her from the food she'd barely touched. "I do as well." He cleared his throat. "But they need to wait."

"I can feel the conflict within you. We can talk about it." Whisterly watched while his eyes filled with tears.

"I can't right now. After everything today, I couldn't get any words or thoughts out that made any sense."

Whisterly took Jack in her arms, her fingers gliding over the muscles stretched tight in his back. "It feels so good to be back here, in your arms." Whisterly lifted her chin to meet his eyes. "We can discuss everything else in bits and pieces. That might make it easier. Let's go to sleep."

"There is something I'd like to know first. You might remember now more than you would later."

Whisterly took his hand, and they walked to the bedroom and sat on the edge of the bed. "Okay. Sure. What is it?"

"Arista and I visited, *um*, Yara. Many times. Once I made the connection with her, and realized the eye color change that happened the day of your death, after that I couldn't stay away." Jack's face tightened. "Do you recall us being there, with you?"

"Eye color change?"

Jack nodded, looking at his hands. "Yara's eye color changed to gray—yours—when your body died. I was the first to notice it."

Whisterly touched the trail of Jack's blood that still stained his ear. "You've been through your own trauma because of me and today's events, Jack." She shook her head. "What they must have done to you to get my true name out of you… I'm not even sure how that part is done."

Jack sniffed. "It's very interesting. I didn't understand much of it myself. I just did as I was told. Then they took part of me and put it in you." He covered her hand with his. "That was the best part." A half smile lifted his mouth. "I like that. Me in you."

"Mother of gods, Jack, I've missed you. And to think I could have lost you today. It's unbearable."

He shook his head. "Anything's bearable, as long as you live."

"I remember you saying that I had the protection of your body, if I ever had need of it, like when Damond attacked us. Looks like I did, again."

"And it's yours, baby."

Whisterly nuzzled against Jack's chest. "In answer to your question, I felt a presence with me. It's hard to describe, since I didn't know who I was, had no connection with the living really. I remember only vague details. Comfort and peace at some times more than others. At the times I was most aware, fear is the emotion I sensed the most. Existing in total isolation is a horror unlike any other."

Jack ran his fingers through her hair and shifted her closer. "Were you aware of Yara at all?"

"Before I left my own body? No. Hers was an empty shell. That's part of the reason I had planned to jump into her body, if the need arose. I didn't want to push anyone out, and I needed someone not infected with PR 251."

"But you didn't sense Yara, the woman?"

"Not in the sense I think you mean…as a living being."

"So we didn't kill her?"

Whisterly searched his face. "No, Jack, she was dead already. Her body just didn't know it."

"I just needed to know."

"You're exhausted. Come to bed with me."

Jack tilted his head toward the chair as Whisterly lay down. He pulled a blanket over her. "Your body needs sleep. I'll be right over here."

She jolted upright again. "Oh, no you don't. Come over here."

Jack folded himself in the chair, throwing a glance at her across the short distance. "A little bossy for your first day back with the living, isn't it?"

"Maybe… Short of casting a spell, I can't force you to come to me, but I can join you." She flung back the bedcover.

He sighed, a smirk resting on his face. "Okay, you win."

"You better believe I do."

Jack tugged off his shirt, lay down on the bed, and Whisterly nestled underneath his chin. "I never thought I'd have this kind of peace again, Jack."

He buried his hand in her hair and kissed her head. "You're home, baby."

She sighed and squeezed in closer, lightly kissing his chest. "Hold me tighter, Jack."

"WHISTERLY, BABY, OPEN your eyes." Jack shook her shoulders again, harder.

She stirred, and Jack released a sigh of relief.

Whisterly's eyelids fluttered open.

He drew her into his arms and shuddered. "God, I thought you were Yara again."

They rocked back and forth. "It's okay," she whispered.

He cupped her cheek. "I don't know how I'll do this every day." He threw on his shirt that he'd tossed off over twelve hours ago. "Let's grab something to eat and take it with us."

"With us where?"

"Where we began. The basement."

"Give me a few minutes to shower to wake up. I'll be right back."

THE HALLS OF the compound were empty as the two traveled the well-known path to the basement, a light breakfast in tow. Jack withdrew his key and unlocked the door, noticing that no mist covered the opening now to the passageway like before, then heaved the door open and led Whisterly inside. Had his wife somehow created that strange fog, a manifestation of her spirit clinging to the life she so desperately fought for? In his mind it made perfect sense. The pair carefully made their way down the steps, crossed the cobblestone path, and ducked into the magic space they'd left just over twelve hours ago.

Whisterly brought light among the darkness with a mumbled spell. The familiar musty odor of the damp room mixed with the candle-wax aroma comforted Jack. This was more how he experienced this place—without the chanting and the life-giving activity of last night—just him, Whisterly, and the grimoire of course. He looked around in search of Whisterly. She returned with two blankets.

"Here. Let's sit on these. I was wondering if they were still around. When Arista was a baby, I used to lay them out so she could play while I worked."

They spread the blankets, and Jack laid out the food he brought. They ate quietly, each absorbed in thought.

"Do you think we'll have company down here?" Jack prodded. "Seems I'm not the only one you gave a key to. Between all of us who have keys and the coven above, it could get crowded pretty quickly."

"You locked the door from the inside, and I've added a spell as well. No one will be coming through from the compound. And the coven has no interest in us, not in the way you're suggesting anyway. They exist in another realm for the coven and their magic. Our daily interactions have no meaning to them, unless they're called into action."

Jack glanced at the mural, which adorned the cave's ceiling. "You mean, like last night."

"Yes." Whisterly nodded. "But at other times too when they're needed or when the crone brings them forth."

He grunted.

"You didn't bring me down here just to eat. Tell me. What's the biggest part of what's upsetting you?"

Jack released a heavy breath and put down the bread-like substance he'd been eating. "That's true. I didn't. I thought this environment might help, where we first kissed." He stood and leaned against the rocky structure, his hands fisted at his side. "It's a miracle we're even here. I know that.

"I'm grateful beyond words." He rasped out. "But now I'm not sure how to get past this…rage… I'm so angry for being left on Earth, for all the time we lost, for our son who has never known us… I thought I could yell at you and get it out." His gaze met hers, a ghost of a smile on his lips, and he shook his head. "But I can't, and it's eating me up inside."

Whisterly walked to his side. "You know all the reasons why I did what I did, even though you don't agree. I'm not sure I made all the right decisions. I felt I'd be sending you to your death if I'd brought you back then, either from the council as the accused murderer of Damond, or by Janus and his army, if you'd gone in search of our son. I did the best I could, based on my love for you. So be angry. But at least you're alive."

His jaw tightened. "Am I? I feel something less than that. My son believes me to be a monster. And I guess, for him, that description fits."

"Let's just be us for now, Jack—the two of us."

Tilting his head back, he searched for words. "We can't erase the years that have come between us. I've done other horrible things, besides deserting my son, disgusting things in the name of war."

"Are you forgetting I was there with you?"

Jack ran his hand through his hair. "No, but I did try to block some of it from you—the atrocities. Every day it's still hard to live with."

"I hurt too, Jack, for the years we've lost, for the people we could never be, and for our son I've not known. But through it all was *you*. My beacon. And without you, nothing else really matters. Remember? You said those words to me at the waterfall."

Jack rested his head against hers. "I remember. And it still holds true for me. I'm not sure though that you'll want what I've become. That old version of Jack is gone."

"I want all of you. Your hurt and anger too. Old version, new, you're still mine. We'll heal each other. We can."

Jack turned away. "You wouldn't say that if you knew…"

"If I knew what?"

Jack hung his head. "Still more… That I've been with another."

"Come here." She cupped his face in her hands, bringing it even with hers. "It's all right. I suspected as much when you blocked me out. We've been apart a long time. I'm glad you had physical comfort when you needed it. That type of intimacy is important to humans."

"Yeah, it is." He avoided her eyes and huffed out a hollow sound. "A poor substitute for you at best though. I hate myself for the betrayal. For my human weakness."

Whisterly reached for him, kissing his shoulder. "I love you. None of that matters to me. We're here *together. Now.* That's what is important."

Jack met her gaze, studying her.

"What is it? My body?"

Longing and sadness warred on his face. "No, you're beautiful. Besides, it's not your body that makes you, *you.* It's what's inside." He pressed her hand against his chest. "And I've got that back. You're here again inside me." His thumb traced the lines around her eyes. "I am glad your eyes are still gray though. I've missed them…" A ragged breath escaped him. "I just want to take in every inch of you, so I can memorize each piece, in case this isn't real… In case I open my eyes, and you're gone… In case I'm dreaming or sick or unconscious on the side of a road somewhere. I don't want to wake up again without you."

"I'm real, Jack. Would it help if I stomped on your feet? I'm not going anywhere."

Jack drew in a deep breath. "That might not be a bad idea. Dance with me."

A smile spread over her face. "I haven't gotten any better at that kind of dancing over the years, and with a different body, I'm probably worse than the last time we danced."

"*Shh*. Come here, baby."

Whisterly fell into the folds of Jack's arms and pulled his forehead to meet hers. As they swayed, each experienced in person the gaps of time they'd lost. Jack took her face in his hands, and they paused, their gazes locked. She made him ache for what he'd thought he'd lost forever. He reached for her hair and coiled it around his fingers.

"What are you waiting for, Jack? Kiss me."

"It's been almost two decades... Jesus, the things I want to do to you..."

"Show me."

He bowed his head. "No. You still don't understand. I'm different... I feel like a caged animal," he whispered.

She lifted his chin, meeting his gaze. "So set it free. I want all of you... Here. It's easy." She kissed along his neck and softly bit his earlobe, then pressed her lips against his, gently caressing. Leaning back, she searched his eyes, waiting. "There. Do you remember?"

His heart hammered loudly in his chest, his breath leaving him in short puffs of air, and a frantic desire surged through him. "God, I need you." His mouth crushed against hers as he lifted her, her legs circling his waist. Jack slammed them against the wall, putting out his arm to keep from hitting Whisterly with the full force of his weight. She moaned, moving against him, drawing their bodies closer as Jack ravaged her neck with a trail of kisses, then bit her exposed shoulder.

The pair slid to the floor. Whisterly yanked Jack's shirt over his head. Jack felt Whisterly's smile reverberate through his thoughts, creating a tingling sensation that traveled the length of his body.

Now, clothes no longer an obstacle, her hands explored the taut muscles of his chest and inched below his waist.

He relieved his wife of the remainder of her clothing. "All the waiting… All the dreaming," he choked out, his voice hoarse in her ear. "The wanting …"

"It's over, Jack. I'm here."

"No. It'll never be over," he murmured. "All that time… Gone… I'll never have enough." Jack's mouth traveled over her skin, kissing, tasting. As a tremor coursed through her, Jack moaned and pulled her swiftly to him.

"Gods, yes, Jack… I've missed you," she gasped. Her hands scaled down the length of his spine. A spasm sparked, rocking her in his arms.

He tightened his grip on her, his breath heaving, then his body went slack, his hands clinging to her. *Baby…*

Whisterly stroked his cheek, their bodies still trembling.

"I never thought I'd have this again. You. Our minds and bodies as one." He stared into the depth of her eyes. "My God, Whisterly, you've saved me."

WHISTERLY DOSED ON Jack's chest. He stroked her hair, content for the moment just to hold her. It all still felt like an illusion, like any minute he'd wake up back on Earth, all this recent time on Remeon only a horrible trick of his mind. Something similar had happened before, during his despair. During the war.

She'd nestled herself in his thoughts. He'd missed this part of her most of all. Sharing what no one else on Earth had ever experienced. A piece of her soul. When Whisterly's body had died, his head had been like a static empty cavity. A void. He'd been sure that night, when he'd visited Harry, that Jack would finally put an end to it all. Then again at the waterfall—it would have been so easy… Life was empty without the best part of himself? *Her.*

Is it strange that her body against mine is unfamiliar yet not at the same time? As her thoughts wrestle with the maze of my mind, they bring rest, calming the storm within me.

Jack pressed a kiss to her forehead and resettled Whisterly beside him. She wrinkled her nose in her sleep, and he could feel her thoughts shifting and churning. She would wake soon. The cover he'd pulled over them fluffed into the air, then floated back down. A little puff of warm air created from their mingled body heat sought escape, hitting his face. He tunneled deeper, pulling her down also, relishing in their solitude. *Let's try this again. Slowly this time.*

"*Mmmm…*" Her hand drifted lazily down his chest.

Jack's eyes roamed her body while he explored, delighting in her eagerness under his touch. He'd meant what he had said earlier. Funny, it didn't matter much that her appearance wasn't the same, not to him anyway. Because what made Whisterly his was what was deep inside her, and he already possessed her essence completely. This was just her facade for now. Delicious and beautiful, but she was so much more. When her shudder echoed through him, Jack drew her to him once again. *Don't try to send me away again. I'm not leaving without you. Ever… I'll die first.*

He heard her sigh, her breath warm against his ear. *Jack…* She found his lips.

He groaned in her mouth. *Baby.*

He possessed her soul, and she, his. This must be as close as he'd get to heaven this side of Earth or Remeon. He closed his eyes, cherishing these moments with her. Whisterly snuggled closer in his arms. Tucking her under his chin, he released a pent-up breath, and at peace for the first time in recent history, he drifted to sleep.

Jack woke to Whisterly scarfing down the remainder of the food he'd brought with him. "Hungry?"

She licked her fingers and broke off a bite for him. "Yes, and this isn't enough."

He perched himself up on an elbow and broke out into a broad grin. "That's a good sign. Let's head back. We'll stop for more food on the way. You'll need your strength." Jack winked at her, and the two hastily dressed.

The early morning greeted them as they closed the wooden door to the basement behind them. After stopping at the gathering area for more food, they arrived at their quarters.

"It seems we've missed another whole day."

A playful smile crossed her lips. "I'm sure the day did fine without us."

"Let's have a shower, eat, and then figure out the new holographic technology you've got in there. Maybe we can stay awake and get off this vampire schedule."

Her eyebrows rose. "I guess we'll need to return to real life eventually." She peered at his neck, fingering her way up and down one side.

"Yes. It's still there. Only a small scar now. Healed nicely, thanks to your care."

A darkness appeared to shroud her face. "I learned a lot that day. But I hate the fact that I attacked you, leaving you with that horrible bite."

"Without that first experience, you'd never have learned to do what you did, jump into another body to survive. And we wouldn't be standing here, now, together."

Whisterly kissed the barely visible scar, grasped his hand, and they walked to the shower.

An hour later, showered and towel-dried, Jack sniffed at the clothes he'd thrown into the corner the previous day. They reeked of smoke and sweat and were covered in bloodstains. Whisterly, dressed already, laid out the food on the bed. "What would you say to another picnic?"

"Sounds good. I need to get my clothes though." He chuckled. "It's not like I've got a lot. But I do need something clean to put on." He slid the dirty shirt back on, a suiting match for his dirty pants temporarily. "Be right back, baby."

Jack hustled through the halls to his room. Hoping that he'd not wake Stephen, Jack crept inside and eased the door shut. Throwing off his dirty clothes again and shoving them in his bag, he redressed and stowed in his pocket the small box he'd brought with him from Earth, along with Sam's dog tags that Vinique had returned to him.

On the desk, he spotted the book Arista had given him, puzzled how it got back here, and grabbed that along with the remainder of his clothes and filled his bag.

Stephen sat up, rubbing at his eyes. "Oh, hi, Jack. I was wondering when you might show up."

"Sorry to wake you. I'll be outta here in no time."

Stephen shrugged. "No rush. Don't forget that cool book. Arista gave it to me to leave for you, when you came back for your things. Said you left it in the hospital room."

Jack nodded, remembering. "Ah, I guess I did... A lot happened that day. Must have left it in the confusion." Jack spotted Whisterly's letters to Arista and added them to his bag. Scanning the room, he checked for anything else important he may have forgotten.

"Hey, I didn't get to say anything to you the other night. But I'm happy for you and Whisterly. Glad things are working out and that you're both all right."

Jack crossed the room and shook Stephen's hand. "Thank you. Appears to be the case, doesn't it? I'll see you around."

"Jack, hold up a minute."

"Sure. What is it?"

"Uh, do you think we... I mean, do you think you'd still have time for us to..."

"Anytime. Just let me know when the holographic suite is calling for you, and I'll be there."

"Thanks, Jack."

He lifted his chin in a clipped nod. "You bet."

JACK TOOK HIS time on the short walk back to his new quarters; the small box poking his leg, reminding him of its presence with each step. *Where do we go from here? And what's my place in it?*

When he returned, Whisterly had turned on the new device Arista had had installed.

Jack's eyes widened as he took in the technology from their bedroom door. "You started without me."

"No, not really. I just turned it on." She patted the space beside her on the bed. "Come see."

Jack grabbed a bite from the spread Whisterly had arranged at the bottom of the bed. "That's pretty incredible."

"Isn't it amazing? I dimmed the lights so we could see it better."

He perched himself against the back of the bed and guided Whisterly in front of him, wrapping his arms around her waist. She leaned back against him. "Tell me about it."

"Well, this is our solar system. Remeon is just there. See?" She pointed. "And our two moons."

Jack sucked in his breath. "Wow… Can you see Earth with that thing also?"

"I believe so. Should be able to display any planet we've visited and plotted maps for by speaking or keying in a site or destination." Whisterly typed *Earth* into the console.

"Perfect, almost like we're looking down from above." Basking in the glow of his home planet, Jack dug into his pants pocket and pulled out two items.

"What do you have there?"

"Close your eyes." Jack laid Sam's dog tags around Whisterly's neck, then kissed her nape. "Back where they belong."

Whisterly felt the cool bumpy metal underneath her fingers. "Sam's dog tags—I was wondering what happened to these. I assumed Arista had them."

"No, Vinique returned them to me when I came back. I'd planned to give the set to Arista though. But now they're yours again."

"Oh, Jack—" Whisterly turned around and faced a small box open before her. "What's that? It's beautiful…"

Jack leaned in and pressed his lips to hers, catching her breathless. "It's the ring I've wanted to give to you for as long as I can remember." He paused, trying to gauge her reaction. "Well, say something. Do you like it?"

Her eyes sparkled, and she threw her arms around his neck. "Like it? It's wonderful. Put it on me!" She extended a shaky hand, and Jack glided it over her finger. Twisting her hand from side to side in front of her face, she gazed at the diamond from all angles. "I love it."

"I can't believe, after all these years, I can finally put it on your finger." Jack raised her hand to his lips and kissed it. "You're mine, Whisterly, until the end of time itself."

She gazed into Jack's eyes and stroked his cheek. "I *am* yours, Jack Livingston. I'm so glad you've put up with me."

"I'm not convinced," he teased, a wicked smile sliding across his mouth.

"Then I've got work to do," she warned, her eyes gleaming as she pushed him playfully against the bed.

God, was this how it felt to be truly happy? He'd forgotten—tucked away that essence of joy that was the two of them, burying it deep so the scorching pain wouldn't rise to the surface in the long years of her physical absence. Warmth emanated from his chest. Experiencing her love again had brought him full circle, closing a wound that had been slashed open for so long he'd gotten used to the horrible festering ache, the driving need.

No more.

His gaze caressed her body. Burying his hand in her hair, he pulled back, giving him full access. "Better," he murmured, kissing a path along her neck. "I need so much more of you Baby."

"Jack..."

He cupped her face and took her mouth slow and deep, letting the heat and telepathic sensations spool between them. "It's a new beginning for us. Let's think about nothing else for now."

CHAPTER 15

SIMON LEANED BACK in his chair, trying to focus on the conversation before him. Travis's mouth was moving, going on about the training drills they'd all participated in. He and Errol had done well arranging and carrying out the maneuvers. The men were in good shape. Watching from the sidelines, Simon had ascertained whose combat abilities were improving and who needed remedial work.

Only afterward, as he had a conversation with Errol, did the impact hit. Not wanting to have another episode, this time in front of the men, he'd sent them all ahead. Simon chose a different path and tramped deeper into the forest.

Someone or something bid him to them. He'd had no choice in the matter and had no knowledge as to how to deny them access to his presence. This summoning had been different, unlike the previous callings; still, he wanted a say in the matter. Even now trying to decipher it all was a muddled mess. The hooded beings, the old woman, Jack, Arista, Vinique, Belle, even Stephen had been there.

When the old woman pulled him forth, it had felt true and real in a sense that nothing else had in his entire life. Then the moment passed. And he'd been back with his men, the scent of fire and blood from the summoned event still mingling with his clothes and hair, dampness clinging to his skin.

Closing his eyes, he breathed deeply, willing the recent memory back to him, hoping to digest it slowly this time. His vision clouded. The aroma of the place lured him in. Dizzy from his efforts, he sank to a log, and, when the fuzziness cleared, he could view the spectacle clearly. Only the woman prone in middle of the group baffled him. Who was she?

He watched, silently taking in every word. Then he heard "Use it, and bring Whisterly back." *What? How in the gods of the universe could it be possible?*

Arista—supported by Vinique, Belle, the old woman, and the hooded women—performed spell after spell, held together in a trance. The concoction bubbled under his nose, and he gagged, bending over and retching in the grass. Gathering himself again, he viewed Belle attending Jack, who'd swallowed the nasty stuff.

The droning of the women echoed in his ears, punctuated here and there by the voices of Arista and the crone. Simon found he couldn't stop his body from moving back and forth, joined under the spell and power of the witches. Jack rose and moved toward the unknown woman in the center of the room.

The din rose to a chillingly high pitch. Simon fought against the pounding; as he did so, a convulsion struck, radiating down his spine. He sucked in a breath and held it, unwilling to stop the vision from unfolding, needing to see the end. Sweat dripped from his forehead, and his chest tightened, aching for air.

Then, silence.

Jack kissed the woman. She woke... It was Whisterly? How could she be *alive?*

This power. The ability to bring back the dead. Would it be his as well? Somehow?

Think of it... All that I could do with this...

He yanked at his collar, watching her rise with aid. *She didn't look like Whisterly...*

Simon attempted to reach Whisterly's thoughts, although he knew it to be next to impossible, at least it used to be. Still, just the same—worth a try. Maybe, with time and the new information at his disposal… a path to his mother would reveal itself.

The chaos in his mind reached a fevered buzz. He had to concentrate, but it was coming at him too fast. Simon could control it better if nothing else interfered with his thoughts. Clearly he was losing the battle. Bits and pieces of the teachings in his head sprung to life, unbidden. The trees swayed, haughty in their rough dance, spiraling, wrenching back and forth even in the unmoving air. Darkness and light alternated, casting shadows unfit for the advancing evening. The ground cracked under his feet, and the earth rumbled, heaving a large groan. He resettled in a new position.

Make it stop.

The scene of Whisterly, Jack, Arista, and the witch gathering disappeared. Suddenly a fire erupted, slowly oozing from his fingertips. He bent down, rubbing his hands in the dirt, but instead of smothering the flames, they burned hotter. Tongues of red, yellow, and blue streaked high, catching limbs and leaves alike.

Fanned from the wind still billowing through the small copse, the forest burned fast. Smoky ash scorched his throat and seared his nose. Simon blocked the images parading through his mind and reached instinctively for only one thought. *Rain.* He delved deep, recalling a memory of being trapped in a heavy thunderstorm as a child, Mila urging him through the downpour to the safety of the Night Dwellers' cave.

He shut his eyes tight and willed the storm to him. First one drop, then another. He clinched his fists by his side…then tighter… his nails biting deep into his skin. Beads of blood trickled from his hands to the ground, and the sky opened up, engulfing him in a deluge.

Simon fell to his knees and lifted his face skyward, panting, relief sliding from him along with the torrents of rain. Dazed, he surveyed the damage he'd caused, a smoke-filled mist rising around him. He gasped in bursts of breath. The potential of these new abilities energized him. He'd be unstoppable if the sloppiness of his learning improved.

Again, the private society he'd just witnessed bringing Whisterly back to life churned his thoughts. Gods… Someone, somewhere could be encouraged to help him. Couldn't they? Everyone wants something. Leaning back with only the sky before him, he issued a silent plea.

Help me!

Burning everything in sight—what would be next? The power itself was less scary than its clumsy use. A sneer twisted Simon's mouth. Mother, Father, and Sister, aren't we just one big happy family…

"Commander!"

"Here. I'm here, Travis." Simon rose slowly, trying to keep his balance.

"Sir, are you all right?"

Simon watched as Travis scanned the evening sky with apparent dread. Simon swallowed a laugh. "I am," he managed. "Everyone accounted for? No injuries I trust?"

"Uh, no, sir. I mean, besides you, sir."

Simon assessed how he must look to Travis. Angry blisters flared on his fingertips; sooty ash covered his forearms, and his feet were bare. Torn clothes stuck to his body, drops of blood still seeping from his palms. *Disheveled* didn't begin to cover it. "Believe me. It looks worse than it is."

Travis raised his eyebrows in what must have been sheer disbelief. "Any idea how this phenomenon occurred, sir?"

"No." Simon met his eyes. "Not a clue."

"I don't mind confiding that what happened spooked the troops. We've not seen anything like this happen, ever." He slowly walked alongside his commander.

"Agreed. But it's over now. Try not to make too much of it, and the men will follow your lead."

"Do you think it's the work of the Day Watchers?"

Simon shrugged. "I wouldn't doubt it one bit."

The pair neared the cave entrance. "May I get you anything, Commander?"

"No. Let me know if any further disturbances arise though and inform the men all is well."

Travis nodded. "I'll see to it."

Lesson learned. Don't kill yourself while learning your enemy's craft, or the sweet revenge you've been planning will be enjoyed by another.

KIX RETIRED TO his quarters for the evening, although the night was young. Since midday a worsening unease had plagued his thoughts, and all things considered, he believed it best to be alone. Sometimes this foreboding he experienced meant nothing, but occasionally, well… entirely the opposite was true.

He flipped on the holographic monitor and dimmed the lights. Earth shone before him, the object of his study for much of his adult life. Perhaps feigning ignorance weighed on him more now, or maybe the boldness of the time freed some of his inhibitions.

Ever since he could remember, he'd been taught to deny his humanity, while still learning all about Earth's society. With the tools at his disposal, the task hadn't been difficult. Here and there, he'd helped where he could.

Unlike the rest of Remeon, he knew Jack hadn't been the first human to come and stay, to try and make a life—Kix's father had.

Covering up the deception had been easy with the skills his father possessed and which had been passed down to him. Before his father's death, Kix's parents had led a full life, in Earthly terms anyway. And continuing to fulfill his father's mission had been

Kix's lifelong work, that and filling a seat on the Remeon ruling council.

His counterparts on Earth thrived on the intelligence he forwarded. The United States' space program hadn't yet formally begun, but it would soon, most likely helped along by his tidbits of communication. In exchange, his people on Earth enjoyed their relative freedom. It was a small sacrifice really, so that their secret order would survive. Over the centuries Earth's history had shown how harshly they'd dealt with his kind. Now he provided a checks-and-balance, as his father had begun before him.

Igni.

A small light sputtered to life between his fingers. He twisted the glowing fragments into a ball and set it on the table beside him. Last night he'd been disappointed when he'd not finished his study. His latest intel on Jack Livingston had been a long time coming and its reading—fascinating. Tracking him from his early years until now had been only one of Kix's many assignments.

The man had a keen sense of people. Kix would give him that. A more brilliant military mind he'd never seen. Too bad Jack's timing to return had been so awful. Approaching him again might help, easing him into the idea that Kix mating with Arista would be best for all. But, if not, there were other means. Relatively speaking, a small price to pay.

Without Kix's help, Jack would have been dead before his illustrious military career had even began. Surely he'd see reason.

Far away a beckoning tugged at the council member's core. Faint at first, then undeniably formidable. He closed his eyes, and his mind sought the source.

Simon...

A wry smile split his lips. *What an interesting, unexpected development...*

WHISTERLY DRANK IN the vision before her. Dappled bits of sun coursed over the muscles of Jack's shoulder, bathing his skin in warmth and light. Scars littered his upper torso. Upon closer inspection, some had faded to a dull gray, the change in skin color barely noticeable; others, more recently borne, burrowed deeper into his skin, still an angry reminder of combat—or maybe a battle of another kind.

His body had transformed in the years they'd physically been apart. A fully grown man when she'd sent him through the portal for the last time, he'd been lean from repeated testing and his time in a coma, but strong nevertheless. Now older, his muscles rippled beneath her fingers, refined from years of hard work and meticulous training for combat, then honed from the battles themselves.

She leaned against him, letting his body heat mingle with hers, planting soft kisses up the length of his arm, then nipped at his neck, before starting down the center of his chest. Dog tags hung around his neck, along with his key to the basement. Had he been wearing these dog tags yesterday? She flipped them over, examining and comparing them to her set—Sam's. A lighter sheen reflected from the ones she wore. His sparkled brighter and, of course, bore Jack's name.

His eyes opened, finding hers.

Her fingertips lingered on the muscles of his chest, tracing small circles on her way down his torso.

"You're going to make me late to meet Stephen, Mrs. Livingston," he murmured in her ear, his voice still thick with sleep.

"Really?" Her fingers continued their downward trek, her nails lightly grazing his skin. "Is that a problem? Being a few minutes late?"

The corner of his mouth lifted in an easy smile. "It is. I'm not late. Ever."

"*Mmm.*" Her lips brushed against his. "You could take your chances that I'll still be waiting here for you when you return, but, that's not likely…"

"Or I could communicate to Stephen to meet up an hour from now instead." He pressed their bodies together, the rough skin of his hands stroking the length of her spine, his breath hot in her ear. "The interruption is taken care of," he said, slowly tasting her neck.

"An hour?" she whispered. "That might just do." She bit his bottom lip, and he groaned, pulling her on top of him, their fingers lacing. Her teeth raked along his shoulder, sending a shudder pulsing through him, tingling her own skin as the sensation passed between their thoughts. *Then again, maybe not.*

Baby…

He clutched her, a raw longing reflected in the deep blue pools of his eyes, drawing her in. She ached with her need for him. Maneuvering still lower, she arched one brow. "Lie still."

His thumb trailed across her lips. He shivered, and his hand fisted in her hair.

My turn, Jack. The hour is mine.

In the end, Jack had kept his reputation intact, leaving her minutes before his rescheduled time with Stephen. Her smile warmed her insides. Before he'd left, he'd reclaimed a portion of the hour to use on his own terms. Heat rose to her cheeks. How had she been without him all these years?

Before long her daughter would be joining her. Whisterly had planned to make Jack some coffee before he left. But their time had been better spent. Still, Arista had learned to make her father coffee—both he and Stephen thrived on it. So Whisterly would learn, practicing first on her little one.

She rummaged through the kitchen, found a pot and the coffee she'd asked Jack to pick up yesterday. The short preparation done, she flicked on the heat source, then left the kitchen to find something to wear.

The brew's aroma filled her chambers, bubbling and gurgling as she dressed. It hadn't been too difficult. But she'd reserve judgment until they'd taste-tested it.

Mother, open our adjoining door.

Coming, little one.

Whisterly twisted the lever, grateful for the added privacy the double doors gave them both, allowing mother and daughter to be close but still maintaining their separateness. Arista, as the reigning council chair, had guards protecting her rooms also, but this additional detail aided in her ease of movement, and ultimately in access to her mother.

The council.

Whisterly had not given it much thought since her return to the living. Naturally her attention had been focused on Jack and Arista. The past few days had given her a needed respite, swept up in the reunion with her love and their daughter. Did she want to return as the council chair, as something less maybe? Or not at all, relinquishing control to her daughter, who, although young, appeared to have run things well in Whisterly's absence.

She let her mind drift to the possibility of returning. The thought lit a desire deep within her core. Bringing calm from chaos, Whisterly excelled at it, but she possessed other talents as well. This passage of power from her daughter back to her would bring many difficulties. The first and largest hurdle, her physical appearance, after her confirmed death, which might dissolve the ruling body into turmoil.

With a well-thought-out strategy, even this could be overcome. They could ease the council into an understanding that would work for them and Remeonites as a whole, eventually. But now, her life with Jack and their time together needed priority. Their love and desire for a life together had been the reason for every decision she'd made, even those which Jack had vehemently disagreed with. Clearly, as a couple, they still had work to do.

Whisterly embraced Arista, kissing her cheek before pulling away and studying her face. Lines stretched across her daughter's forehead and bunched around the corners of her eyes, the latter accompanied with small bags underneath. She appeared tired but not overwhelmingly so. Maybe the decision should be left totally up to her daughter.

Arista and Vinique made a tenacious team. And little Belle… Whisterly had felt her power when they'd met. Now Belle had proven her strength, obtained from a most unlikely source. Her actions during the reintegration process had most likely saved Jack. The youngster's future held so many possibilities.

"Coffee? You've inspired me to learn how to make it," Whisterly said, a smile lingering in her voice. "Personally, I'd rather have tea, but I have a sinking suspicion I'll be drinking more coffee going forward."

"I'd love some. Let me get it for us."

Arista returned, carrying a small platter with two cups of steaming-hot coffee, plus cream and sugar.

"Thank you, dear." Whisterly accepted her cup and took a drink, scrunching her nose afterward, pondering the liquid.

"Try a little cream. You'll appreciate the flavor more."

Whisterly doctored her drink, then, after another sip, nodded in appreciation. "*Mmm.* Pretty good… And I love the aroma." Whisterly set down her cup and grasped her daughter's hand. "I'm so glad you and your father have met and are enjoying each other's company."

Arista's eyes twinkled, immediately filling with tears. "Papa's incredible. I can see what drew you toward him." She took a deep breath, gaining back control. "I just wish we'd known each other sooner."

Whisterly squeezed her daughter's hand. "I know, and I'm sorry. With his life at stake, I erred on the side of abundant caution, in the hope he could return to us one day." Whisterly pulled her gaze from her daughter's. "I'm fairly certain that wasn't the worst shock you had from my letters."

"No, but it was the best so far." Arista took a deep drink, eyeing her mother from over the rim. "Only through two and parts of several more. The impact from the first two made me slow down. I wanted to try to understand your reasoning. I thought, with more reflection and care, I could assimilate the contents better."

"And?"

Arista shrugged, replacing her cup. "After what Simon did to Stephen, I don't believe I could ever think of him as a brother." A shadow passed over her eyes. "He disgusts me."

Whisterly lowered her voice. "He's never had the love that you've had, little one. Still, you'll always share a blood connection. Perhaps one day we could work toward a reconciliation."

Arista's forehead contorted, and her mouth straightened into a hard line. "I doubt I'll want to participate in that, Mother, but maybe, one day, I'll tolerate him better." She cleared her throat and blinked away tears. "I mated with Stephen," she blurted out, "completely without his knowledge. And I think I'm only just beginning to understand some of the reasons you made the decisions you did."

"Your father told me." Whisterly took her cup and walked to the window. Watching the activity unfold below, she sipped slowly, letting the warm liquid inch through her. "I, unlike most people, uniquely understand at least some of your reasons for doing so." She reached out a hand to her daughter in invitation.

Swiping at her eyes, Arista joined her mother.

"You've accomplished so much already, little one. The night I was betrayed, you, Vinique, and Belle gained Stephen's release from the Night Dwellers, which ultimately led to the cure being finalized, healing our people. It's a future we've dreamed of for so long."

"One that you pioneered, Mother. I was only finishing what you could not."

Whisterly flashed a wry smile at her daughter. "*Only*, my ass. How about planning my return after just recently learning of your uncommon bloodline?"

Arista's mouth gaped open. "Without Papa and Vinique, I'd have been lost."

"Papa? How did he help?"

"His letter to me about my identity as a witch… He read it to me, in person, the one he'd written to me years ago. He came at just the time I needed it." Tears spilled down her cheeks.

"Gods, I'd almost forgotten about those. I'm glad you found them."

"Vinique got them to me."

Whisterly pulled her daughter to her breast, and they rocked together.

"Mother, I don't want to be without him ever again."

A tendril of unease crept up Whisterly's spine. "I know, little one. Me neither."

"YOU'VE IMPROVED A lot, Stephen. The extra practice is doing you good."

Stephen wiped the sweat from his forehead, a smile stretching on his face. "Thanks."

"I haven't seen you wear your braces in several days, and you worked out today without them. Feel okay?"

"Yeah. I haven't worn them in a while. I'd say I was done with them, but I'm pretty sure that's not the case. For now anyway, it feels good to be free of them."

"Well done." Jack slapped Stephen on the back. "I'm stopping in here for a drink. Do you want to join me?"

Stephen glanced at the gathering area. "Nah. I'll pass. Thanks anyway. You wore me out. I'm going to head back."

"All right. Catch you later."

Jack veered toward the mass of people. Even though he preferred solitude, the gathering area had a way of drawing him in. Fractured light poured in from the tall windows, dousing the Remeonites and the large room with its rays. Trees branches bent, swaying with the crowds' movement between the gregarious groups, their strategic positions giving the illusion of privacy. Marveling at how a telepathic society could be so noisy, Jack grabbed a bite and a drink and scanned the space for a secluded corner.

His gaze trailed the perimeter, then drew deeper in as he focused on the details of his craft: the planes, angles, the symmetry; and what a feat it must have been to bring them all together. His thoughts delved into the minutiae of all that held the structure together. Yes…he nodded appraisingly, I could replicate something like this on Earth, except on a much smaller scale.

Folding himself into a chair bathed in the light, he sighed. The trees stretched high above him, the tall windows drinking in the sun, infusing the entire room with its warmth. Tilting his head back, he allowed a pleasing dizziness to wash over his skin, willing the heat to spread deep inside his body. The buzz of conversation fell away around him. Thoughts of his house tucked away in the woods, Daniel, and Harry popped into his mind. God, how he missed them.

His mind drifted further, lulled by the peace that pulsed through his blood.

Daniel ran on a path to intercept him. "Papa, come quick!"

Jack had gone to his son, who'd whispered in his ear, "*Shh*. Don't scare them away."

Daniel warily eyed the gun at Jack's side.

Jack took his son's hand and let him guide them, weaving in and out of the brush, ducking past low-hanging limbs. Daniel pointed ahead, beyond a small copse of trees. A doe and its fawn chewed leaves from a nearby bush.

"Watch them, son," Jack murmured under his breath. "Study their reactions." Seconds later the doe's ears pricked back, her head moving as she frantically scanned for predators. "She knows we're here."

A larger deer, a buck, strutted through the underbrush, joining the other two, cautiously sniffing the air.

Jack glanced toward Daniel. "You'll not have long. Do you want to take a shot?"

A horror-filled look filled his son's eyes. "No, Papa. He's their daddy, isn't he?"

The doe and fawn scampered away; the buck chuffed air, raised his head high, and stomped his hoof before following its mate. The moment slipped away.

"I suppose he is, son. But we're hunters, remember?"

Daniel bobbed his head. "I guess, but they're a family, and we're not that hungry."

Jack scoffed and ruffled his son's curls. "Not yet anyway. What would you like to hunt, if not deer?" He slowed his pace as he walked so Daniel could keep up.

Daniel shrugged. "I don't want to fight the animals, unless they're fighting me."

Jack paused, leaned his weapon against a tree, and led his son to his knee. "I see." His gaze met his son's wide-eyed stare. "We might starve if everyone thought that way, son."

He giggled, the solemn lines of his face bending into a smile. "You wouldn't let that happen."

Jack lowered his head, hiding his own expression, stood, and grabbed his gun. "Let's set up some target practice then."

"Sure, Papa." Daniel squirmed away and ran ahead, dried leaves crunching under his feet, freed from the need to be quiet.

"Maybe another day for your first deer…"

Jack's chest tightened at the memory. He reached out, connected with Harry.

Harry, you'll never guess where I am. Well, maybe you will…

Jack. How are you? And you're in the gathering area… I've still got it.

I'm…healing… You?

I couldn't be happier for you both, Jack. Reading your thoughts…it's been nothing short of a miracle. You and Whisterly, you've proven you're capable of absolutely anything.

Maybe. That's yet to be seen. She is pretty much perfect though.

I'll bet so. Daniel is great. We talk about you every day. But don't worry about him. He's comfortable and happy, knowing that you'll be home soon.

Good to hear. He's been on my mind today. What else, Harry? You're hiding something.

Any clue when you'll be back? I'd rather tell you in person.

No. None. So spill it.

Okay. Well, we'll have a little one of our own in about seven months. I'm so happy I don't know what to do with myself.

Jack stood up, as if he could see Harry across the room, almost toppling the table at his knees. *That's great, Harry! Wonderful news, man.*

Isn't it? Not the same without you here to celebrate though.

Give Maggie a kiss from me. And Daniel too. Tell him that I love him. And tell him that I miss him. Tell him…

I know, Jack. I will. Be safe. And I mean that. I worry about you. Somehow I think I'd feel better about things if I were there with you too.

We've been through this, but thanks. I wouldn't trust Daniel to anyone else but you two.

Yeah, I know. He needs you too. So take care. Know your son is well. And come back soon. Oh, think about bringing that wife of yours… Maybe she'd like to visit Earth or even stay for a while.

Wouldn't that be something?

It would, indeed.

Congratulations again. I can't wait to meet the little guy—or girl. I'll talk to you again soon, Harry.

Jack choked back tears, situating himself again in his seat. *My Harry's gonna be a dad…*

His thoughts returned to Daniel and their life together. *Damn, the kid grows so fast. He'll probably be a foot taller when—*

A shadow edged over the table.

Jack turned.

"Well, we meet again. Do you have another excuse to leave, or may I join you this time?"

Shit. Jack gestured to the chair beside him. "Suit yourself, but I won't be staying long."

Kix thrust out his hand, and Jack reached out automatically, his mind searching for an exit. Jack froze and studied their hands still clasped together, then lifted his gaze to meet Kix's.

"So now have I gotten your attention, Jack?"

Jack's mouth fell to a thin line, his thoughts racing. "You have."

Kix settled in his seat, the man's smug smile revealing his enjoyment in Jack's silence. The possibilities quickly tallied before him. Only one made any kind of sense, with his admittedly limited knowledge base of Kix.

"I can see you're getting there, Jack."

A flash of understanding wrenched at his core. The handshake wouldn't have startled him so much on Earth. Occasionally he met men and didn't know they were Freemasons. Recognizing their bond then, the relationship would move forward on a shared knowledge base, steeped in history and based on faith in a supreme being. It was their way.

Here Jack kept his defenses high, his mind working furiously behind them. His gaze met the council member's. "How? Or were you just going to drop this on me and leave me to wonder?"

"Well, no, of course not. It is what it is. An introduction. However, what I have to speak with you about is much bigger than this one common bond we share."

Jack raised his brows. "An Earthly bond…"

"We have more in common than you could possibly know, yet more differences than you'd ever imagine."

"You seem to enjoy speaking in riddles. If you want to talk, then do so. As I said, I have somewhere I need to be." Jack scooted back his chair and straightened, hoping to call the man's bluff—if, indeed, it was that—or maybe Kix only sought information and was baiting Jack. Either way he needed to be careful.

"Sure, let's cut to the heart of the matter."

Jack towered over him, waiting.

"I have information on your son, Simon. Now, before we continue, we should go somewhere more discreet. Follow me."

CHAPTER 16

THE MAN'S EYES held something Jack couldn't reconcile, and Kix's mind was unreadable as well. Unlike with their first meeting when Jack had been a teenager, his telepathy skills were up to the task, and still nothing. Following Kix down several corridors, Jack poked his head left, then right, and realized that he personally didn't recall ever being in this section of the compound. "Your chambers are somewhat out of the way, aren't they?"

"I suppose, but, like you, I prefer privacy, when it can be had."

Kix halted before a door. Jack swore he caught a familiar hand motion.

"*Igni.*"

He paused behind the man. *What was that?*

"Well, Jack, I suppose when I'm finished, I'll have laid all my cards on the table, so to speak. It'll be your move."

"I guess we'll see."

He pointed to several chairs. "Sit, Jack, please."

Jack's gaze swept the perimeter of the room. Books filled tall shelves. Drawn to their mystery, he fought the urge to investigate.

"No, please, take a look. You might see some old friends."

Jack quickly spotted two novels he knew well, *All Quiet on the Western Front* and *Farewell to Arms*. Kix's library appeared to contain books from Earth—many, as a matter of fact. Joining those two books were *Gone with the Wind, Brave New World,* and *The*

Grapes of Wrath. His mind strained, willing this to make some kind of sense.

Kix chuckled. "As you might have surmised by now, Arista is not the first Remeonite with mixed blood."

A combination of dirty clothes, alcohol, and the mustiness of old books brought an interesting aroma to the room. With no natural light and little air movement, Kix's chambers felt tight, even though they were quite spacious.

Jack scrutinized the man. It was true; Kix had saved Jack and Harry that day on the gun range when Damond had attacked them both. Kix's well-timed diversion broke Damond's hold on Jack, giving Harry the time he needed to get Jack away. Then later Kix had helped Vinique and Whisterly investigate the murder charge against Jack, eventually clearing his name, after Jack's departure.

Did Whisterly know of Kix's parentage? And if so, why hadn't she told Jack over the years? Their daily conversations had often included her council business.

"My father was a Freemason. A Remeonite sweep brought him here, just like you, but much longer ago. Garth was his name. He met and fell in love with my mother, a Remeonite, Jessilla. I lost her to PR 251 longer ago than I care to remember and then my father to old age. He lived longer than most from Earth though, since he was a warlock."

Jack choked on his own spit, then coughed.

"Are you all right? How about a drink?"

"Yes, I guess it's the dust from the books."

"Here. A bit more light for you."

Jack looked on as flames burst from the man's fingers. After throwing the hot mass in a container, a warm glow permeated throughout the room. Jack could see more clearly, his eyes drawn now to haphazard items that lay strewn about the room, appearing to be works in progress; of what, Jack couldn't tell.

Kix lifted a bottle of Jim Beam in the air. "You'll be familiar with this." He filled two glasses, gave Jack his, and took his own to a large overstuffed chair, which had the appearance of being old but comfortable.

Jack knocked back his drink and set down the glass.

"Feel free to help yourself to another."

"Don't mind if I do. Thanks."

"Me and my family deal in intelligence. Over the years, this, uh, service, bought my father's safety from those who would have harmed him."

Jack's brows knit together.

"You remember how it was when you were here last. Brutal. Now think how it might have been even before that time, how much worse, how much more difficult to survive."

Jack savored the second drink, nursing it while he listened. "So you sell Remeonite secrets to Earth, in exchange for your family's safety. Do I have that right? *Treason.*"

"That sounds a bit harsh. I share bits of information to help with Earth's space exploration program mostly. And never the entirety of Remeon's data stores, but just enough to send the humans in the correct direction for their program."

Jack leaned forward, his hands on his knees, his mind racing. "What did you say? Earth has a space program?"

"Not officially yet, but they will. Soon."

"Which country? How is the information transfer accomplished?"

"Without going into too much detail, I'll just say from warlock to warlock. And I'll not divulge the recipient of the data at this time."

Silence pooled between the men. No one spoke as each finished his drink.

"Earth has a large population of warlocks and witches?"

A hearty laugh left the council member as Kix rose, lifting the bottle again in invitation. Jack nodded. "Faeries and elves too for that matter. Is that so hard to believe after what you've experienced here?"

"No. I guess not. I know of one other of which you speak, from Earth that is. But you're not aware of large numbers surely."

"That's not information I'm prepared to share."

Jack swallowed his drink in one gulp, relishing the burn as the liquid went down his throat. He eyed the empty glass. *That's probably enough drink.* He shook his head to clear it. *Or not nearly enough.*

"Arista is aware of your status as a warlock, I assume?"

"She is but only just recently so. We will balance each other on the council, just like her mother and I did. You see, we had an understanding. We helped each other where we could. It just made sense. Our exposure would only bring panic and chaos like we haven't seen since the Night Dwellers' departure."

An understanding... With Whisterly... "Does Arista know of your information exchange as well?"

Kix chuckled. "I like the way you think, Jack. No, she does not. But here's where the story gets really interesting—with new information." The smile on Kix's face broadened. "Your son reached out to me."

Jack fought to keep his expression neutral. *Damn it! Why didn't Whisterly talk to me about Kix? How much does he really know about Arista and Simon?* "Continue. I'm listening..."

"I don't even think he meant to connect with me. Basic instinct drew him. I'm a Remeonite, as far as he's aware, and a warlock, which he was able to sense. Simon is a Remeonite and a warlock. He's doesn't know that we're both part human. His innate power sought a like source, simple as that. He's in dire need of training. The potential within him cannot be ignored. It must be harnessed."

"And I suppose you want to train him."

"I could easily determine he'd almost killed himself, and others, while experimenting." Kix shook his head. "To say he's a danger is putting it mildly."

"I'm not sure how I can help with this. What do you want from me?"

"Come now, Jack. With your stellar military background, you know the advantage of keeping an opponent close, closer even than an ally."

"He will have the same thoughts for you as well, to twist your involvement on the council to serve the Night Dwellers' agenda." Jack narrowed his eyes through a glare at the man. "And with your experience as a traitor, it'll come second nature."

Kix huffed and filled his own glass again. He inclined his head toward Jack, who held up his hand. "Or we could leave him alone and pray he doesn't accidentally kill us all learning his craft."

Sweat formed on Jack's forehead. Relatively speaking, Arista and his wife had been safe from others here on Remeon. Would Simon or Kix expose them? Whisterly's words from the night she'd attacked Jack, while practicing jumping into a corpse, echoed in his head. Witches used to be hunted, tortured, and killed here on Remeon, very similar to Earth's history, it sounded like. His body convulsed at the thought, his mind careening through all the possible ways he knew, and had used, to painfully torture a body while the heart still beat.

"I would have a unique opportunity, one that I could use to our council's advantage. Just think. Molding a young magically gifted mind… My training could change Simon's outlook, ultimately bringing the Night Dwellers back to us. The perfect solution, isn't it?"

"Would the joy of coercion, mind control, and magic be your only forms of compensation, or were you looking for something else specifically?"

Kix cocked his head. "Your sarcasm aside, Jack, I have only the purest intentions for our council and Remeon's future. We do want to keep that on track… Whisterly, and now Arista, have worked so hard, along with the council, keeping us moving forward as a healed society. Now a recovering race, what could be better than bringing the two sides back together?"

"Blackmail. Pure and simple. Did your father teach you that as well?"

"I'm not taking any other action than I normally would. And, with the highest hopes for Remeon and Earth, who you now know have already formed an alliance. Don't you see? Our destinies are already intertwined."

Jack's fingers twitched, curled into a ball, and his heart thudded loudly. What he wouldn't give to pound this man into the ground.

"There is one consideration I'd like."

Jack raised a brow. "And that is?"

"Help arranging a mating."

"Shouldn't you bring that to the council? Or to Arista?"

"Typically, but in this case, I wanted to speak to you first. Arista is the mate I'm seeking."

Jack met his gaze with a dead-eyed stare. "That won't happen. You can't have her."

"I believe you'll see the wisdom in my choice eventually. Imagine... What we could do together... We'd be a great team."

Enough. Jack got to his feet and headed in the direction of the door, not wanting to lose his temper in front of this... being. "I'll be going now. Thanks for, uh... showing me your books." He slammed the empty glass on a side table. "And especially the whiskey." Jack rounded on Kix. "Tell me. Have you ever actually been to Earth?"

"No. I haven't. Heard many stories though from my father."

"I thought not," Jack spat. "You know little about being a Freemason either."

"Don't be foolish, Jack. The future will be secure, and your family will play a pivotal role." Kix followed him to the door. "We'll talk again soon."

Whisterly, where are you?

Just leaving Vinique. What's wrong?

We need to talk.

I can sense your anger.

Good. I'd hate for it to go to waste.

Whatever it is, we'll handle it.

His gut churned. Would his family ever truly be safe? Over the course of less than an hour, his confidence, most recently gained, was eroding fast.

JACK BURST THROUGH the doors leading to the suite of rooms he shared with Whisterly. She sat perched on the window seat, staring at the crowd, milling about their business below. With a tilt of her head, she urged him to join her.

Tension hammered through his veins.

"Sit?"

He shook his head. "I can't sit."

Whisterly patted the space beside her. "Give it a try. I'll help too. Come on."

"I'd rather be mad. I'll sit later."

But even as he paced like a trapped animal, Jack sensed her methods working, soothing him.

He rounded on her from their bedroom door. "How do you do that? I wasn't done being mad at you."

Her mouth lifted at the edges. "I know... Do you really want to know?"

Four steps later he leaned against the wall next her. His hand trailed down his face. "Yes, I do."

"Put simply, I wrapped your thoughts inside my own."

"You smother my madness, you mean?"

She laughed softly. "Well, that's one way to put it, I guess. The calm presence suppresses the spike in your negative thoughts, bringing you back into a more normal equilibrium."

Sorrow and the remnants of anger warred on his face. "Are all of you destined to be in danger constantly?"

"I got the gist of the basic conversation. Are you ready to talk to me about it now?"

He nodded. "Why in God's name didn't you tell me about Kix?" Lines folded deep into his forehead. "He thoroughly enjoyed laying all that on me."

"I guess, honestly, I've not thought about it in so long that I forgot you didn't already know."

"Pretty important stuff, him being from Earth and a warlock and all…"

"And I'm sorry. The last time you went through the portal, I didn't know. But you're right. I should have talked to you about it later."

"Can you tell if he senses you're back?"

"He doesn't, not yet anyway. And he does have a history of being reasonable on the council. While dealing with a new baby, and my illness, he was invaluable."

"Yeah. I'm sure."

"The rest he and I confided over time. First he let me know he was a warlock. That was soon after he'd helped to clear your name. Over the years we've supported each other in council business. Neither of us wants to be exposed, so the balance has been beneficial."

"And his parentage?"

"We didn't discuss that piece until Stephen's visit to Remeon, much later." She quieted, introspective. "After you left, he offered sympathy, with much more…understanding…than anyone else."

Jack scoffed. "I'll bet, your knight in shining amour."

"Hardly. I was lovesick for you, had Arista to care for, and ill myself. Not a desirable potential mate by any means." She extended her arm to Jack. "How about now?"

He squeezed her offered hand and positioned himself at the opposite end of the window seat, across from Whisterly.

"Much later, during Stephen's visit, Kix let knowledge slip about Earth in discussions with me. When I picked up on it, he confided in me about his father and the beginnings of Earth's space program, as well as his role in it."

"You let him continue to send data to Earth?"

"No. I did not, even though I desperately needed allies. Many on the council were not happy with me. He was just one more. But he maintained the front of support, at the time."

"I'm sorry. That's about the time a few of the council members were plotting to betray you. Must have been awful."

"Abysmal."

"He is back at it now though, trading information to his contacts on Earth. Arista isn't aware. He confirmed it, flat-out."

"We can fix that."

"What about the offer of mating with Arista and that Simon's magic is so out of control he unknowingly reached out to the man?" He grunted and kicked a pillow, knocking it to the floor. "Simon's dangerous, baby. That's something Kix *is* right about."

"Obviously Kix can't mate Arista. But as to his guidance for Simon, as a fellow warlock, that's logical. Our son has been immersed. Simon can't go back if he wants to survive as a warlock. The body changes in response to the immersion. If the, uh, subject doesn't adapt, severe sickness results with hallucinations and haphazard spells. My best guess is that Simon's already gone through most of those symptoms. Since he was temporarily banned from any study with the coven, his essence is reaching out for another of his kind—Kix."

"I see. So Simon really could die."

"He could, indeed. Most likely due to magic poorly handled."

"His misdirected magic is the biggest threat to all. Is it possible the coven would reconsider? At least with them, everyone could keep an eye on his skill level."

"They'd not allow his evil spirit to enter. If I had to bet, I'd say they would tear him out of the grimoire before they'd welcome him back in. With his history of treachery, he'd have to earn his way into favor again. That would be my guess."

"So we give him up to Kix?"

"Let me think on it. I'll take it up with the coven. Then decide as a group. Kix won't expose Simon right away. Kix has got too much to lose. And he wants Arista."

Jack sighed, the weight of his thoughts gnawing within him.

Whisterly dug her toes under a pillow, reaching Jack's feet. Jack lay her foot in his lap and pressed his thumb into her heel. Radiating outward with his fingers, he worked his way to her toes.

"Ah, Jack, that feels so good."

He gave a brief smile; then his expression darkened. "This could be our chance to show Simon what good he could make of himself."

"I'm not so sure. The patterns of behavior he's exhibited in the past leave no room for interpretation. His goal is to take over the council and merge us back with the Night Dwellers, with himself at the helm, just as Janus had envisioned. Maybe someone with a healthy emotional tie to him would have a better chance at getting through to him. The hatred he has for me runs too deep and, by association, with Arista also. Did Kix talk to you about what Simon actually communicated to him?"

Jack stopped, considering, then picked up Whisterly's other foot. "He didn't say. But I got the feeling Kix hadn't responded to Simon yet."

"What about blackmail? I hadn't thought about this before, but Simon's apparition most likely got pulled into my reintegration. Being bound to the grimoire, he would have been called, just like you and Arista. So, like it or not, he's been privy to what happened there. Probably still in the process of sorting it all out."

Jack rubbed the pads of Whisterly's feet, her facial expressions encouraging him.

"If Simon intends to out me to the council, with or without Kix's help, causing Arista to be overthrown, leaving the council chair up for grabs—"

"To Arista's mate or the next in line…"

"And then, with control of the council, well, Simon could just walk the Night Dwellers right through the door. Or control the Day Watchers with magic, if they don't comply to his wishes."

"How about we take a less direct approach?"

"Meaning?"

"*Belle.* She's one amazing little lady. I've experienced her aid firsthand."

"The idea has merit, Jack. We are all too exposed. Let's look into it."

Whisterly stretched against Jack's hands, and he tugged her leg toward him. "Now what else should I rub? I thought I'd work my way up, being at the bottom and all."

"*Mmm.* No argument here. Work your way up."

Jack stroked Whisterly's shins. First one leg, then the other.

"Where did you learn to do this?"

"When I trained to fight before the war. Worked well for cramps and the like. Then later, when I served in the military, I had the chance to put what I'd learned to good use. Oftentimes, when men were badly injured, massage was the only comfort we could give them on the battlefield. Nurses at the front trained me also, gave some additional tips.

"A touch means more than a thousand words when you're dying. To know that you're not alone, that someone who cares is close, well, death can be peaceful, even relaxing. It's amazing how the mind works on pain. I've known men who had a leg or arm blown off and didn't feel a thing. The mind closes, shuts down, yet those same men could feel someone massaging their temple or forehead." Jack glanced out the window, a wistful melancholy washing over him as he remembered the lives lost.

"Sounds like you did all you could for them at the time."

Unease inched up his throat. "I did what little I could. Death is part of war. The men were my responsibility."

Whisterly reached for him, moving aside hair that had fallen across his face. "Look at you. You've almost worked your way up here beside me. I'd say that's progress since, when you first came in, you wouldn't cross the room."

Jack had Whisterly's legs draped over his lap, working intently on her thighs. "I was mad as hell. When someone threatens my family, generally anger is my first response, followed closely by beating them to a pulp. Sorry I directed it at you."

"It's forgotten already. Could you teach me? Massage therapy?"

"Could you teach me about control of negative thoughts? I mean, unless it's a big witch secret."

"No witchcraft involved. I believe I could be persuaded. And, Jack, we'll handle the rest." She slid her hand down his cheek. "We always do."

I know we will. Turn over, baby. Jack moved his hands to Whisterly's back, his deep strokes eliciting a moan. He sensed her mind drifting while her thoughts eased into sleep. A few mumbled words escaped her; then her eyelids fluttered and shut.

Jack leaned his head back on the window listening to the calm of Whisterly's thoughts as she slept. She'd melted the last of his anger buildup. He stretched a leg toward his bag and scooted it toward him, not wanting to disturb Whisterly.

Still partially open, he grabbed the flap and lifted the whole thing to his lap. *Gotta be in here somewhere…* He dug deeper. *Ah, there it is.* Jack pulled Daniel's comic book free. *For a second I thought I'd lost it.* The bag slipped to the floor.

Settling in again, he rearranged Whisterly's legs over him and flipped open the cover. Instantly the images jumped to life as memories collided on the page—he and Daniel reading together side by side; his son huddled in his bed, reading by flashlight, thinking his father didn't know he was awake; lazy picnics playing catch and poring over comic book characters with his son—all here hidden between these pages. One page became two, then the next and the next, until Jack fell asleep, murmuring words to his son that only one of them would hear.

ARISTA OPENED THE door of her chambers to her mother. "Please join us."

Whisterly smiled, choosing a seat next to Belle.

Belle grinned back, her feet just barely reaching the floor as she shuffled them back and forth.

"Coffee, Mother? Stephen says I'm quite good at making it now."

"Better than me, little one. Your father says so. I'd love a cup."

Vinique leaned over to squeeze her sister's hand. "Good to see you looking so well, Whisterly." Vinique's eyebrows rose. "Rested?"

"Loving care mostly and, yes, some rest…"

Arista returned and handed her mother a steaming cup.

"*Mmm.* Before long your father will have me addicted as well."

"So," Arista began, "we've come together at my mother's request to quickly address a rising concern. And even though the three of us have briefly spoken about this issue, we need to come up with a plan to confront it. Utmost is Simon. Temporarily banned from the grimoire, he's nevertheless been immersed, and his powers are developing and dangerous to us all. Also Kix, a warlock himself, has offered to train him, but his involvement brings with it much deeper dilemmas."

"Belle," Whisterly began, "Before we start, I want to thank you for all you did for me and Jack. You realize you saved his life, don't you?"

Belle's eyes widened as all three sets of eyes settled on hers. "Well, his soul reached out for me. I felt his pain."

"That's extraordinary. Do you know how that happens?"

She shrugged. "The way it always happens, I guess."

Arista scrunched her forehead. "Can you tell us more? Has it happened before?"

"Oh, sure. People's hurt, well, it's drawn to me. I don't know how…"

"Do you know how you make them better?"

Belle's feet shifted faster, making loud skidding noises as they hit the floor. "I touch them. When I do that, their broken bits come into me."

"Think back. Can you remember what hurt Papa? What you fixed?"

Belle's head bobbed. "Yes, his heart."

Vinique, Whisterly, and Arista shared a glance. "What did you do?" Arista prompted.

"I put my hands on his heart. His pain went away."

"Have you done this before? At home?"

"All the time. People feel bad a lot. If they're sad, I give them a happy thought and pull bad ones from them."

"Have you talked to your parents about this?" Vinique interjected. "Do they know about this… ability of yours?"

Belle scooted back in her chair, folding her knees to her chest. "I don't know. But Ma always says, just being around me makes people happy."

"Belle, this skill you have, it must be tied to your magic. You pull the essence from the Earth and share its natural healing with those around you. Those with Elven blood often carry a healing power inherently within them. I believe that is why you're so skillful with that particular type of magic. Do you understand?"

She nodded. "I guess so. I don't think I've ever thought about it this hard."

The three older women laughed. "I'll bet not. But try now, concentrate. When we were trying to locate Stephen, do you remember?"

"I do." Belle's voice shook as she spoke.

"That night when you found him, could you feel his pain?"

Tears filled her eyes and color slid from her face. "Yes," she whispered.

Whisterly stretched out her arms, and Belle fell into them. "It's okay. You saved him that day. And you healed Jack."

Belle released a shuddered breath.

"The magic you used helped to bring me back." Whisterly pulled away and met Belle's watery gaze. "Will you continue to assist us? I understand if you'd rather go home. Truly. Take your time. You don't have to answer now."

Silence threaded the four together, each lost in their own thoughts.

Belle sniffed and wiped her eyes with the back of her hand. "I already know. I don't need to think about it. I want to stay, for now anyway."

Arista released a pent-up breath and leaned over to hug Belle. "Let me know if you change your mind. Do you promise?"

Belle's solemn gaze rose to meet Arista's. "I promise."

"Okay." Whisterly sighed. "You're welcome to stay during our meeting, Belle, if you wish. We need to continue our business. Or you can have snack. It's up to you."

Belle propelled herself from her seat and scurried to the kitchen.

"I guess we have our answer." Arista rose. "I think I'll join her and bring us a little something to eat."

"Need a hand with that?" Vinique asked.

"No. It's already prepared. Be right back."

Arista returned to find the two women already buried in discussion once again.

"Thank you, little one." Whisterly lifted her head toward her daughter. "Ready to tackle the rest of this?"

"We've got the biggest hurdle out of the way, relatively speaking." Arista set the platter down between the three of them. "As long as we can fully protect Belle, her talents will go a long way toward helping with Simon, if your theory is correct, Mother."

"Belle can buy us the time needed to address the related concerns, all of which involve Kix."

"First things first." Vinique spoke up. "I'll offer to mate with him."

Arista and Whisterly stared at her, mouths agape.

"Absolutely not. It's me who he wants so he can co-lead the council. I'll need to deal with him."

"But our mating makes sense though," Vinique continued. "And if our plans follow through as we expect, I'll never go through with the ceremony."

"With Arista's plan to make the mating contingent on the reveal of his information source, we'll catch the leak as well."

"Something he wants…something we want… It should placate him enough to maintain the agreement we've had for almost two decades," Whisterly added.

Vinique eyed her sister. "And if it doesn't?"

"We'll go immediately to plan B and banish him to Earth for good. After wiping his memory of his life here on Remeon, he'll discover his humanity," Arista said. "Are we all in agreement?"

Vinique and Whisterly nodded in affirmation. The three breathed a collective sigh.

"Vinique, want to fill us in on the new council members?"

"Absolutely. We have three candidates already confirmed by the full council. Just in need of a final sign off. You both have seen their dossiers. Whisterly, I doubt you've have the time to fully read them yet. We can wait until you've had more time."

"No need for that. I'll have my decision to you by tomorrow."

"All right. Mother, Vinique, do either of you have anything else? If not, I'll move forward with planning for the upcoming meeting."

"Yes, dear. I do have something else."

"Okay, Mother. What is it?"

"My return to the council. I've given it considerable thought."

Arista turned to Vinique and waited with bated breath.

As if seeking her words, Whisterly paused. Finally she continued, with sorrow—or was it resignation warring for control of her face? "When the coven knit me back together—my consciousness, my being, together with my abilities, all embedded within this new body again—any who attempted to connect with me, who knew me from before, would believe me to be Whisterly. This awareness would make its way to the council, eventually sparking concerns of witchcraft." Her gaze settled on Arista and Vinique. "The fears and allegations would not only rest on me but you both also, as my blood family. We know all too well where that would lead, and I'll not take us down that path. At all costs our line of succession and both of you must be protected."

"But, Mother, Simon knows of this and will use it against—"

Whisterly held up her hand. "Yes, and I have a few ideas to deal with this threat with the coven, after we've met to further discuss this part." She paused, her gaze encompassing them both. "I've communicated with Grandmother, to be certain this procedure would work, and she believes it will. My telepathic signature can be permanently disguised so any I come in contact with will never know I am Whisterly. To Remeonites, I'll remain safely...dead."

"Maybe we could bring you back on the council at that point? As a regular member?"

"I suppose that's possible. But, even if not, I'll always be available to confer with you both anytime. And I'm not sure how I'd feel about coming back to the council as something…less…than I once was."

Arista knelt at her mother's feet. "We're with you whatever you decide, in full support of you either way."

"How soon would you plan to do this, uh, procedure?" Vinique asked, her voice drifting in softly behind Arista.

"As soon as possible. Exposure is a very real risk. I've been so tied up with you both and Jack… I should have been thinking more clearly."

"Mother, I expect coming back to life is difficult work."

"Oh, it is—work that I'm most grateful for. I never wanted to leave you all. Now, though, I need to protect you going forward. Ultimately, as a council chair, you are my first responsibility. It's the very least I can do."

Arista bowed her head.

"Officially, since I'm alive again, at this moment, I *am* the council chair. So, as my final act, I'd like to advance the plans we've set forth today. If we agree between us, as the reigning leadership of the group, we can carry the motion with no further vote. My vote, of course, will need to be silent and secret. Then I will resign from my brief return as council chair."

Arista lifted her head to meet her mother's eyes, let out a soft breath, then glanced at Vinique. "Shall we vote?"

"Yes, I agree," Vinique said.

"Me as well, Mother."

"Then the motion carries. I'll be as involved in the council's plans as you'd both like." The solemn lines of her face softened into a smile. "Now, how about I refresh our drinks?"

"Please, Mother. That would be lovely. It should still be warming in the kitchen. We've details yet to work out. Would you join us for that as well?"

"Absolutely."

CHAPTER 17

"**J**ACK?"

Jack jerked his chin as he heard the door to their chambers clicked closed and locked.

"In the kitchen."

Whisterly poked her head in. "Well, look at you."

A smile lit his eyes. "What?"

"Cooking? I could get used to this."

"Who do you think cooks for Daniel and me at home?" Jack stirred a bubbling pot. "I hate to break it to you—no servants at my house."

"Daniel... I can't wait to meet him, Jack." She kissed him, breathing in the mixture of aromas surrounding them both. Spices tickled her nose and mingled with Jack's distinctly male scent.

He leaned into her touch. "I want that too. You'd love him."

"I already do." She lifted the lid off the simmering pot. "What is it?"

"Stew. Truly, I'm not sure of everything in it." He shrugged. "A lot of guesswork. Hope you're feeling adventurous. We'll see how it turns out."

"Can you turn the heat down a little? There's something I'd like to talk about before we eat."

"Sure. Done." He sat at the table, then guided Whisterly to his lap.

"Tomorrow the coven will alter my telepathic signature."

Jack scrunched his face. "What does that mean?"

"The easy way to explain it is that those I connect with telepathically wouldn't know me as Whisterly. Today the possibility exists that a chance encounter could expose me. And lead to difficult questions for Arista and Vinique—ones that could ultimately put them in jeopardy, kicking off a chain reaction, risking the coven and all we've worked for over the centuries."

"I see." Jack rubbed her arm. "We haven't really talked about what your return would mean for you and your work. Does that mean you'll quit your service to the council?"

Whisterly scanned Jack's face, attempting to read his reaction without taking in his thoughts. "Not completely. I'll still be available to Arista and Vinique whenever they need me, but leading the people of Remeon would be their responsibility, not mine."

Whisterly watched Jack fumble for words, while he tried to fight the smile consuming his face. "I, uh…don't see a downside to this plan."

She lifted a brow. "Try to contain your enthusiasm."

"I am. It's not working."

"For me, the downside would be, in the eyes of the people, I would stay gone forever. To them, I'd be someone else, not the leader they once knew."

He squeezed her against him. "If you'd rather fight and keep your identity public so you can return, I'll help any way I can, battling right beside you."

"I know you would. It's what you always do. But, clearly this time, not what you want."

He raised her chin so their gazes met. "Your happiness and our family's are all that matters to me. If this is the path you feel led to follow, let's do it."

She shook her head. "It isn't. Not when I consider what I could have instead."

"What?" Jack rose, lifting her with him. "Does this mean what I think it does?"

She giggled and nuzzled his neck. "A visit to Earth? Yes. From there we'll have to see. Remeon is still my home."

He spun them around and held her tighter, lowering his lips to hers. "I'll take it! It's a start."

"In some ways. In others, a completion."

"Baby, it's not the end, far from it."

"Time is continuous, so no real beginning or end, but 'Whisterly' will be no more."

"Just a different name to others. You'll still be Whisterly to all of us who love you. After this, though, how will I know you…recognize your new telepathic signature?"

"With a simple adjustment, it will be easy for you, Arista, and Vinique to adapt. Everyone else, except the coven of course, would be kept in the dark forever, regarding my return."

Whisterly's stomach growled. Jack's lips grazed her forehead before sitting her back down. "I'll bring us some dinner."

Whisterly ate a large mouthful of the stew, aware of Jack watching her, waiting for a reaction. "This is really quite good. I think I'll keep you around."

He leaned back in his chair. "Thanks, but no guarantee I can replicate it."

After they finished, Whisterly cleared their bowls. "How about I make us some coffee? We can sit in here. It's more comfortable. And there is something else I wanted to discuss with you." She searched his eyes. "About Simon."

"Okay. And coffee sounds good. I can make it, if you'd like."

"No, I'm getting better at."

"That's what I hear. I'll make a coffee lover out of you yet."

Whisterly rattled around in the kitchen, and before long the drink's rich aroma filled their chambers.

"Here you go." She handed Jack his cup and set hers on the table. "Tell me what you think." Her feet slid underneath her as she settled in next to Jack.

"I've had coffee that tastes like watered-down piss, dirt, and everything in between. I'm sure this is way better than that." He took a sip, feigned a cough, and gagged.

"Really? Is it that bad?"

A smirk crossed his face. "Sorry, I couldn't resist."

"Ugh, Jack." She turned to loud sucking noises just as he displayed his empty cup.

"More please."

"If you insist."

"I wholeheartedly do."

"Here's your refill. Don't drink it just on my account."

He kissed her on the cheek. "It's good, baby. Really it is."

A slow smile curved her lips. "I think I like this playful side of you Jack. It will be a relief when we aren't constantly worried about one of us dying."

His lips pulled back in a grin. "I second that."

"Getting back to what I was saying, after tomorrow, Simon will be the chief avenue of vulnerability we have. Him and Kix."

"I agree."

"We have a plan to deal with Kix, which involves Simon also. I'm thinking of something additional to ensure our safety."

"Go on."

"You're aware that Simon's been temporarily banned from the physical grimoire and the coven. But, since he's already been immersed, that action does very little to curtail his activity in the magical arts. Since he's still bound by blood, just as you and me and Arista are, he was summoned during my reintegration."

"It doesn't sound like there's much we can do about it."

"There are more… final…steps we could take."

"And those are?"

306 | J.W. GARRETT

"First, he could be ripped from the grimoire. This would have unknown repercussions for us as well. To my knowledge it hasn't ever been done. The consequences for Simon, however, would be final—the beginning of the end of his power."

"And the second?"

"A temporary measure, and, even worse, we'd need him physically here for the coven and me to work on him. We'd erase his memory, giving us time to exert our influence over Simon, without all that's come between us through the years. As a warlock though, his memories are destined to return. The interval of time at our disposal is uncertain. After his memories return, the strategy could backfire when he realizes he's been deceived."

Jack eyed her over the cup's edge, then turned it upside down. "See? Empty again. I told you that I liked it." He sat back and crossed his leg over one knee. "Option two sounds like the better course of action, if my vote carries any weight."

"Sure it does. Depending on how our time goes during the memory-lapse phase, Simon may be even more intent on his evil ways, but there is the chance we could have some sort of positive effect on him."

"Then there's the little problem of getting him here. He won't willingly submit to it. Simon left no uncertainty as to his feelings for me the last time we communicated."

"It's no secret how he's felt about me over the years either. Clearly it will do no good to hide my identity through disguising my telepathic signature if Simon can still wreak havoc with this information. And he can."

Jack sat up straighter and folded Whisterly's hands into his. "Think what this could mean for us—all of us. A second chance."

Whisterly studied her husband, trying to give a name to the flurry of emotions she witnessed on his face. Sadness, pain, hope, anger—it appeared they all lingered there.

"How long would we have? Any kind of guess?" Jack asked.

"A couple months maybe."

"Let's brainstorm ways we could lure him here."

"Or capture him. Our troops are trained for this kind of op. Stephen was returned to us using just this sort of maneuver."

"I could go, alone, or pick a small team to accompany me."

Whisterly pulled back. "Jack, no. You're too close to the situation. You know that."

"You bet I do. And I'd pit my experience up against any in your armed forces."

"No one would doubt your expertise, Jack."

"Give me this opportunity back, baby."

"It's no longer my decision to make. We can discuss options with Arista and Vinique tomorrow."

The muscles in his shoulders tightened, his lips thinning to a straight line. "I won't allow someone else to make arrangements regarding how best to apprehend my son. Send your men to me, and if they have suggestions worthy of merit, I'll consider them." He huffed out a breath. "Damn it, Whisterly, I won't screw up twice when it comes to decisions about finding my son. He and Arista are why I'm here." His voice softened. "And you of course."

He took her in his arms and brushed his lips against hers, instantly heightening her attention. "In my wildest dreams I never believed you'd be mine again, but night after night I hoped and prayed for that miracle, many of those nights barely hanging on by a thread. I need to let that same dream live now for our son. Don't take it from me."

Whisterly leaned back, and Jack's gaze drilled into hers. In them Whisterly saw no room for further debate.

"Even he deserves hope."

She ran her hand along the back of Jack's neck, smoothing the hair along his nape, and kissed his cheek.

"I need to fix this." His eyes glistened with unshed tears even as his jaw muscles worked.

"Okay, Jack." She laid her head on his chest, the beat of his heart loud and steady in her ear, his arms wrapping her in a tight hug. "Okay."

A COOL WIND whispered across the back of Arista's neck. She'd ached to be free from the confines of the compound, even if only for a few moments. In her heart she knew it wasn't, not really, but today's actions had felt so…final. With Whisterly's unique telepathic signature gone, the memory of her mother's death clawed toward Arista again. Whisterly would still be here, of course, praise the gods, but in a different manner, never to return to the council chair she once commanded.

Great-Grandmother had even managed to transform Whisterly's telepathic signature into a new identity for Yara. One where she'd begun a life with Jack. One where she'd had a miraculous recovery from a long term injury. Planting these memories in the collective consciousness of Remeonites through their telepathic network ingrained the changes, as if they had always been. For Whisterly and their family it was just another in a series of adjustments toward a unique new normal.

Arista pushed down the memories of her mother's death as they fought for space in her head. That time period, horrible as it had been, served its purpose, forging her as Remeon's new council leader. Although her challenges sometimes tallied more than her wins, over time this would change. Experience and her mother had been the best teachers. Both remained assets.

After the telepathic signature adjustment, Jack had swiftly tucked Whisterly away. Tonight he'd been in full protection mode. No doubt about it…deep within he held his own elite force, and all who dealt with him confronted it. At times it was his keen awareness or the integrity he brought to any encounter. At other times, when the situation warranted, an urgent brutality surfaced to wipe out any who threatened his family.

Tempered only by the love he had for Whisterly, for his daughter, and his family and friends, Arista understood Jack would die for her or his ideals that he'd fought for so tenaciously. But tonight he would be the only one able to ease the sadness hidden in her mother's heart. No one else wielded the same power over her soul to remind Whisterly how much she was loved and cherished. Jack possessed the only key.

The sights and sounds accompanying her late-night stroll eased her tension while she walked. A small ball of light between her fingers gave off only enough glow to see her way but not attract attention. Eluding her posse of guards earlier this evening presented a difficulty or two at first, but in the end, she'd had them searching in circles, lost in the confused circuitry of their own tracking devices from a little spell she'd hurled their way. However well-intentioned they were, her solitude didn't include them. With a twist of her fingers, she coiled her fire tighter, illuminating her path more clearly.

The farther she walked, the easier the events of the day shrugged from her. Crawling under branches and over underbrush, her footing sure, the tiny clearing unfolded before her, just as she had remembered. Branches clung to the growth high above, pulling limbs and debris from the path, leaving a clear line of sight, while still providing an oasis for her.

Muttering words under her breath with a sleight of her hand, she shielded the area from view, and, free at last, she drew a breath, then exhaled, reveling in the nighttime air and sky that were her companions.

Bugs and nocturnal animals chirped and hummed, their songs lulling Arista into a soothing peace. The council, her duties, the unending demands, and the chaos of the past few weeks fell away. The moons above beamed a passage, spotlighting the small patch of earth beneath her feet.

She lifted her face upward, glimpsed the brilliant whorls of light littering the sky, then closed her eyes, spoke her wish, just like her mother had taught her... *Whisper the wish, count to three, turn your spell, there you'll be.* Her eyes drifted shut. The stillness echoed her heartbeat in even thumps inside her ears. Arista tucked away the memory with a smile. *Even before I knew I was a witch, my mother spoke to me of magic and spells.*

Arista? Where are you? I know you're out here.

Her eyes snapped open, the spell of her serenity broken. She lifted the veil that kept her location secret.

Here. Follow my thoughts. I'll lead you.

Breathless, he waded into the hideaway.

"Stephen, why are you here?"

"Why am I here? What are you doing here is really the question, isn't it? Ditching your guards in the middle of the night? What exactly did you have in mind?"

"*Shh.* Calm down. I had in mind a few moments to myself."

He closed the distance between them. "It could be dangerous, love. I know what happened earlier with your mother upset you. I only wanted to be sure you were all right."

"I took the appropriate precautions. I'll be fine." Her gaze lifted and touched his. "Thanks for the concern, but it's not necessary."

Worry wrinkled his forehead. "Of course it's necessary. You're... you're precious to me." His thumb scaled down her cheek.

A shiver sparked through her skin. "At least kiss me when you do that."

"Gladly," he whispered in her ear, his hand on the small of her back, urging her closer.

Dense air hugged the moment of silence clinging between them. He covered her mouth with his and kissed her soft and slow.

Arista inched back. "*Mmm*, Stephen." Needing more of him, she anchored her hands in his shirt and pulled him toward her again. His mouth responded, pressing into hers harder, deeper.

Her fingers trailed down his arms, then slid under his shirt. His roamed down her back. At her waist, he stopped, groping at the fabric stuck there. They fumbled, falling a step backward against a tree.

"Arista," he murmured against her neck, "you're driving me insane."

"Yes, finally..."

She bent her head to the side, giving him better access. He kissed down her shoulder, his mouth and tongue exploring.

Their bodies tangled together. Arista maneuvered a hand below his waist. He moaned, and she moved her hips against him.

"Arista," he panted. "I can't think straight when you do that."

"We're mated. It's okay." His hand sunk into her hair as he kissed a trail along her collar bone. "Don't stop, Stephen." Arista's mouth worked at his neck.

He shuddered. "God, Arista, not like this." He pulled her hands free. Clinging to each other, they slumped to the ground. "I don't want to take you like some crazed animal out here in the woods." Catching his breath, Stephen leaned his forehead against hers. "Well, actually, I do want to take you like an animal, God help me. But I don't want that for you."

She heaved a deep sigh and rested her head against his chest. "Then when? When will it ever be right for us?" Her glassy-eyed gaze lifted to meet his.

"Soon love." A tear drifted down her cheek, and his thumb brushed it away. "I want to do right by you."

"You are the best kind of right for me."

Strong arms wrapped her in a hug.

Arista pulled away, a small smile lifting her lips. "Your heart's beating really fast."

"I know." He raised her chin and kissed her hard on the mouth, biting her bottom lip. "I told you what you do to me."

Shh… Stephen, something is wrong. She lifted a finger to her lips. *Don't talk.*

I can feel it now too.

Gods! No… It's Simon!

Thomas… A crackling erupted inside Stephen's thoughts.

I forgot to cloak us again. Stephen, I wish we had more time. This is my fault.

We will have more time, love. Believe in us.

The leaves rustled. Simon, Errol, and a third man Stephen didn't recognize poked their heads into the clearing.

"I could hear you guys going at it." A grin crossed Simon's face. "Imagine my surprise. Figured I'd give you time to finish. What's wrong with you, Stephen? A little slow with the ladies? Or maybe she just doesn't do it for you."

"You disgusting bastard!" Stephen reached for the knife in his boot.

"No, no, no… Last time we met, you left me with a nasty souvenir. Not again."

Arista lifted her arms and whispered a spell under her breath. The air stilled, and the pain in Stephen's head receded.

At least I can make this part right. He won't get you again. You're protected.

No! Arista. Protect yourself. Nobody else here but you matters.

"Neat trick, sis. Errol, give her the injection. Then we'll be on our way." He licked his lips. "Oh, have I got plans for us."

Errol took a step, a syringe readied in his hand.

Arista thrust out her hand. The wind stirred, tossing Errol to his back.

"Cool, sis. I'm still learning. Maybe you could teach me a thing or two." Simon smothered a laugh, sarcasm dripping from his words, then motioned with his hand. "Now, Travis. Go." The man beside him disappeared.

Arista, love, watch behind you… Let me loose so I can help!

She backed against a tree, her hand splayed out, the rush of wind keeping Simon and Errol at bay. *I need more. Gods help me…* Arista snapped her fingers, igniting a spark. She grabbed the tree trunk behind her, the fire announcing itself with a sizzling hiss. The small spark ignited a flame, spitting smoke as it grew, snaking its way through the tree.

That's it, Arista… You're doing a great job. Let me go now though. I can't reach anyone with this thing around me either… Behind you!

Travis grabbed Arista by the hair, yanking her backward. Her hand groped for her attacker. Travis screamed when Arista gripped his shoulder, searing his skin. His features contorted, Travis approached again. This time, her hand dug into his face, crackling the skin where her fingers touched.

The wind died down. Simon and Errol crawled toward her.

The protection around Stephen held.

Tongues of fire shot out in all directions, encompassing Arista and Travis. Travis slumped to the ground. Arista gasped for breath. But before she could return her attention to Simon and Errol, Travis plunged the syringe in her thigh, then collapsed, ash and burnt leaves puffing up in a filthy black cloud around him.

Simon coughed and attempted to cover his face from the thickening smoke. "Errol, grab Travis. I'll get Arista. Move. Now!"

"Are you sure, Commander? He looks like toast. He won't make it."

"I can arrange for you to share his fate instead, if you wish."

"Uh, sir, no, sir. I've got him, sir."

Arista's eyes flickered, fighting the drug's effects. *Stephen?*

I'm here. You did good. I'll be right behind you. I'm gonna get you free.

Her eyelids closed.

The small band disappeared, thudding slowly through the underbrush.

Damn it to hell! Many long minutes later, the field around Stephen dissipated. He glanced the direction Arista had been carried away, then judged the distance back to the compound. And setting off at a run after her, he contacted Jack.

CHAPTER 18

JACK'S EYES DARTED open. Whisterly had slept finally, her warm body curled against his. They had talked until late into the night, the assurances he'd given making little difference. But his touch had accomplished what his words could not. He kissed the top of her head, breathing in her scent. He'd never tire of the way her cool freshness hit him, like a walk at dawn on a spring morning. And it had been the same tonight—Whisterly's telepathic signature or not, it made no difference.

He closed his eyes again and sighed. It wasn't time to get up, still very early in the wee morning hours. Jack turned over, shifting Whisterly with him. He laced his fingers between hers and listened to her rhythmic breathing, which normally eased him back to sleep if he was restless. Whisterly's thoughts mingled with his, drawing him back to her. Still, the peace he'd had before escaped him.

An agitation gnawed at him. What was it? Intuitively trusting his instincts, he scoured the room, attempting to sense any unwelcome or unnatural presence.

Jack! It's Arista. She needs you.

Stephen? What is it? What's wrong?

Simon—he's captured her.

Baby, wake up. He extricated himself from Whisterly.

Details—give them to me now, Stephen!

While he listened, he dressed, holstered his pistol at his side, checked and stowed his ammunition, and slid his knife in his boot.

Whisterly, fully dressed now also, silently watched Jack, the soldier, prepare. "Arista is not only our daughter but the council chair. Our forces will be sent for her. Vinique will alert them. We'd know by now if they had gone to rescue her."

Jack eyed her over his shoulder. "They shouldn't have to rescue her. Her guards should have prevented this attack."

"Yes, I agree. Although our Arista is pretty good at not being found when the mood hits her. I should know."

"They're professionals or should be. It's inexcusable."

"We'll figure out what happened."

"I think I've got a pretty good idea already, but I'll clarify with Stephen when I see him."

"Jack, they are mated."

He huffed. "That doesn't give either of them license to be stupid."

"Need I remind you of a particular couple, deeply in love, who got themselves in trouble and nearly killed…all because they couldn't keep their hands off each other?"

"No, I don't need reminding. I lived it. And I still can't keep my hands off you. Shows how well I learned that lesson, huh?"

She snaked her arms around his waist from behind and kissed his shoulder. "Looks like you're all set."

"Not quite." Jack took a mental assessment and paused. "Baby, I need more guns, more ammo, and a vehicle. And time. Give me three hours before you alert your forces."

"I've decided. I'm going with you. Vinique can send our team out."

He took her by her arms and sat her on the bed, kneeling before her. "No. I need you here. So I don't have to worry about you too. There's no time to debate this."

"You're planning on going in there without the help of witchcraft then, aren't you? Just shooting your way in and out? Against Simon's untrained magic? And Arista is most likely drugged. She'll not be able to help much, if at all."

"Whatever aid you and Vinique can give us from here, I'd welcome."

"We will, of course, but it might not be much. The dampening fields the Night Dwellers have in place deter outside telepathic communication, and I'm not sure how effective my magic would even be from this distance. Belle was most successful with her brother before, so we'll use her again. Regardless, it's highly likely you and Stephen will be on your own for the most part, until we send our people in."

An answering grin formed on his face. "That's the way I like it."

She rolled her eyes. "I'm sure you do."

"Will you help me with the guns, or shall I add breaking, entering, and theft to my list of crimes?"

"Of course I'll help."

"That's my girl." He kissed her lips and grabbed her hand. "Let's go."

A SHORT TIME later, the jeep-like vehicle puttered and spat as it idled. Three rifles, extra ammunition, and several detonation devices filled the back, along with an additional bulletproof vest for Stephen. Jack had picked his and already wore it. "Give me three hours. If you haven't heard from me by then, send in your men. Well, even if you have heard from me, send your men in. If we've not been successful by then, most likely my plan hasn't worked."

"Just concentrate on getting yourself, Stephen, and our daughter back in one piece. If you can bring Simon without threatening you, or her, then that's okay too."

"Last time you made this decision, I had to live with it. Now it's my turn, my chance to set things right. If my plan works, we'll bring both Arista and Simon home. Have the coven ready to erase Simon's memories. It's our only hope of a fresh start with him."

Jack caught her solemn nod even as the early morning wind whipped her hair about her face. She leaned in and kissed him. And when she pulled away, Jack grabbed her wrist and kissed her again.

"*Mmm...* Hurry back, Jack Livingston. I've got a lifetime's worth of plans for us waiting for you."

He winked. "As soon as I can, baby."

"Now go bring our daughter home."

Vinique walked out and squeezed her sister's shoulder. They both stared in silence until his vehicle faded from view. "Let's go work on plan B. I have full faith in my husband, but we need to be prepared. And we need to check with Arista's guards. They may have alerted security forces already."

"Ready to get started now?" Vinique asked.

Whisterly tore her gaze from the horizon. "In just a moment. There's something I need to say to Jack."

Jack?

Miss me already?

Jack...with you and Arista both in danger, there's something I felt the need to say.

What is it?

I need to let you know how much our family means to me. I've wanted it for so long, and... I need more of us. This may seem odd now, but we could have more children. Whisterly heard Jack's chuckle race through her thoughts.

I'm serious, Jack. You never saw Arista or Simon growing up. Daniel came to you already a young child. I want to have another, and I'd planned to talk to you about it this morning, so instead I'll leave it in your thoughts to take with you.

Whisterly felt his grin wash over her, and then a pause.

Do you know how long I've waited to hear you say that? We... Us... And for it to make any kind of sense? I'll be back, and I'm bringing our family with me. Don't get me wrong. It's not that I'm not ecstatic about the possibility for future children with you, Mrs. Livingston. I am. But I don't need another child. I have what I need: You, Arista, Daniel, a chance with Simon... I love you. See you soon, baby.

Gods... No matter what happens, just come back to me, Jack.

Count on it.

JACK FOLLOWED STEPHEN'S directions explicitly. When he got close to the cave, he hid the vehicle in the woods, slung the rifles over his shoulder, and shoved the rest of the supplies into a sack, adding it to his load, then jogged the short distance to Stephen, crouched behind a series of boulders.

Stephen breathed a deep sigh. "Jack, thank God you're here."

"I don't know about that, but I'm grateful that you contacted me first, before the Day Watchers sent in their own men."

"You were my first thought—the best chance for getting her back quickly, in my mind anyway."

"Here. Put this on." Jack handed him a vest. "And take this, a bite to eat... I assume you've been out here waiting on me for a while. There's a little bit of coffee left too." Jack passed him a thermos. "Drink fast."

He shivered. "Thanks." Stephen downed the coffee, then reached for one of the three rifles Jack had leaned against a rock, and threw it over his shoulder. "Three?"

"Yeah. I'm going in with two." Jack looked him over, his gaze focusing where his braces would be. "How's that leg?"

"Good." Stephen stretched his legs as he chewed on the dried meat. "Just haven't moved much since they went inside. I didn't want to miss anything."

"Before we talk about the plan to get her out of there, tell me a little, and I do mean a little, as I have a pretty good idea, about how she got taken. It could alter my decisions, but I doubt it."

"Basically she wanted to be alone, so she got rid of her guards, like I told you earlier." He averted his eyes. "I, uh, saw her leave the guards wandering in circles, so I followed. I was concerned for her. It was midnight already."

"*Hmm.* Well, typically, she'd protect herself from outsiders. Did she do that? Do you know?"

"Yes, she did. She had to lower that shield she'd created to let me in."

"I see, and I guess she never put it back in place."

Stephen shook his head. "We were…talking."

Jack held up his hand. "That's enough. The rest isn't important to me except for one thing. If you're to marry Arista, your number one priority has always got to be loving her *and* keeping her safe. She needs *both* together—100 percent of the time."

"Understood. And I will of course. She means everything to me."

Jack scrutinized him, letting the silence between them say what he did not. "Did she use witchcraft against them? Was anyone with Simon hurt?"

"Yeah. Simon had already gotten in my head. So, remembering his previous attack, Arista put up a wall to keep him from hurting me again. From that point on, there was nothing I could do but give her information as they attacked her." He hung his head. "She wouldn't remove the protection so I could help."

Jack patted him on the back, remembering Damond's attack as if it'd been yesterday. "It's okay, son. Clearly she loves you. And you're here right now. What else?"

"I think one of them died from the fire Arista created. They called him Travis. He was burned pretty badly. Errol, the other guy with Simon, I knew from my time here before. But it was Travis who injected her with something right before he died."

"All right. We need to move quickly. Whatever Simon's doing, he'll most likely try it while she's out, when she can't fight back." Jack counted the number of guards in front. Eight men milled about, heavily armed. Jack jerked his head toward the men. "Those are not the kind of odds I'd like. Do you know another way in? Preferably less patrolled?"

"I do. And I know where he'd take her. Underground."

"Good man. We'll use the hand signals we practiced during your training. After we free Arista, I want you to get her outta here. Take the vehicle, hidden just beyond those second set of trees there—see?" Jack pointed into the distance. "And get back to the compound. We only have about an hour and half now before Vinique sends in her own men."

Stephen's gaze darted to his means of escape. "What about you?"

"I'm getting Simon out also."

Stephen's mouth fell open. "What?"

"Listen." Jack crouched nearer to Stephen. "He's not part of your mission. Only Arista is. Let me worry about Simon."

"But—"

"My plan isn't up for debate. So, either head on back to the compound now, or show me to the other entrance. We're wasting time."

Stephen ran his hand through his hair. "I... I'll do whatever you say, Jack, as long as it gets Arista away from that psycho."

Jack extended a hand and helped Stephen to his feet.

"Before we go in, there's more you need to know."

DISTANT RINGING ECHOED in Arista's ears. She blinked. A bright light stung the back of her eyes. "Where am I?"

"Well, princess...you're my guest."

She turned, squinting toward the mocking voice. Ties held her arms and legs down. Scanning the room, Arista attempted to gain her bearings.

"Awake earlier than I'd planned. We're not quite done." A snarl curled his lip. "Not even started actually."

"These won't hold me. Surely you know that."

"No, but another dose of this will."

Simon nodded to a medical attendant, who slid his chair alongside her, syringe in hand.

"Wait." The bonds holding Arista fell to the floor. "Let's...talk."

He held his hand up to the attendant. "Hold up a minute."

A wave of dizziness rolled through her head. She grabbed the edges of the table to steady herself.

"You're right. Took you no time at all to work your way free of those ties." He sneered. "We can do better."

"No, I'm not going anywhere, for now. Telepathic communication can't get through. I can barely sit. You brought me here. So?"

"Pretty good assessment. You're not going anywhere anytime soon." A smile inched up one side of his mouth. "I'm just getting started."

Just keep him talking, that's all you need to do, till you can clear your head and think of an idea to get outta here. "What's your plan?"

Simon scrunched his shoulders in feigned glee. "Ah, now, that, would spoil the surprise, wouldn't it?" He dragged a chair across the floor with a loud screech and sat opposite her. "I can guarantee one thing though. You're not gonna like it."

"Try me."

"Nah. I have a better idea. Let's play a game." Amusement flickered in his eyes, and the accompanying lethal smile sent a chill through her skin. "Everyone loves games."

She blew out a breath. "Okay. What's the game?"

"You'll have five questions to guess my plans for you. Of course you can ask any question you'd like. I may or may not answer it. But, if it pertains to the, uh, procedure, I'll answer, honestly, for the most part."

"*For the most part?* Doesn't sound fair."

"Well, life is only *fair* at the compound. Look around you. You're not there."

"And after the fifth question?"

"You guess. Guess wrong and my fine fellow here will proceed."

"What if I get it right?"

A laugh boomed from his throat. "You won't. But if by some miracle you do, we'll wait for your 'friend' Stephen to show up before we begin. I expect he'll be along anytime now. If there's anything left of him after trying to cross my guards, he can watch."

Gods...

"Oh, and, of course, I get to ask you questions as well."

Arista worked her way into the man's mind, the one with the syringe, Darien. *Smart but, thankfully, highly susceptible to suggestion.* She wedged herself into his thoughts. *Leave. Make an excuse to Simon. Go to your quarters and give yourself that injection intended for me. Do it. Now.*

"Pardon me, Simon. I need a minute," Darien said, pushing his chair under the table, while he slid the syringe meant for Arista in his pocket.

"I don't care. Just make it quick," Simon snapped.

Two guards and Simon... A little better odds. At least for now she could only connect telepathically with others here, like Darien. Jack, Whisterly, and Stephen hadn't responded to her.

The rocky structure affirmed her belief that they were underground. *This place looks just like the room Stephen described to me where he was held, interrogated, and tested.* A metallic odor filled the air, mixed with stale sweat.

Blood and fear.

A tightness rose in her throat. The curve of the room's sides and ceiling meant they were closed in. Sweat broke out on her forehead. Claustrophobia wasn't often an issue for her, but in places like this, it reared its ugly head. She had no idea how far below the surface they were. In her basement at the compound, a room, hall, and staircase were the only barriers to the main floor. Time spent there didn't bother her. Not like this. Here, the walls seemed as if they may crumble on top of her at any second. She yanked at her collar, pulling the moisture away from her.

Simon eyed her. "What's the hold up? Or are you trying to kill me with anticipation?"

"How are your people healing here? The ones sick from PR 251?"

"Interesting choice. Not the best question for your benefit though. The vaccine is working well. The cure is on the horizon for us any day now. New cases are dwindling."

"But the sick are still dying."

"Nope, my turn. How long did it take you to find out after your precious mother's death that she was a lying, power-hungry bitch?"

"She's not. My mother's number one goal has always been to heal the people."

"Compelling spin on it. Seems she's forgotten about half of them."

"She never forgot them. They chose to leave."

Simon shook his head. "Wait. So you're going to pretend you weren't kept in the dark about me?"

"No. I was for a while. Until I could understand the truth." *Guard, there's a noise aboveground. Go now and investigate. Take any others patrolling outside in the hall with you for assistance.*

The guard at the main door opened the door and passed through. He nudged the first man he met. "Come on. Follow me. Trouble above."

"Hey! Where's he going? Idiot... " Simon stood and surveyed the perimeter of the room. *Errol, send more guards down here, at least four. Now!* "And where is that damn doctor?"

Arista caught her breath. The fluidity and grace of his movement stopped her. The tilt of his head, the intensity of his concentration as it mounted, resting in deep lines across his forehead, his decisive movements. *Papa...* She could see Jack everywhere in Simon.

"Simon, I can help you. I know what you're going through."

He faced Arista, his gaze level with hers. "Help me?" The words left him in an icy-tinged bitterness.

"Come with me. Meet your father."

He scoffed. "We're done. You wasted your questions."

Arista raised her arms. A hum bit the silence between them. Items in the room loosened from their hinges, took to the air, swinging themselves in the unnatural wind.

Simon ducked from a wildly spinning chair and lunged for Arista's legs as she wrenched herself off the table. She tumbled to the ground, her ankle trapped in Simon's grip. With her other foot she kicked him in the face, landing a blow to his nose and glancing his left cheek.

Simon held tight, then dug in his pocket, laughing as he produced another fluid-filled syringe. "This isn't the same medication," he gritted out, "but it'll get the job done."

She snapped her fingers and murmured a spell, summoning fire to her. The flame flickered from her finger as it grew, its hot mass licking toward Simon. Arista flung the fire at him, hitting his leg.

He grunted as he yanked the cap off the syringe with his teeth and plunged the drug into her leg.

The buzz ended abruptly. Even in the melee Simon's gaze sought the items as they hung, poised in the air. Suddenly the debris fell, clanging in loud bursts to the ground. He dodged, his feet moving quickly under him, while the flame inched higher along his leg.

Finally, quiet.

"Mother of gods!" He slapped out the fire, the burn sizzling his skin, already oozing and raw, then wiped his nose with the back of his hand. Blood continued to drip down his face. He limped to his unconscious sister and struck her cheek, righted the table, and lifted her on it. "Game time is done. You lose." He heaved a shaky breath and swiped at the blood pooling under his nose, the smell from his own crackled flesh sickening him.

The disarray about him began to fade. He willed it further from his mind, along with his injuries and straightened his stature.

It's time to begin.

STEPHEN LED JACK to the rear opening of the Night Dwellers' cave. He stooped low, his body hidden by vegetation. As they approached, the three men on guard huddled, exchanged words, then dwindled to one.

"All the better for us," Jack mumbled. *Ready?*

Stephen nodded. Jack's hand signals meant it was time. He aimed and fired. The man fell to the ground without a sound. In a bent-over dash, Jack hurried to the man's side and threw his rifle over his shoulder. Stephen followed, pausing alongside the fallen man.

Jack pointed to their path.

Stephen signaled back, when, from the corner of his eye, a flutter of movement made him turn. Another guard arrived, and a silver flash rose with the man's hand. Stephen kicked the knife from the guard's grasp, then reached down, pulled his own knife from his boot, and opened the man's throat, just as he'd practiced in the holosuite.

Jack swiveled at the gurgling noise, giving Stephen a thumbs-up, then quickly moved into the cover of the cave. Stephen wiped his blade on the dead man's shirt and returned his weapon to its sheath. After grabbing the Night Dweller's stray knife from the dirt and sliding it into his vest, he followed Jack.

Adrenaline pulsed through his veins as Stephen led Jack into the depths of the cave. An odd absence of guards accompanied the unease coursing up from his gut. Hugging the wall, the pair continued at a steady pace.

"Hey, you. Identify yourselves at once."

Jack paused, giving a quick hand signal. Stephen ducked into the closest doorway, following Jack's orders. The hallway was so quiet that Stephen could hear the man's boots as they lifted and fell, meeting the floor exactly six times before he caught up with Jack.

"Well, what do you have—"

A swift intake of breath prefaced a sickening crack. The stranger met the floor. Stephen stepped from the room, grabbed the dead man's arms, and dragged him inside, out of sight. With an imperceptible nod of his head, Jack urged them forward.

Flashes of the fight with the Day Watchers months ago resurfaced in his head, a prickling sensation erupting with it. Beads of sweat trickled down his neck. Stephen had been afraid of this; would he alert Simon that they were close because of their bond, or was it just his imagination?

Jack, I'm endangering the mission.

Jack turned, shook his head, and instantly Stephen felt his anxiety ease. Somehow Jack had boosted the shields in Stephen's mind.

He released his breath. *Thanks, man. We're close. I can feel him.*

Their steps slowed. Snippets of broken conversation met their ears. Jack craned his neck around the corner. Stephen's breath caught as he waited for a signal.

One guard...three people inside. This was it. The best opportunity they'd have. *Now.*

Jack loosed his blade.

The guard's eyes widened as he turned to face his attacker, a knife protruding from his neck. He opened his mouth, surely to scream, Stephen thought. But blood trickled from the guard's mouth instead; then his knees buckled, and he hit the floor.

Jack peeled himself from the wall. Stephen took the opposite side of the door opening.

"Give her another dose. Now. I don't want her to wake during the procedure. I'm not up for a repeat performance of her powers."

"Of course if you wish it. But I won't take long. Only a few minutes, and—"

"Silence. Just do it."

Stephen took shallow breaths, watching Jack prepare, aim, then fire. The loaded syringe exploded, the bullet lodging in the doctor's chest. Simon barked orders just as Stephen's bullet hit the doctor's forehead. *No procedure today, you asshole.*

Jack advanced on Simon, his rifle aimed at his head.

Stephen rushed to Arista. The cold fury of his eyes lifted to meet Jack's. "What in God's name were you doing to her, you disgusting piece of filth?"

"Stephen, you arrived just in time for the show. Pull up a seat. Take a load off."

Arista, wake up, love. You're getting outta here. Stephen cut the rope binding her feet, swiveled her around, and waved the medicine under her nose Jack had given him outside along with his weapon. She coughed.

"That's it." He kissed her temple and anchored an arm around her waist, raising her to a stand.

"Sit down, Simon." Jack held his gun inches from his son's skull. "We've some things to discuss." A shadow passed over Jack eyes. "Don't even try it. I'm pretty good at this telepathy thing also."

"Pathetic Stephen and Arista won't get far. Reinforcements are arriving as we speak. So, the more the merrier." Simon rounded on his father, and his face slowly evolved into a grin. "Finally the infamous Jack."

The room filled with guards. Stephen counted ten additional men as he witnessed the silent conversation between father and daughter.

Stephen nodded his acquiescence. He knew his part. Jack concurred with a slight dip of his chin.

Arista closed her eyes. A low rumbling shook the ceiling. Deep crevices formed in the ground, slicing chunks of dirt and rock from under their feet, swallowing the legs of the startled guards as they tried to gain a foothold in the shifting landscape.

Jack tackled his son to the floor, anchoring him there with his gun horizontal against his throat. "About that talk…it'll need to be later." Jack slammed his fist into the side of Simon's face, followed immediately by another. After the third punch, Simon's eyes rolled back in his head, which leaned to the side.

"Papa?"

Standing over his son now, Jack glanced over his shoulder, his breath heaving as his gaze met Arista's. He turned, leaned in, and kissed her forehead, lifting her hair from her face, then took a step back. "Stephen, go, now."

True to his word, Stephen pulled Arista toward him. "We're getting outta here. I promised him, love. Lean on me."

Stephen grabbed Arista's hand and lunged for the door.

"We can't leave him!"

"We can. He'll be right behind us."

Turning one last time, Stephen witnessed Jack hoisting his son over his shoulder, then focused his full attention ahead. More rock slid from the ceiling. Stephen eyed the shifting structure and picked up the pace, disappearing down the nearest corridor.

Jack, hurry. The cave is falling down around us.

I'm coming. Go. Don't wait for me. You gave me your word Stephen. Understood.

Papa!

Stephen half-carried, half-dragged Arista the way he and Jack had come. If she'd been fully recovered, she'd have fought him more. For that he was grateful. In all the confusion, the pair was hardly noticed. The Night Dwellers themselves were fleeing the earthquake, and Stephen and Arista fit right in, hobbling to the cave's exit.

Stephen pointed. "Look. That's the way we entered." Bits of rock cascaded into their path, which Stephen easily skirted. "Our transportation isn't too far."

"No. Wait. Please." Arista twisted in his arms, straining through the dust and rock, her gaze focused backward.

Stephen took her face in his hands. "We can't. I promised him, Arista. I won't fail you again or him." He grazed his lips over her forehead and kissed her mouth quickly before moving forward once more. "Besides, you can best help with Whisterly and Vinique. Once you're with them, I'll come back and do all I can."

Free from the cave, with no one following for the time being, Stephen hurried her along. Arista was walking more under her own power now, and he had no idea what he would do if she decided to use witchcraft against him.

A loud explosion caught their attention. They froze, their gazes glued to the man limping from the crumbling cave, another man slung over his back. Smoke and ash threatened the two as they moved toward the trees, making slow progress, but moving forward nonetheless.

"Papa!" Arista's eyes scanned the approaching form.

Stephen pushed her in the vehicle, slammed in the clutch, and turned over the ignition. Puttering and jerking, their transportation purred to life. Stephen paused, threw another backward glance at Jack as he trudged along. *Damn!* Jack was moving even slower than before, except now two Night Dwellers tailed him, and they were taking shots at Jack. Stephen wiped his face with his forearm, clearing his vision, and looked on for a few more seconds.

He swallowed hard, before his fingers found hers. As their gazes locked, he kissed her hand. Leave with her… Now… That's what he should do, just as he and Jack had decided. Gunfire rattled in his ears, tugging Stephen's attention back to Jack, who swayed side to side under Simon's weight with the Night Dwellers gaining ground.

Throwing the gear shift into Reverse, Stephen's face hardened. "I can't. Sorry, Jack."

Arista flung her arms around Stephen and kissed his neck. "I knew you couldn't leave him."

His breath left his throat as he contemplated the power that a living Simon had over him, and, at that moment of weakness, he wasn't sure if he feared more for Arista's safety, Jack's, or his own. If Simon died, wouldn't they all be better off?

Shit...

One hand on the wheel, the other on his rifle, Stephen's eyes slitted against the smoke and ash, seeking Jack. Stephen skidded the jeep to a stop, jumped from the vehicle, and leaned on a boulder, adjusting the sights on his rifle.

This is it.

Fragmented memories and pieces of thought connected in his head, burning through the miasma of rage surging about his insides, culminating in one word: *Simon.*

I know why I'm here.

Stephen wet his lips, held his breath, then took aim at the limp mass secured around Jack's shoulders, as the man lumbered forward in slow, deliberate steps.

A galloping noise raced in Stephen's ears—his own heartbeat. Time slowed as his gaze slid to Jack's and held. The shot echoed. Then the man crashed to the dirt under the weight he carried.

DEAR READER

I had so much fun writing *Remeon's Crusade*, the latest install-ment in the Realms of Chaos series. I hope you enjoyed reading it as much as I did creating it.

I would love to hear from you! Please consider leaving a book review at your favorite site, or feel free to drop me a note at my website at: *www.jwgarrett.com*

Until next time,
J.W. Garrett

SPECIAL THANKS TO...

My husband who loves and supports me through all things, my mom, sisters, and children—my own little tribe. They have stuck with me through each step of the incredible journey of *Remeon's Crusade*. I'm blessed to have their wisdom behind me.

Denise Barker—Thank you for your commitment to excellence. You are amazing and understand the intricacies of my work like no one ever has.

BHC Press—Thanks to the team at BHC Press! You are a joy to work with in making *Remeon's Crusade* a reality.

Thank you to Jackie who won my newsletter contest by coming up with an amazing character name—Aldwin. Well done!

ABOUT THE AUTHOR

J.W. Garrett is a multi-award winning author and has been writing in one form or another since she was a teenager. Her early love of the fantasy genre goes all the way back to elementary school when she read *The Hobbit* for the very first time, and she's been hooked ever since. She currently lives in Florida with her family where she writes speculative fiction from the sunny beaches of Jacksonville, but she'll always love the mountains of Virginia where she was born.

Her writings include novels for young and old alike, as well as short stories and poetry. Since completing *Remeon's Crusade*, the third installment in her sci-fi fantasy series, Realms of Chaos, she has been hard at work on the next book in the series. When she's not hanging out with her characters, her favorite activities are reading, running, and spending time with family.

Visit the author at:
www.jwgarrett.com
www.bhcpress.com